PAPER DRAGONS

THE RISE OF THE SAND SPIRITS

ALSO BY SIOBHAN McDERMOTT

Paper Dragons:
The Fight for the Hidden Realm

PAPER DRAGONS

THE RISE OF THE SAND SPIRITS

麥舒雲

SIOBHAN McDERMOTT

DELACORTE PRESS

Delacorte Press
An imprint of Random House Children's Books
A division of Penguin Random House LLC
1745 Broadway, New York, NY 10019
penguinrandomhouse.com
rhcbooks.com

Library of Congress Cataloging-in-Publication Data is available upon request.
ISBN 978-0-593-70615-2 (hardcover) — ISBN 978-0-593-70616-9 (lib. bdg.) —
ISBN 978-0-593-70617-6 (ebook)

Manufactured in the United States of America
10 9 8 7 6 5 4 3 2 1

The authorized representative in the EU for product safety and compliance is
Penguin Random House Ireland, Morrison Chambers, 32 Nassau Street,
Dublin D02 YH68, Ireland, https://eu-contact.penguin.ie.

For my McDermott family: Derek, Connie, Ciara, Blathnaid, and *now featuring* James

CHAPTER 1

Zhi Ging leaped to the shore, pebbles scattering beneath her feet. Behind her, Hok Woh's glass stepping stones vanished back beneath the waves, leaving no hint of the underwater realm she'd begun to call home. She smiled up at Pou Pou, the giant floating jellyfish Sintou had sent to keep her company, and nodded toward the clifftops.

"All right, let's see if you're as fast as Gahyau."

They raced up the carved steps, the last of the fog streaming behind Pou Pou's bubble like a twirling comet. Before Zhi Ging could reach the top, the jellyfish shot past, bouncing to a stop in the tall grass. He waggled his tentacles in triumph, exaggerating the final distance between them. Zhi Ging shook her head, snorting as she tried to catch her breath.

"Great, you're somehow faster *and* smugger than Gahyau." But her smile faltered as she peered out across the empty clifftop. Several well-worn paths cut through

1

the grass, each snaking in a different direction. Some vanished into dense forest, while others swept toward distant mountains. Zhi Ging took a half step forward, her earlier confidence wavering as she realized she didn't even know which province Hok Woh bordered.

She ran a nervous hand through Malo's feathers. The little phoenix continued to snore, occasionally hiccupping in his sleep. Her feet suddenly felt rooted to the cliff, unable and unwilling to choose between paths. It could take months to search each province for Reishi and the missing Silhouettes. *What if I go the wrong way?*

She grimaced and turned back toward the sea, searching for the underwater waterfall. Ami had been far too calm when she fell into its depths. What if she managed to escape and return to where she'd trapped the others? Zhi Ging's hands unconsciously curled into fists, the indecision that had locked her in place melting away.

I have to get there before Ami. Wherever there *is.*

She rummaged in her pockets and her fingers brushed against the small folded slip Jack had given her earlier.

"Sintou was right," she murmured, half to herself and half to Pou Pou. "I could use some help. The floating market can cover Wengyuen faster than I can." She unfolded the scrap and let green ink drip onto her shoe. The dye pooled across the surface, forming Jack's smiling face in miniature. He winked up at her, then rippled, transforming into a jade-green arrow. Its pointed tip tugged the cloth, pulling Zhi Ging's left foot forward. She smiled as she veered away from the steps, her shoe marching her confidently along a path that curved around the cliff edge. "I wish we had one of these to find Reishi." She chuckled as the arrow swiveled sharply, pointing to a new path. Just as Zhi Ging turned, a bright flash shot past her ear, ruffling the loose strands along her braid.

It was a pure white starling.

The bird swept past Pou Pou, wings rustling like paper as it flitted over the surprised jellyfish. Malo's eyes snapped open and he tumbled out of Zhi Ging's hood, his tail feathers fanned out in excitement as he waddled furiously after it.

"Wait, get back here!" Zhi Ging cried as both Malo and the starling vanished into the forest. She tried to race after them, but her left shoe wouldn't budge. The green arrow had transformed into a tiny hand, stubbornly clinging to the path. Its message was clear: the forest was *not* the right way to Jack.

Zhi Ging turned to Pou Pou as she struggled to take off her shoe, both hands soon splattered in green ink as the miniature hand morphed back into an arrow that wove furiously between her fingers. "Don't let Malo out of your sight. I'll be right behind you."

The jellyfish shot forward and Zhi Ging pulled hard, as if she was paddling over a particularly steep wave at dragon boat training. The ink finally gave up, and the arrow split in half; it formed a pair of folded green arms, frustration radiating off them.

"I'm sorry!" Zhi Ging whispered as she hopped after Pou Pou. "But we're not leaving without Malo."

A heavy canopy soon blocked out the rising sun, and Zhi Ging shivered, the air between the trees somehow both humid and cold. Without the sea breeze, every twig that broke beneath her shoes seemed to echo, but there was no sign of Malo anywhere.

As her eyes adjusted to the gloom, Zhi Ging realized the trees were different than those back in the glass province. Here the bark was made up of bright stripes of color, streaks of celadon green, hawthorn red, and mandarin orange decorating each trunk. She ran a hand along the closest tree in disbelief. With his multicolored feathers, Malo was going to be even harder to find.

She continued deeper into the forest, finally spotting the top of Pou Pou's bubble floating behind an overturned trunk. As she clambered over the fallen tree, Zhi Ging let out a small laugh. A disgruntled-looking Malo was trapped beneath the jellyfish's bubble, his feet kicking petulantly at the leaves around them. Pou Pou waved a serene tentacle up at her while Malo immediately began to chirp, clearly unimpressed with how they'd teamed up against him.

"Haven't you learned by now not to wander off by yourself?"

Malo blew a raspberry at her, then turned his back on them. Zhi Ging suppressed a smile and gestured for Pou

Pou to release the sulking phoenix. She leaned forward, tickling the feathers at the top of his head. "Hey, you never know, there could still be some thralls lurking around—"

A loud crack echoed through the trees and Zhi Ging crouched down, her heart pounding as visions of gray-eyed thralls possessed by the Fui Gwai filled her mind. *No,* she reminded herself. *The Fui Gwai's not a real spirit. Ami's the one possessing everyone.*

The cracks continued, each one creeping closer toward them. Even Malo was silent as Zhi Ging hurried them to a dense thicket of bushes. She pressed against the leaves and peered through a small gap. A hunched figure shuffled back and forth on the other side.

Every so often, the figure would stoop down, their back to Zhi Ging as they considered the dried curling leaves caught between exposed roots. Although each leaf looked identical to her, some were discarded while others were tossed over a gnarled shoulder to a small but growing collection of kindling in the center of the clearing. The figure twisted, their profile suddenly outlined against the murky haze, and Zhi Ging jerked back.

Even if the shadowy figure wasn't a thrall, it definitely wasn't human. Dark bulbous growths covered its spine, rising up along its back in two diagonal lines. The creature knelt, clinking as it bent over the pile of leaves. Zhi Ging glanced at Pou Pou, but the jellyfish shrugged his tentacles, equally confused by the curious hollow chiming.

5

The creature hit two shards of flint together and sparks leaped out, catching the dry leaves. Light blazed across the clearing, and Zhi Ging blinked in surprise.

It was a boy.

He looked a few years younger than her, with short black hair that stuck out in every direction, as if he was floating underwater. Strapped across his back were two thick silk braids, different-sized porcelain jars strung along their length, fabric looped through their handles.

Zhi Ging tapped lightly against Pou Pou's bubble and gestured away from the strange scene.

Let's get back to the path, she mouthed. The boy might not be dangerous, but he also wasn't going to help them find Jack. Zhi Ging nudged the ink on her shoe, and the folded green arms begrudgingly unfurled, transforming back into an arrow that twisted back and forth as it took in their new surroundings. Her eyes widened in concern when the arrow continued to spin, showing no signs of stopping. She pointed her foot in different directions while Malo pecked at the whirling ink, but it made no difference. It seemed to be lost, no longer sure of the best way to reach Jack.

There was a faint crackle as the boy shook more leaves over the now-dancing flames. Light seeped through the branches around them, and Pou Pou gestured back toward the clearing. The boy was struggling to untie a porcelain jar. After a few clumsy attempts, he finally freed a small ornate jar from the center of the two overlapping braids.

With extreme care, he snapped its thick wax seal and tilted the jar over the fire. Thick clouds began to swirl out, tumbling down toward the flames. The movement made Zhi Ging's breath catch in her throat. For a split second, she was back in Tutor Wun's class, Mynah and Pinderent presenting their cloud-carrying ideas.

She watched, hypnotized, as the cloud curled toward the smoke rising from the fire. The two seemed to collide in slow motion, dense cloud pushing down the wisps of gray, trapping smoke beneath a thick layer of white haze. The smoke coiled beneath its new heavy blanket, unfurling and causing it to billow back up. Zhi Ging stared in amazement as a form began to emerge, sealed in cloud and shaped by smoke.

There was a faint rustle, and the white starling from earlier landed on Pou Pou's bubble. It hopped across the surface, causing the inner water to ripple, and turned to peer directly at Zhi Ging.

She gasped, barely able to believe what she was seeing. Each feather on the starling's body was an elaborate paper cutting, its beak and feet dipped in rich purple ink. Zhi Ging stretched a hand to it, her fingers brushing the delicate cutouts that speckled its pale plumage.

"Where have you come from?" she whispered in awe. The only person she knew who could make paper cuttings come to life like this was her mother. What if, just like the paper dragon that had flown her to safety as a baby, this paper cutting had been created to protect her? The dawn air above Fei Chui had regularly been filled with starling song. Had this paper cutting been hidden among them? Zhi Ging felt hope swell inside her, filling her lungs with glittering light.

What if my mother sent this?

Before she could ask, the bird ruffled its wings and swooped between branches, Malo bounding after it in chase.

"No!" She barreled after him and stumbled into the clearing. The boy looked up, mouth dropping open in surprise as they locked eyes. Zhi Ging felt a brief flicker of relief that he didn't have the gray eyes of a thrall, but her stomach dropped as she saw what was about to happen.

Before she could stop them, the paper starling pierced the shape above the fire. Malo leaped after it but panicked as thick cloud closed in around him. He flapped his wings and the trapped smoke began to swell, distorting the boy's floating shape. The outer cloud flared with golden light, then erupted, smoke roaring out across the clearing. Pou Pou flung his bubble in front of Zhi Ging, shielding her as smoke crashed over them, the thick white surge knocking the boy off his feet.

CHAPTER 2

Zhi Ging scrambled out from behind Pou Pou, spluttering as warm cloud caught in her throat. She rubbed at her face, trying to clear the waxy mixture of smoke and cloud clinging to her eyelashes. Then she sank down, crawling beneath the haze to where she'd last seen Malo and the boy.

To her surprise, the air at the center of the clearing was free of smoke. The boy was already back on his feet, snatching at bits of cloud that had snagged against low-hanging branches. Discolored tendrils swirled between his fingers as he struggled to squeeze the cloud back into its jar. In his panic, several leaves also made their way into the porcelain, where they fizzed against the cloud. Malo wove beneath his feet, small fragments of cloud clasped between his wings as he chirped apologetically.

"What did you do?" The boy turned to stare at Zhi Ging, his face pale.

"I'm so sorry. Malo just ran out and—" She jerked

forward, trying to stop a piece of cloud from floating back out of the jar. The boy flinched and pulled it away from her.

"Are you the Fui Gwai?" he croaked, eyes darting between her bright green fingers and Pou Pou rising over her shoulder.

"What? No, I'm a Silhouette, and this"—Zhi Ging frantically wiped her hands against her cloak—"is just ink." Her eyes flicked to the snuffed-out fire between them. "Let me help you rebuild that."

"It's too late." His voice was suddenly small.

"What do you mean?"

The boy sighed deeply, clasping the porcelain jar tight.

"This was meant to be my cloud ceremony." He looked at her expectantly, his eyes wide with meaning.

"I . . . ," Zhi Ging began hesitantly. "I'm sorry, we don't have those in the glass province. What is that?"

"It's how everyone from Wun-Wun finds out what they're meant to be when they grow up. You only get one chance." His expression crumpled and Zhi Ging felt her stomach knot with guilt. *He looks just how I felt when Iridill got Reishi's Silhouette invitation instead of me.*

She paused, then leaned forward, peering closely at the boy's tanned face. It was hard to tell now that the fire was out, but his cheeks seemed to be spattered with purple freckles. *Were those there before?* They were the exact same shade as the starling's beak. Zhi Ging spun around, but there was no sign of the paper-cutting bird anywhere.

"What, is there cloud stuck to me?" he asked, wiping the back of his hand across his cheeks. The boy yelped as the purple freckles drifted over his fingers, spreading across his palms in a gentle rolling murmuration.

He hopped in place, frantically trying to shake the dots loose. Instead, they whorled along his arm, floating back up to rest across his nose.

"What are these?" he asked, tilting his head back to try to watch the hovering freckles.

"I'm not sure," Zhi Ging admitted, still searching for the paper starling. Suddenly Gertie's amused face flashed across her mind. "But I know someone at the floating market who might!"

"Really?" The boy's face lit up, his cheeks flushing beneath the purple dots. "My father rents a stall each time they land near Wun-Wun. I've never been allowed to explore it properly, though; I just help set up the snow cloud jars, then get sent home. Last time I didn't even get to do that. I was stuck doing extra cloud-stitching practice." He paused, tucking his porcelain jar under one arm before holding out a hand.

"I'm Ehn D'Ippitti." He grimaced, as if he'd just swallowed another mouthful of warm cloud. "Ugh, I don't know why I said that; people only call me that when I'm in trouble. You can call me Dippy."

"I'm Zhi Ging and these"—she pointed at the jellyfish and phoenix beside her—"are Pou Pou and Malo." Malo held up a final wisp of cloud and quacked a sheepish apology. She crouched down to collect it and spotted the green ink on her shoe had almost settled. The arrow now bounced between Dippy and pointing back down the earlier path.

"We were looking for the floating market before Malo ran in here. My friend Jack . . ." Zhi Ging paused, shocked at how much had happened since she'd last seen him. *He doesn't even know Reishi's missing.* "Anyway, once this stops spinning we should know which way to go." She gestured uncertainly at the wriggling arrow.

"Oh, I know!" Dippy beamed. "Today's our province capital's Bao Saan festival. That's where I was heading after my cloud ceremony." He waved toward a cart piled high with porcelain jars, each at least ten times larger than the ones strapped across his back. "The floating market always shows up at that. I'll take you."

The green arrow nodded vigorously, transforming into a thumbs-up at Dippy's offer.

"Thank you!" Zhi Ging clambered onto the cart after Malo, who immediately hopped into the nearest jar, his chirps echoing off porcelain as he searched for hidden sunflower seeds. The donkey at the front of the cart seemed unbothered by the sudden presence of a floating jellyfish and phoenix. He gave them a cursory sniff before setting off, the cart's wheels rattling over tree roots.

As they reached the forest edge, Malo wriggled out of the final jar, shaking his feathers in disappointment. Zhi

Ging gave him a meaningful look, then glanced toward Dippy, who was steering from the front of the cart. The little phoenix sighed and waddled toward the boy, patting his arm tentatively as he quacked a new apology.

"Don't worry, I know you didn't mean it." Dippy ruffled his feathers, his eyes focused on guiding them through the final rainbow-striped trees. His purple freckles swirled down, flowing across his left ear to land on the hand resting on Malo's head.

Dippy turned to look at Zhi Ging and she tried to smile reassuringly, although her entire body tightened in an internal wince.

"I *really* hope Gertie knows what to do about those," she whispered to Pou Pou.

PINGON, THE PROVINCE CAPITAL, WAS MORE THAN half a day's journey from Wun-Wun, and the midday sun soon floated high above them. Zhi Ging stretched out between the spherical jars, letting dappled sunlight warm her face. The sound of cicadas filled the air as they wove between fields blooming with bright yellow cole flowers. She turned to one side, watching the scenery drift by between porcelain jars. A farmer waved at them from a distant field and she smiled back.

Out here, surrounded by the porcelain province's wide plains, the previous night felt like nothing more than a bad dream. It didn't seem possible that a short cart ride was all that separated Ami's disappearance into the underwater waterfall from this moment. Zhi Ging propped herself up on her elbows and tilted her head to Dippy. Now that they were back on the main road, the donkey's reins hung loose beside him. He was hunched over the small jar from before, Malo clapping his wings in encouragement each time Dippy pulled a twig loose from what was left of the cloud. Zhi Ging cleared her throat and scooted up beside him, silently gathering the leaves now scattered around the cart.

"That cloud ceremony you mentioned earlier, can you definitely not try again tomorrow?"

Dippy sighed, purple freckles gliding over the bridge of his nose. "No, it's my tenth birthday today."

"Oh!" Zhi Ging flushed, horrified they'd ruined his day. "I didn't—should we turn back? You don't have to take us to Pingon on your birthday." She stopped as Malo scrambled up her sleeve, tumbling into her hood before wriggling back out with a single sunflower seed clasped in his beak. He placed it carefully on Dippy's lap, attempting to chirp "Happy Birthday."

"How long has that been there?" Zhi Ging murmured, running a dazed hand along her hood. *And why do I get the feeling that's not the only one he's hidden?*

"Don't worry about it, I'm happy to take you. Most birthdays are just another day for people from Wun-Wun. Only our tenth is different." He paused, struggling with a leaf that threatened to tear in half. "When we're born, we spend our first twenty-four hours swaddled inside a cloud to protect us from illness." He spotted Zhi Ging's confused expression and gestured at the jars around them. "Wun-Wun villagers specialize in catching ocean clouds. Healers from all six provinces trade with us, using our clouds in their elixirs," he added proudly. "Anyway, our swaddling cloud is kept in a jar until our tenth birthday. On that morning, we're sent alone into the forest and told to build a fire. That's it, no other instructions." Dippy shook his head. "My father wouldn't even say if I was meant to build it out of leaves, bark, or moss. No villager ever shares how they built theirs, in case it impacts the final cloud shape. We have to go by instinct."

"That doesn't seem fair," Zhi Ging muttered, half to herself. "The Silhouette entrance exam was tough, but at least the Scouts gave us questions on the day. This is like being handed a blank scroll and being told to guess what the questions are."

"It's not that bad." Dippy shrugged. "Everyone gets a shape no matter how they build their fire. You can't normally fail a cloud ceremony . . ." He trailed off, his eyes drifting back to the jar in his hands. Pou Pou floated closer, pointing out a small twig still caught between two gray wisps.

"Thanks. Anyway, once smoke starts rising, we're meant to slowly pour our original swaddling cloud over the fire. I spent all year practicing just in case it spilled out too quickly and I accidentally put it out. I never prepared for a somersaulting duckling, though." Dippy smiled ruefully before patting a sheepish-looking Malo on the head.

"Ocean clouds are really dense, so the smoke gets trapped beneath it. Since they come from seawater, our swaddling clouds form thin salt crusts during the ten years they're stored in jars. The flames burn small cracks into that crust, and smoke seeps into the ocean cloud. The two temperatures collide and the outer cloud rises up, creating a shape unique to your fire. That shape . . ." Dippy exhaled and started again. "That shape shows what you're meant to be. A cart would mean I'd become a cloud carrier like my father and grandfather, while a boat would mean a cloud stitcher, Wun-Wun's version of a fisherman." Dippy's ears flushed red. "Most of my cousins could guess what shape they'd get years before their ceremony, but I'm not really good at any of it. Any time my aunt brought me out to the bay to practice, I'd fall overboard, scattering the ocean clouds."

Zhi Ging's eyes widened, suddenly remembering the boat she had spotted when she and Reishi had first arrived at the clifftop months ago. *Is Dippy the one I saw falling overboard? Were those puffy white fish actually ocean clouds?*

"You never know." Zhi Ging heard her voice squeak with forced optimism as she pulled the final leaf from the jar. "Maybe you'll get a brand-new shape, something no one else in Wun-Wun has ever gotten. At least once Malo and I have helped you rebuild the fire."

"Thanks, but I don't think there's enough swaddling cloud left to try again," he admitted in a quiet voice.

A heavy silence pressed down over the cart, the only sound the faint rattle of wooden wheels trundling along the road. Zhi Ging felt her stomach tighten. She had accidentally taken his future from him, just like Iridill had stolen her original shot at getting get into Hok Woh. She had to make things right.

IT WAS LATE AFTERNOON BEFORE THEY REACHED Pingon. The city was surrounded by a vast moat, the pale green water glinting in the light. Zhi Ging blinked hard, wondering if the bright sun had dazzled her eyes after months of living underwater. The waves breaking across the moat's surface seemed to be frozen in place. She shielded her eyes and peered closer. The rippling water was actually thousands of green ceramic shards, the cracked glaze revealing thick white porcelain.

"What is that?" she asked, waving a hand at the strange sight.

"It's Pingon's celadon moat. They—" The rest of Dippy's sentence was drowned out by a blast of drumbeat that boomed through the city's open gates.

Zhi Ging tore her eyes away from the moat and realized with a start that the gates weren't just flung open, they didn't exist. *How can an entire city be this confident against a thrall attack?*

Dippy caught her eye and nodded to a small bridge that arched over the green ceramic pieces. "They say Pin-gon's moat can rise up, trapping anyone who crosses the bridge with bad intentions inside an unbreakable porcelain shell."

"Have you ever seen it do that?" Zhi Ging asked, not sure if Dippy was being serious.

He pointed to a series of jagged porcelain vases that lined the lower half of the city wall. "No, but my father says those are people trapped waiting for their trial."

Zhi Ging shuddered as her eyes flicked over them. Some of the vases were almost completely hidden beneath long trailing vines. *Just how long are they kept waiting?*

"Um, are Silhouette still welcome?" she asked in a quiet voice. *What if the moat thinks anyone from Hok Woh has bad intentions?*

Dippy frowned, a worried crease spreading across his forehead as the bridge loomed up ahead of them. "I think we should be okay. But maybe we should get off the cart before—"

Pou Pou soared ahead and raised a tentacle from the center of the bridge. His message was clear: *I'll test it.*

The group held their breath as the jellyfish spun from side to side, scanning for rising pieces of porcelain. But thankfully the moat remained frozen.

Zhi Ging breathed a sigh of relief as Pou Pou rejoined them on the cart. She pressed a grateful hand to his bubble, only then noticing he had been shaking, anxious ripples shivering through the water.

Dippy gave them a nervous smile, then urged the donkey forward, over the bridge, and into the chaos of Pingon's Bao Saan festival.

CHAPTER 3

The cart was immediately hit by a wall of loud, infectious music. Drums, gongs, and cymbals reverberated through the air, pulsing through Zhi Ging's entire body until her heartbeat matched their excited rhythm.

"The parade's started!" Dippy whooped, his voice barely audible as he helped them off the cart.

"Maybe it's safer if you stay hidden for now," Zhi Ging suggested as Pou Pou swooped low, dodging the spinning drumstick of an overly enthusiastic musician. The jellyfish nodded, spinning his bubble tighter and tighter until he fitted snugly inside the hollow glass bead at the center of her gold Pan Chang Knot.

Paper lanterns shaped like giant steamed buns hung between eaves, and Zhi Ging had to hold Malo's wing to stop the little phoenix from flying toward them. Although she had initially felt bad for Pou Pou, the streets were so crammed that she soon began to wonder if he actually had more space inside his tiny glass bead. They pressed through the jostling crowds, searching for any sign of the floating market.

Suddenly, Zhi Ging spotted a ribbon of emerald floating high above them. It was a cluster of Gertie's weatherwax bees.

"They'll lead us to the market, come on!" she cried, grabbing Dippy's arm.

They hurried after the bees until the crowds spilled out into Pingon's central square. Stall owners from the floating market had set up along the outer edges but, for once, no one was looking at their colorful silk tents.

Zhi Ging's jaw dropped, and she instinctively clasped Malo with both hands before the phoenix could leap out of her hood. There, rising high above them, were three giant towers covered in pillowy white buns. A single tent sat in the middle tower's shadow, a hastily painted bakery sign hanging above its entrance. Above that, the tent's canopy was a living, shimmering mosaic of emerald-green bees.

Of course Gertie somehow still has the most eye-catching tent. Zhi Ging beamed, dragging Dippy behind her.

"Zhi Ging!" The old woman waved once she spotted them, a slim jade hairpin clasped in her hand like a conductor's baton. Around her, bees hovered in the air clutching buns, waiting for Gertie to direct them to paying customers.

"What are you doing here? Is Reishi with you?"

Zhi Ging bit her lip, feeling the crowd press in. She

couldn't tell the truth here, not when so many people could overhear. If others found out the mysterious gray-eyed spirit possessing villagers had been Ami all along, no one would trust a single Cyo B'Ahon ever again. Certain towns and cities were already suspicious of the immortals living in Hok Woh.

Gertie gasped, and for a split second Zhi Ging wondered if she had read her thoughts.

"Your glove!" The old woman patted Zhi Ging's bare left arm. "I warned you the Cyo B'Ahon wouldn't know how to fix it. Are you here for a new one? I hope you brought the original fabric."

"No, it's not that. Where's Jack? I need to talk to you both."

"Oh, he's over by the Scramble." Gertie jerked her head toward the bun towers. "Now, *who* are you?" she asked, smile widening as she turned her attention to Dippy. "Let me guess, you're someone who constantly wishes they had a simple way to stay warm no matter the weather?"

Zhi Ging let the rest of Gertie's familiar weather-wax pitch wash over her as she stood on her toes, trying to spot Jack. The buns on each tower were marked with a round stamp, their central red symbol changing the higher up the bun was on the bamboo frame. Zhi Ging's gaze continued up until she spotted six women high above the square. They stood in pairs, two on each narrow tower top. Unlike the crowd, who were dressed in shades of blue to celebrate the porcelain province, these women wore shimmering robes of red silk.

While five of them bustled about, one stood with her arms crossed at the center of the middle tower, barking orders at the others. She was the only one with a splash of blue to her outfit, butterflies made from lapis lazuli and cobalt kingfisher feathers decorating the ornate headdress balanced above her sharp widow's peak. Although she was beautiful, a distinct coldness radiated from her features, as if it had been years since her mouth had lifted into a smile or her eyes had looked at anyone with kindness. Her expression soured as she seemed to feel Zhi Ging's gaze. She strode to the tower edge, her dark brown eyes narrowing as she searched the crowd for the source of the attention, the eight gray rings that decorated her fingers gleaming as her hands curled into fists.

"Don't stare at Niotiya, she's the worst of the Matchmakers," Gertie ordered, stepping forward to block Zhi Ging just as the woman's icy scan swept over them. "She'd probably charge you for the honor. The less you have to do with that particular Guild the better."

Gertie glowered at the red-stamped buns covering the towers before handing Zhi Ging and Dippy buns from her own tray, a smiling green bee stamped across each domed surface.

"Niotiya hasn't officially been made Head Matchmaker yet, but she already insists on wearing that ridiculous headdress. Ginsau's still the Guild leader, but she's holding on to her power by a thread. Which is bad news for us." Gertie spotted Zhi Ging's confused expression and waved a hand across the rest of the floating market. "The Matchmakers' Guild has been in charge of trading across Wengyuen for centuries, ever since one of them convinced the province rulers it was 'simply matchmaking between buyers and sellers,'" the old woman quoted through clenched teeth. "I didn't agree with a lot of Ginsau's rulings, but at least she never tried to control where the floating market could land or what we could sell." Gertie's green bees hummed in frustration, and Zhi Ging spotted one shake a tiny foreleg at the Matchmakers, a bun almost slipping from its grip.

"Niotiya refused to let me organize this year's festival buns. Instead, she's brought a batch all the way from her private kitchens in Omophilli. Let's see how many children choose her stale day-old buns over one of mine, though," she muttered, her eyes gleaming. "I've been making buns for the Bao Saan festival for decades. Families are already buying mine rather than waiting for a free tower bun after the Scramble." Gertie gestured at the empty trays stacked around her tent.

"Why are the Matchmakers up there, anyway?" Zhi Ging asked before biting into her bun. Warm, rich lotus seed paste coated her tongue, the delicate nutty flavor just the right level of sweet.

"They're guarding the paper cuttings. Can't have those

disappearing before the Scramble," Dippy explained, trying to keep his own bun away from Malo's eager snuffling.

Zhi Ging's head snapped toward him. "Paper cuttings?"

"Those are the main prize; it's why people take part in the Scramble." Gertie pointed to the top of the closest tower. There, balanced on a stand between the two Matchmakers, was a single white paper cutting of a steamed bun.

"In the Scramble, each climber will race up their chosen tower, filling a cloth sack with as many buns as possible."

Malo chirped in approval from Dippy's shoulder; this was clearly his idea of the perfect sport.

"The first climber to reach the top gets that tower's particular paper cutting, and that's where it gets interesting." Gertie's face creased into a wide grin, wrinkles dancing across her features. "Each level of buns along the tower has a different value, so the higher you climb, the more they're worth. At the end of the race, the three winners have a choice. They can either keep their papercutting bun or trade it for another climber's entire sack of real buns, doubling the amount they earn."

"What's written on the paper cuttings?" Zhi Ging asked, struggling to spot the character cut out across their flat surface.

"It's not what's *on* them; it's what's *in* them that makes the Scramble brilliant," Dippy cut in, his arms flailing with excitement. "All three paper cutting buns have a different reward. One of them, when you break it in half, will shake loose enough gold coins to last a whole year—it's worth more than if you somehow collected every single bun from all three towers. Another bun will shake out a jewel-colored lantern. Once you light it, any passing trader will know to give you a lift in their cart; you can even ask the floating market to carry you between provinces."

"Actually," Gertie cut in gently, careful not to ruin his enthusiasm, "Niotiya has changed that prize. It's now an amulet that supposedly protects against the Fui Gwai."

Zhi Ging and Malo exchanged a sideways glance. She really had to tell Gertie and Jack the truth about Ami. *But how do I do that without Dippy overhearing?*

"Then why would anyone ever swap a paper cutting for a sack of buns?" Zhi Ging asked quickly, feeling Gertie and Dippy turn to her with near identical looks of confusion, puzzled by her silence.

"Ha! That's because of the third paper cutting." Gertie cackled, a delighted glint entering her eyes. "No one knows which of the three towers holds which paper cutting, but there's one bun everyone wants to avoid. Break that in half and all that'll shake out is"—she paused dramatically, waggling her eyebrows—"a cha siu bao." Gertie and Dippy roared with laughter. "One measly pork bun worth less than every other bun collected during the race."

Zhi Ging shook her head, chuckling at the idea. At least everyone had liked when Pinderent and Mynah made custard buns rain down from their homework cloud. Her smile crumpled as she thought of her friends: one frozen in Hok Woh's sick bay and the other still missing. She winced and reached for Gertie's sleeve. "I really need to tell you—"

The square suddenly filled with exploding firecrackers, and the drumming reached a fever pitch, the sound waves almost visible from the way Gertie's bees bounced in the air.

"You two get to the front of the Scramble," Gertie encouraged as the crowd surged past them toward the towers. "Come and find me after with Jack; we'll talk then."

Zhi Ging and Dippy squeezed their way forward until they were just a few feet from the climbers. While some crouched at the base of their chosen tower, others jogged between them, desperately searching for any hint whatsoever of which paper cutting would be waiting for them at the top.

The crowd fell silent as Niotiya peered down from the middle tower. She plucked one of the kingfisher feathers from her headpiece and held it high, a faint breeze threatening to tug it loose from her ringed fingers. In a flash of blue, she slashed the feather down, and the Scramble began.

Each of the climbers had a different strategy. Some frantically grabbed at the lowest buns before even starting their climb, while others shot up, aiming for fewer but higher-value buns. Several tried to snatch multiple buns in each palm before shoving them into the cloth sack tied across their backs, but the buns would slip from their grip, bouncing off climbers farther down the tower. One woman noticed and quickly untied her sack, simply holding it open beneath the more frantic racers above her.

Zhi Ging's eyes darted between the climbers and the cheering crowds at the base of each tower. Where was Jack?

There were screams from the crowd as one climber, already halfway up the middle tower, slipped, buns coming loose beneath their feet. They plummeted down past others before their emergency rope pulled tight, their back to the crowd as the force flipped them upside down. The climber stretched their hands frantically toward the tower's bamboo frame, and their sack ripped, tangling them in cloth while their buns tumbled to the ground.

The crowd around Zhi Ging leaped forward, cheering as they snatched at the more valuable buns, hoping to be the first-ever spectators to win prize money at a Scramble. Only Dippy and Zhi Ging remained standing, Malo flapping his wings in delight as he caught a bun that bounced off someone's head and into his beak.

"Didn't you just eat most of Dippy's bun?" Zhi Ging laughed, her voice trailing off as she stuffed Malo's half-eaten bun into her pocket. A sudden shift had rippled through the square. The entire crowd was now silent, gawping. Zhi Ging turned slowly, following their gaze, and her mouth dropped open.

The three paper cuttings had floated free from their stands. Matchmakers tried to snatch them back, but the paper fluttered between their fingers. The three cuttings twirled between the frozen climbers, drifting down the towers to land softly . . . in Zhi Ging's hood.

Every pair of eyes snapped toward her, and time seemed to stretch, a single moment congealed in confusion.

"Zhi Ging?" The voice was a muffled gasp as the upside-down climber finally pulled the sack from their face.

It was Jack.

He looked down at her, the surprise in his flickering green and blue eyes quickly turning to concern as he took in the crowd's scowling faces.

"Thief!" Niotiya screeched, her imperious voice ripping through the silence. "Get her!"

The spell broke and the crowd roared forward, lunging for Zhi Ging.

CHAPTER 4

D ippy unfroze first and pulled Zhi Ging between the bun towers, weaving amid outstretched arms as he raced away from the square. Gertie's weather-wax bees appeared around them, a blurring wave of green that fought to keep the crowd back.

"Pou Pou!" Zhi Ging yelled as they raced into an alley, the furious pounding of Matchmakers' feet echoing behind them. The jellyfish shot out of her golden Pan Chang, his tentacles curled into protective fists.

"Don't, there're too many of them!" Dippy shouted over his shoulder.

They raced blindly down streets that twisted and splintered, each unknown path threatening to trap them in a dead end.

"What if the moat stops us from leaving?" Zhi Ging cried, the vine-covered vases suddenly flashing across her mind.

Dippy skidded to a stop as they spotted Niotiya and

another Matchmaker blocking the far end of the path. Zhi Ging lurched sideways, dragging them down a narrow lane filled with thick steam. She rushed forward, one arm stretched wide, desperately searching for a way through the blistering haze. The heat turned Pou Pou's bubble opaque, and the giant jellyfish began to spin in confusion, unable to see. Around them the anxious hum of Gertie's bees reverberated against the walls.

"We have to keep going," Zhi Ging urged as Dippy began to splutter, hot air stinging each breath. She stepped toward him and screamed as the floor suddenly crumbled beneath them, an ancient wooden hatch giving way beneath their weight. They tumbled down a flight of stairs into a sweltering basement. Dippy groaned. Several of the porcelain jars tied across his back had broken and heavy ocean cloud spilled down around his ankles.

Zhi Ging yelped, racing to help him up. "Are you okay?"

"Fine," he croaked in relief as his fingers brushed against the small jar that held his swaddling cloud. It had survived the fall. The weather-wax bees buzzed in concern as beads of glistening steam gathered across their wings, weighing them down and making it difficult to fly.

"Get back to Gertie," Zhi Ging urged them. "It's not safe for you down here."

She and Dippy hurried farther into the steam-filled basement, searching for another way out. As her eyes adjusted, Zhi Ging realized they were at the edge of a vast porcelain workshop. The floor tilted away from them at a steep angle, and long cylindrical kilns stretched in different directions, creating a maze-like series of alleys that mirrored the streets of Pingon above them. Zhi Ging jumped as footsteps crunched down the stairs on the other side of the kiln, Niotiya's low voice hissing through the steam.

They hadn't lost the Matchmakers yet.

"Let's just give the paper cuttings back," Dippy whispered, his eyes wide as the Matchmakers began searching the kiln passages, dry earth cracking beneath their silk shoes.

"I'm trying!" Zhi Ging murmured, both hands fumbling in her hood. Each time her fingers brushed against a cutting, it would flit away, refusing to be caught. Malo flapped onto her shoulder to help, but the paper cuttings simply twisted over his outstretched wings, bouncing across his beak to land back in her hood.

A Matchmaker suddenly appeared from the steam in front of them, a torn half bun clenched in each fist. Her scowl deepened as she took in Zhi Ging, the three paper cuttings now rolling up and down her braid like a slide.

"I didn't mean to take them," Zhi Ging babbled, her voice a high squeak. The woman's eyes narrowed, a sinister smile stretching tight across her perfectly painted lips. She leaned forward, not to collect the paper cuttings but to press the red-stamped bun toward Zhi Ging's face.

"You won't cause any more trouble after one of these."

"What are you doing?" Zhi Ging spluttered as the Matchmaker became more insistent, trying to force-feed her the bun. Malo's feathers flared white-hot, and he snatched the bun away. It blazed in his beak and crumbled to ash. At the same time, Pou Pou shot forward, head-butting the woman. His bubble rippled dangerously as the Matchmaker collapsed backward into the steam with a muffled thud, dazed by the force of his blow.

"Malo, stop," Zhi Ging whispered as flames continued to crackle along his wings. "You're evaporating the steam. That's all that's hiding us from the Matchmakers."

"Has he always been able to do that?" Dippy asked in astonishment as Malo's feathers immediately returned to normal.

"Actually, he only started yesterday," Zhi Ging admitted, pulling them between two sloping kilns. They froze as Niotiya and another Matchmaker stalked past the exit ahead of them.

"Just give up!" the shorter Matchmaker called out, wiping steam from her clammy face, heavy eyebrow paint smearing across her cheeks. "We've sealed the staircase; there's no way out."

"Start lighting the dragon kilns," Niotiya barked. "They'll give up pretty quickly once these heat up." She slapped the kiln chamber, and the four gray rings that rested above her knuckles clinked against the brick surface. Zhi Ging pressed back into the steam, then shivered, staring in surprise at the base of the kiln.

We need to turn around, Dippy mouthed, *before the other Matchmaker wakes up.*

"Wait." Zhi Ging watched as the three paper cuttings fluttered down, tumbling over one another beside the kiln. She crouched softly as Niotiya and the other Matchmaker went off in search of firewood. "Put your hand here," she said, spreading her fingers wide between the dancing cuttings.

Dippy jumped in surprise as a cool breeze streamed through a gap between the weathered bricks, flowing out from the heart of the dragon kiln.

"How's it doing that?"

"There must be all sorts of escape routes down here," Zhi Ging said, frantically pressing different bricks. "There's no way people working with fire would build a workshop without several ways out. They'd have to be easy to find while crawling to avoid smoke too." Her fingers brushed a small sliver of celadon fused into the brick, a dragon's face carved across its pale green surface. Zhi Ging pushed its snout and there was a muffled click. Several bricks swung inward to reveal a door.

"Let's go!" Dippy squeezed in after Zhi Ging and pulled the bricks shut behind them. They wasted no time hurrying after Pou Pou, the jellyfish's faint glow illuminating the inside of the escape kiln.

They crawled along the slanted tunnel in tense silence, the scorched earth beneath their hands and feet eventually giving way to thin grains of silt. Zhi Ging blinked up into the new gloom. The kiln had led them to the mouth of a large limestone cavern, hundreds of stalactites reaching down toward their heads.

Zhi Ging lifted Malo back into her hood, the three paper cuttings scooting over to make room for the little phoenix. There was no sound of the Matchmakers following them, but there was also no sound of Pingon's Bao Saan festival above them. Just how far underground were they?

Dippy took a step forward and stumbled, his foot hitting a thin rod half-buried beneath the dull gray sand. He bent down and Pou Pou strengthened his glow, revealing an abandoned metal track leading into the cavern's depths.

"Where do you think that goes?" Dippy asked, his breath clouding in front of him. The breeze was stronger now, tugging wisps free from Zhi Ging's braid.

"Guess we'll find out," she murmured, facing the cold head-on as she stepped onto the track. Wherever that gust was coming from, it had to be a way out.

They followed the track in silence, both straining to hear the first warning sound of Matchmakers emerging from the escape kiln behind them. Eventually the metal track split in half, curving down two identical tunnels.

On the path that swept to the left, a rickety cart had been abandoned between two limestone pillars, thick knotted ropes tangled inside it.

Dippy lifted one out with a puzzled expression. "What animal is meant to steer this?" he asked in a hushed voice. The heavy white cord looked nothing like the reins on his own cart. It was made up of several strange loops, as if designed for a creature with no legs.

"Where *is* the animal?" Zhi Ging whispered back.

They instinctively huddled closer together, peering back at the reins. Several of its loops appeared chewed through, leaving what remained looking like a frayed and tattered Pan Chang Knot.

"Let's keep going," Zhi Ging said with a shudder, squeezing between the cart and pillars toward the cold air whistling down the left tunnel. The breeze grew stronger, forcing them to inch forward with eyes half-shut. The three paper cuttings rose out of her hood, rustling loudly as they tried to shield her face from the worst of the wind. The crackling sound filled the tunnel, and Zhi Ging couldn't help but remember a similar sound from long ago, when a dragon had coiled its scaly tail around her on Fei Chui's jade mountain, lightning swelling between its jaws.

After a while, the path tilted steeply upward, the tunnel walls closing in around them. Their climbing slowed and Dippy had to help each time Zhi Ging's hood caught on a low stalactite.

"At least the Matchmakers don't seem to be following us," he whispered reassuringly as he released her cloak for the fifth time. "And the paper cuttings finally seem happy to leave your side. Maybe we *can* give them back after all."

Zhi Ging watched the three cuttings swooping in front of them, the corners of their paper bending as if beckoning them forward farther into the tunnel.

"Maybe. Although I feel like all of Pingon will still be mad at me for ruining the Scramble," Zhi Ging said with a small grimace.

"At least it's a Scramble no one will ever forget. Who knew you and Malo were just warming up when you interrupted my cloud ceremony," Dippy said with a grin, trying to lighten the mood. "If it makes you feel better, I've accidentally ruined loads of cloud-stitching trips. It's not like you did it on purpose. Once we give back the cuttings, they'll have no reason to stay mad."

His smile faltered when one of the paper-cutting buns bumped into his nose. Dippy nudged it aside, frowning as he watched it rejoin the others.

"Why do you think that Matchmaker tried to feed you a bun?"

Zhi Ging paused while Pou Pou floated ahead, Malo perched atop his bubble. Before she could answer, the phoenix's low reassuring chirps stopped, and the entire tunnel filled with blinding light.

"Malo!" Zhi Ging clambered up the rest of the slope, one arm shielding her eyes from the strength of his glow.

Her free hand hit the top of the rocky climb, and she hauled herself up, wheezing hard. Her fingers brushed against wood and then something solid yet strangely soft.

Zhi Ging blinked away the remaining bright spots, then yelped, snatching her hand back with such force that she almost fell backward onto Dippy. Staring up at her was Iridill's frozen scowling face.

CHAPTER 5

Malo inched forward and tapped his beak against the girl's nose, but there was no reaction. Iridill's eyes were clouded with thick gray smoke, and she was leaning forward out of a cart, her two sidekicks, Cing Yau and Kaolin, squeezed in beside her. Dippy clambered up behind Zhi Ging and gasped, his eyes moving past Iridill as Pou Pou filled the cavern with light.

"Who are they?" His question echoed, reverberating against the frozen Silhouettes packed in tight across eight linked carts that stretched back to the far wall. Water dripped down on them from sharp stalactites, but none of the gray-eyed Silhouettes seemed to even notice.

"Thralls," Zhi Ging whispered. "Possessed Silhouettes." She inched closer, unable to shake the feeling she had stepped into a nightmare version of Hok Woh's dorms.

She tried to lift Iridill's arm, but it was like attempting to bend a carved statue. Although the girl was breathing softly, there was no other sign of life. Zhi Ging watched as the three paper cuttings fluttered over the frozen Silhouettes, tapping each one lightly on the head as if they were checking no one was missing.

Is that what the cuttings were trying to do all along? Zhi Ging wondered. *Lead me here? But how did they know where the Silhouettes were?*

There was a faint grunt as Dippy tried to push the front cart away from the cavern edge, clearly worried Iridill and the others might tip forward. Zhi Ging's mind flashed back to the stone macaque from her first challenge, and she glanced across at Dippy. She and Iridill had struggled to lift that heavy chimera, and Dippy was even smaller than her.

How are we going to move these carts?

Each Silhouette that Zhi Ging recognized caused her stomach to twist, as if she'd swallowed one of Ami's oily gray jellyfish and it was now trying to slither toward her heart. Dippy shuffled ahead in a daze, his features frozen in horror as he counted the motionless Silhouettes.

Zhi Ging staggered to the final cart, her knees threatening to give out.

Mynah and Hiulam had toppled sideways at the back of the cart, the two Silhouettes back-to-back with their arms raised in defiance against some unseen figure. Ami must have frozen them in place once the possession took hold.

"You're here!" Zhi Ging cried, her voice cracking as she reached for her friends, struggling to lift them upright.

For a second, Mynah's cheek patches appeared to flicker a soft yellow before fading back to gray. "I promise I'll work out how to fix this. I'll . . ." She trailed off as a series of marks in the sand caught her eye.

"Dippy," Zhi Ging called out hesitantly, "you haven't already walked around here, have you?" She had to force the question out between her teeth, already dreading the answer.

"No," he replied, his voice growing louder as he hurried to her from the other side of the cart. "I was still counting . . . why?"

Zhi Ging pointed a shaking finger at the faint footprints that circled the final cart. It looked like someone had recently inspected the frozen Silhouettes. The paper cuttings rolled into the cart and began to bounce beside Zhi Ging's friends. She leaned forward into the cart to collect them, and her breath caught in her throat. The Matchmakers' red seal had been stamped across both Mynah's and Hiulam's left palms. The symbol was identical to the one used to decorate the higher-up buns. *What is going on?*

Zhi Ging raced back to Iridill, bending to check the palm of each Silhouette she passed. Every one of them had been marked with a Matchmakers' seal.

"Where were they taking you?" Zhi Ging wondered out loud. She tapped Iridill's hand, the red ink smearing as water continued to drip down from an overhanging stalactite.

"Oh!" Dippy's eyes widened in realization. "I don't

know *where,* but I bet I know *when* they were going to move the carts." He hurried over to Zhi Ging, his knuckles whitening as he gripped the wooden frame. "The Matchmakers never stay for the feast at the end of the Bao Saan festival, when all the uncollected buns from the Scramble are handed out to local children. I bet they were planning to move these carts right after the Scramble winners were announced, when no one would hear them trundling beneath the city."

Zhi Ging breathed in sharply, her head snapping back to Mynah and Hiulam.

"If we'd gotten to Pingon even an hour later, none of them would've been here," she hissed in disbelief. She glanced gratefully at the paper cuttings floating back into her hood. "They must have known there was only one chance to find them."

"Then we've even less time to get everyone out." Dippy grimaced, peering back down the dark tunnel. "Maybe that's why the Matchmakers split up earlier. Some were heading back here instead—we just happened to find a shortcut through that kiln."

"Just a second." Zhi Ging raced back along the carts while Dippy and Pou Pou began searching between limestone pillars for more metal tracks. She counted under her breath as she ran, her eyes darting between the faces in each cart. Every Silhouette from Ami's Perception challenge was there; the only person still missing was Reishi.

"Dippy, can you see anyone else? Not in the carts,

but maybe hidden behind a stalagmite? I'm looking for someone with . . ." Zhi Ging hesitated. She had been about to say *with a beard,* but Reishi could have ageshifted down. What if he now looked eleven again? "He won't be dressed like the others," she said instead. "He'll be in yellow robes."

"No, sorry." Dippy anxiously drummed his fingers on the carts as he made his way to her. "What do we do now? Should we follow this track?" A blast of cold air rippled through his hair as he stopped beside her, each strand swaying like blades of ink-black grass.

Zhi Ging shook her head. "I'm not sure what's at the other end, but it can't be anything good if that's where the Matchmakers planned to take them." She moved to the far cavern wall, where the wind whistled between two wide limestone pillars.

Zhi Ging crouched by the rocks, her eyes streaming as a strong gust hissed over her. Hidden behind one of the pillars was a large hollow in the cavern's sheer surface.

"There's another way out!"

"But how?" Dippy pointed at the end of the metal track. It stopped at least four feet away from the pillars.

"Give me a minute," Zhi Ging said, frowning at the space between the carts and the hollow.

All of a sudden, a loud clang echoed up the tunnel, and the metal track began to rattle. The cavern filled with overlapping arguments, the sound of bickering Matchmakers growing louder by the second.

"Minute's over." Dippy gulped, crunching across the sand toward her. He bent down, gripping a stalagmite as he leaned out of the wide opening in the rock face. Wind soared up from a field far below, the glass post pipe winding between Pavetta shrubs that promised to soften their fall. He took a deep breath, his eyes focused on the large cumulous clusters of white flowers.

"Can't be worse than landing in an ocean cloud," he whispered to himself.

Before Zhi Ging could stop him, Dippy pulled out his porcelain jar and emptied the last of his swaddling cloud across the cavern floor. He tugged expertly at its uncurling corners, tying two edges to the metal tracks before handing the other two corners to Malo and Pou Pou.

"Fly these down to the field—we're going to make an escape slide."

"But your cloud ceremony!" Zhi Ging stared at him, wide-eyed.

Dippy grimaced, then shrugged, plucking a final leaf from the cloud's surface as it stretched past them. "I guess I'd rather an unknown future than the one we're guaranteed if the Matchmakers catch us." He stood up, grabbing the side of the cart. "Come on! I'm not sure how long it'll last."

Zhi Ging scrambled to her feet to help push the carts onto the cloud. Her hair was soon plastered to her face from the effort, and Dippy's purple freckles became clearer than ever as his cheeks turned bright red from pushing. Her breath caught in her throat each time a cart dropped from the track onto the swaddling cloud, the cracks along its salt crust deepening with every thud. Behind them the rumble of the Matchmakers' cart grew louder, Niotiya's sharp voice filling the air.

Once the final cart had landed on the makeshift slide, Dippy raced back to the pillars and peered down, waving at Pou Pou and Malo.

"They're ready! The cloud's stretching all the way to the grass now."

He leaped into the front cart and held out his hand. Zhi Ging gulped and clambered up beside him. They leaned forward, and the three cuttings shot to the last cart, giving it one final push. Zhi Ging shut her eyes as they began to roll toward the sharp drop. For a second, their cart seemed to hover, caught by a strong gust of wind, then Zhi Ging's world tilted sharply forward in a near-vertical drop. The carts shot down the slide, rust sparking as their wheels spun faster than should have been possible.

There was a strange sound as they hurtled downward, like a sudden flash of metallic rain. Zhi Ging peeked through one eye and saw the Silhouettes around her jerking wildly.

"Uh-oh," Dippy whispered, his voice barely audible over the screeching wheels. Zhi Ging opened her eyes fully to see what he was staring at. Large strips of salt crust had begun to fall away as they sped to the ground, leaving patches of dangerously soft cloud between them and the end of the slide.

"Malo, Pou Pou, watch ou—" She didn't even have time to finish her sentence before their cart sank through the cloud, sending the others behind it soaring past in a wild arc. Zhi Ging and Dippy screamed as they tumbled through the air to land in a dense shrub, white petals erupting around them. She struggled to pull herself free, the force of the fall having pushed her down between gnarled branches. Two of the paper cuttings fluttered around her, checking her for injuries.

"Is everyone okay?" she shouted, her voice hoarse and dry.

There was a muffled grunt to her right as Dippy pulled his head out from between whiskery Pavetta blossoms. They stuck to his face, momentarily giving him a beard that rivaled Reishi's.

Zhi Ging looked down at the pair of cuttings now balanced on her wrist. "Where's the third one?"

The closest cutting drooped, tapping its center before shuddering.

Dippy croaked, still coughing up petals, as he pointed back to the base of the cliff. There, scattered directly beneath the cliff, were hundreds of gold coins. *That's what that odd metallic noise was,* Zhi Ging realized, her heart sinking. The paper cutting must have caught on something while pushing the cart and torn open.

Zhi Ging felt frustrated tears blur the edges of her vision. She'd already lost the paper starling that morning. She should have been able to keep the cuttings safe, especially after they helped her find the Silhouettes. She took a half step forward, wondering if she could put it back together. But before she could start searching, Pou Pou shot toward them, gesturing urgently with his tentacles. She and Dippy hurried after the jellyfish. There, beside the last evaporating sliver of ocean cloud, was Malo. The little phoenix was curled into a tight ball, shivering.

"What happened?" White petals scattered around Zhi Ging as she raced forward to scoop him up. "Was he hit by one of the carts?"

Pou Pou shook his body, his tentacles wringing together in concern.

"We need to get back to Wusi," Zhi Ging murmured before turning to the jellyfish. "Can you send a message through the post pipe? Tell the Cyo B'Ahon we need help carrying the Silhouettes back to the sick bay." She eyed the water-filled pipe anxiously. Although she now knew it was filled with jellyfish that could send messages back to Hok Woh, the sight of it still made her skin itch. Zhi Ging grimaced, wondering if she would ever see the sprawling glass pipe as anything other than the dangerous fate she has escaped by fleeing Fei Chui. Would she have made it this long as a post pipe scrubber, or like many others would she have drowned in her first month?

Pou Pou nodded and soared toward the post pipe,

rolling along its glass surface in search of a mailing hatch. Malo coughed and spluttered as Zhi Ging gently lowered him into her hood, the color in his feathers turning pale.

She and Dippy climbed back over the thicket, checking that none of the frozen Silhouettes had been hurt after falling from their carts. In front of them, the post pipe shimmered in the last rays of sunset, the water in the hollow glass barely moving. Zhi Ging ran her hands along it, shuddering at its clammy surface.

Pou Pou squeezed inside, swimming back and forth until he found another jellyfish. They linked tentacles and the smaller one wriggled once he received Pou Pou's message, shooting off farther down the pipe. Zhi Ging was still watching when she heard what sounded like cloaks rustling above her.

"That was fast!" She beamed, holding the mailing hatch open for Pou Pou.

"Um, Zhi Ging"—Dippy's voice was tight and strained and she felt him take a step back—"that's not the Cyo B'Ahon. But I think I know what chewed through those reins earlier."

CHAPTER 6

Ice raced down Zhi Ging's spine as a dark shadow swept over the post pipe. A strange writhing creature loomed above them, like nothing she had ever seen. Its giant body was a thick matted tangle of gray knots from which eight limbs extended out, each one twitching like a tentacle.

The creature had no face, but it seemed to know exactly where the group was. Its two closest tentacles morphed into sharp pincers while the other six stretched down to the ground, slithering toward them at speed. It emitted a constant, steady hiss as it leaned forward, both pincers open. One clamped around Dippy and began to lift him up, gray sand cascading down as the terrified boy struggled to break free.

"No!" Zhi Ging raced forward, Malo leaping out of her hood to help. She watched as flames flickered to life across the tips of his feathers, but then the little phoenix flinched, spluttering violently before plummeting to the ground. She caught him as he fell, a wracking cough shaking his entire body and extinguishing his flames. Pou Pou shot out of the post pipe, a trail of smaller jellyfish rising up behind him as they fought to pull Dippy free.

The creature batted them away with its free pincer, clearly immune to jellyfish stings, and stretched another tentacle past Zhi Ging to pluck Mynah out of a nearby bush. Its other limbs wrapped around overturned carts, dragging out more Silhouettes.

"Let them go!" Zhi Ging screamed. She leaped up, grabbing onto her friend before the pincer could drag the frozen Silhouette away. There was a loud rip, and the creature's gray tentacle snapped under her extra weight, sending Zhi Ging and Mynah crashing down. They rolled as they hit the ground and the remaining paper cuttings tumbled out of her hood.

Zhi Ging watched in horror as gray sand streamed out of the creature's broken limb, its furious hissing now louder than ever. The paper cuttings rustled in confusion, tilting up to take in the monstrous creature, when a tentacle lashed forward like a striking snake and sliced right through them.

"No!" Zhi Ging tried to catch the falling fragments, but the creature wrapped its tentacle tightly around the paper scraps, absorbing them beneath its gray surface. Gold light flared across its body, pulsing toward its broken limb. The falling gray sand slowed and began to thicken in midair, transforming into a new pincer identical to the one it had just lost.

"It's a sand spirit!" Dippy shouted down. "We must have damaged its nest when we landed."

"But how? We're not even near a desert!" Zhi Ging cried, yelping as the original broken pincer began to thump toward her.

She spun out of reach, and a flash of red high up on the rock face caught her eye. A figure stood by the hollow with both arms raised, their fingers mirroring the movement of the spirit's tentacles. Circular bands of gray caught in the light as they raised their hands above a blue headdress. Zhi Ging's mouth dropped open in surprise. It was Niotiya. But how was she controlling the spirit? Not even the Cyo B'Ahon could do that.

A second strong wind rose up around them, and the spirit screeched, sand streaming from its tentacles until they were reduced to spindly spider legs. Its matted body shrank, leaving a single complex knot of gray with eight sharp stubs thrashing at its core.

A buzzing green comet shot toward them, and the air filled with the sound of rustling silk. Zhi Ging looked up as more shadows covered the field, relief flooding through her.

It was the floating market!

Stall owners leaped from their tents, scrambling up the weakened spirit to pull Dippy and the frozen Silhouettes free.

"Get in the tent!" Gertie yelled, holding the entrance open as Jack raced toward Zhi Ging.

She staggered to her feet just as the comet of weather-wax bees barreled into the sand spirit's central knot.

It froze, the spirit's hissing replaced by a sudden deafening silence. Jack skidded to a stop beside Zhi Ging, watching openmouthed as the spirit began to twitch, lurching from side to side as hundreds of bright green bees worked together to untangle its tentacles. Its pincers snapped open, then the spirit erupted. Waves of gray sand cascaded over the floating market as the spirit split into eight loose tendrils. Seven strands immediately twisted into the air, slashing through the deep blue dusk as they raced across the horizon.

"Don't let it escape," Gertie ordered, pointing at the eighth tendril as it slithered over Jack's shoes before attempting to burrow underground. Her weather-wax bees soared forward, their warm bodies glinting as they descended around the fleeing sand. It began to steam, bubbling, as grains melted and fused together like glass. *It's made from heat-sensitive sand,* Zhi Ging realized with a jolt. The bees now hovered about the glistening puddle, their wings beating rapidly to cool the molten glass.

Once it had solidified, Gertie snatched up the glass, fragments of burned earth tumbling through her fingers. The newly formed structure looked like a sea urchin: narrow dark spikes of glass that stretched out from a central dome. Zhi Ging's mouth dropped open as the spikes dimmed to clear glass, the darkness trickling into the hollow dome as individual grains of gray sand.

Gertie's eyes flickered between the spikes, counting them under her breath. "This spirit was determined to escape." She nodded proudly at her bees. "Well done on cooling the glass as quickly as you did."

Gertie held the spirit's new glass cage away from her body as she bundled Zhi Ging, Dippy, and Jack back toward her tent. Around them, stall owners were setting up makeshift hammocks, gently lowering in frozen Silhouettes while Pou Pou kept watch, scanning the skies for more spirit tendrils.

Zhi Ging followed Gertie through the comforting jumbled piles that filled the tent. The old woman finally stopped in front of a cluttered side table covered in spools of thread and silk strips. She snapped her fingers and Dippy yelped in surprise as the fabric immediately began to move, sliding off the surface as order ants made space for the glass cage. Once Gertie had placed it down, a dozen weather-wax bees landed along its spikes, buzzing so furiously that the table itself began to rattle.

"Hush now," Gertie said soothingly. "You've done well trapping the spirit. We won't let it escape."

"I've never seen the bees react like this to anything," Jack said in a hushed voice. "Not even that time someone tried to steal an entire tray of fresh weather wax."

"How did Niotiya get it to attack us?" Zhi Ging asked, careful to avoid the longer spikes as she crouched down to peer into the glass.

"What do you mean?" Gertie's head snapped to her.

"I saw her, back on the mountain. She was moving her arms around, almost like she was showing the sand spirit what to do." Zhi Ging glanced over at Dippy, but he was looking at her in confusion. *Had he not seen the Matchmaker?*

Gertie's expression darkened. "In all my decades I've only come across two sand spirits, and neither of them looked anything like this." She nodded at the cage, where the tendril was still lashing against the glass. "Spirits usually avoid humans. If Niotiya really has summoned one, I wonder what she offered it in return. You'll have to warn Reishi about this."

Zhi Ging's heart dropped. "I can't. Reishi's missing," she croaked. "That's what I've been trying to tell you."

Malo chirped feebly from her hood as Jack and Gertie stared at her in shock.

"Ami tricked him; she pretended that she and the other Silhouettes were attacked after the last challenge, but"— Zhi Ging sat down, nodding gratefully at the small army of order ants that had chosen that moment to scurry over with chairs for everyone—"there never was a Fui Gwai; it was all Ami."

Gertie sucked in a sharp breath and Jack's eyes flashed

54

furiously between green and blue. Even the order ants stopped, turning slowly to form a semicircle around Zhi Ging rather than hurry on to their next task.

"That memory elixir she had? Turns out it was something much worse. Since she was the Dohrnii, none of the other Cyo B'Ahon noticed just how much time she spent in the Seoi Mou Pou. After all, it was her job to look after both Silhouettes and the baby jellyfish. But it turned out she'd actually been stealing jellyfish and using them to possess Silhouettes who failed their challenge, pretending each jellyfish was a droplet of memory elixir."

"She was possessing children right in front of other tutors?" Gertie's face was thunderous, deep seams of fury carving across her usual web of smile lines.

Zhi Ging gulped; the sand spirit could have erupted from the fierceness of Gertie's glare alone.

"And in front of me," Jack whispered, guilt washing over his face. "I never even thought to look."

Gertie's features immediately softened and she shook her head. "None of that, now; you're not responsible for Ami's actions. Those who've been tricked should never feel ashamed—that's reserved for the deceiver. Now"—she turned back to Zhi Ging—"where does Reishi come in?"

"After the last challenge, the mirror maze outside Omophilli, I had to go back to Hok Woh for detention. Ami burst in and told Reishi that the other Silhouettes had been kidnapped by thralls. He raced out with Gahyau to find them and he's been missing ever since. Sintou's convinced Ami must have planned a trap before she fell into the underwater waterfall."

"Is that who you were looking for back in the cavern?" Dippy blurted out, before slapping a purple-freckled hand over his mouth, clearly not meaning to interrupt.

"Yeah. I was hoping we'd find him with the Silhouettes, but he wasn't there." Her voice cracked as she held Malo's outstretched wing.

A brief look of panic flickered over Gertie's face, then she pulled Zhi Ging into a tight hug. "In that case, the floating market will help." She stood up, scanning the jumbled piles, then leaned past Jack to pull a small wooden block out from between several unlit lanterns. A bee floated up from a glass spike and nodded at Gertie as it landed on the block. They bent their heads together in concentration, the old woman muttering instructions under her breath while the bee traced its stinger across the block, thin curls of wood falling like confetti.

"How does this look?" Gertie asked a few minutes later, turning the block to the group.

Zhi Ging blinked in surprise. There, carved into its surface, was a perfect likeness of Reishi's fifty-year-old face, down to his neat beard and the laughter lines that radiated out from his eyes. "It looks just like him."

The bee buzzed happily, delighted with the compliment.

Gertie gestured back toward the table and the order ants reappeared, each carrying a blank slip of paper.

Gertie pulled a thick calligraphy brush from under a tray of dried haw flakes and dipped it into a pot of emerald ink. She swiped the rich ink across Reishi's carved face as the order ants began to line up. Even the sand tendril stopped lashing out, coiling along the inner glass to watch the order ants with interest.

"Remember the slip I gave you last time you visited the market? The one with the face and ink feet?" Gertie murmured, catching Zhi Ging's confused expression. "Well, these are similar. The difference is, rather than leading you straight to me, they'll wander around Wengyuen until they spot the face that matches their stamp." She paused, a smile dancing at the corners of her mouth as she glanced at Jack. "I had to use so many of these for him when he was younger. Once, when Jack was five, he wandered off while we were setting up and we only found him hours later, fast asleep in a field surrounded by cheering slips. It was quite a day for the entire floating market."

Jack laughed, shaking his head. "I'm pretty sure the slips found me after twenty minutes, not 'hours later.' It's not like you to undersell how fast they are."

Gertie chuckled as she stamped Reishi's face across one of the new slips. "What can I say? Your constant wandering over the years helped improve their search times. These should hopefully find Reishi for us—no matter where he is in Wengyuen. They'll last until the next rainfall too, which gives us"—Gertie glanced up at a bouquet of dried flowers balanced above a teak cabinet and counted the open petals along a pale blue flower—"six days. After that, the ink will wash away."

Zhi Ging stared up at the flower, a new thought slowly blooming in her mind. The droplet-shaped petals were the exact same shade of blue as Ami's glasses and, when she tilted her head, each petal revealed itself to be made up of neatly overlapping layers.

"We thought Ami might be working with one other person," Zhi Ging began slowly, still craning her neck at the bouquet, "but what if it's an entire group? What if the Matchmakers' Guild is involved?"

"It'd make sense for Ami to recruit them." Gertie scowled. "Apart from the floating market, no one travels around Wengyuen as much as the Matchmakers. I bet Niotiya would know all the best places to hide thralls in each province."

"But where does the sand spirit come in?" Jack asked, waving a hand toward the glass cage.

A tense silence fell over the group, broken only by Malo's coughing.

The old woman's eyes flashed to the little phoenix and she frowned. "When did this start?" she murmured, running a finger over his shivering feathers.

"Just before we were attacked. I don't know what caused it, though," Zhi Ging admitted.

Dippy shook his head, equally unsure.

Gertie frowned and gently lifted the phoenix out of Zhi Ging's hood. "You poor thing. Let's take a look at—"

Malo yelped in pain, both wings clasping his stomach.

Gertie spun back to Zhi Ging, her expression serious. "What's he eaten today? Quickly, now." She pulled what looked like a handful of cloves out of her pocket and held them out to Malo. "This will help with the pain, but if it's food poisoning I can't start brewing a cure until I know what he's had."

"I, uh . . ." Zhi Ging floundered, flashes of the chase through Pingon and the sand spirit attack threatening to drown out her other memories.

"We shared one of your steamed buns. Right before the Scramble," Dippy suggested before his eyebrows knit together. "But I feel fine. Could he be allergic to the filling?"

Zhi Ging yelped. "That's not the last thing *Malo* ate, though!" She rummaged in her pocket, her fingers shaking as they closed around the half-eaten bun that had fallen out of Jack's bag during the Scramble. She dropped the squashed remains onto the table, the Matchmakers' red seal staining the bun's white surface.

Gertie carefully peeled back the upper half of the bun, stale dough coming loose between her fingers. There was no sign of sesame, red bean, or lotus seed paste in its center. Instead the bun was filled with gray spirit sand.

The group stared at each other in disbelief. Zhi Ging felt her stomach turn—had the bun that the Matchmaker tried to force-feed her been the same?

"The feast!" Jack and Dippy blurted in unison, their faces pale.

Gertie leaped up, racing back to the tent entrance. "Vrile!" She barked at a passing stall owner, causing the young bald man to jump. "Get back to Pingon now! No one there touches the tower buns. Bring back every last one."

"What's going on?" Zhi Ging asked as the weatherwax bees swarmed out to join him. "Surely the Scramble's been over for ages?"

Jack glanced up at the rising moon and winced.

"The Bao Saan feast will be starting soon. Any buns not collected during the Scramble are given out to children across Pingon and—"

"And I doubt the Matchmakers added that spirit sand for *flavor*." Gertie glowered, gesturing for them to follow her through the market. They trailed after her, weaving between the dozens of hammocks that now swung between tents, each one holding a frozen Silhouette. In the distance the rock face was gray—no flash of Matchmaker red.

"We'd better have enough of these," Gertie sighed, fingers drumming a nearby hammock.

"I can help take the Silhouettes back to Hok Woh," Jack offered. "Let me borrow the tent and I'll fly everyone back. It's the safest way to free up more hammocks, and besides"—he grinned—"no one would ever expect me to turn up there tonight."

Gertie hesitated, her expression shifting almost as much as a Cyo B'Ahon trying not to ageshift.

Zhi Ging peered at her in confusion. *Why does she almost look guilty?*

"That might not be true," Gertie said eventually.

"What do you mean?" Jack asked absently, already busy making plans.

"Now that Ami's gone, Hok Woh will need another Dohrnii, someone to look after the Silhouettes."

Jack shrugged. "I'm sure Sintou's got someone in mind."

"I suspect she'll want the previous Dohrnii, the Cyo B'Ahon that Ami replaced."

"Sure, fine, who was that?" Jack asked.

Gertie placed a hand on his shoulder, and when she spoke her voice was barely louder than a whisper.

"Jack, it was you."

CHAPTER 7

Jack's eyes flickered, no longer green and blue but a teal haze. "Is that meant to be a joke? It's not funny."

"I swore to Reishi I'd never say." Gertie sighed deeply, kneading the wrinkles across her face until they folded into one another. "I've raised eight Reverted Cyo B'Ahon over the years and managed to keep that promise every time. Until today."

Jack stood stock-still, barely breathing as he stared up at her. "I was a Cyo B'Ahon?" His voice came out as little more than a croak, struggling to take in anything she was saying.

The old woman nodded, gently folding his hands between her weathered palms. "According to Reishi, you were the only Cyo B'Ahon who could regularly make Sintou laugh." She smiled fondly at him. "Just the way you do with me."

"But Reishi never said. Why didn't he ever tell me?" Jack demanded, pulling free.

Zhi Ging felt her stomach tighten and she tugged Dippy away. Jack was always so confident; it felt wrong for them to see him like this.

"Because you made him promise, right before you Reverted." Gertie's voice floated after them. "That was the only way he could keep visiting, making sure you were growing up happy." There was a long pause and Zhi Ging faltered, suddenly wondering if Jack would have wanted a friend beside him after all. She turned around, but his reply was swallowed up by the layers of fabric that separated them. All she saw was Gertie's face crumple before he darted between two hammocks, vanishing into the market.

ZHI GING AND DIPPY SAT TOGETHER IN SILENCE, feet dangling over the tent entrance as they floated back toward Hok Woh. They flung batches of stamped slips out over the passing valleys and fields, watching as Reishi's inked face glinted up at them, overlapping winds sending the slips in different directions.

When the midnight ocean finally reappeared on the horizon, Zhi Ging glanced back at Jack. He had spent most of the journey curled up at the back of the tent, clutching a sleeping Malo in his arms. Gertie sat beside him now, whispering as she refilled his fifth cup of jasmine tea. Over the past few hours, Jack's head shakes had slowly turned to hesitant nods of understanding. As Zhi Ging watched he gave a small half smile, and Gertie's entire body sagged with obvious relief.

"How do you think he's doing?" Dippy whispered, releasing the last of his slips over a vast waterfall. "Should we go over?"

"Not yet," Zhi Ging murmured, twisting her gold Pan Chang between her fingers. She was desperate to talk to her friend but wasn't sure how much he'd want to say in front of Dippy. She turned back to Dippy and winced, moonlight catching against his open face. "We've not even asked Gertie to look at your freckles yet."

"Don't worry about it—they're not painful." He shook his head and the purple dots flowed across his nose to resettle around his temples. "I'm actually getting used to them, and they definitely made my birthday memorable."

"More memorable than being chased by Matchmakers and attacked by a sand spirit?" Zhi Ging raised an eyebrow, laughing as Dippy gave an exaggerated shudder that sent the freckles ricocheting across his cheeks. "Well, we should still get Gertie to check them before she drops you back at Wun-Wun. Why don't I ask . . ." A flash of gold beneath them caught her eye. She leaned forward, holding on to the side of the tent.

Zhi Ging gasped, pointing at the fluttering silk carriage waiting for them on the shore. "It's Sintou's sedan."

"Wait here," Gertie warned once they landed, hurrying across the pebbles toward the Head of the Cyo B'Ahon. They bent their heads together in urgent discussion, and Zhi Ging was struck by how different the two similar-aged women looked. Decades hidden beneath the waves in Hok Woh had left Sintou with skin so pale she seemed almost unearthly, while Gertie's warm tan sang of a life spent exploring Wengyuen under a blazing sky, layers of memory stamped in sunlight.

Zhi Ging spotted Sintou's features flicker with shock, and for one brief second she caught a glimpse of what the Head of the Cyo B'Ahon must have looked like in her forties. High cheekbones disappeared beneath willow-leaf eyes as Sintou shook her head, returning to her usual age.

"I hope Gertie's not getting in trouble," Jack murmured, coming to sit between Zhi Ging and Dippy. She gave him a grateful smile as he lowered a snoring Malo back into her hood, relieved he was talking again.

You okay? Zhi Ging mouthed, carefully tilting her head toward him. Jack scrunched up his nose and exhaled deeply.

"Don't know about okay, but apparently I'm old," he whispered back, a ghost of a grin tugging at the corner of his mouth.

"Could we ask Pou Pou to listen in for us?" Dippy wondered, glancing at the jellyfish floating above them.

Zhi Ging snorted. "Probably not. He belongs to Sintou."

Dippy went bright red and mouthed, *Will he tell her I just asked that?*

Zhi Ging laughed as Pou Pou bounced on top of his head in a mock scolding. "I think we're safe."

"What do you think they *are* saying?" Jack asked, a

mischievous glint returning to his eyes. "I'm pretty sure I just saw Gertie say *half-price weather-wax*. Maybe she's actually trying to sell the entire tent before the market closes."

The three of them began trying to lip-read the conversation, each suggestion becoming more ridiculous until Jack and Zhi Ging were convinced the two women were talking about the best way to boil bamboo and store bubbles, while Dippy was sure they were competing to see who could list more words that rhymed with "congee." They were still shaking with quiet laughter when Gertie bowed and began to march back to the tent. Behind her Sintou gestured for them to approach.

"Did she mean me too?" Dippy asked as he trailed after Zhi Ging and Jack, staring at the gold-robed Cyo B'Ahon in apprehension.

Gertie herded him gently back to the tent. "This is just for them. The bees have made some fresh egg tarts, so we'll have a little snack while they talk." He hurried after her with obvious relief, smiling as her emerald-green bees rose to greet him; the purple freckles along his arms swirled to mimic their movements.

Zhi Ging hesitated, then spun around, ignoring Sintou's raised eyebrow. "Gertie, can you take a look at Dippy's purple freckles?" she shouted back. "It's my fault he has them."

The old woman sighed good-naturedly and shook her

head. "There you go again: still trying to hide what makes you different. Dippy doesn't need these removed any more than you needed that glove to conceal your gold lines." She smiled thoughtfully at the boy, watching as her bees began to dance in time with his freckles. "In fact, we might be able to find a way to train them, transform them into something no one from Wun-Wun could even dream of."

"Really?" Dippy beamed, his freckles bursting like fireworks around his eyes.

"Absolutely." Gertie smiled, pulling a gold coin from behind his ear. "Besides, after the sand spirit attack, some of my bees found hundreds of these scattered beneath the cliff." She looked up, flashing Zhi Ging a conspiratorial wink. "I can only imagine this was the money you'd already earned selling an entire cart's worth of ocean cloud. It also happens to be more than enough to pay your father for you to join the floating market as an apprentice. If, after a year, you decide you don't like it, I'll remove your freckles and take you back to Wun-Wun."

Dippy shook his head emphatically. "I won't."

"Excellent, in that case, once you've finished your egg tart we can walk back to Wun-Wun and discuss everything with your father."

Zhi Ging waved as Dippy vanished into the tent, surrounded by an excited green cloud of bees. Pou Pou nudged her gently and she hurried to catch up with Jack, who was already standing beside Sintou.

"Now," the Head of the Cyo B'Ahon began, fixing them both with a serious expression, "Zhi Ging, once we've found a way to lift the possession, you are to tell none of the other Silhouettes that Jack used to be a Cyo B'Ahon. That is to remain a secret no matter what."

"Does that mean Jack's coming back? Is he going to be a Silhouette too?" she asked, her heart leaping with excitement. They wouldn't just have to catch up at challenges anymore.

"That is up to him," Sintou explained calmly. "Only Jack can decide if he would like to return to Hok Woh. He never told me why he first chose to Revert."

Zhi Ging's heart sank when her friend refused to meet her eye; the back of his neck flushed red as he stared down at the waves instead.

The silence stretched tight between them and was only broken when other Cyo B'Ahon began to appear from the entrance stepping stone, leaping to the beach with stretchers for the frozen Silhouettes. Zhi Ging spotted Gwong and Yuttou, two members of her dragon boat team, looking at her and Jack curiously as they raced past.

"I—I don't know," Jack mumbled, peering back at Gertie's tent.

Sintou nodded. "Take some time to decide." Her face softened into a warm smile as Pou Pou landed gracefully between their feet. "I'm glad Pou Pou was helpful," she said to Zhi Ging. "I look forward to getting his account of how you found the Silhouettes."

Zhi Ging sighed, still staring at her friend and desperately trying to guess what he was thinking. "We weren't able to find Reishi."

"True, but thanks to your efforts the shoreside Scouts now have a united mission. It'll be easier for them to search for a single Cyo B'Ahon rather than several Silhouettes." She turned back to Pou Pou and gestured to the entrance stepping stone. "Let Wusi know the Silhouettes will be arriving in the sick bay shortly."

"Do you think she could take a look at Malo too?" Zhi Ging asked, holding the sleeping phoenix out toward Sintou. While Gertie's herbs seemed to have eased his shivering, he was still pale, his colorful feathers dimmed as if they'd been dipped in a gray glaze.

The Head of the Cyo B'Ahon frowned, twin lines appearing between her thin eyebrows as she stroked his wing. "Ai'Deng Bou," she called out, and Zhi Ging's former tutor skidded to a stop beside them, an empty stretcher tucked under his arm. "I need you to prioritize getting Malo back to full health. We'll need him if phoenix fire turns out to be the only cure to Ami's possession."

The Fauna tutor nodded and pulled a handful of sunflower seeds from his pocket, but Malo simply peered blearily at them, then spluttered, a small gray cloud billowing out from his beak.

"We think he swallowed some spirit sand," Zhi Ging explained as Ai'Deng Bou's eyebrows shot up.

He lifted Malo out of her arms, gesturing for them

to follow him. "If Malo was an ordinary duckling, I'd recommend magnolia root, but I suspect the spirit sand has dampened the fire in his core," he explained as they rushed down the winding steps, the empty stretcher occasionally hitting the glass like a broken wing. "We need to coax those flames back to life."

Zhi Ging raced after him into Hok Woh's circular main hall, then skidded to a stop, staring back up the empty staircase.

Jack hadn't followed them.

Her heart sank as she held her breath, hoping to hear her friend's footsteps hurrying down the glass. She hesitated, unsure whether to race back up or follow Ai'Deng Bou. *I didn't even say bye. What if Jack decides he wants nothing to do with Hok Woh now? Will he even show up at the next challenge?* She took a half step back toward the stairs, then Malo's pained whimper echoed down the corridor. Zhi Ging winced and raced after Ai'Deng Bou, the guilt at leaving Jack curdling with the worry that had already settled deep in her stomach.

Ai'Deng Bou slid the Silhouette dorm door open and headed straight for the central fireplace, where the orchid-scented flames rose, as if sensing Malo's pain.

Of course! It's also phoenix fire.

A flame coiled past the Cyo B'Ahon's hands, softly stroking Malo's feathers as he was lowered into the fireplace. Almost immediately, the phoenix stopped shivering and Zhi Ging exhaled deeply, only now realizing how long she had been holding her breath.

"If he starts getting worse, come and find me immediately," Ai'Deng Bou ordered, adjusting the stretcher under his arm. "I'll come to check on him once all the others are safely in the sick bay." With that, he sprinted back out to the stairwell, leaving Zhi Ging alone.

She settled down beside the fireplace, watching Malo snuffle in his sleep, pulling flames around him like a blanket. Her eyes began to prickle and she sniffed deeply, clutching her sides tight. First, she hadn't been able to say goodbye to Aapua, her old guardian, who was sent away in Fei Chui's roaming pagoda on the day of her Silhouette exam, and now she'd lost the chance to say goodbye to Jack.

Zhi Ging peered around the empty dorm. For once, there were no softly glowing paper screen doors, revealing which Silhouettes were staying up late to finish homework or had sneaked back from the dining hall with a bowl of warm midnight noodles. There was no soft clink of homei spoons and calligraphy brushes or whispered guesses about what the next challenge would be.

There was just her.

Zhi Ging looked at her screen door, her bed waiting on the other side. But then her eyes slid to Mynah's door beside it: silence radiated through the paper screen. She'd never be able to sleep knowing everyone else was in the sick bay.

Zhi Ging crouched down, straining to hear the faint crackle of flames dancing in the firepit. It almost sounded like distant footsteps racing around the dorm. She squeezed her eyes shut, curling up on the floor as close to Malo as she could.

Mynah and the others are going to wake up any second now, she told herself. *They're going to come back. They have to.*

CHAPTER 8

The next morning, Zhi Ging peeled herself off the dorm floor and rubbed the left side of her face, which was numb after a night pressed against the glass. A note in Ai'Deng Bou's scratchy handwriting had been left beside her, explaining that he had collected Malo for a few extra checkups but that the little phoenix's feathers already seemed to be brightening.

Her stomach rumbled and Zhi Ging grimaced realizing she hadn't eaten anything since Gertie's festival bun the previous afternoon.

At least I don't have to worry about the best homei spoons being taken.

Jellyfish waved at her as she trudged along the corridors, clearly relieved to see at least one Silhouette still in the realm. Zhi Ging raised a hand to the dining hall door, and it slid open to reveal a beaming familiar face.

"Jack!" she yelped, her hunger immediately forgotten.

He spun in front of her, a black Silhouette cloak

flapping, while two bowls teetered and wobbled in his palms.

Once they were comfortably seated, he passed her a bowl and began to explain. "I had a long chat with Gertie last night. Neither of us knows why I Reverted before, but all the clues have to be hidden here in Hok Woh." He flashed Zhi Ging a smile as he handed her a red and brown homei spoon. "And if I come back, it means I don't have to keep smuggling these out with me."

Despite his breezy tone, Zhi Ging knew it had to have been a big decision to leave the floating market. "I'm glad you're here," she said quietly, nudging her shoulder against his.

"How's Malo doing?" he asked, glancing into her empty hood.

"I think he's going to be okay," Zhi Ging admitted with relief. "Ai'Deng Bou has him right now, so he's probably scoffing sunflower seeds." She tapped the homei spoon over her breakfast bowl and the shards tumbled down to become a comforting helping of lou yuk faan. Red porcelain transformed into a generous portion of braised pork balanced above fluffy steamed rice, while a single brown fragment wobbled over the top before cracking open, turning into two halves of a perfectly jammy tea-stained egg.

"What do you think happens now?" Zhi Ging added, sprinkling sesame seeds over her breakfast.

"What do you mean?" Jack bit into a glossy rice noodle

roll, chewing appreciatively before putting his chopsticks down.

"Well, are we still meant to have Perception classes?" Zhi Ging lowered her voice, although there was no one else there. "Ami was going to be our next tutor. Are they really going to go ahead with just the two of us? You've already done all twelve challenges anyway."

"Yeah, but I don't remember passing any of them." Jack shrugged, filling her teacup. "Besides, before your Concealment challenge, Yingzi mentioned she'd changed how she taught that skill. You know, after the original Hok Woh was attacked. What if Perception's also changed?"

Splash.

"What was that?" Zhi Ging looked up at the sound of water sloshing against the glass floor. She spun around and saw Pou Pou waving at them from his basin, water spilling out over the crane's carved glass feet.

She grabbed the last lau sah bao in the steamer and they hurried over to the jellyfish. Pou Pou accepted the custard bun enthusiastically, then turned opaque, elegant brushstrokes shimmering across his body.

Tutor Miraj will lead your lessons this month.
Wait for him in the main hall.
Sintou

"Does that name mean anything to you?" Zhi Ging asked.

"No, I really don't remember anything from before." Jack paused, his eyes flashing blue and green as he tried to explain the unshakable memory loss. "It's like asking you to describe a dream you had when you were three."

"Hmm, maybe seeing Tutor Miraj's face will help."

They hurried out, both curious to meet their new tutor. However, Zhi Ging skidded to a stop at the end of the corridor, pointing out a solitary boy lurching around the main hall. He looked no older than twelve, but his cloak was strangely dated, the pattern stitched along his oversized sleeves a design even Aapau would have called old-fashioned. The boy hummed to himself, both eyes clamped shut as he moved in erratic circles. One leg occasionally swung in new directions, and his entire body swayed wildly as it tried to keep up. He teetered toward one path before spinning toward another corridor that twisted out from the hall.

"I've never seen him before," Zhi Ging whispered, taking a step back as the boy began to career toward them. "He definitely wasn't in the dorms before Ami's challenge."

"Could he be one of the Silhouettes from the catacombs?" Jack asked. He grabbed Zhi Ging's arm as the boy's outstretched hands swung inches from their faces. "Let's get Wusi," he hissed. "We don't want a thrall loose around Hok Woh."

"No need." The boy's eyes snapped open, causing them both to jump.

Zhi Ging was relieved to see his irises were a rich dark brown, not the all-consuming gray of a possessed thrall. The boy ageshifted up to sixty and gestured for them to step out of the shadows.

"Sorry about that. I hadn't quite considered how bizarre I'd look," he said with a wry chuckle, his dated robes now much more suited to his lined face. "I'm Tutor Miraj. I'm afraid I left my classroom to fetch you and now I can't remember the way back. It's been centuries since I wandered over to this part of Hok Woh. I was hoping if I ageshifted down, muscle memory would kick in." He hesitated, then pointed at the corridor next to theirs. "I *think* it's this way."

THEY SPENT THE NEXT TWO HOURS WANDERING around Hok Woh, Tutor Miraj ageshifting in frustration each time they arrived at another dead end. Occasionally he was forced to knock against a glass wall, asking a passing jellyfish for directions. Jack caught Zhi Ging's eye as they once again spun around to retrace their footsteps.

"At least I'm getting the scenic welcome tour," he whispered. "I've really enjoyed walking down this corridor three times."

Zhi Ging snorted, gazing up at the now-extremely-familiar statues around them. "Just you wait—it gets *really* exciting on the fifth wander past."

Tutor Miraj's face finally lit up as they passed a glass statue of two cranes in flight.

"That's more like it! Right, I know where we are now."
He began to take long, confident strides, almost sprinting
as he led them down three more twisting corridors. The
Cyo B'Ahon finally came to a stop, pointing to a door
made up of mirrored panels at the very end of the corridor. "After you." He beamed, sweeping his arm in a dramatic flourish.

Zhi Ging and Jack walked forward, their confusion
growing with each step. The door was tiny, no larger
than one of the books in the library. Tutor Miraj was still
standing at the corridor entrance, smiling encouragingly
at them.

"I don't think we're going to fit," Zhi Ging said, crouching down beside the miniature door. Even then, her chin
was a good foot higher than the top of the frame.

"Oh, dear me, I see we'll be beginning with the very
basics of Perception today." Tutor Miraj chuckled, tilting
his head with an indulgent smile. He gestured for the two
Silhouettes to rejoin him at the corridor entrance. "Hopefully, by the end of our month together, you'll be able to
do this for yourselves but, at least for today, let me open
the door for you. Now, you both took one look at that door
and thought, *Absolutely not, this is far too small.* At the same
time, the door took one look at you and thought, *No way,
they're far too big.* What we want to do now is change *both*
perceptions." Tutor Miraj held out his palms, then slowly
and deliberately brought the two hands together. "Both
you and the door currently agree there's the same issue,

which'll make it easier to find a harmonious solution. All we need to do is nudge the balance between perceived and genuine reality. They should still overlap, of course, but they don't need to be identical."

He pulled the two Silhouettes farther down the corridor until their reflections fitted neatly within the door's mirrored panels. Tutor Miraj shut one eye and stretched out his hand while his miniature reflection did the same. He pushed his hand sharply to the left and the door slid open, revealing his classroom.

"Now," he said, leading them back toward the door, "holding two perceptions simultaneously can be tricky and gives some people a rather nasty headache. I recommend closing your eyes until we reach the classroom."

Zhi Ging shut hers tight, bracing herself to hit the wall above the door. Instead, she felt the doorframe creak as they stepped through, the space expanding to welcome them.

"No way," Jack whispered beside her.

Zhi Ging opened her eyes. They were now standing at the top of a vast circular amphitheater.

Thick banners of silk covered the ceiling and walls, the fabric spooling out across the floor. In the center was a large, water-filled pipe that stretched up from the floor and vanished into the silks.

"Please sit on opposite sides of the room," Tutor Miraj instructed.

Zhi Ging giggled as Jack settled on the far side of

the glass pipe, his features suddenly magnified so his nose stretched to fill its width. Tutor Miraj leaped to one side and pulled a lever. Jellyfish poured into the water, their white glow filling the amphitheater as they danced around, waving at the two Silhouettes.

"Now, we lost a bit of time getting here, so I'm going to dive straight into the main part of this morning's lesson. There's something odd about what you're looking at," Tutor Miraj said, still clutching the lever. "What is it?"

Zhi Ging and Jack were silent, both peering intently at the glass in front of them.

"Is it the jellyfish?" Zhi Ging guessed, flashing back to the mirror maze from Ami's Perception challenge. "Is there actually only one and the rest are reflections?"

"Creative, but I'm afraid not. How about you, Master Oltryds? You figured it out the last time you were my student."

"I, uh . . ." The pipe seemed to flash green and blue as he shifted awkwardly in his seat. "Is it actually just filled with air? Are these jellyfish that can float without bubbles?"

"Dearie me, and that's it—we're out of Silhouettes to guess." Tutor Miraj shook his head.

"Are you going to tell us?" Zhi Ging asked.

"Trust me, you'll get a big clue in three . . . two . . ."

She felt something hit her ear and stared in surprise as her braid stood straight up, reaching past the top of her head.

Tutor Miraj finally let go of the lever, ageshifting back down to twenty as he shot up to the ceiling. Zhi Ging's mouth dropped open as he pulled another lever and the silk curtains drew back.

The entire classroom had spun upside down. What had been the floor was now the ceiling, while all around them was ocean. A pod of pink dolphins swam past, clicking excitedly as they spotted the Silhouettes.

"Never get distracted. Once you choose the wrong focus"—Tutor Miraj tapped the glass pipe—"you'll lose all perception of what's really going on around you." He nodded at the jellyfish as they floated back out of the pipe, their white glows flashing in time with their silent chuckles. "I spent last night reading through the materials Ami had planned for your lessons. I never should have let her take over as Perception tutor. No wonder no Silhouette's chosen this as their specialty skill in years." He paused, ageshifting back up to sixty. "It's true that inward and outward perception are important, but perception doesn't stop there, as Ami tried to claim. I can see now she was trying to keep half the knowledge for herself. Deliberately, I suspect." Tutor Miraj shook his head in frustration before continuing. "I'm going to teach you what to *do* with outward perceptions. What use is it to simply know what others think of you? In our role as Wengyuen's guardians, Cyo B'Ahon need to help change perceptions across provinces. Perception isn't a simple mirror, where what you see is what you get. No, it's like water—it can flow and adapt. Over the next four weeks, I'm going to teach you how to wear different perceptions like a cloak."

He strode briskly around the water pipe, his reflection rippling before he reemerged on the other side.

Zhi Ging's eyes widened. His musty cloak was gone, replaced by bright yellow robes, identical to those Reishi had worn while overseeing Silhouette entrance exams.

"I'm usually shoreside as a Scout, but let's see if I can still improve talent as well as spot it."

THAT EVENING, POU POU DELIVERED ANOTHER message, and Zhi Ging and Jack hurried along the corridor to Sintou's office, the secret glass entrance already open for them.

"Malo!" Zhi Ging cheered as she stepped into the room.

The Head of the Cyo B'Ahon looked up from the six-pointed checkerboard in front of her, where the little phoenix was currently rolling each glass marble over in search of hidden sunflower seeds. Tutor Miraj waved from the chair facing Sintou, quickly flicking one of his pieces sideways while she was distracted. Above him, the trapped white flame that lived behind the glass walls of Sintou's office flared, twisting together to spell out the word "cheat" in bright burning letters.

The Head of the Cyo B'Ahon chuckled as Tutor Miraj sheepishly returned his marble to its original space. "You'll have to try harder than that." She stood up and poured two small cups of tea for Zhi Ging and Jack. "I hope you've both settled back. I—"

"Has anyone found Reishi yet?" Zhi Ging blurted out. The question had been bubbling inside her all day.

The flame above Sintou dimmed momentarily.

"I'm afraid not," she admitted. "However, there has been some good news." She pulled a slightly water-damaged scroll from her sleeve. "Bucbou and the other dragon boat captains have spent the past twenty-four hours circling the underwater waterfall, and there's been no sign whatsoever of Ami. It's safe to say she won't be escaping. Not even one of Ai'Deng Bou's pink dolphins could hold their breath for that long." She handed the scroll to Malo, who bounced over the checkerboard to share it with them, glass marbles raining down in his wake. Tutor Miraj pretended to look disappointed that the game was over, but Zhi Ging watched him flash a smile at the passing phoenix and drop a handful of sunflower seeds under the table.

"But everyone's still frozen?" Jack asked as he skimmed over Bucbou's report, raising his voice over Malo's excited chirps. Apart from a single bright flash several hours earlier, the underwater waterfall had remained the same, hungrily pulling sand and silt into its depths. Nothing had traveled back out.

"Unfortunately," Sintou sighed. "Which does bring me back to my earlier theory that Ami wasn't working alone."

"I think it's the Matchmakers," Zhi Ging said. "One of them tried to force me to eat a bun filled with spirit sand, and I spotted Niotiya when the sand spirit attacked us; she was controlling it."

Tutor Miraj ageshifted down in surprise, both eyebrows nearly touching the very top of his head. "That shouldn't be possible," he spluttered. "Sand spirits are rarely interested in humans and *never* attack unless provoked."

"Yes, but Dohrniis are also meant to protect Silhouettes, not possess them," Sintou said with a frown. "Ami's proven that exceptions do exist and can be extremely dangerous." She stood up, her gold robes rustling as she began to pace her office. "If Ami was working with the Matchmakers and they've discovered a cluster of sand spirits willing to hurt others . . ." She cast a meaningful look at Tutor Miraj. "How many Scouts do we currently have in the paper province?"

"At least two, but potentially more now that the others are searching for Reishi. I'll alert their jellyfish." He ageshifted back to sixty and pushed back his seat.

"Thank you. Please take Miss Yeung back to the dorms on your way. I wish to speak with Jack about his return to Hok Woh."

Zhi Ging tried to catch her friend's eye as Tutor Miraj bustled her toward the door, but the white flame behind Jack cast his face in shadows. "What would it mean,"

Zhi Ging pressed, "if sand spirits were working with the Matchmakers?"

Tutor Miraj sighed and lowered his voice as the door slid shut behind them.

"The Matchmakers' Guild are smart. They mastered the ability to use perception as a shield years ago. While most people across Wengyuen have gentle, almost romantic perceptions of them, they now hold more power than any single shoreside ruler. Sintou needs to ensure that this perception is still just a shield and hasn't become a weapon."

FOR THE NEXT TWO WEEKS ZHI GING AND JACK continued their lessons with Tutor Miraj, learning how to sidestep first impressions and adapt attention. He rarely assigned homework, but the novelty of testing how fast they could run before the classroom door's perception changed soon wore thin; their collection of bumps and bruises grew each morning.

One night, long after she'd said goodnight to Jack, Zhi Ging lay awake in her room, struggling to fall asleep. She rolled over, frowning at the small indent beside her pillow where Malo used to rest.

Now that Malo had fully recovered, Wusi had asked the little phoenix to stay in the sick bay, helping her trial new phoenix-flame-based elixirs for the possessed Silhouettes. After another hour spent tossing and turning, Zhi

Ging gave up and kicked her blankets loose. She slipped on her cloak and crept out of the dorm, sneaking along the dark corridors to find Malo.

Once she reached the sick bay, Zhi Ging paused, her hand hovering above the door. She was hit by a similar wave of hesitation each time she visited. This moment, right before the door slid open, was her last chance to imagine her friends were awake and waiting for her on the other side. That hope, as fragile as glass itself, would shatter once she entered, only to slowly rebuild ahead of her next visit. Zhi Ging exhaled deeply and stepped inside. Wusi was snoring in a chair, the exhausted healer's face pale after another day of experimenting. A half-finished yellow scarf was pooled on the floor beside her, knitting needles barely visible through the thick wool. Only her jellyfish, Heisiu, was still awake. When he spotted Zhi Ging he shrugged, waving a tentacle for her to come in.

She ducked beneath the numerous roving lanterns that now filled the room. The idea had come to Wusi after she'd learned how Ai'Deng Bou had cured Malo. Day and night, red lanterns filled with phoenix fire now floated between the frozen Silhouettes, the heat and smoke hopefully healing them while they slept.

Zhi Ging picked her way toward the far wall where Malo was curled up in a makeshift nest, snoring loudly from a pillow squeezed into a bamboo steamer. She stroked his feathers, staring through the glass into the dark ocean beyond.

The last time they'd been in the sick bay together was to watch a dragon boat race during Zhi Ging's detention. "Do you think there'll be a race this month?" she whispered, smiling down at him. Malo hiccupped in his sleep, his feet waggling in the air as he chased sunflower seeds in his dreams.

Zhi Ging turned back toward the beds, stopping to check on Pinderent, Mynah, and Hiulam. After the excitement of finding the missing Silhouettes, she had hoped her friends would be swapping homei spoons by the time she and Jack finished their first lesson. Instead, days had dragged by with no sign of recovery. She sighed, looking down at their bandaged faces, thick strips of gauze still wrapped around their eyes. Wusi had tried different salves for each Silhouette every night, but nothing had worked.

She adjusted Mynah's pillow, then traipsed back to Malo, wondering if there was a spare blanket in the store cupboard. She'd rather sleep on the sick bay floor than alone in her room. Zhi Ging settled in, leaning her head against the nearest bed as she lifted Malo's bamboo steamer onto her lap.

With eyes half closed, she turned back to the ocean. Zhi Ging yelped, her feet kicking frantically beneath her, pushing away from the glass wall. A blurred face was swimming toward them through the dark water.

"Ami!" she screamed, struggling to pull herself up. The Cyo B'Ahon had escaped the underwater waterfall!

A passing lantern hit Zhi Ging's cheek, its shadow causing the hazy face to wink out. She scrambled forward, pressing her hands against the cold glass as she tried to catch another glimpse of Ami. Had she imagined it? Had it just been her reflection?

High above her, clouds parted and moonlight poured down through the water, the face reappearing in sharp focus. A mouth shimmered into sight and a hoarse voice breathed over Zhi Ging's shoulder.

"What did you do this time, NoGlow?"

Zhi Ging spun around. The face had been a reflection after all, just not hers.

Iridill was awake.

CHAPTER 9

Z hi Ging stumbled backward into the wall.
"Ugh, be louder, why don't you?" Iridill groaned,
clutching at her bandages while the glass reverberated across the sick bay.

Malo jerked awake and chirped in dazed confusion,
his beak swinging between the two girls.

"Wusi!" Zhi Ging croaked, her back still pinned to
the wall. Heisiu twisted in his basin and began frantically
splashing water over the healer. She grunted mid-snore
and looked up in confusion, her chair crashing down behind her once she spotted Iridill.

The healer raced to the Silhouette, snatching up the
handwritten chart clipped to her bed. "Dried lantana petals, glutinous rice flour, crushed longan seeds, and bamboo charred by phoenix fire," she murmured, scanning
the cure she'd trialed earlier that day. "Heisiu," she called
over her shoulder as she began expertly removing the bandages around Iridill's eyes, "start preparing that salve for

the rest of the beds. I want new bandages on every Silhouette within the hour. Zhi Ging, you can help. In fact, Heisiu, wake Jack and—"

She broke off as the final bandage fell away.

"What? Why are you both staring at me?" Iridill snapped, as irritable as if she'd just woken from a long nap rather than a powerful possession. When neither Zhi Ging nor Wusi replied, her face filled with panic. "Is it my hair?" A hand anxiously shot up, her fingers racing through glossy black strands. She stopped, glaring at them in obvious frustration.

"Seriously, what is going on? NoGlow, why are you both staring at me like that?"

Zhi Ging felt sick to her stomach, unable to look away despite Iridill's glare. *This doesn't make any sense.*

The door flew open and Jack raced toward them.

"I just heard from Heisiu! Who woke up? Should I—" He stopped dead, a passing lantern bumping against his cheek.

"What, what is it?" Iridill demanded, worry now creeping into her voice.

"Your eyes." Jack stepped forward, his irises flashing frantically between green and blue. "They're like mine now."

"ARE YOU SURE YOU'RE ALL RIGHT?" ZHI GING pressed, grimacing at the untouched feast spread out in front of Jack. After Sintou had arrived at the sick bay, they'd been told to wait in the dining hall. Hours later they still hadn't heard from any of the Cyo B'Ahon.

"All I ever wanted was to find others who had eyes like mine," Jack muttered, stabbing a chopstick into a siu long bao, the dumpling's hot soup spilling out across the table. "But it turns out *I'm* not even meant to have eyes like this." He pressed his forehead against the table, wrapping both arms over his head to avoid Zhi Ging's gaze. "If Wusi's right, the green and blue are just leftover signs of a possession. Proof of being attacked by Ami."

"But the colors also prove you defeated her!" Zhi Ging said, pulling him back up. She slid a bowl of grass jelly forward and thrust a spoon into his unresisting hand. "Iridill's eyes only look like yours now because of Wusi's cure. No one did that for you—you did it yourself."

Jack was silent for a moment, prodding the wobbly black dessert in front of him.

"But when did Ami do it?" he muttered. "Was it before or after I left Hok Woh? What if I only Reverted because I was possessed?"

Zhi Ging grimaced, unsure what to say. She had hated being the only one in Fei Chui whose hair didn't glow near dragons, but at least that difference was one she'd been born with. One she actually shared with most of Wengyuen. What Jack had thought was a link to his family had turned out to be nothing more than the final traces of a curse.

"Maybe Wusi will find a way to lift the color from

91

everyone's eyes. Get them all back to normal," she said, trying to find a way to cheer him up.

Instead, Jack's face crumpled. "But I've only ever had blue and green eyes. That *is* my normal."

Zhi Ging winced, wishing she could take back her clumsy comment. There was a faint tap beside Jack's foot and they looked down to see Pou Pou waving at them from beneath the glass floor. The jellyfish gestured for them to follow and shot back toward the sick bay, his large body leaving a glowing trail through the water.

The sick bay had been completely transformed: the neat rows of Silhouette-filled beds now curved around the tower in a circle, individual Pan Chang Knots pinned to the foot of each bed to help identify gauze-covered faces. Iridill and four others had large crocheted blankets made up of bright yellow squares draped over them, making it easy to spot which Silhouettes had begun to wake up.

"Why can't I have a green one?" Zhi Ging heard Iridill whine as Heisiu stretched out from his basin, tentacles straightening the edge of her blanket. "You know my father's the Lead Glassmith, from the glass province. We're meant to wear green, not yellow."

"Yes, but I'm from the gold province and I prefer yellow," Wusi's voice called back, sounding surprisingly far away. Zhi Ging glanced around and saw the biggest change to the room was actually beside Jack. Wusi and Sintou now stood in a brand-new shimmering wing, the space easily twice as large as the original sick bay. The outer layer of cooling glass rippled as seawater swelled over it, and Malo sat between them, the tips of his feathers still glowing as he worked his way through a small mountain of sunflower seeds.

The new wing had a near-identical circle of Silhouette-filled beds, but unlike those in the original sick bay, these had no Pan Chang Knots to help identify the still-frozen faces.

"Wusi and I agreed it would be best for Silhouettes from previous years to have their own separate dorm as they begin to wake up," Sintou explained, catching Zhi Ging's and Jack's baffled expressions. "Things will be confusing enough without them discovering their old bedrooms have been filled by someone new."

"Having that dorm here will also make it easier for me to keep a close eye on their recovery," Wusi added. "The longer a possession's been in place, the trickier it is to remove. I'll need to run multiple checks to know Ami's power isn't lurking deep inside, waiting for the right moment to flare back up."

Zhi Ging felt Jack shift beside her, crossing his arms tight around himself. Without knowing exactly when Ami had possessed him, there was no way to tell just how long he had been under her control.

Sintou's gaze snapped to him, taking in his pale face and anxiously flickering eyes. "Jack—Master Oltryds, all Silhouettes who wake up will be asked to return to the sick bay each night after dinner. This will allow Wusi time to conduct her various tests and ensure all are recovering well. I would like to extend that invitation to you. We will keep the five recently awoken Silhouettes"—she was interrupted by Heisiu's excited splashes as two paper province Silhouettes began to splutter, rubbing at their bandages in confusion—"*seven* Silhouettes," the Head of the Cyo B'Ahon corrected smoothly, "in the sick bay overnight, and depending on Wusi's expert opinion they might soon join you both back at the dorm and in Tutor Miraj's classroom." Pale patches of pink and orange filtered down through the glass ceiling, warm dawn light breaking across the ocean surface high above them. "Before you leave, Wusi has a request."

The healer nodded, gesturing for Zhi Ging and Jack to join her by Heisiu's basin. "Pou Pou has already shared the details of what happened earlier in Pingon, but the waking Silhouettes don't seem to have much memory beyond completing Ami's Perception challenge. It would be best for them to hear what happened from a fellow Silhouette." Behind Wusi, Iridill's cheeks flushed, clearly frustrated by her own memory loss. She scowled when she caught Zhi Ging's eye, a strange glint of what almost looked like jealousy darting across her pinched features.

Zhi Ging tried to focus on what the healer was saying, but flashes of the possessed Silhouettes trapped within the water-filled walls of the catacombs, dark glass shattering as they leaped for her, mouths filled with writhing tentacles, and Ami's mercury eyes and jellyfish-scarred arms, each raised welt controlling a different Silhouette, filled her mind. She shuddered, fighting to push the memories away and refocus on Wusi.

Iridill's lucky she can't remember.

"—easiest method. I always use him for this when checking a patient's vitals. It's much safer than writing information down on a scroll that can be misplaced. So, when you're ready, just speak directly into his tentacle."

Jack nodded, then caught Zhi Ging's confused expression. "Should we do a quick test first?" he suggested pointedly, realizing she hadn't heard a word of Wusi's instructions. "You know, to make sure Heisiu can definitely record our voices too." He pointed to the jellyfish, who had raised a single tentacle toward them. "We don't want to go through everything just to realize it hasn't worked. But you're right, Wusi, a jellyfish recording of our voices would be much easier than you explaining to each new Silhouette that wakes up."

". . . to each new Silhouette that wakes up." Both Jack and Zhi Ging jumped and turned to the basin. Heisiu had stretched his tentacle tight against the glass. It now vibrated like one of the strings on the erhu Zhi Ging had played at the iceberg instrumental, an exact copy of Jack's voice radiating off it. She beamed, eyes flicking to the bed where Mynah was still frozen. Although the sound didn't make her friend sit up, Zhi Ging was convinced she spotted a warm buttery yellow flash across the girl's arm patches.

Mynah's going to love this when she wakes up.

Zhi Ging breathed in sharply, realizing this was the very first time she'd thought "when" rather than "if." She leaned toward Heisiu, eager to start. More memories of Ami's betrayal—the oily gray jellyfish placed on her tongue, Malo melting the spiral staircase as they fled Hok Woh, and using the silk dragon head to lure Ami to the underwater waterfall—flooded her mind. However, this time the memories didn't make her wince. Instead, Zhi Ging realized with a smile that rather than hurting her, she could now use them to help her friends.

CHAPTER 10

"Tere you are! You miss one month thanks to your ridiculous detention and immediately forget about training?!"

Zhi Ging jumped, noodles slipping from her chopsticks to land beside a delighted Malo. She and Jack spun around to see Bucbou marching toward them, two racing paddles tucked under an arm.

"It'll do neither of you any good spending all day and night trapped inside Hok Woh. Especially now. Time to get back out on a dragon boat." She flung the green paddle to Zhi Ging before turning to Jack, a smile briefly crossing her face. "Welcome back."

She twirled the second paddle in her hand, its white paint flashing like a shark fin. "I heard you still can't remember your first life in Hok Woh, so let me help refresh your memory. You never made it past your initial trial. In fact, you somehow paddled so much water into the folds of the silk dragon that the entire boat tilted forward and capsized. Some of Team Si Cau still talk about it in hushed tones, amazed anyone messed up that badly." She paused as Zhi Ging tried, and failed, to turn her sudden snort into a cough. "Lucky for you, but less so for them, Team Si Cau is still a crew member short for tonight's group training, and you're the only conscious Silhouette who hasn't been snapped up for a team yet."

She handed him the white paddle, then pulled out her whistle, its shrill blast echoing through the corridors as Bucbou marched them back up to the surface, her brisk pace forcing them to take the steps two at a time.

Zhi Ging was still trying to catch her breath as she reached the final step. In front of her six dragon boats glimmered under the full moon, with familiar Cyo B'Ahon and Silhouettes gathered in each one.

"Hiulam! When did you wake up?" she shouted in excitement. The girl gave a dramatic double-handed wave from the front of Team Bolei's glass dragon boat, her black Silhouette cloak barely visible under the giant yellow knitted scarf Wusi had wrapped her in. Just like Iridill, her eyes now flickered between green and blue. Zhi Ging leaped between the stepping stones and onto the boat, hugging her friend tight.

"Careful," Hiulam said, laughing. In her right hand was a small flask filled with a pungent peat-black elixir. "Wusi will murder me if I don't finish every last drop. She's already annoyed Bucbou, and the other captains pulled us out of the sick bay. I was only allowed out after

Gwong promised to make sure I didn't accidentally spill any overboard." She blew on it and Zhi Ging took a step back, pinching her nose as thick steam flowed over her.

"How does that smell worse than our musty race cloaks?"

"I wouldn't be surprised if Wusi blitzed one of them into this." Hiulam gave an exaggerated grimace before offering her the flask. "Ever wanted to try a liquid that somehow tastes furry?"

Zhi Ging laughed, backing away with both hands up.

"Of course you've still not finished yours," a voice drawled from a nearby dragon boat.

Zhi Ging frowned as she spotted Iridill in Team Tsadeu's boat. The girl was also wrapped in a hand-knitted scarf, but Zhi Ging was secretly smug to see Hiulam's was considerably longer than Iridill's.

"And why is Jack still here?" Iridill continued, jabbing a finger at him as two Cyo B'Ahon helped him on to the silk dragon boat. His eyes flickered as several other Silhouettes turned to him in confusion, finally recognizing him as the same Jack who had previously collected them for their monthly challenges.

"I passed a Scout exam while you were still frozen," he said quickly, twisting the white paddle in his hands.

"Is it really that unbelievable he could pass?" Zhi Ging asked, raising her voice as she glowered at Iridill.

The other girl flushed, knowing what Zhi Ging really meant: *We both know Jack passed* your *exam for you.*

"Ignore her," Hiulam whispered. "She's just annoyed I got to come along tonight." She paused, a proud gleam filling her eyes as she adjusted her scarf. "I only woke up this morning, but Wusi agreed to let me join after I spent all afternoon practicing new drumbeats for Team Bolei against the side of my bed."

Zhi Ging grinned, imagining how eager the healer would have been for even an hour's peace and quiet after that.

"Hang on! You're not even our team's Drummer." She snorted. "You only did that one time when Gu Sao was away."

Hiulam grinned mischievously. "Yeah, but Wusi doesn't need to know that."

Zhi Ging shook her head in amazement, then looked around, finally spotting Gwong, Yuttou, and B'ei Gun also on the boat. Another Silhouette she recognized as Ailing waved sheepishly from Pinderent's old seat. Her smile faltered when she accidentally locked eyes with B'ei Gun, their team's Steerer. He had been one of the Cyo B'Ahon who had been suspicious of her arrival as the Second Silhouette, convinced Sintou was planning to name her as the next Head of the Cyo B'Ahon. *Does he still think I can't be trusted?* The Steerer looked away, his expression hidden as he turned to face the dark water.

"Are we training tonight or what?" Hiulam asked, taking a swig of her herbal elixir before spluttering at the bitter taste.

"All right," Bucbou called over the growing babble between dragon boats. "The other captains and I have been given a new assignment from Sintou, which means training's going to look pretty different. In fact, there's not going to be a dragon boat race for a while." She leaped over the glass dragon to land beside Ailing and gestured for B'ei Gun to steer them away from the shore. Zhi Ging was relieved when all six boats veered to the left, swerving away from the underwater waterfall.

"Our new assignment is to find a safe way to return the Silhouettes home." She held up a hand before the protests could begin. "We won't return anyone until Wusi's absolutely certain their possession won't come back, but, while she's working on that we'll be finding the best routes through Wengyeun that don't involve roads."

"Why can't we use roads?" Gwong asked, the confusion on his face mirrored in the crew of several boats.

"Because . . ." Bucbou frowned and shut her eyes, clearly trying to decide what details she could share. "There's a chance Ami wasn't working alone, and her . . . collaborators may or may not have teamed up with creatures that will be difficult to escape from on roads. These creatures can't reach us through the water, though; their power would literally dissolve."

Zhi Ging caught Jack's eye and he nodded as she mouthed, *Sand spirits.*

"On top of that," the Cyo B'Ahon continued, looking toward the dark shore in the distance, "we don't know for sure that every thrall froze after Ami fell into the underwater waterfall. The more we can do to avoid the roads marked by previous attacks, the better. To get Silhouettes home safely, we plan to operate in total darkness, sailing through the rivers and tributaries that connect Wengyuen, and that"—she paused, staring deep into the eyes of every single crew member—"will include learning to row up waterfalls."

Zhi Ging and Hiulam exchanged an apprehensive look; rowing over breaking waves was difficult enough. Bucbou ignored their winces and jabbed her paddle toward Team Tsadeu, causing Iridill to flinch in surprise.

"There are already three older Silhouettes from the carved lacquer province who've woken up. From our guesses, at least two of them first arrived in Hok Woh seventy years ago. It's our duty to return the Silhouettes who have spent years, perhaps even decades, hidden as Ami's thralls. Sintou has declared it's only right we return them to their surviving families and arrange new apprenticeships for each and every one of them. Until Wusi's sign-off, we'll train with a scale model of the various waterways that link Hok Woh to the six provinces."

Bucbou pressed her hand to the water, and miniature jellyfish rose up around the boats. Rather than following the familiar racecourse pattern, they spread out across the ocean's surface, filling the dark water with glowing rivers and tributaries.

"Do you remember anything from being a thrall?" Zhi

Ging asked Hiulam as the dragon boats began to line up behind Team Tsadeu. "Did you see Reishi?"

"What do you mean? Didn't everyone come back?"

"Well, everyone from our dorm did, but there's still no sign of him."

Before Hiulam could reply, Bucbou hit the side of the boat with her paddle, demanding everyone's attention.

"We'll start with the waterfall that separates the northwestern section of the carved lacquer province from the sea." Bucbou pointed at a distant shimmering patch of jellyfish, floating together to create a glowing X. Directly beside them, the six bamboo stands usually filled with cheering crowds during races had been stacked on top of one another. Zhi Ging craned her head back as the wooden structure stretched up to the moon. "Until we master that, we won't be able to reach the landlocked gold and paper provinces."

In front of them, the Steerer on Team Chi Hei bent down to the water, his features illuminated by glowing jellyfish. It was Ai'Deng Bou. He pulled a dekzi from his sleeve, lowering one end of the thin bamboo flute into the water. His cheeks puffed out, but the only sound Zhi Ging could hear was the faint pop of bubbles dancing across the ocean's surface. The boats bobbed silently for a moment, the Silhouettes glancing around in confusion.

Hiulam suddenly shrieked, pointing at a large dome rising up in front of Ai'Deng Bou, water cascading off it.

Yuttou whooped, shaking Gwong's shoulders as she

pointed at the gargantuan jellyfish now spinning in front of them. "I *told* you he was working on a new chimera!"

"Most jellyfish are already ninety-five percent water, so all I did was nudge that up a smidge and give Seoizyu here an extra four percent seawater," Ai'Deng Bou explained.

All six dragon heads seemed to bow in greeting as Seoizyu lifted a shy tentacle, the movement sending waves billowing out to the shore.

Ai'Deng Bou caught Zhi Ging's shocked expression and chuckled. "You look very surprised for someone who met her chimera cousin just a few months ago. That salamander from your Fauna challenge was my original prototype. I was searching for an animal that could keep its shape while in water form, and it turned out the answer was, quite literally, staring me in the face as I paced Hok Woh's corridors."

He pulled a rice paper map of Wengyuen from his pocket, waving it to catch the jellyfish's attention. Seoizyu turned slowly to him, stretching a watery tentacle out over Team Tsadeu to collect it. The movement created a shower of seawater, and Team Syun Zi paddled backward frantically, desperate to protect their paper dragon head.

The rice paper sank through Seoizyu's tentacle, an internal current dragging it up toward the chimera's liquid core. For a split second the intricate map of Wengyuen flashed across her body, then the jellyfish sank, vanishing back beneath the waves.

"Where did she go?" Jack asked, leaning out of the silk dragon boat.

In the distance the sea surface erupted and Seoizyu reappeared floating upside down, her tentacles stretching up along the stacked bamboo stands to hook over the top. Water thundered down in tumbling rapids and hid the jellyfish's body under heavy mist.

"Won't the dragon boat paddles hurt Seoizyu?" Zhi Ging asked.

"Not at all. That extra four percent seawater makes sure of that. Seoizyu will feel as much pain as a puddle does when you jump in—which is none at all."

Bucbou cut between them, whistle already in her mouth. "Excellent, let's get started."

The dragon boats hurried back into line, Team Chi Hei waiting impatiently as Team Tsadeu attempted the vertical climb first. However, neither the carved lacquer nor porcelain dragon boats made it more than a few feet up the makeshift waterfall before crashing back down. Each time a boat capsized, training had to pause, Bucbou tapping her foot impatiently as miniature jellyfish hurried forward with baskets filled with hydrophobic pebbles. Water erupted between fingers as crew members rubbed the water-hating stones across drenched cloaks, their clothes drying in seconds. When Jack and the rest of Team Si Cau didn't even make it past the plunge pool, the captain on Team Syun Zi began to shake his head. He ageshifted down and flung his paddle overboard, narrowly missing the paper dragon head. Although it made no more than a soft splash, all faces turned to him in concern.

"Why are we even trying? We're never going to be able to climb that." He jabbed a finger at the waterfall. "The waterways might be safer, but this is a waste of time! I say we just fight the sand spirits now, before they get to us."

Bucbou blew furiously on her whistle, the shrill sound barely audible over the frantic whispers that erupted across each boat. Zhi Ging spun around, trying to spot Jack through the billowing cloaks of ageshifting Cyo B'Ahon.

"That's enough!" Bucbou barked, eyes flicking toward the Silhouettes. "Training ends now—for everyone."

CHAPTER 11

"Anyone?" Zhi Ging asked as Hiulam stepped back into the dorm later that week.

The other Silhouettes streamed in around her friend, Iridill smirking when she spotted Zhi Ging alone beside the central fireplace.

"You missed the best Cure Club tonight, NoGlow." She smirked, flicking the tail of her bright yellow scarf over her shoulder. It narrowly missed Cing Yau's face, and the other girl was forced to duck swiftly while her own scarf flapped around her. Every newly unfrozen Silhouette now wore one around their neck; Wusi's bobbly knitting was appearing all across Hok Woh. Iridill glanced down at the paper cuttings surrounding Zhi Ging, her mouth twisting into a sneer. "Cute, have you cut out new friends to keep you company?"

Zhi Ging flushed, snatching up the delicate cuttings. She kept her face blank, refusing to let Iridill see just how much her comment had stung. While some of the other Silhouettes had woken a little more anxious or timid than before, Iridill seemed worse, lashing out at others—particularly Zhi Ging—every chance she got.

After the first couple of checkups with Wusi, the others had nicknamed their nightly trips to the sick bay "Cure Club," and, at least to Zhi Ging, that's exactly what it had started to feel like. A secret club that only she wasn't allowed to join.

The others would come back each night chatting excitedly about which of the older Silhouettes had woken up. Two nights earlier, a gold province Silhouette had come bouncing back into the dorm after discovering one of the older Silhouettes was his great-great-great-aunt. During lessons, dozens of notes would be passed around Zhi Ging, inside jokes that made no sense to her but would cause giggles to erupt across Tutor Miraj's amphitheater.

Dinners were the worst, with Silhouettes shouting across tables, asking who was heading to Cure Club early, and chatting excitedly about who they thought might wake up next. Zhi Ging was always the last to know when a Silhouette, either current or old, had woken up; she was forced to wait for Hiulam and Jack to tell her once they got back from the sick bay. Even Malo got to join Cure Club. Wusi was keen to have the little phoenix there in case she spotted gray streaks creeping back across someone's eyes.

"Ignore her," Hiulam said, sitting beside Zhi Ging. She leaned across to smooth out the crumpled paper cuttings in her friend's palm. "I'd rather have been here. Even an hour of anticurrent drills with Bucbou would have been better. Cure Club was really boring—like it always is," she added loudly, glaring back at Iridill. "No one else woke up, and once we had our next disgusting dose of elixir, Wusi made us spend the rest of the hour helping to wash and dry the sick bay bandages."

"That was just you, because you somehow knocked over five bowls before finishing your own elixir," Iridill snapped. "The rest of us got to hang out in the other dorm with the old Silhouettes. Anyway, I'm glad no one else woke up; we're all so bored of hearing your recorded voice, NoGlow." Iridill's eyes narrowed. Unlike Jack's, Iridill's blue and green irises reminded Zhi Ging of a particularly toxic toadstool Aapau used to warn her about on the jade mountain. "Besides, all the best Silhouettes are already awake."

Zhi Ging leaped up and Hiulam put out an arm to stop her. Although Zhi Ging knew Iridill was trying to rattle her, the worry that had weighed down on her all month as she waited for Mynah and Pinderent to wake up now twisted into a prickling anger.

"Hey!" Iridill squealed as Malo flew over the other Silhouettes to land with a thud on top of her head. The little phoenix beat his wings wildly, Iridill's long glossy hair tangling and knotting beneath his feet.

"Get off me!" She flung her cloak hood up, knocking him free. She pawed at her hair, trying to smooth it back before snatching Cing Yau's and Kaolin's arms, dragging them into her room and slamming the screen door shut.

"I said a *subtle* distraction, Malo," Jack groaned, shaking his head as he pushed through the other Silhouettes who had stopped to watch. He was the only one apart from Zhi Ging without a yellow scarf.

But at least his eyes match everyone else's, a small part of her grumbled.

The little phoenix ruffled his feathers and held out a wing, a flame flickering to life along it. He chirped in protest, nodding his beak toward the fire.

"I guess you're right," Zhi Ging said with an amused smile. "Iridill was lucky you only decided to have a little dance." She scooped him up and placed him back in her hood. "No sign of Mynah or Pinderent waking up?" she asked, looking between Jack and Hiulam.

Jack shrugged. "The last salve didn't work. But Mynah's cheek patches have started flashing brighter and for longer now, which Wusi says is a good sign."

"Maybe it'll happen while we're at our challenge tomorrow," Hiulam added. "I tried to ask a few of the older Silhouettes what their Recall challenges had been, but Wusi stopped me and gave me even more bandages to scrub." She turned to Zhi Ging, smiling widely. "Actually, if Sintou still won't let you come along to Cure Club, why don't you join my brand-new, much cooler Scrub Club." She waggled her fingers in a dramatic *ta-da*.

Zhi Ging snorted, tucking the paper cuttings back into

her pocket. "You know what? The dorm suddenly doesn't seem as bad."

THE NEXT MORNING, THE SILHOUETTES CLAMBERED out of the entrance stepping stone and onto the red junk. A few hesitated, looking at Jack in confusion, clearly wondering if he was still going to lead them to their next challenge.

He laughed, raising both palms. "Don't look at me. I *really* don't know where we're going this time."

Malo chirped and leaped out of Zhi Ging's hood to explore the teak boat. She smiled as he waddled determinedly past the central mast, glad he'd finally been allowed to come along to challenges. The little phoenix reappeared on the other side of the main bat-like sail, joined by two red-crowned cranes, his feathers ruffling in excitement at having found new friends. The cranes dipped their elegant black necks toward the staring Silhouettes, while Malo bounced beneath them, only just reaching halfway up their long legs.

Three Cyo B'Ahon emerged from behind the same sail and stood beside the cranes, surveying the group. While two were currently in their late forties, the third was no more than fifteen. She waved hesitantly, barely taller than some of the nearby Silhouettes.

"My name's Zinnia, and I'm specializing in Recall with your next tutor. These are G'Aam and Wuyan." She gestured to the Cyo B'Ahon towering beside her. "They're

Prediction Cyo B'Ahon specializing in preemptive defense and will chaperone Silhouettes to and from all challenges from now on."

One of them, Zhi Ging wasn't sure whether it was G'Aam or Wuyan, nodded as Zinnia spoke, raising the familiar hooped gold rope up for the Silhouettes to see. Meanwhile, the other Prediction Cyo B'Ahon ignored them entirely, his eyes scanning between the clouds and the waves lapping against the junk.

Zinnia glanced up at them, then plowed on when it was clear neither Cyo B'Ahon planned to add to her introduction.

"We'll also be joined by their combat cranes, as extra security for our journey today."

"What can catch us while we're floating?" Iridill asked, her sneer only half hiding the worry that bubbled beneath her question.

"It's just a precaution," Zinnia said hurriedly, the tip of her nose turning pink. She nodded at the Cyo B'Ahon and they ageshifted down, shrugging on black robes to become indistinguishable from the current Silhouettes. Zinnia smiled and pulled out a crumpled lantern, its surface a collage of faded theater flyers.

The group settled into their golden hoops and lifted up, Malo quacking in excitement as the sea breeze raced through his feathers. Zhi Ging laughed as he pirouetted and tumbled through the air between the combat cranes. Her shadow drifted out over the ocean and she glanced back to where Seoizyu, the giant jellyfish, had vanished after dragon boat training. The six bamboo towers that made up the makeshift waterfall were still there, swaying gently over calm waves. She frowned at the structure as they soared toward the porcelain province. No one had worked out how to climb the waterfall yet, but she would.

THE GROUP LANDED AT A DISTANT HARBOR, A giant glowing ship docked in front of them. It was at least six stories high, warm light pouring out of every window while bright red pillars and beams held up jade-green tiles and golden carvings of twisting dragon tails. A gleaming pagoda emerged from its roof, causing it to look less like a boat and more like a floating palace.

"Oh, I've been on one of these before!" a silk province Silhouette shouted in excitement. "It's a hoi sin fong, a floating restaurant. My parents took me to one to celebrate passing my entrance exam. There were stages on each level so you could watch performers while enjoying the seafood banquet. That ship wasn't even half as big as this one, though."

Zinnia led them to a gangplank where another Cyo B'Ahon was waiting. Zhi Ging blinked in surprise as the woman turned to smile at them. Unlike her previous tutors, or anyone else in Hok Woh, this woman's entire face had been swept in white pigment and her lips stained a dark red. Deep pink blossomed around her black-lined eyes, the color dusting her cheekbones and stretching up toward thick dark eyebrows. An ornate headdress fanned from ear to ear, large white pearls studded between curling patterns stitched in cerulean silk.

"Welcome to your Recall challenge. My name is Wuiyam. I hope you find today memorable," she said, a small smile tugging at the corners of her mouth. There was a strange echo to the Cyo B'Ahon's voice; each word was doubled slightly as if the listener immediately remembered what she'd said. To Zhi Ging, it was almost musical, like the tutor was speaking in harmony with herself.

"Recall is all about knowing when, and how, to look back. For those of you who make it through today's challenge, you'll quickly discover that memories can be deceptive. I'll teach you how to recall information at a second's notice, even if you initially only had a fleeting glance." Wuiyam pulled a series of opera tickets from her sleeve, handing them out among the Silhouettes. "For today's challenge, you'll be sitting in on a Binlim practice. This ship won't set sail until tomorrow, so you'll be seeing the very first performance. On each of your tickets is your assigned booth for the challenge, which we've set up just for today. G'Aam and Wuyan will take you to the right performance floor."

Jack glanced over at Zhi Ging's ticket as they filed passed Wuiyam into the floating restaurant. He beamed, waving his ticket in front of her. "Oh, Zhi Ging, look! You're next to me."

They followed the two guardian Cyo B'Ahon down narrow hallways that still gleamed with fresh paint and into a large banquet hall. Wide circular tables were stacked against the far wall, waiting to be set up. G'Aam and Wuyan pointed in silence to the temporary booths that formed a crescent around the hall's stage, a number pinned to each screen door.

"Good luck," Zhi Ging whispered to Hiulam and Jack before double-checking the number on her own ticket. She hurried into booth eighteen, and Malo immediately leaped onto the wooden seat, snuffling under the thin silk cushion.

"We're the first performance, remember?" Zhi Ging said with a laugh, scooping him into her lap. "No one's even had a chance to leave crumbs yet." The smell of wet paint was even stronger inside the booth, wafting up from its blue wooden sill.

Drumming filled the air and a Binlim performer stepped through the heavy curtains. They wore a curved head-piece covered in red pom-poms and two long pheasant tail feathers that stretched down their back. Although their robes were covered with embroidered dragon scales, the most eye-catching part of the Binlim performer was their face. It was hidden behind a cobalt-blue mask, with red and black highlighting an exaggerated snarl.

Wuiyam appeared beside the performer as they continued to pace the stage, prowling like a tiger in front of the Silhouettes.

"Your challenge this month is simple. Remember the masks," Wuiyam called, before vanishing behind the curtain, her echoing voice even more noticeable in the theater.

Masks? Zhi Ging thought. *Just how many are there?*

The music sharpened, cymbals and drums filling the banquet hall as the Binlim performer leaped to life and strutted around the stage. They waved their sleeve over their face and suddenly the blue mask vanished, replaced by a red mask decorated with swirling white eyebrows.

There was a collective gasp as the Silhouettes leaned forward. Zhi Ging struggled to keep track as the Binlim performer sped up, a new mask appearing on their face each time they turned toward a different booth. At one point they spun in three wide circles, masks flashing between colors with each rotation.

Too late, Zhi Ging began whispering the mask order to herself, trying to keep the jumbled colors right in her mind. She could hear several Silhouettes frantically rushing around their empty booths, looking for something to write with.

Zhi Ging's eyes began to stream, her vision blurring, but she refused to blink. The Binlim performer was shifting so quickly now that a single blink could cost her two mask changes. Finally the performance came to an end, and the performer's last green mask vanished, their true face shining out at the Silhouettes.

Zhi Ging leaped up. There, in the center of the stage, was Wuiyam. But how was that possible? The tutor had stood right beside the Binlim performer and they had never stepped off the stage.

"Silhouette number one." Wuiyam pointed to the first booth and a spotlight swung toward it, revealing a wide-eyed Kaolin still gaping at their tutor in confusion. "You're up—time to test your Recall."

Kaolin gulped before following Wuiyam backstage. The other Silhouettes were silent, straining to hear the muffled conversation drifting through the crack between the thick curtains.

"Silhouette number two." They jumped as Wuiyam's strange echoing voice bounced around the hall less than five minutes later. Zhi Ging waved as Hiulam hurried across the stage, Malo flapping his wings in encouragement.

While the Silhouettes continued to count down, Zhi Ging repeated the list of masks in her head, determined not to forget a single one. She fidgeted with the opera ticket, tearing the thin paper into strips.

"Silhouette number eighteen."

Zhi Ging winced, blinded by the swinging stage lights.

"Wait here," she whispered to Malo before scrambling out of her booth, fingers sticking against the sill's still-tacky paint. Zhi Ging's heart pounded in her ears as she stepped through the curtains, shuffling forward until her eyes adjusted to the gloom. At the back of the room, Wuiyam gestured for her to take a seat in front of a table laid out with fifty masks.

The Cyo B'Ahon leaned forward, still dressed in her Binlim robes. "Did you enjoy the performance, number eighteen?"

Zhi Ging nodded, trying not to interrupt the looping order of masks in her head.

"Let's begin with an easy question. Which was the final mask?" Wuiyam spread her hands over the options, her long sleeves brushing the bright faces.

Zhi Ging looked down and tapped the top-right mask, its green surface decorated with thick red swirls.

"Correct." Once again, Wuiyam's voice had an odd double echo to it, now louder than ever. The Cyo B'Ahon flipped the mask over and there, scrawled across its inner surface, was the next question. *Which was the eleventh mask?*

Zhi Ging paused, her heart racing. She hesitated for a moment, speeding through the first eleven colors in her internal chant before tapping on a dark purple mask. Wuiyam nodded and turned the mask over. Zhi Ging carried on selecting masks this way, murmuring under her breath until the chant began to blur on her tongue, running together until it sounded less like words and more like a strange babbling flurry of *blueredbluewhiteyellowgreen.* They continued in near silence, Zhi Ging quietly tapping at masks until there were only two left on the table.

"Now, number eighteen, which was your own mask? The eighteenth mask." Wuiyam leaned forward, her eyes glittering in interest.

Zhi Ging froze. *I don't remember.* The remaining masks

were nearly identical; the only difference between the two yellow faces was the color around the eyes—one was black, the other a rich blue. Zhi Ging shut her eyes, frantically trying to pull more detail from her memory. One had appeared as the fifth mask, while the other was the eighteenth, but which was which?

"This is not a timed challenge, but I encourage you to make your choice soon." Wuiyam sat back, her gaze drifting over Zhi Ging's hunched shoulders to the booths visible between the stage curtains. "The longer you wait, the harder it may be for the remaining Silhouettes to hold the mask order in their minds."

Zhi Ging grimaced. Jack was meant to go after her. She tried to shut her eyes, but the two masks had merged now, a blended version appearing and becoming the only mask she could remember. Wuiyam gave a disappointed sigh and Zhi Ging looked down, her hands twisting frantically in her lap. Was this it? Was she about to fail a challenge and be sent back to Fei Chui?

Her hands swam into focus and Zhi Ging froze, staring at the blue smudges that covered her fingertips. *Where did those come from?* She lifted a hand to her face, and the smell of damp paint drifted up from her fingers. Zhi Ging stared at her blue-tinged skin as memory fragments began to stitch together. *It must've been from when I touched the sill just now . . .* She frowned, trying to remember exactly what Wuiyam had said earlier.

"These booths," she muttered, "you said that they'd

been set up for today's challenge. So why would you waste time painting them?" She glanced between her fingers, the final two masks on the table, and the Cyo B'Ahon, who was now staring at her with an inscrutable expression. Zhi Ging's eyes flicked in a looping triangle between the three. *There's something I'm missing, but what is it?*

She drummed her stained fingers on the table, then froze, staring up at Wuiyam, her eyes wide. "You *told* us how to pass!" Zhi Ging spun around, laughing in wonder as she gazed out across the colorful booths visible through the curtain crack. "You said Recall was all about knowing *when* to look back," Zhi Ging began, "and that's all we had to do." She shook her head, smiling back at the eighteenth booth, where Malo's beak peeked over the blue sill. "You've painted the booths to match the order of the Binlim masks." It was only now, looking back, that she saw the rest of her booth front had been painted a bright yellow, identical to that of the masks in front of her. *I wonder how many others spotted that.*

"This"—Zhi Ging smiled, tapping the matching mask— "is number eighteen."

Wuiyam beamed. "Congratulations. I look forward to seeing you in class tomorrow. Now I just have one quick question before I call Silhouette number nineteen in." Her eyes glinted as she looked at Zhi Ging. "How did I switch places with the original Binlim performer? I've had some creative guesses so far, but no Silhouette has solved it."

Zhi Ging peered up at the Cyo B'Ahon; she had been

wondering that ever since Wuiyam removed that final mask.

"*Did* you switch places?" she asked slowly, trying to untangle the thought teetering at the edge of her mind. "The Binlim performer never stepped offstage."

"Are you sure? Can you really trust your memory when you were so focused on tracking the masks?"

Zhi Ging bit her lip, doubting herself.

"Not to worry, number eighteen—as I said, you've already passed. I just thought I'd ask. I'm honestly glad I didn't get another accusation of spirit magic," she added with a snort. Wuiyam waved a hand to release Zhi Ging. As she did, her sleeve brushed the eighteenth mask, causing it to glance off the other yellow mask, creating a faint echo as they hit together. Zhi Ging stopped, her gaze now fixed on the two masks with their near-identical designs.

"You're the Recall tutor, right?" she asked, a sudden idea jolting through her.

Wuiyam nodded, curiosity dancing at the corners of her eyes.

"Then what's my name?" Zhi Ging said, her heart racing as the Cyo B'Ahon raised a painted black brow in confusion. "You can recall information from a fleeting glance, that's what you said. Well, what's my name? Jack said it as we walked past you earlier."

Wuiyam's eyes flicked to a dark corner of the room, an impressed smile twitching at her mouth. "I can't recall," the Cyo B'Ahon admitted.

"But not because you didn't hear, right?" Zhi Ging pressed as it all began to click into place. "I didn't misremember; you were definitely on the stage at the same time. It's not impossible because my memory was wrong. It's impossible *and* my memory was right." She held up the two yellow masks, never taking her eyes off Wuiyam. "I think . . . there are *two* Recall tutors."

Wuiyam clapped her hands in delight, the feathers on her elaborate headdress dancing.

"Well done!" The unique echo in her voice grew louder, and Zhi Ging spun to see an identical Cyo B'Ahon stepping out of the shadows. *Twins!*

"No, not twins," both women said in unison, as if reading her thoughts. "I simply replicated myself. I learned how by studying the jellyfish in Reishi's lab. Most people, even Cyo B'Ahon, can only remember around sixty percent of what they experience. I realized if there were two of me, I could remember every single part of my day. All I'd need to do is have a quick catch-up with myself each night." The two Wuiyams laughed, the echo almost impossible to hear now that they were side by side.

"Congratulations again, Zhi Ging," the new Wuiyam said, while the one in Binlim robes began replacing the masks on the table. She pointed at a small door at the back of the hall. "You can wait with the other successful Silhouettes."

CHAPTER 12

"Where are we going? Our Chau better not be out there," Iridill grumbled, pulling her hood tight until only her scowling mouth was visible. The Silhouettes had been squeezed into four small rowing boats and were now sailing upstream through heavy fog. The canopy above each boat drummed with constant rain, and the fabric had noticeably darkened since they had started sailing.

"Anyone know what province we're even in?" Zhi Ging asked, trying to spot the shoreline through the fog.

"I'm guessing either silk, porcelain, or glass." Jack shrugged. "Those have the most rivers."

"Wow, helpful," Iridill sneered. "I don't see why we couldn't have waited back in the floating restaurant until this rain stopped."

"You're still not as soggy as when your dragon boat team slid back down the waterfall," Hiulam called over from the next boat, an innocent smile plastered across her face.

"We're here!" The two Wuiyams jumped off the front boat in tandem, waving at a group who had been hidden by rain seconds earlier. As the Silhouettes hurried after their double tutor, Zhi Ging spotted the waiting figures. Each had a cormorant perched on their shoulder. Malo quacked, and the birds dipped their long beaks in greeting, thick rain droplets sliding off their black feathers.

"They almost look like the combat cranes," Zhi Ging whispered to Jack and Hiulam. "But with tiny little legs."

"So what you would look like as a bird, then?" Hiulam said, ruffling the top of Zhi Ging's head while Jack snorted loudly.

"Eh, we're pretty much the same height." Zhi Ging laughed, rolling her eyes before turning back to the others.

A large barrel-chested man stood at the front of the group. "You've timed this visit perfectly, Wuiyam," he said, tilting his conical hat up to get a better look at the Silhouettes. His face was weathered but welcoming, a neatly trimmed mustache twitching as he spoke. "I'm Wengyuen's Chief Ricetorian. Our role as Ricetorians is to collect and preserve moments from across all six provinces." Behind him, four other Ricetorians began to unravel a thin shimmering net.

"We make these from the finest spider silk," he continued, draping the net over his arm. "As you'll learn from Wuiyam, all forms of water can hold memory. We aim to collect as many droplets as we can before they evaporate." He flicked his wrist and the net swung out, blooming open like a glistening lily pad to encompass the Silhouettes.

There were squeals around Zhi Ging as the net covered them in thousands of overlapping silver wisps. The Chief Ricetorian raised his arm, and all five cormorants rose as one, catching the edges of the net in their beaks. Every single water droplet clung to the net as the birds lifted it up, and the Silhouettes went from scrambling against the shining threads to patting suddenly dry robes in bafflement.

Above them, the cormorants flew in a complicated dance, folding the droplet-filled net between them until it was small enough to fit into a glass jar being held up by the youngest Ricetorian. She smiled at the Silhouettes as she swiftly added a cork stopper. "Want to see what happens next?"

The Ricetorians led them through dense fog that began to change temperature, slowly rising to a warm steam that hinted at freshly baked cakes. A small bakery emerged through the sweet-scented air, rich honey light shining down from the lanterns strung between the roof's wooden panels. The younger Ricetorian hurried forward and held the door open for the Silhouettes, ushering them inside.

Zhi Ging's stomach rumbled as she stepped into the shop, immediately wrapped in the lush velvety scents of pandan cake and pineapple buns. Malo's beak dropped open in wonder as he spotted a counter that ran along three walls of the bakery. Egg tarts, coconut-dusted jellies, and mango-filled mochi gleamed like precious gems under the lantern light.

"Keep moving." The Chief Ricetorian chuckled, pushing open a second door that led into the bakery's back garden. "We'll come back, I promise, but you'll want to see what happens with the collected raindrops first."

The Silhouettes gathered in a wide circle as the Ricetorians unfurled the water-studded net. The cormorants swooped above them, pulling a bamboo canopy out from the bakery roof to stop new rain mixing with the collected droplets. The Chief Ricetorian directed the others as they laid the net out across soft grass, careful not to let a single drop slide off. Under the glow of lanterns, the net gleamed as if covered in diamonds.

He then bustled over to a large barrel filled with rice and lowered in a chipped porcelain bowl. The Chief Ricetorian whistled and the cormorants dived down, landing on his wide-brimmed hat as they took turns plucking individual grains from the bowl. One by one they flew over the net, sprinkling single pieces of rice into each of the raindrops.

Malo looked on in awe, his wings unconsciously copying their movements as he watched their swooping choreographed dance. Once each droplet had been studded with a small fragment of white, the Chief Ricetorian nodded and the others lowered lanterns to the net, causing the grains of rice to swirl in the center of each warming raindrop.

"Look!" Jack shouted, pointing to a far corner of the net.

Zhi Ging stood on her toes, peering over the jostling Silhouettes. Tiny green sprouts had begun to erupt out of the droplets, young rice stalks in various shades of green shooting up from the net. Within a few minutes, the entire net had disappeared and was hidden beneath a rich tapestry of rice leaves.

An image rippled across the shades of green. It was them! The Silhouettes captured at the exact moment the Ricetorians' net had been cast over them. The stalks swayed and Zhi Ging watched as her rice image moved, placing a protective hand over Malo. Beside her in the image, Jack prodded a thread in amusement while Iridill pushed stray hairs back under her hood. The scene repeated on a short three-second loop, restarting each time the rice stalks bent in a new direction.

"The rain captures an exact moment, preserving the memory in a raindrop, and the rice brings it to life," the Chief Ricetorian explained. "While the spider silk nets can be reused, the memories themselves are stored in the droplets, meaning they can only be used once." He gestured to a small workshop attached to the back of the bakery. "Let's show you what happens with the rice we harvest from the droplets."

The Silhouettes squeezed in behind him, and three

new Ricetorians smiled up at them, each holding a heavy wooden mallet. Between them was a large mortar filled with steaming rice dough, the curved structure taking up most of the workshop.

"Right, who'd like a go turning this into mochi?" the closest Ricetorian asked, twirling the mallet.

Every single Silhouette's hand shot up, causing Malo to jump. He buried himself in Zhi Ging's hood as the Chief Ricetorian's booming laugh echoed across the workshop.

"Don't worry, you'll all get a go. It takes more work than you'd think turning this into Ricetorian-quality memory mochi, better known as memochi." He scanned the eager faces, gesturing for Zhi Ging, Jack, and a young carved lacquer Silhouette to take the first go. Zhi Ging puffed out her cheeks as she took the mallet; it was much heavier than she expected.

"Now, I want each of you to take turns hitting the dough as hard as you can." The Chief Ricetorian's eyes twinkled. "This memochi is your Chau, after all, so let's make it the best batch this bakery's ever seen. Watch how it's done."

He pulled a fourth mallet from one of the workshop shelves and slammed it down into the warm dough. A burst of sunlight escaped from beneath his mallet, heat radiating over Zhi Ging's face before vanishing back into the rice.

"This rice was grown from raindrops that captured the glass province's first spring sunrise of the year," he explained. "The beams of sunlight have been stored in the grains ever since. Once we've transformed this dough to memochi, the warm light will be infused throughout the rice cakes. Your turn." He nodded, waving his mallet at the trio.

They took turns, speeding up as their confidence grew, until all three mallets moved in a blur, flashes of sunlight dancing across their faces with each swing. A few minutes later, the Ricetorians called up a new set of Silhouettes, and Zhi Ging handed her mallet to Hiulam, who swung it enthusiastically.

Once every Silhouette had taken part, the Chief Ricetorian pulled a piece of memochi toward himself. The Silhouettes were silent, waiting for his verdict as it stretched upward, sunlight glinting along the thick glutinous dough. He looked up at them, one eyebrow raised, before beaming proudly. "Absolutely perfect."

The other Ricetorians hurried forward, clapping hands covered in cornstarch. They molded the memochi into identical spheres, placing each one onto a tray, which was then handed out to the Silhouettes.

"Try one," the two Wuiyams said enthusiastically.

Zhi Ging took a bite, and her eyes widened. She was suddenly transported back to a sunrise on Fei Chui's jade mountain, the cloud sea transforming into an ocean of pure gold as the sun rose beneath its surface. The vision faded as she swallowed the rice cake, but her entire body felt wrapped in warmth. She took another bite, and this time the Glassmith's workshop glinted around her, its stained glass walls glowing in the rising spring light. She reached a hand to the glass but touched bakery walls instead.

"Powerful, right?" The Chief Ricetorian nodded appreciatively, passing Zhi Ging a neatly wrapped gift box filled with fresh memochi. "Everyone needs memory aids from time to time, and memochi can be enjoyed by everyone, even old Ricetorians like him." He chuckled, pointing at the eldest Ricetorian in the workshop, who was happily enjoying his memochi despite having no teeth.

Zhi Ging tucked the box into her pocket. *Maybe a taste of sunlight will help Mynah and Pinderent finally wake up.*

CHAPTER 13

The Silhouettes squeezed down the library aisle, staring up at the bookshelves that stretched to the ceiling.

"Did Wuiyam give us the wrong directions?" Zhi Ging asked, tapping the outer glass wall.

"I hope not," a familiar voice called out. "Wusi sent me here too."

"Mynah!" Zhi Ging spun around, immediately recognizing her friend's voice.

The girl beamed back at her, her cheeks flashing yellow and green as Malo leaped out of Zhi Ging's hood, tumbling over himself in his excitement to welcome her back.

"When did you wake up? How are you feeling? Do you get to come back to the dorm now?" Zhi Ging asked, her questions spilling out over one another.

"Annoyingly, I woke up an hour after you all left for the Recall challenge. Wusi kept me overnight, just to be safe, but she said I can start coming to lessons." She picked Malo up and glanced at the other recently cured Silhouettes, their eyes also flashing green and blue above bobbly yellow scarves. "Oh, wow, awkward matching. One or forty of us should go back and change."

Iridill scowled and blinked hard, as if her determination would finally remove the blue and green from her previously brown eyes.

"Clearly everyone spent their time in the sick bay wishing they were more like me," Jack added with a snort. Mynah did a double take, her mouth dropping open in surprise.

"Jack! I didn't know you'd be here! Did you finally take the Silhouette exam? Oh, this is brilliant. You can tell the truth now—did you *really* never know what our challenges were? Wait, do you know what the rest of the challenges for this year are going to be?" Her cheek patches flashed through a full rainbow of colors, each question getting faster and faster as she spoke without taking a breath.

"Pinderent woke up this morning too!" she continued, spinning back to Zhi Ging before Jack could answer any of her questions. "Wusi said we could visit after class."

"No way!" Zhi Ging glanced at the library entrance, suddenly impatient for class to be over. *Is there time to visit Pinderent now?*

She turned back to Mynah, scrambling in her cloak pocket. "I saved both of you some memochi from the last Chau."

"Ah, I knew I woke up at the right time!" Mynah smiled, tickling Malo before dropping him back in Zhi Ging's hood.

To their left, a bookshelf rumbled, creaking open to reveal both Wuiyams. They were now dressed in matching coral robes, their dramatic makeup from the challenge replaced with delicate pink eye shadow that haloed up to their eyebrows.

"Right this way, little Silhouettes," they said, their voices in near-perfect harmony. The Recall tutors gestured toward the top of a large spiral staircase that curled down five levels before reaching a polished glass floor.

Mynah grabbed Zhi Ging's arm as they hurried after the others. "You have to tell me what I missed at yesterday's challenge," she whispered, her eyes darting between the identical Cyo B'Ahon while her cheek patches flashed dark purple.

"Welcome to Recall," Wuiyam announced, their voices only a millisecond out of sync as one tutor focused on shutting the bookshelf door behind them. "Over the next month, I'll show you how to track down lost memories and bring them back as clear as if you're experiencing them for the first time. We'll also explore how the different provinces across Wengyuen have learned to store memories in objects. There's much to learn, and not just from the Ricetorians and their delicious memochi." She pointed at a cabinet filled with dozens of glittering headdresses. "I personally like to spend most of my year shoreside, refining my skills with opera and theater performers. They have some of the best instinctive recall you'll ever encounter. Now, depending on how quickly we progress in the first fortnight, I'll teach you how some in the gold province are transforming empty mines into echo chambers—contracts, and agreements repeated endlessly against the cave walls—while those from the silk province have mastered how to bottle memories as scents." She pointed back at the bookshelf door. "Imagine an entire library aisle of information stored in a bottle that fits in the palm of your hand, a single spray releasing the memories fresh in your mind."

The Silhouettes murmured excitedly among themselves. Zhi Ging's heart leaped; with Wuiyam's help she might finally know if she really did see Niotiya controlling that sand spirit. Beside her, Jack was staring intently at the tutors. She could almost hear his thoughts. What if Wuiyam could help him track down his memories from before he Reverted?

"Now, a quick show of hands," Wuiyam continued. "How many of you here have spent more than ten months in Hok Woh?"

Only Mynah and three other Silhouettes raised their hands.

"Excellent, the first lesson is always much less exciting when the answer's none of you." The Wuiyam by the door pulled a glass lever, and dozens of silk banners unfurled above the spiral staircase, the fabric brushing against the banister. "The other tutors will never admit it, but Recall is the most important of the twelve skills when it comes to ageshifting. If your body can't remember how it looked and felt at younger ages, how can it ever return to them? So today, ahead of your graduation, why don't we have a secret practice?" Her eyes sparkled, the pink eye shadow creasing to look like petals fanning out over her face.

"Do you think we'll actually be able to do it?" Mynah asked, her cheek patches a bright sunflower yellow as excited whispers rippled through the group.

"Occasionally, eleventh- and final-month Silhouettes can manage a small flicker. After your graduation ceremony, you spend your first few months as a Cyo B'Ahon with me." Wuiyam's two sets of hands pointed at each other. "I'll coach you through how to combine your twelve skills to ageshift. Once you've got it, it's no harder than breathing, but even some of your other tutors needed help when they first became Cyo B'Ahon. And besides"—a mischievous glint entered her eyes—"I'm the one in charge of ageshift training. What am I going to do, tell on myself for letting you try early?" Her laughter echoed across itself, both her faces shining in identical amusement.

Mynah grabbed Zhi Ging's arm, her eyes wide. "Okay, I'm still really excited for your memochi, but how amazing is this? And no"—she laughed as Malo's optimistic face immediately popped out of Zhi Ging's hood—"that doesn't mean you can have my rice cake, Malo."

"He already had more than enough last night." Zhi Ging snorted, remembering how the sunlight had shone through his feathers in rainbow hues back in the dorm. He had transformed the entire room into a glowing palette until Iridill complained the light was interrupting her sleep.

"Everyone get in line," Wuiyam continued, tapping the banister. "Final-month Silhouettes first, followed by eleventh-month and so on."

"That's not fair," Iridill whined as Silhouettes began to line up in front of her. "Why do they get to go first?"

Zhi Ging glanced between the two Wuiyams and held back a laugh. She'd been wrong about there being no differences between them; only one kept her face blank. The other tutor rolled her eyes before continuing as if she'd not heard Iridill's outburst.

"Poor recall is the most common blocker to ageshifting. That squeezed, claustrophobic sensation you get in your head when struggling with something difficult? Well, I'm going to teach you how to use that. That feeling happens because your brain is stretching itself, rummaging through every single one of your memories—both clear and forgotten—to try to solve the problem. When you start ageshift training, it can almost feel like your brain can't breathe; the difficulty of the problem threatens to smother it. However, as long as you don't panic, your brain will start pulling from the rest of your body as it sifts through memories. Not only will you remember, but your body will also recall how it felt and return to that earlier age." The Wuiyam closest to the spiral staircase leaned forward and pulled the first silk banner toward the Silhouettes. "These puzzle banners each have a different memory-based problem. Try to solve each one as you slide down. We won't try to ageshift you down too quickly, but let's see if some of you can shake even a few months."

Zhi Ging stood on her tiptoes, trying to peer over the shoulders of the Silhouettes ahead of her. A splatter of dark ink filled the center of its red silk surface, but she couldn't make out any writing. Instead, when she tilted her head and squinted, the splash mark almost looked like an abstract jellyfish.

Wuiyam caught her confused frown and smiled. "You won't be able to read any of the questions until it's your turn." She shook her head at the Silhouettes. "I've worked hard with Neoi Syu, the Calligraphy tutor, to create an ink that can only be read when faced directly. Until you're sliding down the banister yourself, it'll look like nothing more than spatters."

"Which is better for all of you anyway," the other Wuiyam added from the back of the group. "If you read the questions too early, your mind won't be scrambling for the answers and your chances of ageshifting will drop."

She strode to the front of the line and hopped onto the banister. Wuiyam winked, then slid down the spiral staircase, ageshifting each time she passed under a banner. She leaped off at the bottom and waved back up at them, now looking younger than most of the Silhouettes.

"All right," the baby-faced Wuiyam continued, not bothering to raise her voice as the Wuiyam still standing with the Silhouettes mirrored her words. "Your turn—one at a time now."

Oimaa, a final-month Silhouette, stepped forward and perched cautiously at the edge of the banister. Her knuckles were white as they gripped the wood on either side. There was a short pause, then Wuiyam shuffled forward, bending low so she was face-to-face with the Silhouette. "You'll need to loosen your grip a bit. Otherwise you'll never reach the bottom."

"I hate heights," Oimaa admitted, her cheeks flushing the same shade of pink as the tutor's eye shadow.

"Nothing embarrassing about that; Sintou hates them too. Why do you think Hok Woh's underwater? Let's slide down together." The tutor hopped up in front of Oimaa, ageshifting down so they were the same height before encouraging the Silhouette to grab hold of her robes. "Ready?"

Oimaa took a deep breath and nodded. Wuiyam leaned forward, sliding down at speed. The others broke out of their line, leaning over the banister to watch them go. Oimaa yelped, flinging one hand over her eyes as they veered around the second floor, banners fluttering above them. They eventually came to a stop by the other Wui-yam, Oimaa shaking as she was helped off the banister.

"Right. One quick tip I forgot to mention: please try to keep your eyes open!" the two Wuiyams shouted up. "Otherwise there really isn't much chance of ageshifting."

The next Silhouette was able to scan the puzzle banners but had no better luck at ageshifting. However, there were excited cheers from the small group below as Mynah slid toward the ground floor.

"We had a partial face flicker!" Wuiyam called up excitedly. "Miss Niu definitely looked at least a couple months younger between the final two banners." The tutor held up Mynah's hand in triumph and a dazed smile splashed across the Silhouette's face. Malo flapped his wings together, chirping his congratulations.

Soon tenth- and ninth-month Silhouettes were also on the lower level, eagerly crowding around Mynah and a gold province Silhouette named Hoi Dak, the only two who had managed a slight ageshift.

"Go, Zhi Ging!" Mynah and Hiulam cried as she stepped toward the banister. Before Zhi Ging could place her hand on its surface, Iridill barged forward, slamming her hand over the curving wood.

"You can wait, NoGlow. After all, I was the *first* Fei Chui Silhouette." She leaped onto the banister and pushed down before Zhi Ging could even respond. The group was silent as she leaped off at the bottom. Iridill flung her arms wide as she looked around in frustration. "I definitely ageshifted, why is no one congratulating me?" she snapped, glancing back up to Kaolin and Cing Yau for support. The two Silhouettes obediently began to clap, but both Wuiyams shook their heads.

"I'm afraid you've mistaken airspeed for ageshifting, Miss Seoipin. Although I agree your behavior at the top of the banister was that of someone considerably less mature than your age."

Iridill flushed, slouching to the back of the group with her arms folded.

Zhi Ging turned to Malo as she stepped back up to the banister. "Do you want to slide down with me or fly ahead?"

The little phoenix chirped, wriggling out of her hood to roll onto the banister. He turned and patted the space behind him, watching her expectantly.

"OK, here we go." She laughed. Although Zhi Ging had watched the others, it felt even faster once she was the one racing down. The ink on the first banner shimmered as she approached it, stretching to form her first question. Before Zhi Ging had even finished reading, the next banner whipped past. She spun around, trying to catch the second half of the missed question when the third banner zoomed past overhead.

The speed made her eyes water, and she struggled to keep them open long enough to read the remaining puzzle banners. Snippets flashed before her until she finally skidded to a stop at the end of the banister. Malo slid off, immediately hopping back up the stairs for another turn.

"At least one of us enjoyed that." Zhi Ging winced, leaning against Mynah as she waited for the room to stop spinning.

The rest of the Silhouettes slid down, each having no more success than Zhi Ging, until finally only Jack was left at the top of the stairs. His eyes flashed frantically between blue and green as he slid down. There was a collective gasp from the group when on the third floor he noticeably shrank, his robes suddenly loose. It only lasted one bend, though, and he was back to his usual age by the time he staggered off.

Zhi Ging stepped forward to congratulate him but was pushed aside as every other Silhouette rushed forward, surrounding her friend.

"That was amazing! How did you do that?" Oimaa cried, nearly hitting Hiulam as she swung her arms wide.

"Haven't you only been here a month?" Cing Yau asked in awe.

Zhi Ging tried to catch Jack's eye but he was too distracted. Something unfamiliar coiled in her stomach, and she spotted Wuiyam looking at her curiously. Zhi Ging turned away, trying to push down the bubbling jealousy, but each fawning question made it harder to drown out the bitter voice in her head.

Jack's already been a Cyo B'Ahon; of course he can ageshift. This isn't fair.

CHAPTER 14

"Mynah, I said *one* guest. You know he's still recovering," Wusi grumbled as Zhi Ging, Mynah, Hiulam, and Malo bundled past her toward Pinderent's bed.

He smiled feebly at them, a large cup of elixir clutched in his hands.

"Oof, good luck," Hiulam said, scrunching her nose at its steaming black surface. "I thought I'd be used to that after a few weeks, but the bitter taste still gives me nightmares."

"I actually don't mind it," Pinderent said with a faint laugh, taking a small gulp before shuddering. "Ugh, no, never mind. It's gotten worse since the first sip."

Hiulam nodded knowingly. "That's when the muddy carpet taste really kicks in."

Zhi Ging glanced back at the healer, checking that her attention was on a new batch of the thick medicine.

"We brought snacks," she whispered, pulling the

memochi gift box from her cloak pocket. "Don't let Wusi see!"

"Amazing! All I've had today is plain congee."

"You know they're both made from rice, though, right?" Zhi Ging giggled as he sniffed the memochi deeply, leaving a perfect circle of cornstarch dusting on the tip of his nose.

"Yeah, but these are clearly the better rice option." Pinderent bit into it, and his eyes widened. "Whoa, okay, this is even better than I remember mochi being."

"It's memochi," Zhi Ging said, breaking off some of her own to share with Malo. "The Ricetorians promised to send us more soon too."

"Just you wait," Hiulam added enthusiastically, "that new batch is going to be made with rice grown from the net they used on us." She smiled at Mynah's and Pinderent's confused expressions. "Don't worry, once you bite into that memochi the net'll make sense."

"Yeah, it'll be like you were at the Chau with us." Zhi Ging nodded, handing Mynah another piece. The group sat in companionable silence while they finished the memochi, taking turns to push Malo's snuffling beak out of the box. Zhi Ging glanced around at her friends, knowing the comfortable warmth filling her wasn't just from the sunlight-infused memochi. She'd missed this.

Pinderent sighed contentedly as he shook the now-empty box. "So what else happened while I was asleep?" he asked.

"Turns out Malo's actually a phoenix!" Zhi Ging said excitedly.

"What? No way, that's so cool."

Malo flapped a wing in fake modesty, clearly delighted by the attention.

"Yeah, all the lanterns in here are filled with his phoenix fire," Zhi Ging explained, batting one away as it floated toward them.

"I had eight of those around me when I woke up." Pinderent snorted. "It was so confusing."

"Oh, you'll never guess what, Jack's a Silhouette now too! And—" Mynah began.

"And he can ageshift!" Hiulam interrupted. "It's amazing. The only other two who managed it were Mynah and Hoi Dak, and they've both nearly finished their Silhouette years."

Pinderent's jaw dropped as he turned back to Mynah, clearly impressed. She took a dramatic bow, genuine excitement and pride mixed into the flourish.

"Where is Jack, anyway?" Pinderent asked after the group had indulged Mynah in a miniround of applause.

"Oh, he's still in the dining hall. Surrounded by his new fans," Zhi Ging muttered.

Hiulam shot her a look, surprised by her sour tone.

Zhi Ging bit into her final memochi, swallowing the other sentences clamoring to be said. She'd thought it would be easy to keep Jack's secret, but the truth had begun to rattle between her teeth. No one had ever given her this much attention for being Fei Chui's Second Silhouette. She glanced away, not liking the thoughts swirling through her mind but unable to stop them.

"Was there anyone else missing from class?" Pinderent asked, looking at the empty beds around him. While a few others were still frozen, they were older Silhouettes in the other dorm, their beds carefully pushed back ahead of that night's Cure Club.

"I don't think so." Zhi Ging shook her head, trying to peer through the dappled glass. This was as close as she could get to seeing what happened in Cure Club. Soft cushions were scattered across the floor, while plates of freshly baked almond cookies were stacked in the center of the room, waiting for the others to arrive from dinner. A few of the older Silhouettes were already snacking on them, crumbs sticking to their fingers while they sketched out their time trapped as thralls. The two Wuiyams wove between them, encouraging the Silhouettes to add more detail to their blurred watercolors.

Zhi Ging was still watching when Wusi bustled past, carrying a tray laden with various steaming elixirs. The healer paused beside the group, her gaze drifting meaningfully toward the empty box of memochi on Pinderent's bed. They jerked to life, four sets of sleeves and one set of wings leaping forward to sweep it out of sight. By the time Zhi Ging looked back up, Wusi had drawn a wooden screen across the sick bay, blocking the other dorm from sight.

"Hiulam," the healer's voice called out, "since you're here early, why don't you have your dose of elixir now?" Her arm appeared around the screen, a cup filled to the brim with what looked like steaming black sludge in her hand.

Hiulam winced, sliding off the bed to crouch behind the others. "Can one of you tell her I've gone?" she hissed.

"I don't think that'll work," Mynah whispered back, her arm patches flashing navy as she pointed at the floor. Heisiu, the healer's jellyfish, was swimming toward them beneath the glass. He stopped directly beside Hiulam's feet, tapping a tentacle against the sole of her shoe before pointing to Wusi.

"Ugh, fine. I'll be right back."

The others exchanged sympathetic looks as Hiulam traipsed back over, holding the pungent cup as far from her nose as physically possible.

"Here's to you rejoining Team Bolei soon. Training isn't the same without you," Hiulam said, clinking her cup with Pinderent's half-empty one.

"There aren't even races now." Zhi Ging sighed. "It's just endless drills while we try to work out how to climb a waterfall. Bucbou is making us practice before—" She broke off as something clicked into place. "Pinderent," she began slowly, not really wanting to know the answer, "has Wusi mentioned what'll happen after she's sure you've recovered?"

"She said she'd tell me at Cure Club, but I heard some

of the older Silhouettes whispering about it at lunch." He nodded at the new dorm. "Once Wusi's sure the possession won't come back, I'll get added to the list."

"The list?" Mynah asked, her cheek patches fading to dark gray.

"The list of failed Silhouettes who need to be escorted home. I think they're planning to start with the ones who were thralls the longest, but that still means I'll probably leave Hok Woh in a few months. Hey, it's still more time than I should've had," he quickly added, spotting their crestfallen expressions. "I can't come to classes, and I'll need to move into the new dorms after tonight, but at least I'll be able to see you guys at meals."

"I'm sorry, Pinderent," Zhi Ging blurted out. "It's my fault you failed the Concealment challenge. If I hadn't given you that weather wax, you'd never have become the Komodo dragon's main target. I'm going to fix things, I promise."

"It's okay. Just make sure you visit me back in the glass province once you're a super-important and powerful Cyo B'Ahon." He smiled weakly.

The glass beneath Zhi Ging's feet clinked, and she looked down. It was Heisiu again.

"Oh, but I don't need any elixir."

"Cure Club is about to start," Wusi called out, her voice sailing over the wooden screen. "Time for you to go back to your own dorm, Zhi Ging."

"Wait, why don't you get to join?" Mynah asked in

confusion, her arm patches shifting between blue and pink.

"Because she was never a thrall," Wuiyam said, stepping through the screen door. Other Silhouettes began to stream into the sick bay, their excited cheers echoing along the glass as they spotted the almond cookies. "Zhi Ging doesn't need to take any of Wusi's elixirs and—"

"And there's a risk she'll muddle the others' memories," the other half of Wuiyam finished, brushing crumbs from her fingers. "As I explained in class today, untrained memories are far too malleable. Until we've built an accurate picture of exactly what happened, having Zhi Ging in the room while Silhouettes share their own hazy memories might cause confusion. Cure Club isn't just a chance for cookies; there's a lot of hard work involved."

"Doesn't sound that hard," Zhi Ging muttered as Kaolin's and Cing Yau's nasal laughter bounced over the wooden screen. There were delighted coos as Malo waddled into the dorm, his arrival rewarded with the distinct sound of sunflower seeds dancing across the floor. Buttery light shone through the screen, the Silhouettes' yellow scarves reflected by the polished walls until the spherical room resembled a rich harvest moon. "Everyone just seems to sit around eating snacks while phoenix-fire lanterns float about," she pushed. "There's already phoenix fire back in the dorm fireplace; why can't Cure Club happen there?"

"It's just one hour," Wusi said soothingly as she

ushered Mynah and Pinderent past. "You never seemed to mind spending time away from the others while helping Reishi with his air rail research. This is no different."

"But I got to pick that." Zhi Ging sighed as she trudged back down the tower stairs. "I never had a choice about Cure Club."

ZHI GING TRAIPSED ALONG THE CORRIDOR, BARELY paying attention to where her feet were taking her. Hok Woh's corridors were surprisingly silent once all the other Silhouettes were tucked away in the sick bay. She soon realized she could even hear the soft ripple of jellyfish passing on the other side of the glass. Zhi Ging turned to watch, but her eyes widened in confusion. A thick stripe of yellow paint had been smeared over the glass, stretching the full length of the empty corridor. It had been slashed above her head, luminous streaks dripping down over her wide-eyed reflection and across the glass floor. The jellyfish on the other side of the wall were rubbing at the paint in frustration, their tentacles ineffectively trying to wipe it away.

"Where did you come from?" Zhi Ging hurried back, retracing her steps to find where the paint started. There was a faint splat as she raced past the dragon boat equipment room, and Zhi Ging realized too late that she had run through a large puddle of yellow, the sunny dye seeping beneath the unlocked door and across her shoes.

"Great, just what I needed," she grumbled, turning

to the far wall while she removed her shoes. Her hand pressed the still-tacky paint above her and it squelched, droplets landing along her braid. She flicked her hood up with her spare hand before it could do more damage.

"There they are!" a voice bellowed behind her. "I knew they wouldn't stay away. Thieves always come sneaking back." The equipment room burst open and two Cyo B'Ahon stormed out, clutching empty paint pots.

"Do you have any idea how expensive glowing paint is? It's exclusively for racing paddles, not smearing over walls!" Sycee, the captain for Team Wong Gam, roared. "Just because you Silhouettes don't have a Dohrnii right now doesn't mean you can do whatever you want."

Zhi Ging froze, seeing their eyes dart between her paint-stained hands and shoes. There was no way they'd believe it hadn't been her.

There was only one thing to do.

Zhi Ging took a deep breath and sprinted, both hands tugging her hood tightly over her face. The popping sound of Cyo B'Ahon ageshifting down in frustration echoed after her and she was still breathing hard when she burst into the dorm a few minutes later. Zhi Ging flung herself through her bedroom door and slammed it shut before lying flat on the floor. She held her breath as Sycee and the other Cyo B'Ahon thundered in a few seconds later.

"We need to talk to Wusi," Sycee muttered as she began yanking bedroom doors open at random. "Find out if any of the Silhouettes didn't bother showing up for tonight's Cure Club."

"Or left early," the other Cyo B'Ahon added. "That's the fifth pot of yellow paint on corridor walls this week."

Sycee cursed furiously under her breath, and Zhi Ging's heart stuttered as the captain's tall shadow paused in front of her own door. The captain drummed her fingers on the screen, then pulled away.

"I don't care how many challenges they have left," Sycee snarled as they turned back into the corridor. "Once we find them, they're on the first dragon boat home with the other failed Silhouettes."

CHAPTER 15

"So who do you think it is?" Zhi Ging asked once Mynah sat down for lunch. For the past week, all any of the Silhouettes could talk about was the paint thief, trying to guess whether it was one of them or an older Silhouette. More yellow stripes had appeared each day, despite Sycee organizing crew members to keep watch over the equipment room.

"I'm not bothered about who they are. I just want to know *why* they're doing it," Mynah said as her homei spoon transformed into a comforting helping of wonton noodles. She scooped up a generous helping of thin shrimp roe noodles and waved her chopsticks. "I don't get why someone would risk being sent home over yellow lines. You'd think they'd at least try something different, like a caricature of some tutors, but no, it's just the same boring old line over and over again."

"Maybe it's some sort of code?" Jack mused. "The lines might be a secret symbol."

"They kind of look like our scarves," Pinderent murmured, tugging the wool from around his neck and laying it flat across the table.

Zhi Ging could see what he meant; the thick bright lines that had started to decorate the corridors definitely did have a scarf-like look about them. She frowned down at the table, wondering if the lines and scarves were linked in some way. *At least it's not another Cure Club inside joke everyone else is in on.*

Jack glanced up at her and, for a split second Zhi Ging worried she'd said that last thought out loud. Although he was the only other Silhouette without a scarf, she still couldn't shake the jealousy that had coiled like brambles around her since he had ageshifted. What was the point of Jack coming back to Hok Woh if he spent all his time talking to other Silhouettes and going to Cure Club without her? She jabbed at the siu mai in her bowl, poking a chopstick through the steamed pork and prawn dumpling.

Maybe he's talking to others because you've *been ignoring him?* a small part of Zhi Ging whispered, its reproachful voice muffled beneath the coarse jealousy. She felt her cheeks flush and her shoulders tighten, knowing it was true.

She had deliberately sat beside Hiulam just now, even though Jack had gestured at the spare seat beside him. Zhi Ging leaned across the table to refill his tea, a tiny peace offering that she hoped he would accept, even if he didn't understand why she had been distant all week.

"Thanks," he said, smiling directly at her.

Zhi Ging nodded back, feeling some of the brambles break apart, their thorns no longer pressing deep into her shoulders.

"Have any of you heard the latest rumor?" he continued after taking a long sip. "I heard Kaolin telling people at breakfast that it's not paint at all. It's actually thick paste to stop water flooding through cracks in the walls."

Zhi Ging snorted. "Oh! That explains why I saw a group of silk province Silhouettes racing down a painted corridor earlier."

"Did you notice there's lines on both sides of the sick bay stairs now?" Hiulam added. "There was definitely only one earlier this week."

"Maybe it's actually Wusi behind them." Mynah giggled. "She's run out of recovered Silhouettes to make scarves for, so now she just has to paint them." She slurped up her noodles while the others laughed, but her eyes suddenly widened as her arm and cheek patches turned slate gray. The chopsticks dropped from her hand and she began to choke.

Zhi Ging leaped toward her friend and began thumping her hard on the back. "Someone get Wusi!" she shouted as Silhouettes at nearby tables stopped talking, turning to them in shock. Out of the corner of her eye, she spotted Pou Pou rise up from his basin before darting into the wall to alert the healer's jellyfish.

"I'm . . . ," Mynah began, her face pale. "I'm okay, I just . . ." She waved her hand toward a cup of cooling tea and Pinderent leaned forward, almost knocking it over in his rush to hand it to her.

"Miss Niu!" Wusi came racing into the dining hall, a stream of paper lanterns trailing behind her, bright phoenix fire flashing as they jostled together.

"I'm fine, really," Mynah croaked in embarrassment, her arm patches now bright tangerine as the healer tilted her face up, peering closely for any sign of gray in her pupils.

"Let me be the judge of that. Sick bay, now."

"I'll come with you," Zhi Ging whispered, grabbing her friend's hand.

Mynah nodded and squeezed it gratefully as they hurried out, trying to ignore the deafening silence that followed after them. Every Silhouette in the hall had gone quiet, homei spoons and chopsticks lying forgotten on tables. Zhi Ging couldn't help but shudder as forty faces swiveled to watch them go. It was eerily similar to how the Silhouettes had moved as thralls while trapped inside the catacomb's hollow walls. This time, though, it wasn't just her fear filling the room. Instead the air was heavy with a single, cloying worry. What if the possession was coming back?

"WHAT HAPPENED?" ZHI GING ASKED SOFTLY ONCE Mynah had finished her second helping of elixir. She had been forced to wait by Heisiu's basin while Wusi checked over her friend, speaking with Mynah in urgent, hushed whispers. The others would be back in class now, but she didn't want to leave until she knew Mynah was all right.

The other girl sighed, rolling the empty cup between her hands. She hesitated and glanced over at Wusi, who was already busy preparing the next batch for that night's Cure Club.

"It was horrible," she whispered. "I've not eaten noodles since I woke up, and I don't think I ever will again."

"What do you mean?" Zhi Ging asked in confusion, sitting down on the edge of Mynah's bed.

"It's just . . ." The other girl grimaced, her cheek patches flowing between blue and gray as she tried to explain. "You saw what the thralls looked like, right?"

Zhi Ging nodded, her stomach tightening as she remembered the gray-eyed faces turning toward her, their silent screaming mouths filled with jellyfish tentacles.

"Well, in Cure Club the two Wuiyams are trying to help us collect our thrall memories. I've not been able to remember much, only Iridill and a few others have, but"—Mynah shook her head and pulled the bedcovers up to her chin—"when I ate those noodles, I suddenly remembered *everything*. The way they moved over my tongue was awful, just like the jellyfish Ami tricked me into eating at the Perception Chau."

Zhi Ging sat stock-still, scared to even breathe in case it interrupted her friend. Behind her Wusi looked up sharply and gestured for Heisiu to start recording, a tentacle stretched out toward the Silhouette's bed.

"Once I took that first bite it was like I'd gone back to being a thrall with a jellyfish wriggling inside my mouth. I'm so glad Ami didn't get you at the Chau." She grimaced, her patches dulling to a tarnished rust. "When I was a thrall, I couldn't control anything. Not my movements or even my emotions. Instead all I could feel was Ami's thoughts. A low constant thrum of anger that rattled against my skull. Each time I tried to fight it, one of the jellyfish tentacles would lash out, knocking me back." Mynah paused, rubbing her eyes. "There were others there too, though, not just Ami. Just before the jellyfish took over, I remember seeing a group burst into the Chau banquet hall. But . . ." Her voice caught in her throat, and she turned back to Zhi Ging, her face crumpling. "It makes no sense; they looked just like Omophilli Matchmakers. My great-aunt is the Head Matchmaker; why would she let them hurt us?"

Zhi Ging gaped at her, unsure what she could say to help. "Maybe Niotiya wasn't involved," she said feebly, trying to ignore the memory of the Matchmaker watching over the sand spirit attack.

"Who?" Mynah asked, looking back at her in confusion.

"Niotiya, the Head Matchmaker? Isn't she your great-aunt?" Zhi Ging whispered, worried her friend might have lost more of her memories.

"She's not my great-aunt. Ginsau is," Mynah said slowly. "There was a Matchmaker with that name when

I was growing up in the Guild, but my great-aunt never liked her very much. Apparently, her punishments for junior Matchmakers were always too extreme."

Zhi Ging frowned before remembering what Gertie had said before the Scramble. She hesitated, wondering whether to tell Mynah about Niotiya's growing power. She lowered her voice so Heisiu couldn't hear. "What did your great-aunt mean by 'extreme'?"

"I'm not sure," Mynah admitted, unconsciously rubbing her left palm. "But I got woken up a few times by junior Matchmakers crying." Her fingers brushed against the exact spot that had been marked by the Matchmakers' stamp. "There's no way I'm going back to Omophilli if Niotiya's in charge."

"I'M JUST SAYING IT'S SUSPICIOUS, THAT'S ALL." IRI- dill's voice floated along the corridor as Zhi Ging made her way back down the stairs later that evening. Her stomach rumbled from missing dinner, the handful of cookies she'd shared with Mynah had been nowhere near enough.

For once, Zhi Ging didn't feel jealous. Mynah had been right; she was lucky not to visit the sick bay each night. Lucky not to have been possessed at Ami's Chau. After seeing how the memory had affected her friend, Zhi Ging no longer felt like she was missing out on a fun secret club. She winced at how selfish she must have seemed to her friends, complaining about how even Malo got to join them while she was stuck in the dorm alone. She had thought it was just an hour of hanging out, but the cookies were a small comfort when the others had to drink that peaty elixir and confront their time under Ami's control. Zhi Ging sighed, embarrassed it had taken seeing Mynah's reaction to the noodles to realize how difficult Cure Club must actually be for the Silhouettes who had started to remember their time as thralls. *What if Hiulam or Pinderent have been dealing with horrible memories the entire time I've been complaining? I never even asked.*

She rounded the corner and nearly crashed into a group of yellow-scarved Silhouettes.

Iridill glowered at her from the center of the group. "Excuse you, NoGlow. What are you even doing here? Don't tell me you're trying to sneak into Cure Club *again*."

Zhi Ging felt her cheeks flush red as she shook her head. "No, I was actually just leav—"

"Look at her hands!" Cing Yau yelped, jabbing a finger at Zhi Ging's flour-covered arms. "It *is* her! She's stealing Team Si Cau's white paint now!"

"What are you talking about?" Zhi Ging asked in bafflement before clapping her hands together to create a soft cloud. "It's just flour. Mynah and I helped Wusi make the next batch of almond cookies for all of you."

"Convenient." Kaolin snorted before tapping the yellow line daubed on the wall beside him. "Is it just me or do these only appear when the rest of us are at Cure Club?"

"And why"—Iridill shoved her way forward and snatched at Zhi Ging's cloak, tugging the gold Pan Chang

Knot up—"do you *still* have a different knot than everyone else? One that's almost the exact same color as the painted lines? Let me guess." She sneered, her eyes flashing dark blue and green as she released the Pan Chang. "You hated that no one cared about Hok Woh's precious Second Silhouette anymore, not after we started waking up. So you decided to ruin the walls just to get some attention."

"That doesn't even make sense!" Zhi Ging had to shout to be heard over the shocked whispers that rippled among the rest of the group. "Sintou *gave* me this Pan Chang after Ami took mine. And why would I try to be sent home? Once Sycee catches the paint thief, there's no way they'll get to stay."

Iridill's eyes narrowed, clearly not believing her. "Now that you mention it, why *did* Ami want your Pan Chang? Didn't she make that white knot specifically for you in the first place?" She took a step forward, peering down her nose at Zhi Ging. "Why are you the only Silhouette who didn't get possessed? The only one not at the Chau when we were attacked?" She paused dramatically, checking she had the group's full attention before flinging down her final accusation. "How do we know the person Ami was working with wasn't you? Is that what you're doing while we're all at Cure Club, trying to find a way to reverse Wusi's elixir?"

Zhi Ging went pale. It was so ridiculous she didn't know how to answer. She could hear more Silhouettes' footsteps echoing toward them, voices calling out and asking why the stairwell was blocked. If she tried to argue now, everyone from the dorm would hear. She tugged at her braid, pulling it out from her hood and twisting it anxiously.

Surprise flashed across Iridill's face as she glanced at a spot just behind Zhi Ging's shoulder. Her eyes narrowed and her mouth twitched into a wide smirk as she leaned forward, lowering her voice so only Zhi Ging could hear.

"You tried to threaten me last month. Big mistake. If you *ever* even hint again that Jack got me into Hok Woh, I'll show everyone the yellow paint inside your hood. If I have to leave, so will you."

CHAPTER 16

Thick fog covered the sea as the Silhouettes stepped out of the entrance stepping stone a few days later. It was the evening of their Perseverance challenge and a sharp breeze whipped at those already on the red junk, a prophecy of snow whirling between them. Zhi Ging hopped from foot to foot, peering at the jittery faces around her. It was the first time a challenge had started after dusk, and the group's collective nerves had been building all day.

Mynah clambered up beside Zhi Ging, her cheek patches a frosty shade of blue. "Why has the challenge been left until now? I couldn't enjoy my dinner at all, *and* I got the only baked-pork-chop-rice homei spoon," she grumbled.

"Wait, I thought you finished that?" Jack said, an eyebrow raised in confusion.

"I said I didn't enjoy it—not that I didn't finish it!" Mynah huffed good-naturedly. "The Perseverance tutor owes me a second spoon."

"I'm glad you woke up before this challenge, though," Zhi Ging murmured as she huddled closer to Mynah. Her friend's cheek patches softened and returned to warm buttery yellow.

"Oh, this is definitely better than being frozen," she agreed. "Although Wusi's now trying to get me to eat a bowl of noodles at every Cure Club, until they stop feeling like jellyfish tentacles." She paused, her cheeks flushing orange. "Another reason why I'm owed a new homei spoon! Am I not allowed to enjoy noodles *or* rice now?" she said with exaggerated indignation.

Once the final Silhouette had boarded the junk, Heisiu floated out from behind the red sail, a lantern balanced above his head like a crown. It was a sturdy structure, woven together with dozens of bamboo saplings.

"Wait, it's definitely Perseverance and not Flora today, right?" Zhi Ging asked Jack, looking at the lantern in concern.

"Oh no, do you only have the right thing to cheat your way through Perseverance, NoGlow?" Iridill sneered, adjusting her yellow scarf.

Zhi Ging glared at her but spun back around as the two guardian Cyo B'Ahon and their cranes joined Heisiu at the front of the boat.

"Who are they?" Mynah asked, nudging her.

"G'Aam and Wuyan; they're Prediction specialists," Huilam explained, leaning over Zhi Ging's shoulder. "They don't speak, but Sintou has ordered them and their combat cranes to keep watch over all our challenges just in case there's an attack."

"Hi, I'm Mynah. Which one are you, G'Aam or Wuyan? You look a bit like my second uncle, actually. Are you also from the paper province? Why do you have a crane instead of a jellyfish? Or do all Prediction Cyo B'Ahon have both?" Mynah asked as one of them mutely handed her a golden hoop. He ignored her questions, but his crane looked around in disappointment, clearly searching for Malo.

"Sorry," Zhi Ging whispered as she stepped into her own hoop. "He's keeping Pinderent and the older Silhouettes company tonight, but I'll try to bring him next time."

THE LANTERN BROUGHT THEM DOWN ON THE SIDE of a frozen mountain. Heavy snow made the air shimmer, causing the Silhouettes' faces to blur even though they were just inches apart. They shivered and instinctively huddled closer, the hoops clattering down around them as the rope's ocean spray transformed to ice. No matter which way the Silhouettes turned, sharp gusts of wind lashed their faces, stinging their noses and ears. Zhi Ging winced and flung her hood up as a flurry of snowflakes slid down the back of her neck. *I really wish we had Malo and his fire right now.*

She became convinced she could hear a faint plink each time she closed her eyes as icicles coated her eyelashes. It had been nowhere near this cold at the iceberg instrumental. Even G'Aam and Wuyan were forced to pull their cloaks tight around themselves.

"Welcome, everyone." Wusi appeared through the snow, wrapped in a thick fur-lined cape. She smiled at the shivering Silhouettes and gestured for them to step closer.

"As I'm sure you've worked out, I'm your next tutor. This evening's challenge is all about simple perseverance. Namely"—she gestured at the mountain around them, both upturned palms immediately filling with snowflakes—"what you can and can't tolerate."

The Silhouettes watched in silent confusion as she drew a line in the snow, separating herself from them. "To pass my challenge, you need to stay on your side of the line until midnight—which is four hours away." Wusi stepped to the side, pointing at a series of steps barely visible through the heavy snow. "For those who find this challenge too difficult, the way to the nearest village, and warmth, is down there." The group inched forward, careful to keep their feet firmly behind the line as they peered down the cliff.

Nestled at the bottom of the valley was a small village. The rooftops were free of snow, and rich light flooded out from each window. Mynah leaned out farther, one hand clutching Zhi Ging's shoulder as her stomach rumbled. The smell of pan-fried dumplings and roast goose drifted up from several chimneys.

"G'Aam, Wuyan, and their combat cranes will keep you safe until the end of your challenge."

The two Prediction Cyo B'Ahon swept toward them, rolling back their broad sleeves to reveal thick rows of jade bracelets that stretched from wrist to elbow on each arm. Wusi pulled an identical piece of jade from her pocket. "Now, as Hok Woh's healer, I don't want to see any of you in the sick bay after this challenge. Outside of Cure Club, that is," she added, flashing them a quick smile, but the Silhouettes were too focused on keeping their teeth from chattering to notice her joke. "These bracelets will track your heart rate. If you become dangerously cold, your jade will begin to shake. If it snaps in half, you must leave the challenge immediately, for your own safety. Unfortunately, that will also mean you don't quite have the knack for perseverance." Wusi bent down and opened a large cloth bag by her feet. Inside it were dozens of thick winter capes identical to her own. "I'll leave these here for anyone whose jade does snap. All you have to do is put one on, then make your way to the village. They know to feed any Silhouettes who arrive tonight. I'll see the successful Silhouettes in four hours." Wusi nodded at the group, then vanished back down the steps. Heisiu waved after her, his bubble barely visible through the heavy snow.

Zhi Ging looked uncertainly at her friends as G'Aam and Wuyan began sliding jade bracelets onto Silhouettes' wrists. *Is this really it? We just spend four hours standing here?*

She glanced down at her bracelet, tracing her fingers over the polished circular stone. The two Cyo B'Ahon finished just as fresh snow clouds rolled over the horizon;

as blue light washed over the group, the temperature noticeably dropped. Instinctively several Silhouettes tucked their bracelets under their scarves to keep them away from the falling snow.

"Hey, have you seen that?" Hiulam giggled, nodding toward the back of the group.

Zhi Ging snorted. Iridill, Cing Yau, and Kaolin looked like a trio of particularly frustrated flamingos, each with one hand tucked into an armpit as they hopped on a single foot, clearly convinced they could keep warm by having fewer shoes in the snow.

"Hold still, Kaolin," Iridill snapped as she attempted to balance her foot on top of his shoe. "We'll take turns, but I'm going first."

"Let's try to get to the middle of the group," Zhi Ging whispered, tugging Hiulam, Mynah, and Jack behind her. Hopefully they would be better sheltered from the winds there.

"Is this seriously it?" a paper province Silhouette called out after fifteen minutes had passed. "How did Sintou allow this as a challenge? We could genuinely freeze."

Mynah scoffed at the idea, but a tall Silhouette beside her glowered, wrapping the edge of his cloak around his jade bracelet. "It happens, you know," he snapped. "Every winter there's stories of people vanishing in these mountains and being found frozen months later."

"Even the floating market doesn't stop here," Jack muttered between chattering teeth.

Thunk.

Every Silhouette went silent as two halves of jade landed in the snow, the rich green now a pale lichen. There was a frantic rustling as Silhouettes disentangled themselves from cloaks and scarves, desperate not to see a bare wrist on their ice-numbed arms. Zhi Ging breathed a sigh of relief that it wasn't hers.

"Oh," came a small voice from the edge of the group. A carved lacquer province Silhouette bent down and picked up the snapped jade. "That was mine."

G'Aam hurried forward and wrapped a cape around the shivering girl. Heisiu floated forward, fern-like patches of frost springing up across the surface of his bubble as he guided her toward the steps.

Time slowed to a crawl as Zhi Ging struggled to stay warm. Her cloak was white now, the thick layer of snow clinging to its surface making it hard to move. The scent of warm dumplings rising up from the village was almost hypnotic, each inhale causing Zhi Ging's stomach to clench tighter. Cold tingled across her fingers, the feeling the exact opposite of sensing air rails. Rather than something solid flickering to life beneath them, it felt like the fingers themselves were fading away.

"I think my patches have frozen over," Mynah whispered, prodding frantically at a numb cheek. A glimpse of her wrist revealed her arm patches were also icy white.

Thunk.

Thunk, thunk.

Three more jade bracelets snapped in quick succession, rolling between shoes.

Zhi Ging watched through snow-coated eyelashes as Heisiu once again led the Silhouettes toward the steps, icicles reappearing across his bubble each time he floated back and forth. She stared hard at the jellyfish as he drifted back to his resting spot, trying to shake the cold turning her mind to slush. Heisiu spun in his bubble until he was facing her group, waving a supportive tentacle at them.

"Wait." Mynah lurched forward and, for a second Zhi Ging thought her friend was about to faint. Instead, the girl pushed through the huddle, staring at the jellyfish. Her patches crackled, then flooded emerald green beneath the snowflakes sticking to her face. She pulled back her sleeve, causing her jade bracelet to rattle dangerously, but Mynah simply smiled and picked up her pace, snow cascading off her cloak.

"Where are you going?" Jack cried, trying to pull her back to the warmth of the group, but his frozen fingers refused to bend.

"Leave her," Iridill snapped from her clumsy tangle with Cing Yau and Kaolin, the three Silhouettes hopping into the center of the group to claim Mynah's spot. "The cold's clearly short-circuited her brain."

Zhi Ging hurried forward, not understanding what had happened to her friend. Her eyes darted to the shrinking gap between Mynah and Heisiu. *What am I missing?*

"How come I can see your tentacles?" Mynah demanded,

pointing an accusing finger at the jellyfish. "You should be a solid ball of ice by now. Why hasn't your bubble frozen over?"

Snow crunched underfoot as she stomped toward him. She almost slipped as she hit a near-invisible snowbank, but she never took her eyes off Heisiu. Once at the top, Mynah reached toward him, jade glinting at her wrist. Thick seams of gray now covered its surface, only seconds left before it snapped.

"Your bracelet!" Zhi Ging cried, her stomach plummeting as a lightning streak of white crackled across the length of the stone. The others looked on in shock as Mynah did absolutely nothing to shield her bracelet from the cold. Instead, she crouched down, holding her hand directly beneath the jellyfish's bubble.

Iridill gasped, her eyes flashing wildly as Mynah's bracelet stopped rattling. Rich green flooded its surface, perfectly matching the proud color now filling her arm patches.

Mynah stood up and beamed at the opened-mouthed Silhouettes.

"I know how we pass the challenge."

CHAPTER 17

True to her word, Wusi reappeared at midnight, a bamboo lantern illuminating the baskets of food clutched in her arms. She jolted to a stop, eyebrows shooting up in surprise as she scanned the empty mountainside. There wasn't a single Silhouette in sight.

"Over here!" Mynah's voice called out. The faint sound of splashing water and muffled giggles tumbled through the icy breeze. The tutor followed after the noise, smiling to herself as she spotted the faint footprints that now covered the steep snowbank. Wusi followed them, then came to a stop, blinking rapidly before doubling up with laughter.

The Silhouettes waved up at their new tutor from the middle of a large hot spring, their cheeks rosy from the warm water. Their dark cloaks bobbed around them, making them look like sprouting mushrooms, while the two combat cranes waded between them. G'Aam and Wuyan stood at either end of the hot spring, twin domes of fresh snow rising up from their statue-still heads. It almost looked like the Cyo B'Ahon were wearing matching white party hats. Mynah splashed to the edge of the hot spring, her jade bracelet now such a deep emerald green that it rivaled Gertie's crown of weather-wax bees.

"I knew it didn't make sense that Heisui wasn't freezing," she explained proudly, shaking warm droplets from her hair. "Even my patches were losing color, but there was barely any ice on his bubble."

Zhi Ging kicked up, floating on her back as she marveled at how lucky they were that Mynah had not only woken up in time for the challenge but taken a chance in climbing the snowbank. *Would I have solved it?* She had assumed it was snow blurring the jellyfish when they first landed, but it had actually been hot steam making him shimmer.

"Well done." Wusi nodded, an impressed glint dancing across her eyes as she considered Mynah. "Now, why don't I get Heisui to fetch you all some hydrophobic pebbles?" The jellyfish soared back to the bundle of capes, rummaging beneath them to lift out a carved lacquer box filled with the familiar smooth stones.

Once the Silhouettes had dried off, Wusi opened a basket to reveal a container filled with slices of roast goose over steamed rice.

"I hear I owe you a homei spoon too." She chuckled as she handed the dish to Mynah.

"I'll take two if you've one spare. Those baked-pork-

172

chop-rice ones are seriously rare," Mynah said, her cheek patches bright teal. Heisiu floated around the group and Silhouettes grabbed the containers balanced above his bubble. There were excited yelps around Zhi Ging as the scent of soy sauce chicken wings, soft-shell crab with fried mantou, and scallion pancakes filled the air. Even G'Aam and Wuyan nudged each other enthusiastically when they were passed a container filled with spicy dan dan noodles.

Wusi smiled at the group, raising her voice over the sound of their enthusiastic chewing.

"This is usually the challenge that catches out the most Silhouettes. True perseverance isn't a bullheaded refusal to change; the ability to bend must always be found at its core—much like this bamboo." The Cyo B'Ahon tilted her head to the challenge lantern. "Just because you bow to a storm doesn't mean it defeats you. It only defeats you when you refuse to adapt." She clapped her hands together and the Silhouettes paused in their feasting, many still with chopsticks in their mouths. "True perseverance is also impossible without what you're about to witness in your Chau. Not even an immortal Cyo B'Ahon can keep going indefinitely; perseverance is only possible if you look after both your body and mind. Sleep, and in particular dreams, are essential."

THE GROUP ARRIVED AT THE EDGE OF A THICK BAM-
boo forest at the bottom of the valley. Miniature red

173

lanterns had been tied along the lower branches, their gentle light revealing a well-worn path through the trees. Every so often the soft harmonic sound of a guzheng being played rippled between the leaves, its calming melody causing Zhi Ging and several others to yawn. There had been no time to rest between their meal and the post-midnight walk down the mountain.

Wusi gathered the Silhouettes around her while G'Aam and his combat crane stepped onto the path, scouting ahead for danger. "Now, I need everyone to remain completely silent during the first half of this Chau," she said in hushed tones. "We've been invited to a REM Cycle. You're very lucky. If your challenge had taken place even one night later, we wouldn't have experienced this. It only happens once every full moon."

"What's a REM Cycle?" Zhi Ging whispered as Mynah nudged her in excitement.

"Not a clue—all I know is I'm suddenly way less tired." Mynah stretched her arms wide, patches of yellow flashing around her sleeves.

G'Aam and his crane reappeared and nodded, gesturing that the route was safe.

Music swelled as they wound along the path, a soothing lullaby lifting up from the guzheng's strings.

A few moments later, Zhi Ging and the others stepped into a wide clearing. The glade was filled with a complex bamboo frame, its intricate wooden canopy towering high above them. Small fires crackled safely from pits along the edge of the clearing, and a thick lavender haze filled the forest floor, obscuring the base of the structure behind soft curling wisps of lilac smoke.

"Acrobats!" Jack said in a hushed, excited voice, pointing higher up.

Zhi Ging followed his gaze and spotted four slender figures balanced on the bamboo beams. One caught her eye and waved, the light of the full moon catching his fingers and causing them to sparkle.

Wusi held a finger to her lips and gestured for the Silhouettes to sit down. Zhi Ging stifled a giggle as the scented haze lapped against her chin, the purple mist almost reaching the top of certain Silhouettes' heads. Suddenly she gasped and grabbed Mynah's arm, pointing directly in front of them.

Beneath the acrobat's bamboo platform were dozens of sleeping people.

As one, the four acrobats lifted their left wrists to the night sky, revealing a flash of shimmering silk, before diving forward into the air. The silk ribbons unspooled behind them as they somersaulted toward the sleeping figures, spinning in perfect circles as they plunged toward the clearing. Zhi Ging leaned forward, unconsciously holding her breath until the silk pulled tight, the acrobats stopping inches above the snoring group. She could see the four figures more clearly now, their expressions focused as they swayed above the others. They pulled thin tweezers from their waistband and plucked something from the sleeping faces. Zhi Ging squinted, struggling to see what they had taken.

Wusi waggled a hand at the Silhouettes, catching their attention to explain.

"They're collecting good dreams." She tapped the inner corner of her eye. "When a dream ends, it diffuses out of your body, but its core stays behind as a single grain of sleep."

Zhi Ging's own eyes widened in amazement and she turned back to the acrobats. After the closest one had collected all the sleep from the face below him, he placed it into a cloth pouch and pulled himself back up the silk ribbon. Once he reached the bamboo platform, he raced across the thin beams before diving back down to another snoring figure. At one point a small child stirred, and the acrobats quickly stopped, flinging handfuls of dried lavender into the firepits. The sweet smoke soon soothed the child, and even Wusi had to waft the purple mist away, the scent tugging at her eyelids. Behind Zhi Ging, Hiulam yawned before quickly flapping both hands in front of her face. Heisiu drifted down, dozing in the lower half of his bubble.

Once all the sleep had been collected, the four acrobats swung toward one another. They clasped hands and began to spin, building momentum until they were able to soar over the far corners of the sleeping crowd. They untied themselves from the silk ribbons and stepped through the haze toward the Silhouettes.

"Thank you for being so silent," the lead acrobat murmured, her voice as soft as the smoke itself. "If you follow us, we can show you what we do with the collected dreams."

The acrobats led them away from the clearing, twisting down a new path toward a calm lake. The full moon glistened in the center of the water, brighter than any lantern in the bamboo forest. The four acrobats stepped onto sampans, holding out their hands to help the Silhouettes board the small wooden boats. "Who would you like to do the honors?" the lead acrobat asked Wusi, gesturing toward a weathered box floating in the center of the moon's reflection.

Each Silhouette sat up a little straighter as Wusi's eyes roved between them, their jade bracelets jangling softly as they waved their hands, hoping to be picked.

"It has to be Mynah," Wusi said with a smile.

The acrobat steering Mynah's boat rowed forward, expertly gliding over the reflection so it barely rippled. He spun the sampan so the box floated right beside her arm.

"I wonder if we could get him to replace B'ei Gun," Hiulam whispered to Zhi Ging in amazement. "I couldn't even feel that steering."

Zhi Ging nodded distractedly and watched as Mynah leaned forward to pull the box up, glowing moon water cascading from it in sparkling droplets. Connected to its base was a thick frayed rope, its woven surface covered with clusters of oysters. As their shells came in contact with the moonlight, they opened wide, each revealing a sea-blue pearl.

"These," the lead acrobat explained, "are REMedy pearls. Rather than growing from a grain of sand, they're formed around grains of sleep. Anyone who uses one is guaranteed a night of deep, healing sleep and restorative dreams." She nodded back at the path that led to the clearing.

"Those gathered beneath the bamboo make this all possible. Most have family members who are ill and need a REMedy pearl, but others are just volunteers, returning the favor after benefiting from a pearl in the past."

Another acrobat leaned forward, lowering a small glass bowl into the moon's reflection. As he lifted it back up, the doubled reflection made it look like the moon had its very own pearl. He hummed to himself as he gently emptied his collected grains of sleep into the bowl. The surface immediately began to shimmer, and he leaned forward carefully, handing it to the next sampan.

"Come on," the acrobat beside Mynah encouraged, waving at the rest of their boat. "We'll need to pull the entire rope up to collect the REMedy pearls."

Zhi Ging and the others rushed forward, tugging at the worn rope until it clattered on board.

"Careful now," the lead acrobat called out. "Make sure to be gentle when removing the pearls. We want to disturb the oysters as little as possible."

Zhi Ging crouched down and delicately eased a blue

pearl from an open oyster. It gleamed with inner light, moonlight infused through its core. The REMedy pearl shone in her palm, and for a second she saw a glimpse of the dream contained within it: a child with wings flying between clouds.

Once all the pearls had been collected, the acrobats demonstrated how to place new grains of sleep, freshly cleaned in the bowl of moonlight, into the empty oyster shells.

"Ugh, I thought Chaus were meant to be rewards, not drudge work," Iridill muttered; she wiped slime from her fingers as she handled the rope of oysters, searching for one that was still open and not busy with its new grain of sleep.

Wusi frowned at her, but the lead acrobat smiled calmly.

"Not to worry, little one, we know how hard you all worked to receive tonight's Chau. As this challenge has stolen an uninterrupted night from you"—she lowered a slender hand into the collected bowl of pearls—"we will send you home with one REMedy pearl each. It will grant you a night of undisturbed sleep; simply hold it in your palm when you want to drift off." She took in Iridill's unimpressed scowl and raised a curious eyebrow. "I can tell you've suffered from many sleepless nights. Surely you can understand that for those who have persevered through weeks or months of illness, a single night of deep sleep is worth more than any other pearl in Wengyuen."

"No I haven't." Iridill flushed crimson, her knuckles whitening around the pearl that had been handed to her. "And if I ever have, it's just because the dorm is filled with loud, selfish snorers."

Zhi Ging and Mynah exchanged a confused look. Why was Iridill being so defensive?

"I'm afraid each pearl only works once, so choose when to use it carefully," the lead acrobat warned as the rest were passed around. Zhi Ging clutched hers tightly, concerned by the calculating look that suddenly twitched across Iridill's face. Although they hadn't had their Prediction classes yet, she couldn't shake the feeling she knew exactly what was going to happen back in the dorm. Zhi Ging shoved her REMedy pearl deep inside her cloak pocket, determined to keep it safe from Iridill.

"This is why we must repeat the REM Cycle each month," the lead acrobat continued. "Even then there are barely enough to supply a fraction of the pearls needed in healers' homes and sick bays across the six provinces."

"Why don't more people in Wengyuen take part in the REM Cycle?" Jack asked, his pearl glinting as he rolled it between his palms. "Surely you'd have enough then."

"We're trying. At the moment we're reliant on volunteers, which is tricky. In recent years, fewer and fewer people are willing to risk a night sleeping in the forest, especially with the threat of a Fui Gwai attack hovering over them. It can also be difficult to worry about another's perseverance when you're struggling with your own."

There was a moment of thoughtful silence among the Silhouettes.

"Why are they blue?" Mynah asked, breaking the hush as she held a pearl up to her right eye. For a split second both eyes were an identical shade of sea blue.

"We're not sure why the oysters add that color," the lead acrobat admitted with a small smile. "But we like to think it's the perfect color for perseverance. After all, waves will keep leaping toward the shore no matter how hard the moon pulls."

CHAPTER 18

The next morning, a bleary-eyed Zhi Ging thumped down for breakfast.

"Whoa." Pinderent whistled, taking in the identical dark circles under her, Jack's, and Hiulam's eyes. "You all look like Ai'Deng Bou tried to turn you into pandas. What happened? I'm glad I wasn't allowed to join the challenge now."

"Yeah, yeah, rub it in," Hiulam said, yawning loudly as she pulled a homei spoon toward her. It shattered in her bowl to become a comforting helping of congee.

"Our Chau didn't finish until well after midnight," Zhi Ging explained, a sesame-seed-covered zaa loeng slipping out from between her chopsticks. The rice noodle roll splashed into a dish of soy sauce, causing Malo to chirp in annoyance as it splattered over his feathers.

"Where's Mynah?" Pinderent asked as Zhi Ging dabbed at the little phoenix with her cloak sleeve. "I thought she'd be here, showing off her new Cyo B'Ahon robes. Perseverance was her twelfth challenge."

Zhi Ging's eyes widened. "I completely forgot! That's so excit—" She stopped, looking back at Jack and Hiulam in confusion. "Wait, I'm not imagining things, am I? Mynah was definitely at the Chau, right?"

"Yeah." Hiulam nodded, her nose scrunching up in bewilderment. "Why didn't Wusi send her back for her graduation ceremony?"

Malo quacked, flapping a wing at the dining hall entrance. An equally tired-looking Mynah was traipsing toward them, still wearing her Silhouette cloak. The group immediately made space and she flopped down between Zhi Ging and Pinderent, her cheek patches ink black with exhaustion as she rested her forehead against the table.

"Mynah," Zhi Ging asked gently, addressing the top of her friend's head, "why are you still in a Silhouette cloak?"

Mynah sighed, peeling her face off the table, her arm patches deep blue as she looked around the room. "Well," she began, forcing a smile, "the good news for Pinderent is we're going to spend a lot more time together. I'm moving into the new dorm with you today."

"Wait, why?" Zhi Ging interrupted, unable to keep the panic from her voice as she looked around the rest of the table. Were more of the Cure Club Silhouettes about to be moved out?

183

"Aren't new Cyo B'Ahon given their own rooms in Hok Woh?" Jack asked in surprise.

"So, technically, that was my last challenge." Mynah stabbed a single chopstick into a nearby siu mai, waving the pork and prawn dumpling in the air. "The problem is, I've only actually done eleven. I was still in the sick bay when all of you did the Recall challenge. Sintou says I can't graduate and become a full Cyo B'Ahon until I've passed all twelve."

"But that's not your fault!" Zhi Ging cried. "How is that fair?"

"I know," Mynah said bitterly. "Hoi Dak and Oimaa should also have graduated last night." She tilted her head, and Zhi Ging spotted two similarly miserable-looking Silhouettes at the next table staring unblinkingly into bowls of congee while their friends tried to comfort them.

"Wusi spent the last hour explaining it to us. We have to wait until the *next* group of Silhouettes take the Recall challenge. Which means all of you now get to become Cyo B'Ahon before me!" She winced, cheek patches flashing navy as she glanced at Pinderent. "Sorry, I meant . . ."

"Don't worry about it." He shrugged, shooting her a shaky smile. "I'm fine with not becoming immortal, really. I'm just going to miss dragon boat racing. There's not really any way to race across the cloud sea."

Mynah gave him a quick one-armed hug, then continued in a softer tone. "Anyway, until then we can either go along to classes again, with the small bonus of not needing to redo homework." She twirled her siu-mai-topped chopstick in fake celebration, Malo's eyes widening as he watched it spin above him. "Or spend our days in the new dorm, reading library books. *In strict silence, Miss Niu,*" she added in near-perfect imitation of Wusi's voice.

"What'll you pick?" Zhi Ging asked, trying to keep her face neutral. Classes wouldn't be the same without Mynah, but would she sit through lessons again if it was her choice?

Mynah bit into the siu mai, frowning as she considered the question. Beside her, Pinderent reached over to top up everyone's tea. She looked up, eyes widening in sudden delight. "Well, I think I'll come along to some classes, depending on how interesting I found them last time, but"—she paused, a slow smile spreading across her face—"maybe I'll spend this morning helping Suwun. She's one of the older Silhouettes from the porcelain province," Mynah added, turning to Zhi Ging. "She was telling us at Cure Club a few nights ago that she hid a stash of homei spoons during her time here. Unfortunately Hok Woh's expanded so much in the ninety years she's been frozen that she now has no idea where they are. If I can help her find them, we'll be rich! Well, rich in snacks." She grinned. "Wanna help, Pinderent?"

"Sorry, I promised to join Team Bolei for extra dragon boat training this morning."

"What?" Zhi Ging and Hiulam cried in unison. "Why weren't we invited?"

"Because you still have class," a voice above them said, chuckling. They spun around to see Gwong standing behind them, two paddles tucked under an arm. "Although if you'd like to complain directly to Bucbou . . ." He gestured back at the dining hall door, his free arm stretching out in a dramatic flourish.

"I'll take my chances with Wusi's elixir instead," Hiulam said with an exaggerated shudder. The Cyo B'Ahon's loud booming laughter was still echoing around the glass walls long after they left for class.

WUSI'S CLASSROOM TURNED OUT TO BE TUCKED halfway up the spiral staircase leading to the sick bay. Hidden beneath a thick stripe of yellow paint, the door only became visible as Heisiu bobbed toward them through the water-filled wall, his soft white glow causing the frame to glint.

"I should have used my REMedy pearl last night," Hiulam groaned as they filed in. "I swear I didn't fall asleep until two hours ago."

"No way," Zhi Ging said with a laugh. "I definitely heard you snoring and sleep-talking about dragon boat training from my room. And you're a whole level away from me in the dorms."

Malo ruffled his feathers in agreement.

"What can I say? I'm a dedicated member of the team." Hiulam beamed, dusting imaginary fluff from her cloak. "Although I guess we now know who the selfish snorer

Iridill was complaining about was." She sighed, glancing over at her.

"Where did she get those?" Zhi Ging scowled as she followed her friend's gaze and spotted several REMedy pearls adorning Iridill's scarf.

"She went around every door on our level last night," Jack murmured, squeezing in between them, "demanding we hand ours over. Apparently, she deserved them more since she's shared the most memories at Cure Club."

Zhi Ging spluttered in surprise. "And people actually agreed?" There were at least eight pearls shining around Iridill's neck.

"She threatened that if we didn't, she'd tell Sycee and the other captains that we were working with *you* on the painted yellow lines." He rolled his eyes before nodding at some of the younger gold province Silhouettes. "I ignored her, but I guess the threat worked."

"She can't do that," Zhi Ging muttered, her hand unconsciously reaching for her hood. After Iridill had threatened her last month, she'd stayed up all night, frantically scrubbing away the yellow flecks. The monthly worry of failing a challenge and being asked to leave Hok Woh was already bad enough. *If I can find out who's really behind the yellow lines, Iridill won't be able to threaten anyone.*

The door slid open and Wusi ushered them into a room that should have been spacious but, over the years, had been crammed with numerous apothecary cabinets, their rows of wooden drawers strained to bursting. Several other Perseverance Cyo B'Ahon were gathering ingredients from the various cabinets, their smooth coordinated movements reminding Zhi Ging of Gertie's emerald-green bees. Toward the back of the classroom, a heavy clay pot bubbled away, the all-too-familiar scent of bitter black elixir filling the air with pungent steam.

"Ugh, drinking that for the past few weeks has been way more of a Perseverance challenge than last night's snow." Hiulam shuddered, stepping behind Jack in case Wusi called her forward for another helping.

Instead, the tutor gestured for the Silhouettes to take their seats at the desks squeezed between cabinets. "Welcome, everyone." She caught quite a few of the Silhouettes looking apprehensively at the medicine pot. "Don't worry, this is simply for those still in the sick bay upstairs. We won't begin each lesson with an enforced elixir."

Zhi Ging smiled as Hiulam, and several others exhaled loudly.

"No, instead I'm going to spend the next month teaching you the power of perseverance. This is one of the most misunderstood of the twelve skills needed to become a Cyo B'Ahon. People across all six provinces have confused true perseverance with single-minded repetition. That interpretation of the skill often leads to nothing more than tunnel vision." She shook her head before pushing aside a ceiling-high apothecary cabinet. It screeched along the polished floor, revealing a panel of dark glass fused into the wall. Wusi pulled chalk from her robes and began to scrawl across the glossy board, underlining key points as she wrote.

True perseverance requires both flexibility and inner kindness.

"Guess Iridill won't be specializing in this, then," Zhi Ging accidentally muttered out loud. She glanced over at her, relieved the girl hadn't heard, as Jack shook with silent laughter.

"Many Silhouettes who choose to specialize with me after graduation go on to become healers. Apart from Scouts, we're the only group Sintou allows to regularly travel shoreside. There aren't enough healers in Wengyuen, so we occasionally send Perseverance Cyo B'Ahon out. The four acrobats you met last night are currently spending a century shoreside for me. Unfortunately we've found that if our healers stay for more than a hundred years, it becomes obvious they're not ordinary shoreside folk. We've a few others who'll be returning within the next year. They'll spend a decade back home in Hok Woh and then ageshift down and re-begin in the province of their choice."

Wusi paused as another healer reached past her for a jar of ginseng roots. "I'm not the true master of perseverance; those trapped in sick bays across Wengyuen are. Every day they spend with their lives on hold, bodies in pain, is a demonstration of pure perseverance." The tutor placed the chalk back in her pocket and began counting the students. "Unlike your previous lessons, Perseverance will need a bit more commitment. As usual, you'll have lessons from eight thirty until four, with an hour's break for lunch. However, for the rest of the month, I'll be requesting groups of three stay back after Cure Club to help the other Perseverance specialists bottle drafts and elixirs for our shoreside counterparts."

The other healers stopped grinding and boiling ingredients and waved at the Silhouettes. Zhi Ging immediately grabbed Jack and Hiulam as Wusi began to sort them into groups, not wanting a repeat of Tutor Wun's disastrous pairing with Iridill.

"What elixirs are we sending shoreside?" Jack asked, peering closely into a nearby pot, its sparkling amber surface reminding Zhi Ging of the aventurine glass the Lead Glassmith specialized in.

Wusi's smile faltered as she clasped her hands together. "Unfortunately, the Matchmakers have been making increasingly poor and lazy matches in the past few years. That has resulted in a string of broken hearts across each province." She paused, head snapping toward the sound of Iridill's snort. "You may find that entertaining, Miss Seoipin, but each broken heart requires time from our healers, who are busy enough as it is. If it wasn't for their recent hard work, you could very well be one of the poor Silhouettes still frozen in the sick bay above us." Wusi strode forward until she was standing directly above Iridill's desk. "Now, I *know* I didn't include any decorations in the scarves I knitted." She lifted up the edge of the wool, eight REMedy pearls shimmering like orbs of pure ocean water along its bobbled surface. She unlooped the scarf from around Iridill's neck and folded it neatly. "Why don't you stay behind at lunch, Miss Seoipin? See if we can work out where these pearls actually belong."

Zhi Ging heard a deep sigh of relief behind her, and several Silhouettes visibly brightened.

"Speaking of working things out," Wusi continued, ignoring Iridill's withering pout, "I'm delighted to say one of our newest Perseverance Cyo B'Ahon may have found a way to lift the blue and green from everyone's eyes. D'Amask, why don't you explain?"

A bashful-looking Cyo B'Ahon squeezed out from between two cabinets, a heavy ceramic kettle balanced in his arms. He nodded at the Silhouettes, glasses sliding down his broad nose. "I'm infusing fresh mountain snow from your challenge with plum blossoms, pine nuts, and finger citron. We need to wait for the snow to naturally melt, absorbing the purifying qualities of these aromatics as it does. We'll then bring it to a boil with phoenix fire and"—he raised the kettle, using its spout to push his glasses back up—"I'm hopeful that after a few servings the blue and green will begin to fade, removing the very last of Ami's possession."

"How long until the snow melts?" Iridill asked, sitting up from her usual slouch.

D'Amask scrabbled for the teapot lid, mumbling under his breath as he peered in at the collected snow. "I'd say it'll be ready by the final Cure Club of this week."

A delighted ripple rushed across the Silhouettes, and Zhi Ging spotted Iridill's normal scowl vanish, replaced by what could only be described as a genuine excitement. Zhi Ging nudged Jack. "Just one more week! You'll finally know what your eyes are meant to look like." She beamed, her smile only faltering when she spotted his frown. "What is it?" she asked, leaning as close to his desk as she could. His eyes were flickering rapidly, two miniature kettles reflected in teal.

"If it works, the failed Silhouettes will start being sent home. There'll be no reason for him to stay in the other dorm."

"Him?" Zhi Ging's stomach dropped as she realized who Jack meant, her gaze drifting up to the sick bay dorm above them

Pinderent.

CHAPTER 19

Zhi Ging frowned at her bedroom ceiling, dozens of paper cuttings floating high above her. They dangled from thin ribbons: paper dragons, tigers, horses, and roosters chasing each other on an infinite loop. She twisted the two cords of her gold Pan Chang tight as she watched them sway back and forth, wondering what color everyone's eyes would be once they got back from Cure Club. Wusi had announced before dinner that the last of the snow had finally melted and each Silhouette would be given a cup of phoenix-fire-brewed tea that evening.

Two nights earlier than expected.

Her stomach twisted tight, knowing the countdown for Pinderent may have finally begun. The only small relief was the dragon boats. Although the Cyo B'Ahon on each team had started training throughout the day, not a single boat had yet made it up Seoizyu's tentacles to the top of the makeshift waterfall. Until that happened, none of the older Silhouettes would be leaving.

She leaped up as the dorm doors flew open, the excited babble of Silhouettes bouncing across the room. Zhi Ging hurried out and nearly crashed straight into Iridill.

"Ugh, back off," the other girl snapped.

Zhi Ging blinked hard, peering intently at the narrowed eyes in front of her. They were still green and blue. She smiled in relief, which just caused Iridill to glower further.

"What are you smirking at?" the other girl snarled. "At least my weirdness has a cure, NoGlow. I was possessed; what's your excuse?"

Zhi Ging's eyebrows shot up, thrown by the viciousness of Iridill's attack.

"I wasn't smirking," she said slowly, wondering what she had missed at Cure Club to make Iridill so furious.

"Whatever." The other Silhouette barged past her before turning back to the rest of the dorm. Iridill pulled her cloak back to reveal pockets stuffed with swiped sesame brittle and coconut cookies. "I say we keep Cure Club going—sleepover in my room!" Cing Yau, Kaolin, and a handful of porcelain province Silhouettes knocked past Zhi Ging as they followed Iridill up to her room.

"What was all that about?" Zhi Ging muttered as Jack came to check on her.

He shrugged, his eyes flashing their familiar green and blue. "Oh, she's just mad about the tea."

"Did it not taste nice?" she asked, surprised anything could be worse than the peaty black elixir.

"I wouldn't know. Once Malo finished boiling it with his phoenix fire, it took much longer to cool down than any of the healers expected. Only a few cups had stopped bubbling by the time Cure Club was meant to finish, so Wusi offered them to the older Silhouettes. No one from this dorm got to try any."

"Did Pinderent . . . ?"

He nodded, knowing what she was about to ask.

"Yeah, he got the last cup. I didn't see if the tea worked, though. D'Amask did warn us we might need a few helpings for the color to fade. Guess we'll find out tomorrow."

"WUSI'D BETTER LET THEM OUT SOON," BUCBOU muttered, drumming her fingers impatiently against her race paddle. Zhi Ging nodded, staring unblinking at the entrance stepping stone, her stomach tense as she waited for the other Silhouettes to step through.

Pinderent hadn't joined them at breakfast. Instead, Pou Pou had been instructed to take enough homei spoons back up for everyone in the new dorm. The jellyfish had then returned with a message that, on Sintou's request, dragon boat training would be postponed until after that night's Cure Club—D'Amask's tea taking priority over waterfall training.

Zhi Ging had been the unlucky Silhouette forced to pass that message on to Bucbou when the captain had stormed into the dorms an hour earlier, demanding to know why the Silhouettes on all six teams were late.

"Finally," Yuttou sighed as the sound of chatter drifted up through the glass steps.

Zhi Ging leaped up, sending the boat rocking, but she ignored Bucbou's glare as she squeezed past the others, leaping onto the glass dragon head to try to spot Pinderent.

He appeared seconds later, his gangly frame towering over Hiulam. His eyes were still green and blue, but Zhi Ging's breath caught in her throat when she saw them flicker to a familiar brown between blinks. The tea was working.

She glanced back down at the dragon boat, suddenly filled with a wild urge to sink it. Her foot itched to stamp down hard against its teak frame, images of panels shattering under her shoe filling her mind. If tonight's dragon boat training went well, Pinderent could be gone in days.

Bucbou's shrill whistle cut through the air before Zhi Ging's thoughts could spiral further. The captain swung her green paddle in an arc, directing the Silhouettes toward their various teams.

Iridill barged past Pinderent, her eyes still a stubborn deep blue and green, and she thumped down beside the other Pacer on Team Tsadeu.

"All right, everyone!" Bucbou shouted, cutting over the final few conversations. "It's a late start to training, but don't for a second think that means we'll be wrapping up early. Team Chi Hei, you're up first. Let's see what you've come up with since the last session."

The porcelain province Cyo B'Ahon roared in unison, glowing blue paddles flashing as they made their way toward Seoizyu. The enormous jellyfish rose up in front them, dwarfing the boat until it looked no larger than a child's toy.

Over the sea breeze, Zhi Ging could hear proud cooing from Ai'Deng Bou, the team Steerer, as he waved up at his jellyfish. The team expertly navigated around the plunge pool, the hollow dragon head chiming as heavy water drummed the blue and white porcelain. Zhi Ging leaned forward and held her breath as the boat began to climb, the team's swift paddle strokes pushing them higher and higher. They inched their way up the near-vertical rapids, the other dragon boats falling silent as they watched on in wonder.

Suddenly, Seoizyu twitched her giant tentacles. The torrents shifted and split, hitting Ai'Deng Bou hard in the chest. He cried out, ageshifting down in shock from the blow. In his younger hands the oar rattled against the currents and the boat listed sharply to the left. The dragon's horns and whiskers snapped loose and crew members were forced to fling their hands up, protecting themselves from the shards of porcelain now raining down over them. Blue paddles vanished beneath the water, shooting back down toward the plunge pool. What was left of the dragon head began to tear free from the teak frame. It tilted back toward the crew, threatening to crush the Drummer. The two Pacers leaped forward, shoes skidding beneath them as they tried to hold the heavy porcelain back without tumbling from the boat themselves.

Zhi Ging felt her knuckles tighten around the side of her boat, horrified guilt flooding through her. She had wanted to damage a dragon boat, but not like this. Not when actual Cyo B'Ahon could be hurt. Ageshifting wouldn't protect anyone from permanent injuries. To her left, Team Si Cau had begun frantically unwrapping their silk dragon head, the fabric billowing up to catch the other crew members before they plummeted deep into the plunge pool.

"Seoizyu, stop!" Ai'Deng Bou called out. Immediately, the entire waterfall stilled, the jellyfish's tentacles gliding back down the bamboo frame in gentle ripples so the dragon boat hit the water with no more than a soft splash. The crew was silent as they examined the extent of the waterfall's destruction. Their team captain stood up, pressing a shaking hand to the destroyed dragon head.

"That was too close, Bucbou," he cried. "We won't have Ai'Deng Bou's protection at the real waterfall. We need to seriously consider another way." He hesitated, glancing down at the unspooling silk now floating between dragon boats. "Maybe others here have a point." He nodded at the captain of Team Syun Zi. "I know Sintou suggested the waterways to protect Silhouettes from sand spirit attacks, but what's worse? A potential spirit attack or guaranteed death on the waterfall? No one's been able to make it to the top of Seoizyu's waterfall, not even you."

"No!" Bucbou snapped, her green paddle clattering down beside Pinderent. "We're Cyo B'Ahon; we're not about to be defeated by water." She leaped onto the glass dragon head, feet balanced between its antler-like horns. "We'll take a break for a week while we wait for a new porcelain dragon head to arrive, but training restarts then. I suggest you all use that time to work out how to scale the waterfall because"—she took a deep breath, her piercing eyes blazing over the boats around her—"whichever crew member finds a way will take my position as captain of Team Bolei."

"NO WAY," MYNAH BREATHED AS ZHI GING RACED through what had happened at training, Pinderent and Hiulam adding extra detail as she spoke. The dining hall was empty, theirs the only table piled high with half-eaten plates as the night stretched toward midnight.

"I can't believe she's willing to give up being captain." Jack shook his head, handing Zhi Ging the final bowl of grass jelly. Malo chirped in excitement, waddling over with a spoon clenched in his beak.

"I know!" Pinderent said, eyes wide in amazement. "When I first joined, B'ei Gun told me Bucbou had been captain for over three hundred years."

"Ugh, B'ei Gun'd better not solve the waterfall problem!" Zhi Ging groaned, filling Malo's spoon with jelly. "He'll kick me off the team if he becomes captain."

Pinderent was silent for a moment, rolling his empty teacup back and forth between his hands. He took a deep breath, then placed it down, his neck turning bright red as he faced the others. "Do you think it has to be a Cyo B'Ahon who becomes captain? It's just," he continued quickly, and Zhi Ging couldn't tell if he was speeding up in case someone interrupted or to stop himself from backing out, "Bucbou said 'crew member,' not Cyo B'Ahon, right?"

Zhi Ging nodded. "You're right! 'Crew member' could mean anyone on the boat, whether they're a Cyo B'Ahon, Silhouette, or—" She broke off, unsure what to call Pinderent now.

"This is how you stay in Hok Woh!" Mynah yelled, slamming both hands down on the table as she leaped up, her arm and cheek patches flashing through rainbow hues. "They can't send you away if you're in charge of an entire dragon boat team."

"Do you have any idea how to get over the waterfall?" Jack asked.

Pinderent exhaled slowly. "I've had a few ideas, but I think it'd be much easier if I could see the actual waterfall."

Zhi Ging glanced down, her grass jelly still wobbling from when Mynah had whacked the table. The dark black cubes rippled back and forth like waves, her friends' faces reflected in their silky surface. "Maybe we should go and see it, then," she murmured, prodding a cube. "It's not like we'd have to swim . . ." Zhi Ging looked up, peering meaningfully at Pinderent.

Understanding rushed across his face and Hiulam hooted in excitement.

"What?" Mynah demanded, her eyes darting between the three Team Bolei Silhouettes. "What are we doing?"

Pinderent leaned across the table and pulled the others into a tight huddle. Malo wriggled between their linked arms, anxious not to be left out. Pinderent glanced over his shoulder, double-checking that no one had stepped into the dining hall, then turned back, his eyes brighter than Zhi Ging had ever seen.

"We're going to steal a dragon boat."

CHAPTER 20

A distant thundering rumbled over the sound of
paddles splashing out of sync.

"I think we're almost there!" Jack shouted,
raising his voice from the back of the dragon boat and
clenching the Steerer's oar tightly.

Zhi Ging sighed with relief, her arms creaking as she
copied the speed set by Pinderent and Mynah. Getting
the silk dragon boat out of its entrance stepping stone had
been easy enough, but rowing a boat made for eight with
just five pairs of hands and one set of wings had turned
out to be far trickier than the group expected.

After drifting dangerously close to Wun-Wun's shore,
its stony beach threatening to ground them before they
even started, Zhi Ging and Hiulam had been forced to
jump out, icy currents attempting to drag them under as
they pushed the boat back into deeper water. Although
Malo's flames had dried their cloaks, the freezing water
had seeped into Zhi Ging's bones, and each gust of sea

air sent goose bumps rippling along her arms. The little phoenix sat on top of the boat's drum, his feet kicking out a chaotic but enthusiastic rhythm.

Mynah heaved against her paddle, still unused to holding its water-slicked handle. Every few strokes, Pinderent was forced to lean over, his own paddle stretching past her, to help straighten their boat. Although he could row faster than most Cyo B'Ahon, to the envy of many other Pacers, his strength was now a disadvantage. Months of practice meant that each of his strokes was easily three times stronger than Mynah's, causing their boat to spin in wide circles until Pinderent pulled back on his own paddling.

Zhi Ging craned her neck, trying to see past the craggy cliff. A thin crescent moon was the only sliver of light above them, the sky and sea merging in an ink-black horizon. The sound of crashing water was definitely getting louder now. Their dragon boat rocked from side to side as a new current hit them, attempting to push them back from the bay. They curved around a final sea stack and Zhi Ging's mouth dropped open.

The waterfall was enormous, easily three times as wide as the practice one created by Seoizyu's tentacles. Sharp jagged rocks sprouted out on either side, the force of the water sharpening the limestone to resemble the curved fangs of a roaring sea dragon. An endless cascade pounded down, white fists pummeling the plunge pool surface, ensuring nothing could ever rise back up. Zhi

Ging shuddered, unable to drag her eyes away from the heavy torrents. *If we fall, we'll be trapped forever.* A memory of Ami tumbling into the underwater waterfall sliced across her mind, and she grimaced, clutching her gold Pan Chang tight.

In front of her Pinderent and Mynah had stopped rowing entirely, their necks tilting higher and higher as they tried to spot the top of the waterfall through the thick spray that shrouded the upper rapids in dense white mist. Zhi Ging became aware of Hiulam trying to speak, but her voice was drowned out by the water crashing down the cliffside.

"What was that?" she shouted back, her voice straining as she leaned across the dragon boat.

"I said I hope these are enough!" Hiulam repeated, gesturing at the lanterns scattered between their feet. Although Pinderent had refused to tell them his full plan, he and Mynah had first sneaked back to their dorm, bundling ten sick bay lanterns beneath their cloaks while Heisui snored in his basin. The red paper that covered each lantern was now dappled with waterfall spray, dark patches seeping across the surface.

"Keep those covered," Pinderent called back, shrugging off his Silhouette cloak and flinging it over the lanterns. The others followed suit, creating a protective mountain of fabric in the center of the boat.

"Are you going to tell us your plan now?" Jack asked,

twisting his oar back and forth to keep the dragon boat away from the worst of the deluge.

The other boy nodded before picking his way toward the front of the boat. "I got the idea from how Zhi Ging tricked Ami using the silk dragon head." He hesitated before correcting himself. "Well, it's not exactly the same. This boat, once it has a full Cyo B'Ahon crew and homebound Silhouettes, would be far too heavy for Malo to carry over the waterfall." The little phoenix gave an offended chirp, flexing his wings as he stamped an indignant foot on the drum. "Sorry, I meant too unfair, not too heavy," Pinderent corrected, smiling as Malo ruffled his feathers. "I do think there's something of Malo's we can use, though: phoenix fire! The lanterns are too light to lift the wooden boat, but if we gather them together under the silk, the trapped heat should help the silk float upward, lifting us over the waterfall."

"That's genius!" Mynah beamed, flinging her paddle into the boat, clearly relieved the rowing portion of the night was over. "So what should we do first, light the lanterns or unfold the dragon head?"

Pinderent held out his palm, watching it immediately fill with glistening drops of spray.

"Silk first. The lanterns will be hard to light with this much water in the air."

Mynah leaped from her seat, wobbling slightly as she made her way to the front of the boat. She grabbed the dragon's silk horns and tugged them loose, her arm patches flaring green as the fabric billowed free. Zhi Ging and Hiulam took the edges from her and stretched the silk above their heads and along the length of the boat. Jack then pulled the fabric over himself, knotting its corners tight around the dragon boat's tail. Once the silk was safely secured, the five Silhouettes crouched near the center of the boat, their eyes slowly adjusting to the darkness. Zhi Ging inched forward with both arms outstretched, the sound of the waterfall now partially muffled above her.

"Malo, would you do the honors?" Pinderent asked, reaching under the jumbled pile of cloaks to pull out a crumpled lantern.

The little phoenix nodded, and delicate flames flickered along his wing. He dipped it beneath the lantern's paper covering, chirping proudly as the inner candle sparked and flared to life.

Soon all ten lanterns filled the boat with a soft rosy glow, candlelight illuminating the shimmering silk canopy. The temperature rose, and when Zhi Ging shut her eyes she could almost imagine she was being bathed in sunbeams rather than crouching by a waterfall at midnight. She sighed with relief as her earlier chill finally lifted.

"How long until we start floating?" Hiulam asked, stifling a yawn as the soothing warmth tugged at her eyelids.

"It should have started by now," Pinderent murmured, peering along the edges of the boat. "We must be losing heat somewhere." He shuffled forward, the silk canopy rustling against the top of his head and causing his hair to spark with static.

"How did that happen?" He pointed at a small tear in the fabric where cold sea air was whistling through.

Zhi Ging shivered, the eerie hissing causing unwanted memories to rise up. She peered at the tear, her eyes narrowing as she noticed threads of silk caught on the paddle beneath it. *Why does it look like it was torn from the outside?*

Zhi Ging opened her mouth but was suddenly thrown sideways, her right shoulder slamming into the teak frame as their boat tilted dangerously, threatening to capsize. Blinding pain crackled along her arm as she struggled to get back to her feet.

"What was that?" Mynah screamed, hands punching the silk as she tried to pull it loose. "Something out there just hit us."

"Well, don't make it easier for it to spot us!" Hiulam yelled as she helped lift Pinderent back up.

He groaned, clutching his head, and Zhi Ging winced when she spotted the cracked paddle beneath him. Malo was hiccupping anxiously in Jack's arms, bright light pulsing across his feathers.

Crrssshhh.

The Silhouettes screamed as a dark shadow sliced through the top of the silk canopy. The fabric split in half, tearing away to reveal the sharp tip of a gray tentacle. An all-too-familiar hissing filled the air, swelling against the waterfall's threatening rumble. No longer trapped under silk, the ten lanterns floated up, illuminating the creature.

The sand spirit leaned forward, its eight tentacles leaving trails of gray as they slithered across the boat.

Zhi Ging snatched at the broken paddle, raising the splintered wood high as she swung a protective hand out in front of her friends. "Get back!" she screamed as two of its tentacles transformed into pincers, snapping hungrily at Pinderent and Hiulam.

Jack leaped up, desperately twisting the Steerer's oar to try to shake the spirit loose. They exchanged panicked looks and Zhi Ging knew he was thinking the exact same thing as her. *How does it have all eight legs again? Did the tendril escape Gertie's cage? Or are there more sand spirits?*

The hissing intensified and their dragon boat suddenly lifted into the air, six tentacles raising them up toward the spirit's gnarled, knotted core. Zhi Ging shrieked as they were flipped upside down, the Silhouettes shaken loose to thud down across the creature's faceless body. The spirit tossed the boat toward the waterfall plunge pool, where it immediately shattered, its thick teak panels pulverized beneath the thundering rapids.

"No!" Pinderent shrieked, his face ghostly pale.

Malo swooped down, his flaming wings turning the water's surface to steam as he frantically searched for salvageable pieces. Zhi Ging felt her stomach lurch, and the half paddle slipped from her hand.

Their only way back to Hok Woh was gone.

The spirit began to twist around them. Matted gray tendrils snarled between their limbs, pulling them down through its sandy surface. Mynah's arm and cheek patches leached to a panicked slate gray, identical to the spirit's own sand, and Zhi Ging gasped, for a second convinced her friend had begun to dissolve.

"Malo, help!" she cried, spluttering as a shower of gray sand rained down over them. The little phoenix soared up, a blazing ribbon of fire trailing behind him, but it was no use. Each time he attempted to hit the spirit, its tendrils simply parted around him, sending him tumbling through thin air. Jack was forced to duck as the phoenix whistled over his head, barely missing the Silhouette after a giant hole appeared in the center of the spirit's tentacles.

High above them, the waterfall spray parted, and Zhi Ging caught a glimpse of red and blue. The flash of color vanished almost as quickly as it had appeared. She glanced at the others, but they were too focused on fighting the tendrils, spluttering as they flailed to stay above the spirit's writhing gray sand.

The spirit turned to Malo, tentacles curling over the Silhouettes' heads as it teased the phoenix, goading him to try to save them. Zhi Ging felt the upper half of her body tilt forward sharply as the spirit spun in the air, the tendrils wrapped tight around their torsos the only thing stopping them from falling straight into the waterfall's plunge pool. Beside her, Hiulam continued to scrabble in the sand, so focused on clawing her way out that she hadn't even noticed the new danger. A single pincer began to dance between the five Silhouettes, tapping each of them in some sort of spinning countdown. Jack reached forward and closed his hand tight around Zhi Ging's.

"We need to hold on to each other!" he shouted, his flashing eyes never leaving the spirit's twisting movements. "I don't know what's going to happen once that pincer stops, but it's not going to be good."

Zhi Ging nodded and began to reach her free arm down toward Hiulam when the spirit stilled, its pincer coming to a final halt above Mynah. The other girl screamed, gray sand erupting out across the spirit's gnarled body as she was pulled free and held out directly above the plunge pool. Malo screeched, his body vanishing within a fierce ball of light as he raced toward her. A strong gust of sea breeze rattled over the spirit, sending grains of gray sand flying out over the phoenix. They flared, the heat of his flames transforming them into droplets of molten glass. Light filled the bay as the glowing beads rained down into the waves, and Zhi Ging realized with a start that the spirit was now floating at the very edge of the waterfall, its body no more than an arm's length from the torrents ready to pull them under. Her eyes widened as the sand directly behind Mynah began to ripple, as if tensed to erupt.

It was a trap!

The spirit wasn't planning to drop Mynah at all. It

wanted to panic Malo and trick him into flying straight into the waterfall.

"Wait, stop!" Zhi Ging cried, terror crackling through her words as Malo shot toward them, his eyes focused on the pincer clamped around Mynah. Time seemed to slow as Zhi Ging snatched her hand out from Jack's grip and lunged forward. She reached desperately for Malo, but the tendrils around her body tightened, causing her to slam hard into the spirit's surface. The phoenix's head turned in confusion as he soared past, but he was going too fast to slow down.

There was a long drawn-out *thwump* as the pincer holding Mynah jerked aside. Malo shrieked in panic, finally spotting the waterfall through the hole in the spirit's body. He flung a wing back toward Zhi Ging as he hurtled through, his eyes wide with fear.

CHAPTER 21

Water erupted up from the plunge pool, cocooning Malo in a shimmering geyser. The little phoenix spun within it and came to a stop inches from the actual waterfall, protected within the new rippling column. The sand spirit hissed as more ribbons of water shot up, trapping it within a dome of overlapping bands. It skittered from side to side, careful not to let its tentacles brush its new aqueous cage. Above it, Malo somersaulted through the water, his feathers returning to their normal rainbow hue as he kicked his way up to the top of the dome.

"Seoizyu, bring it down," a familiar voice ordered from across the bay.

Zhi Ging's eyes snapped toward the speaker just as the glass dragon boat surged around the cliffside. Bucbou stood behind its horns, fury radiating off her. She swung her paddle up, its wooden blade whistling through the air as she crouched, ready to pounce. Suspended between dark waves and the midnight sky, the glass dragon almost seemed to be flying, the writhing sand spirit reflected in its polished eyes.

Seoizyu nodded, then began to slowly lower her tentacles, forcing the spirit toward the ocean surface. Zhi Ging felt the tendrils around her loosen, the sand spirit now focused on finding a way out. Its hiss reached piercing new levels, each piece of sand swept away by the waves causing the earsplitting sound to rise in volume.

"Grab on!" Bucbou yelled, leaping onto the glass dragon's snout. She gestured for Ai'Deng Bou to steer the boat closer, then blew her whistle, the shrill sound cutting across the spirit's frantic hissing. Her paddle slammed forward, batting away a half-formed pincer, and toward Zhi Ging. As one, the four Central Paddlers swung their paddles between Seoizyu's tentacles, stretching them out toward the other Silhouettes. The sand beneath Zhi Ging was bubbling now, individual grains dancing like hydrophobic pebbles as the space between Seoizyu's tentacles and the ocean surface continued to shrink.

Zhi Ging grabbed the paddle, taking a deep breath and shutting her eyes as Bucbou pulled her onto the boat. Warm water cascaded over her as she passed through the giant jellyfish, and Malo glided down one of Seoizyu's larger tentacles to land with a small splash in her hood. The duckling nuzzled against her, his feathers wrapping around the back of her neck in a relieved hug.

Behind her the sand spirit gave one final hiss, then

dissolved, currents of gray sand lapping harmlessly against the side of their boat. Jack, Mynah, Hiulam, and Pinderent thumped down beside her, and one of the Central Paddlers immediately leaped forward, placing heavy cloaks around their shivering bodies. The group was silent, the only sound the gentle plink of water dripping off the end of Pinderent's nose. Zhi Ging eventually became aware of footsteps stopping in front of her. She looked up and saw Bucbou looming above them, a sodden paper lantern from the sick bay clutched in her hand. The captain glared down at the five Silhouettes, Malo quietly curling over the edge of Zhi Ging's hood to hide from the Cyo B'Ahon's gaze.

"So," Bucbou began, her low voice sharpened to steel, "which one of you is going to explain this particularly *idiotic* plan to Sintou?"

THE HEAD OF THE CYO B'AHON SCRUTINIZED THE SI-lent group in front of her. The white flame trapped behind her office walls hovered directly above them, a blinding spotlight on the five Silhouettes. Zhi Ging shuffled uncomfortably, trying to use the tip of her shoe to wipe away the seawater that had begun to pool around them.

"Just what exactly were you hoping to achieve tonight?" Sintou's voice was terse as she examined the broken lantern. "This is not what either Bucbou or I had in mind when she offered to hand over her captaincy. From what I understand, if it hadn't been for these *stolen* sick bay lanterns, Bucbou never would have found you in time. I shudder to think how tonight would have ended if the lanterns hadn't risen up, alerting the Cyo B'Ahon to your location."

"I just thought—" Pinderent began.

"It's my fault," Zhi Ging interrupted, worried that—despite his flickering eyes—Pinderent would be sent home immediately if he took the blame. "I convinced the others to take the dragon boat." Her cheeks burned as the Head of the Cyo B'Ahon turned the full force of her gaze on her. Zhi Ging plowed on, speaking to her reflection in the puddle. "I never meant for Team Si Cau's boat to be destroyed. I'll do whatever the crew needs to help rebuild it. I—"

Sintou held up a gnarled finger, commanding silence. Deep creases ran down either side of her mouth as she frowned at the group. "Although only one of you had the initial idea, every single one of you chose to get into that boat. You are incredibly lucky Seoizyu spotted it being released from its stepping stone and alerted Ai'Deng Bou." She drummed her fingers on her checkerboard, deliberating. "You will all remain in detention until a new dragon boat has been carved and delivered to Bucbou."

"Together?" Zhi Ging blurted, unable to keep the small flutter of excitement from bursting out.

Sintou arched an eyebrow, causing deep wrinkles to

ripple across her forehead. "No, Miss Yeung. Detention is a punishment, not a reward. We've already seen what happens when the five of you spend more time together than necessary. No, your detentions will be split." She narrowed her eyes, then pointed at Pinderent, Hiulam, and Mynah. "The three of you will scrub the remaining yellow lines painted across Hok Woh's walls. Pou Pou's been doing his best, but there's too many for a single jellyfish. Meanwhile"—she turned back to Zhi Ging— "you, Miss Yeung, and Master Oltryds will spend your evenings assisting Neoi Syu, the Calligraphy tutor. She's been requesting additional support in the lantern archive. You will help her cross-examine the writing on former Silhouette lanterns against the handwriting samples Wusi provides from the older Silhouettes. Unfortunately those who spent longer as thralls are still struggling to remember which province they're from, despite Wuiyam's best efforts." The Head of the Cyo B'Ahon leaned back in her seat, the trapped flame curling behind her. "I recommend you all return to your respective dorms immediately. The others will be waking for breakfast soon."

NEOI SYU WAS WAITING FOR JACK AND ZHI GING outside the dining hall the following evening. She nodded politely as the other Silhouettes flowed past on their way to Cure Club, glancing up at the young Cyo B'Ahon in curiosity. A large carved lacquer box was tucked under

216

one arm, and she handed it to Jack as they stopped in front of her.

"Welcome back," she whispered to him once the other Silhouettes were out of earshot. "Now, let's see how many samples you both get through tonight." Her lavender robes were decorated with a border of shifting characters, the black embroidery stretching and shrinking to create a flowing banner of her conversation. As Zhi Ging watched, a small line of lilac wriggled out between the larger characters along her sleeve. However, rather than repeating Neoi Syu's sentence, these words glinted briefly before curling back into a decorative row of pine trees: *Brave move, annoying both Sintou and Bucbou this soon after returning.*

Zhi Ging's mouth dropped open, willing the purple pines to repeat their message. Was that what Neoi Syu had wanted to say? The Cyo B'Ahon caught her shocked expression and winked before marching down the corridors at such a pace that they were forced to jog behind her.

After a few minutes, they rounded a corner, and Zhi Ging realized with a jolt that they were marching along the same corridor Ami had taken her to before the thrall attack. She held her breath as they walked past the now-repaired crane sculpture, its glass wings patched together with thin bands of gold. It didn't feel possible that there was a tunnel hidden behind it.

The Calligraphy tutor eventually stopped in front of

a large sculpture of a paper lantern, the glass stained red to match the Silhouette lanterns that hung in the dorms. Neoi Syu pressed both hands to the center of the glass, then pushed forward, the circular lantern splitting in half to reveal a vast room.

Jellyfish floated above the silent archive, their soft glow filtering through the ceiling to reveal glimmering patches of dust that drifted through the air. Six trees rose up from the center of the room, their gray trunks arranged in a smooth crescent. Every branch was covered in what looked like enormous blossoms, and it was only when a bloom of jellyfish sailed overhead that Zhi Ging realized what they really were. The trees were decorated with thousands of Silhouette lanterns, brightly dyed ribbons in province colors identifying where each lantern was from.

Neoi Syu lifted the carved lacquer box out of Jack's hands, removing its lid to reveal a stack of scrolls. The ink on the first page was still damp, and Zhi Ging couldn't help but smile at a very Malo-shaped beak print. After Sintou had assigned their detention, the Head of the Cyo B'Ahon had given the little phoenix strict instructions to return to the sick bay and share more fire for the final few frozen Silhouettes.

"He was rather enthusiastic in helping Wusi collect these," Neoi Syu said, her mouth twitching into a smile. "He actually knocked an inkwell over himself right as we were finishing up. Luckily I managed to snatch the scrolls away before they were ruined. When I left, he was having a time-out in Heisui's basin while the jellyfish tried to scrub the ink out from between his feathers." She chuckled, and once again the lilac embroidery wriggled to life, a second message dancing between the main sentence being transcribed along her robe's border: *Heisiu's going to be even more eager for detention to end than either of you.*

"We've had the older Silhouettes share samples of their writing at Cure Club," Neoi Syu continued, handing a bundle of scrolls to Zhi Ging and Jack. "You need to match each of their scrolls to one of the lanterns in this room." She paused as they were momentarily plunged into gloom while the passing jellyfish veered farther down the hallway. "Unfortunately, you won't be allowed any sort of fire-based light to complete the search. A single flame could ignite an entire tree's worth of lanterns. You'll need to work in sprints, checking handwriting each time a bloom of jellyfish passes."

Zhi Ging looked dubiously from the scrolls to the red lanterns hanging from the lower branches.

"How do we even start?"

"Ah, that's the main challenge of your detention, I'm afraid. Although I would recommend—" She broke off, her gaze suddenly flicking to her left hand. Her eyes widened as she read the jellyfish message scrawling itself across her palm. Zhi Ging tried to read it upside down, but the characters were hurried and impossible to make out. Neoi Syu clapped her hands together, concealing the message, and flashed a smile at the two Silhouettes. "I'll be right back. Wusi's requesting my help in the sick bay."

Zhi Ging groaned, wondering what Malo had done now. She frowned as a small glimmer of purple darted up and down the border of Neoi Syu's robe. Without the glow of the jellyfish, the Cyo B'Ahon's unspoken sentence had been impossible to read.

Once the lantern door shut behind the tutor, Jack dropped his pile of scrolls back into the box. "Quick, before she comes back. Let's see if we can find my lantern first," he said, his eyes flashing excitedly between green and blue. "It might help me remember arriving at Hok Woh."

"What does your handwriting look like again?" Zhi Ging asked as they hurried to the closest tree, a thick yellow ribbon for the silk province tied around its wide trunk.

Jack paused, rummaging in his pockets for a brush, but they were both empty. He sighed and hurried past the tree toward the far wall. He exhaled onto its glass surface and used a finger to write across the newly clouded glass.

HELLO, IT IS I, THE INCREDIBLE JACK OLTRYDS, AND THIS IS WHAT MY HANDWRITING LOOKS LIKE.

He hesitated for a moment then scrawled a second line beneath the first.

Zhi Ging squinted hard at his writing until it faded back to clear glass.

"Okay, I think I can remember that," she murmured, a smile twitching at the side of her mouth. "Worst case, we can take Iridill's lantern with us tomorrow and use the answers you fixed to find your handwriting match."

"I can't believe you brought that up!" He snorted, shaking his head in mock outrage. "What do you think our detention would be right now if I'd also admitted that to Sintou?" he added with an exaggerated shudder.

"Ugh, let's never find out! We were lucky not to end up as Wusi's taste testers for new elixirs." Zhi Ging winced. She peered at the branches as Jack circled the trunk, looking for the easiest way to climb up. She stretched onto her toes, spotting an exam date scrawled across the closest ribbon.

"Ami only arrived at Hok Woh around a hundred years ago," she began, "so if you were Dohrnii before her, then we at least know you got to Hok Woh before that."

"That rules out"—Jack pulled himself up, clambering between branches as the glow of passing jellyfish shimmered above him—"these three branches."

Before he could continue, the main door flew open and Jack jumped, his foot slipping. He fell the short distance to the floor and scrambled up beside Zhi Ging, one arm stretched out protectively as he scanned the empty corridor, as if half expecting the sand spirit. Instead, an ink-stained Malo stared up at them, one foot still sticking out in front of him from when he'd kicked the door open. He gave a muffled chirp, a scrap of scroll rolled up in his beak.

"What does it say?" Jack asked as Zhi Ging tugged it loose.

"I—I can't read it very well." She squinted at the paper; it had been rolled too quickly, the ink characters smearing across the paper.

C–ME TO TH– S–CK BA–, S–0–T –S B–CK
NE–I SY–

"Why does Neoi Syu need us back at the sick bay just because an older Silhouette's woken up?" Jack asked. "We could pick up their handwriting scroll after Cure Club."

"I don't think that says 'Silhouette,'" Zhi Ging whispered, her heart starting to race. "The smudged word's too short. I think . . . it says 'Scout.'" She looked up at Jack, excitement flooding through her as Malo began to hop in anticipation.

"Reishi!"

CHAPTER 22

Zhi Ging and Jack raced back to the sick bay, Malo waddling furiously behind them. They almost crashed into a group of Cyo B'Ahon as they rounded a corner, the corridor filling with the popping sound of ageshifting adults as they swerved past.

"No running!" a furious now-thirteen-year-old tutor shouted after them, but they had already turned down the next bend.

Wusi was waiting for them at the sick bay entrance, a relieved smile on her face as she ushered them in. Behind her, a heavy wooden screen had been pulled across the new dorm, blocking those currently in Cure Club from looking into the sick bay. Meanwhile, sitting up in the only occupied bed was a familiar figure, his left arm in a sling. A steaming cup of black elixir was balanced above a jellyfish-filled bubble while he spoke with Neoi Syu.

"Reishi!" Zhi Ging yelled, skidding to a stop just before she reached his bed.

Gahyau spun expertly out of the way to avoid elixir spilling over all of them. The Scout was pale, and there were several deep scratches along the side of his cheek, but his eyes curved into welcoming crescent moons as he smiled.

"Take my seat—we'll restart your detention tomorrow," Neoi Syu urged, before giving Reishi's hand a friendly squeeze. "I'll leave you to it. Sintou'll be here in a moment." Her robes shimmered as she stood up, the thin lilac characters dancing along her collar. *And I've been holding my breath since Wusi brought that elixir over.* She slipped out of the sick bay, giving the healer's latest batch of medicine a wide berth.

"Don't tell me you're already back in detention, Zhi Ging." Reishi shook his head, his amused chuckle turning into a cough. "Surely you didn't actually enjoy scrubbing the tanks last time?"

"Actually, it's not just me in detention," Zhi Ging said with a laugh, stepping aside to reveal Jack.

Reishi ageshifted down in surprise when he spotted the other Silhouette.

"Jack! What are—why are you—when did this . . . ?" His flustered half questions petered out, his expression suddenly more uncertain than Zhi Ging had ever seen.

"Do you know?" he asked quietly.

Jack nodded, tugging at his cloak sleeves. "And I want to say thanks for keeping this for me after I Reverted." He smiled at Reishi. "Gertie told me the truth. I can't believe

I thought we were just lucky a random Silhouette's old cloak fitted me."

"I'm just glad I checked its pockets before I handed it over," Reishi said with a faint grin, ageshifting back up. "There was a crumpled scrap in your handwriting that would have been a bit of a giveaway." He winced as the sudden height change pulled his sling tight. Before Jack could help him adjust the shoulder strap, Sintou swept into the sick bay. Pou Pou floated after her, and there was a faint *splish* as the two bubbles merged, Sintou's jellyfish patting Gahyau in greeting before giving the two Silhouettes a quick wave. Wusi hurried over with a chair for Sintou, the Head of the Cyo B'Ahon's golden robes billowing around her as she leaned forward on the low wooden seat.

"Tell me everything," Sintou commanded.

"Gahyau and I had just made it off the final stepping stone when figures emerged out of the mist. At first I thought they were thralls, but they kept shifting, their bodies blurred. All we could hear was a constant hissing."

Zhi Ging gasped. "More sand spirits!"

"More?" Reishi raised a concerned eyebrow.

"It's all right—they've not entered Hok Woh." Sintou waved an impatient hand. "They can update you on their encounter later. Continue."

Reishi glanced between Zhi Ging and Jack, then nodded. "I grabbed hold of one only to discover it was actually the tentacle of a giant eight-legged creature. It lifted into the air, trapping us between pincers as it soared over the bay. We only broke free at the gold province border, plummeting into the Jyuging River. The spirit chased after us, its strange, knotted limbs flattening out across the water's surface until it looked like the entire river was covered by a swarm of furious gray wasps."

"How did you manage to get away?" Jack asked in a hushed whisper.

Reishi nodded at Gahyau. "It was all thanks to him. Once we were in the river, we knew I'd only have a few minutes before breathing became impossible. Gahyau created a new bubble, filled with air rather than water, and lowered it over my head."

"But it's been months," Sintou pressed. "Why did it take this long for you to make it back?"

Reishi paused, pressing his free hand against his sling as his entire body began to shudder, the pain of the memory deepening the lines across his face. Gahyau rolled the bubble over, a tentacle patting the Cyo B'Ahon's shaking hand. "It was the spirit sand," he explained in a strained whisper. "I must have accidentally swallowed some during the initial struggle. It did something strange to me." He took a long draft of his elixir, steam curling around his face. "Even before we fell into the river, I could feel my mind beginning to haze, gray static filling the corners of my vision."

He turned abruptly to Sintou, his expression urgent. "We need to investigate Omophilli. There was something drawing me to the paper province capital, as if the swallowed sand was pulling me toward it. The only way I could fight that impulse was by ageshifting down. But each time I ageshifted, the grainy hypnotic static would eventually find a way to reach me, leaving that age unreliable. It wasn't long before I ran out of ages to safely return to."

Zhi Ging's heart began to pound, and she clenched her hands as the flash of red and blue she'd spotted by the waterfall flared through her mind. Now that she thought about it, it was just like the glimpse of Niotiya she'd seen at the first spirit attack. The Matchmaker who was based in Omophilli . . . had she been there last night? She opened her mouth to speak, but Jack shook his head furtively, his eyes darting to the sick bay door. Zhi Ging knew what he meant. If she interrupted now, especially to remind Sintou about last night's disastrous dragon boat theft, the Cyo B'Ahon might send them back to detention, meaning they'd miss the rest of Reishi's explanation.

"I spent weeks trying to shake the possession eating at the corners of my mind," Reishi continued, his gaze distant. "Each time I tried to head back to Hok Woh, the sand would thrum along my skull, thundering through my bones until taking more than a dozen steps would fill me with such intense nausea that I'd be forced to stop."

Zhi Ging hugged Malo tight, the little phoenix pressing his beak into her robes. *Is this how he felt after eating that spirit-sand-filled bun?*

"Without Gahyau I wouldn't have survived," Reishi

admitted. "I woke up multiple times with his bubble pressed against my chest, stopping me from sleepwalking to Omophilli. But the possession finally took hold one night when I accidentally ageshifted back to eleven in my sleep, long after it had stopped being a safe year. When I came to, I was in a cavern filled with gray-faced children. Many of them were shivering, clutching their stomachs as if they'd been poisoned, while women in red capes marched between them."

"Buns!" Zhi Ging croaked, unable to stop herself. "The same thing happened to Malo after he ate one of the Matchmaker buns at Pingon's Scramble. They were filled with spirit sand."

"But Gertie sent Vrile to stop anyone else from eating them," Jack reminded her, his eyebrows furrowed in confusion.

Reishi's expression darkened as he took in the new information.

"This wasn't in the porcelain province," he said slowly. "From the style of their clothes, most of these children were from the carved lacquer province." The weight of his words sank into the pit of Zhi Ging's stomach. *Just how many spirit sand buns did the Matchmakers make?*

"Gahyau is the only reason I escaped late last night. Once he found me, he was able to guide me to a narrow hollow high up the cavern's side." Reishi paused as the jellyfish nudged him, his tentacles weaving in a complicated mime that Zhi Ging couldn't quite understand.

"Oh yes! In a far corner of the cavern an eight-legged sand spirit was placing children into carts. Matchmakers would roam between them, snatching children up by the top of their heads, peering closely between their faces and a scroll before stamping the child's palm."

Zhi Ging rubbed at her hand, itching to ask if they had looked like the red characters she'd spotted stamped on the frozen Silhouettes' palms. *Dippy and I never found out what those meant . . .*

"But why are sand spirits involved?" Sintou interrupted. "We've never been able to get a spirit to collaborate with us, despite the Folklore tutor's best efforts. What are the Matchmakers offering that we can't?"

"I'm not sure 'offering' is the right word," Reishi muttered. "I got the sense the Matchmakers have found some way to control them."

The two Cyo B'Ahon exchanged a tense look.

"The six provinces have had a pact against spirit summoning for the past thousand years. I was the one to oversee it." Sintou frowned. "No rulers or guilds were to engage in it. I know most turn a blind eye to villagers summoning local spirits to help with harvests, but no one with significant power is allowed to call on them. Why are the Matchmakers willing to risk breaking that pact now?"

"What about the others?" Zhi Ging interrupted, still rubbing her palm. *What if Mynah and Hiulam had been in the carts?* Her next question pressed against a heavy silence that suddenly filled the room. "Are they still there?"

Reishi sighed, his already gray face becoming somber. "Unfortunately, the escape route Gahyau found for me was too small for the others. I had to ageshift down to five just to squeeze through." He winced, his eyes darting to Jack. "Dangerously close to Reverting age." He took a deep draft of his elixir before continuing, and Zhi Ging couldn't tell if he was grimacing from the taste or the memory he was about to share.

"Once I got out, Gahyau crept back into the cavern. It was a gamble, but we knew we had to split up to work out what the Matchmakers were up to. The carts were already moving by the time he returned, and under cover of darkness he followed them all the way to Omophilli. He only lost them after the children were bundled into the Matchmakers' Guild Hall."

"I doubt they're still there," Sintou muttered. "There's been rumors for years that the Matchmakers have tunnels snaking out beneath the Guild Hall. I suspect they've numerous ways of traveling around the paper province capital without being spotted." The Head of the Cyo B'Ahon stood up. "I'll inform the shoreside Scouts; the sooner they can begin searching Omophilli the better."

"What was on the scroll?" Jack suddenly asked, his voice barely audible.

The two Cyo B'Ahon stopped, staring at him in confusion.

"You said the Matchmakers were checking faces against a scroll?"

Reishi's eyes flicked to Zhi Ging, and there was a strange hesitation before he shook his head. "I—I'm afraid Gahyau didn't get a good look," he said without meeting their gaze. Out of the corner of her eye, Zhi Ging saw Gahyau take one of Pou Pou's tentacles. The larger jellyfish shuddered, then Sintou glanced down. Shock slashed across her face, and her expression hardened as she read the message coiling across her palm.

"I think that's enough questioning for tonight. Zhi Ging, Jack, I suggest you return to your final thirty minutes of detention."

Zhi Ging felt her stomach tighten as Wusi ushered them out of the sick bay. She paused at the door, glancing back at the Cyo B'Ahons' carefully blank faces.

Why had Reishi lied?

CHAPTER 23

For the next week, Zhi Ging and Jack continued to rifle through handwriting samples, impatiently searching through old lanterns for a Silhouette match.

"This is impossible," Jack muttered. He slid down a tree trunk to land with a heavy thud beside Zhi Ging. "What if Wusi and Neoi Syu are having a great laugh back in the sick bay, scribbling out fake Silhouette samples?" He exhaled loudly, batting several lower-hanging lanterns out of his way.

Zhi Ging grimaced in sympathy. She knew exactly why her friend was finding the nightly detention so annoying. After all, she'd been dealing with the exact same itching frustration for months, missing out on each new inside joke from Cure Club.

"I could see Neoi Syu doing that; Wusi not so much," a voice murmured from the door.

The two Silhouettes spun around and spotted Reishi smiling at them, the sling around his arm finally gone.

"I'm afraid I'm about to make your detention even more difficult, Jack." He turned to Zhi Ging, tapping the glass door with a bundle of scrolls. "It's high time we restarted our air rail research, wouldn't you say?"

"THERE'S SOMETHING I HAVE TO ADMIT," REISHI said, pausing with a hand on his lab door.

Zhi Ging's head snapped up, staring at him in surprise. He had been silent for most of the walk through Hok Woh, humming to himself and occasionally nodding at the jellyfish passing by on the other side of the glass walls. *Is he finally going to share what Gahyau saw on the scroll?* she wondered. Reishi beamed at her, oblivious to her thoughts. "You're not the only Silhouette I've kidnapped from detention tonight."

The glass door slid open to reveal Pinderent, smiling broadly at them. Behind him, the tanks that usually filled Reishi's lab had been pushed to the far corners, great slabs of glass balanced precariously on top of one another. Several of the jellyfish waved, welcoming Zhi Ging back, but others floated with their tentacles crossed, glowering down at a wooden structure that dominated the center of the lab.

Zhi Ging let out a gasp as she recognized its shape. "Is that Team Bolei's dragon boat?"

"Correct. We've left its glass head in there for now." Reishi gestured to a large tank, where dozens of miniature jellyfish were using the dragon's glass whiskers as twirling slides, their tentacles waggling in excitement as they scooted down.

"I've been trying to work out a way to re-create its frame, but lighter," Pinderent explained. "I think that's where we're all going wrong at training."

"Have you been working on this all day?" Zhi Ging asked, eyeing the dozens of sketches scattered across the lab floor.

Pinderent blushed as Reishi chuckled.

"Oh, you're not giving your friend nearly enough credit! Pinderent has been working on these designs every time you've been in class. While I was recovering in the sick bay, I noticed he was the only Silhouette in the new dorm who constantly looked busy. Most of the others were more focused on training Heisiu to perform tricks. Your friend Mynah has almost gotten that jellyfish to perfect a double cartwheel." He gave an impressed harrumph before continuing. "Anyway, once Pinderent agreed to show me what he was working on, I knew I had to help." The Cyo B'Ahon paused, running a hand through his short beard. "Having said that, I've not quite gotten Bucbou's approval. Although I'm sure she'll be less furious once the new and improved silk dragon boat arrives. Until then, though, perhaps we can keep this between the three of us."

Zhi Ging nodded, biting down a smile as she remembered how horrified Reishi had looked when she'd been late for her very first dragon boat tryout with Bucbou. *Guess even Cyo B'Ahon can be scared of something.*

"What's this one?" she asked, bending to pick up a sketch. The longer she could delay failing to find air rails the better.

"That was one of my first ideas," Pinderent said, waving a dismissive hand. "I thought if Seoizyu came with us, she could just raise us over the actual waterfall."

Zhi Ging's mouth dropped open. "Why haven't we done that? We could've saved weeks of training!"

Pinderent shook his head. "Reishi checked with Ai'Deng Bou, and apparently the captains were warned before the first training that it wouldn't work. Watch." He pulled over a small glass tank, dropping a miniature dragon boat and fake waterfall onto its surface. The water rippled and a crystal-clear jellyfish wrapped a tentacle around it.

"Like Seoizyu, this jellyfish has been created with a higher percentage of water," Reishi explained. "Although that gives him certain strengthened powers, it also means he can only focus on one task at a time. If he's raising his tentacles over a waterfall, he won't have enough energy to also lift a filled dragon boat." Zhi Ging and Malo watched as the jellyfish raised his tentacles over the scale model of the waterfall before splashing back down once Reishi nudged the toy boat toward him. "It doesn't hurt either jellyfish, but it means we can't use them to help us over the waterfall."

Zhi Ging sighed in frustration. "So what's your next dragon boat idea?" she asked. It felt good to see Pinderent this excited. He'd been quiet at every meal since their failed waterfall trip, but maybe what she'd assumed was disappointment had actually been focus.

"Well." Pinderent's dark brown eyes lit up; there was almost no trace of blue and green left after multiple nights of D'Amask's tea. "That's where you come in. If you can work out how to find the air rails, we might be able to get the dragon boats to travel along them."

"Remember I once told you we'd need dragon talons to find the air rails? Well, if you can find them, then this dragon"—Reishi smacked the side of the boat in enthusiasm—"won't need claws at all! So long, dragon boat, hello . . . dragon float!" He chuckled to himself while behind him Gahyau rolled his tentacles good-naturedly at the terrible pun.

"I can try," Zhi Ging began hesitantly, splaying her fingers wide. It had been months since she had attempted to find an air rail. She could barely remember the last time her hands had filled with swirling gold lines.

"Just one second!" Reishi cried, scrambling past her to pull heavy wooden screens in front of the glass tanks, hiding them from view. Several of the jellyfish shook their tentacles in protest, annoyed to be missing the long-awaited return of the air rail sessions. Malo flew to the top of a screen, chirping a promise to reenact each of Zhi Ging's attempts for the blocked jellyfish.

"Just in case you do find an air rail," Reishi said when he spotted Zhi Ging's confused expression. "I don't want you or Pinderent being hit by breaking glass." He pressed back against a nearby screen, catching several jellyfish working together to try to push it away. "And I also don't want any of my jellyfish to need a new tank," he added loudly, nodding in satisfaction as tentacles vanished back behind the screen.

Zhi Ging took a deep breath and shut her eyes. She moved her arm in a careful circle, trying to imagine thick golden beams beneath her fingers. The seconds trickled into minutes and eventually congealed into a heavy silence. Zhi Ging clenched and unclenched her fist but there was no sign of the air rails.

"Would it help if you were in the boat?" Pinderent asked.

She sighed without much enthusiasm. "Maybe."

Zhi Ging sat cross-legged at the front of the boat, in the glass dragon head's usual position. This time, when she shut her eyes, she imagined that she herself was a dragon, flying high above the cloud sea. The image flickered to the dragon boat that had rescued them from the sand spirit, its solid teak body suspended over ink-black waves as if it was flying through the night sky. She ran her right hand along its cracked frame, trapped grains of sand tickling her fingers.

Zhi Ging froze.

There, at the edge of her left hand, was a whisper of an invisible beam. It felt like the curling glass whiskers of the

237

Lead Glassmith's dragon door, but as she inched her hand across it, she heard Reishi and Pinderent gasp.

"It was right there!" Reishi cried, the excitement in his voice spilling over Zhi Ging.

She smiled, tightening her grip around the beam.

"See if you can open your eyes," Pinderent urged.

Zhi Ging slowly opened her left eye. Her gaze trailed along her arm, and her breath caught in her throat. The air rail was visible under her palm, one half stretching harmlessly toward a wooden screen while the other flowed directly into the ceiling.

Reishi and Pinderent walked around it in awe.

"Well, this is a new problem," Reishi murmured. "I always assumed the air rails flowed in straight lines, but this"—he flicked his wrist, his fingers mirroring its swooping form—"this'll make it just that bit harder to lift the dragon boat."

Malo flew over, not wanting to miss out. He landed on the upper end of the air rail, shuffling along it before sliding down its curved length to the others. Zhi Ging laughed as he hurtled down, and her concentration slipped. The air rail vanished, the gold evaporating as Malo landed with a small thump into her lap.

"Sorry about that," she whispered. "But you can still tell the jellyfish you landed gracefully?"

The little phoenix nodded, his cheek feathers puffed out in agreement.

"Let's see if you can find it again," Reishi said enthusiastically. "I think—"

Splaaaat.

They stopped, looking around for the source of the sudden strange sound. Several of the jellyfish in the upper tanks pulled themselves up, peering over the top of the wooden screen in curiosity.

"The rail didn't hit any of the tanks, did it?" Pinderent asked, crouching down to check the lab floor for water.

"I don't think so," Zhi Ging murmured, stepping out of the dragon boat. "It doesn't sound like it's coming from inside the lab—"

Shrrrrrrr.

They spun around, finally spotting the source. There, on the other side of the lab's thick glass, was a shadowy figure. Their features were blurred, but the object in their hands was unmistakable. A brush smothered in glowing yellow paint was being dragged across the outer wall.

"Paint thief!" Pinderent yelped, barreling toward the door. "You're the reason my detention keeps getting longer."

Zhi Ging and Malo raced after him, but Reishi was faster. He flung his lab door open just as the thief reached the entrance.

"Got you!" Reishi leaped out, his hand closing around their outstretched hand. The thief jerked back, paintbrush clattering out of their grip to leave a thick streak of yellow across the front of Reishi's robes. He ageshifted down in shock, now identical height with the paint thief as he dabbed at his ruined clothes.

Zhi Ging skidded to a stop, her mouth dropping open in shock.

"You?" she croaked, blinking hard at the face in front of her.

CHAPTER 24

Iridill refused to meet their gaze. Instead, she stared down at the floor, a small blob of glowing yellow paint clinging to the tip of her nose. She halfheartedly tried to pull free from Reishi's grip, cheeks flushing red as jellyfish began to gather behind the glass, floating above the freshly painted line to watch the scene unfold.

"But why?" Pinderent asked in a daze, crouching down to pick up the brush. He unconsciously pulled a cloth from his pocket and began to wipe it clean, the last few weeks of paint scrubbing kicking in instinctively.

While he waded through confusion, Zhi Ging could feel a very different emotion rising through her. Her initial shock curdled, thickening into layers of brittle anger.

"You tried to convince others it was me!" she snapped, taking a step toward Iridill. "You knew Sycee wanted to send the thief home, but you didn't stop. Instead, you painted even more lines around Hok Woh and tried to pin them on me."

"You don't get it." Iridill jerked her head up, her eyes flashing a bright blue and green. She winced and dropped her gaze before continuing, speaking directly into her thick yellow scarf. "Every time I look at—what if it never works? At least yours is hidden here. Every corridor is horrible."

"What?" Zhi Ging frowned, suddenly wondering if Iridill was actually sleepwalking. Her sentences didn't even make sense. They were like the mutters she occasionally heard back in the dorm when a Silhouette was having a nightmare.

Reishi frowned and took a half step sideways so he was standing right beside Iridill. His oversized robes flapped around his now-twelve-year-old frame as he peered at the clear glass behind Zhi Ging, then twisted his head back down the paint-lined corridor.

"Hmmm." His frown deepened and he slowly began to ageshift back up, growing an extra foot so he was once again face-to-face with the watching jellyfish. "Ah!"

All three Silhouettes jumped in surprise as he ageshifted back down, robes billowing around him until he was once again Iridill's height. He released his grip around her wrist and turned to Zhi Ging and Pinderent. "Please return to your dorms. I'll be speaking with Miss Seoipin about this. Alone."

"SO DO YOU THINK SHE'S BEEN SENT HOME?" HIU-lam asked as they filed out of Wusi's classroom for lunch the next day. "I didn't see her in the dorm this morning."

Jack nodded. "She's definitely gone. Cing Yau and Kaolin were so quiet; normally the three of them spend all class snorting at each other's notes."

"Yeah, there's no way Sycee would let her stay," Zhi Ging agreed.

For the first time in months, she felt calm. Life in Hok Woh was going to be so much easier without Iridill's constant snide comments. They hung back, waiting for the others to pass before turning right and climbing up to the sick bay to collect Mynah and Pinderent from the other dorm.

"But why did she do it?" Zhi Ging wondered, unable to shake the small thorn of curiosity that had been rattling around the back of her mind all night.

"Other than trying to get you kicked out of Hok Woh? Who cares? I'm just wondering who'll get her room. I bet . . . No way!" Hiulam skidded to a stop at the top of the stairs.

Zhi Ging peered over her shoulder and her mouth dropped open. There, in the center of the sick bay, were Reishi and Iridill, calmly sipping from cups of tea.

"What's going on?" Zhi Ging demanded, the unfairness of it all crackling down her back like dragon lightning. "Why is she still here?" She jabbed a finger at Iridill before turning to Reishi.

"Miss Yeung," Wusi snapped, appearing behind them on the stairs, "I'll have no raised voices in the sick bay. If you can't follow that simple rule, I recommend you return to the dining hall with the others."

"But, Iridill, the yellow paint," Zhi Ging began, hating how flustered she sounded. She took a deep breath and crossed her arms, forcing her jumbled thoughts to slow down. "Does Sycee know?" she asked, flinging down her trump card. Out of the corner of her eye, she saw Iridill flush deep red, the color clashing with her blue and green eyes. But her triumph fizzled out immediately when Reishi nodded.

"Yes, Sycee knows. As does every other dragon boat captain. And Sintou."

Wusi bustled past the group, spinning them back toward the stairs. "Any final questions before lunch?" she asked, her tone making it clear it was extremely unlikely any would actually be answered.

"But it's not fair," Zhi Ging mumbled, holding on to the doorframe. "I would have been sent home." She looked back at Iridill and Reishi in confusion, a strange prickling filling her throat as if she'd swallowed dozens of coarse lychee husks. *Why am I the one getting in trouble?*

Reishi sighed and stood up, gesturing down the stairs. "Let's have a chat, Zhi Ging."

They walked in silence to his lab, each yellow-streaked wall they passed causing Zhi Ging's frown to deepen. Gahyau waved as they stepped inside, but the jellyfish's tentacle drooped when he spotted Zhi Ging's tightly folded arms. He rolled his bubble between two narrow tanks, clearly wanting no part in their argument.

"What's going on?" she demanded, swiveling to face Reishi.

The Cyo B'Ahon gestured to his desk, and she thumped down in her usual chair, feeling a small spark of triumph as ink splattered across his scroll. Reishi said nothing but simply dabbed the stain away.

"Why is she still here?" she pressed, annoyed by his calmness. "Iridill never got in trouble after writing that nasty message and flooding my room before our first challenge, and now after splashing paint all over Hok Woh she's being given cups of tea?" Zhi Ging snorted, furious at the unfairness of it all. "Is it because she's the Lead Glassmith's daughter?"

"I can understand your frustration," Reishi sighed, shaking his head. "But I need you to believe me when I say there is more to this than you realize. Iridill is . . ." He began again: "There is a reason why Cyo B'Ahon, and not Silhouettes, decide on final punishments, Zhi Ging. I promise you she's not receiving preferential treatment." He paused as she scoffed. "In fact, thanks to you and Pinderent catching her yesterday, Iridill is finally receiving the *correct* treatment."

"What do you mean?" Zhi Ging asked as she uncrossed her arms, unable to stop the curiosity from sneaking in.

"I'm afraid that will remain between Iridill and Wusi, who has, ah . . ." His eyes flicked to a message scrawling across his palm in silver lines. "Wusi has just spoken with the rest of your friends. We would appreciate if you could keep Iridill's identity as the paint thief secret. No need for the rest of your class to know."

Zhi Ging huffed. "But why? I bet she's been bragging to Kaolin and Cing Yau about it for weeks."

Reishi raised an eyebrow, staring at her with such a somber expression that she couldn't help but shrink back into her chair. "I can assure you it is not something she is proud of, Miss Yeung. I appreciate you are not friends, but compassion should never be conditional."

Zhi Ging lowered her head, feeling an embarrassed blush creeping up the back of her neck. How had the conversation spiraled so quickly? Right now, all she wanted to do was hide from Reishi's disappointed frown.

"Fine," she muttered, eyes down as she pushed her chair back. "I promise."

BY THE END OF THE MONTH, ZHI GING, PINDERENT, and Reishi were still no closer to solving how to get the dragon boat to travel along air rails. No matter how hard she focused, the rails would never support any more than her own weight.

Pinderent sighed as they walked back to the sick bay. "I think we need to find an even lighter material for the boats."

"Once we add a single Cyo B'Ahon, though, it'll already

be too heavy." Zhi Ging shook her head, batting a floating lantern aside as they stepped through the door.

Jack leaned out from the new dorm, waving one of the ideas that had been strewn across Pinderent's bed. For the past week, he and Hiulam had started adding their own sketches after detention. Wusi had rolled her eyes when they first crept into the other dorm after Cure Club but she said nothing apart from "Fine by me. Makes it easier to find you for your next elixir dose, Hiulam."

The stack of scrolls covering Pinderent's bed had grown each night. Some had potential, like Jack's idea of asking Gertie to lend them tents from the floating market, while others, like Mynah's unforgettable let's-just-fill-the-entire-waterfall-with-rice-so-it-becomes-climbable-congee, had been useful for nothing apart from making the group howl with laughter, quickly switching to silent shaking hiccups when Wusi shushed them.

"What do you think of this one, Heisiu?" Zhi Ging asked, holding up her latest idea to the healer's jellyfish. Over the past few visits, he had become their unofficial judge, selecting the best and worst ideas.

The jellyfish tapped a contemplative tentacle against the side of his basin, then curled a tentacle down.

"Ooh, bad luck!" Mynah said, taking a bite of memo-chi. "My turn. How about this?" With a dramatic flour-ish, her scroll unrolled to reveal a dragon boat team where each crew member's paddle had been replaced by what looked like giant jellyfish tentacles, each tentacle sticking to the rocks on either side of the waterfall.

Pinderent almost choked on his latest dose of black elixir. "What is that?"

"Eh? It's obviously the best idea we've had all week," Mynah huffed in fake outrage, her bright yellow cheek patches giving her away.

Zhi Ging stared hard at the illustration, and something niggled at her. Could there be a sea creature solution? She frowned as the rest of the thought sank back down to the depths of her mind, refusing to reveal itself.

The night before, she had attempted to create a paper cutting of a boat while Reishi supervised, hoping she might have inherited her mother's powers. However, it had simply floated down to the lab floor. There hadn't even been a flicker of gold along her arms.

"So what do we think tomorrow's challenge will be?" Hiulam asked once Heisiu had judged the rest of their sketches.

"It's Calligraphy, right?" Pinderent said. "I have to say it's much more fun guessing what the challenge will be when I don't actually have to take part."

"I don't mind what the challenge is as long as it's not cross-checking handwriting in the lantern archive." Jack leaned back against the bed behind them. He stopped, frowning at the empty sheets.

"Hey, where's Suwun gone?" He paused, spotting Zhi Ging's blank expression. "She was in Cure Club with us. The older Silhouette who told Mynah she hid homei spoons somewhere in Hok Woh, remember?"

Wusi paused in her herb preparation, shooting the group a confused look.

"Didn't Neoi Syu tell you? The first porcelain province Silhouettes were sent home this evening. We're beginning with those who've been kept from home the longest and there's no need to travel past any waterfalls to reach their coastal villages."

They fell silent, all eyes turning to Pinderent. His knuckles tightened around the final scroll as the unspoken question seeped through the group. How much longer did he have left in Hok Woh?

CHAPTER 25

The next morning, the Silhouettes clambered back out of the entrance stepping stone to be greeted by G'Aam and Wuyan. Zhi Ging waved as a combat crane emerged between them, a lantern covered in swirling calligraphy swinging from its beak.

The two guardian Cyo B'Ahon handed out gold hoops in silence, and the group lifted up from the junk. They swept over the porcelain province, the narrow Batzuk River curling beneath them. It wound between banks filled with hydrophobic pebbles, the small stones bursting up like fireworks every time water lapped against the winding shores.

The Silhouettes fell silent, the only sound an excited murmur as friends pointed out each new burst. Zhi Ging tried to let the pebbles distract her, but it wasn't just pre-challenge nerves coiling tight in her stomach. This was the river being used to return the more coastal porcelain province Silhouettes. How long would it be until they found a way back up to the cloud sea? *Will Pinderent even be here by our next challenge?*

The group eventually landed in a lemon grove high up in the gold province. The air was thick with the scent of incense as G'Aam and Wuyan gestured to a small pavilion nestled between the trees, encouraging the Silhouettes to step inside.

Every pillar inside the wooden pavilion had been covered in paper banners, rich calligraphy brushstrokes sweeping across their surface. Above them a warm glow spilled over the Silhouettes from dozens of red paper lanterns that filled the ceiling and cascaded down the pillars in rosy bubbles of light. An oversized saffron lantern swung from the center of the cluster; in any other room it would have been the focus of their attention, but not here.

Their next tutor sat directly in front of a giant yellow fan, its gold embroidery a detailed illustration of G'Ilding, the province capital. It swayed gently in the breeze, fluttering like a giant peacock's tail behind the Cyo B'Ahon.

"Welcome." The Calligraphy tutor's eyes darted to Zhi Ging and Jack. "For those I've yet had the pleasure to meet, my name is Neoi Syu. Your challenge today will be focused on Calligraphy." She paused, staring intently at the Silhouettes. "Please don't misunderstand the power of this skill. Calligraphy covers so much more than you think. It's the power of language and the closest anyone shoreside will ever come to achieving immortality." She pointed at the rustling banners. "Through writing, an ordinary villager's thoughts can live on forever. To become a Cyo B'Ahon, though, you'll also need to learn to read between the lines and see the unspoken message lurking behind letters."

Hiulam gasped, and Zhi Ging's eyes darted to Neoi Syu's robes, where the tutor's sentences were once again running along her sleeve borders in thick black characters. *Some of you may notice I'm a big fan of secret messages.* The lilac embroidery glinted before innocently curling back into a decorative row of pine trees.

"Calligraphy is collaborative; it's one of the few skills that rely on others. Without someone else reading it, its power stays dormant. Good calligraphy can shape reality, but it also relies on being read to *become* reality." She paused, noticing the baffled faces of several Silhouettes. "Don't worry, I'll explain what I mean to those who pass today's challenge."

Zhi Ging gulped, and the Silhouettes around her stood a little straighter. Only Hiulam seemed unperturbed; she bounced from foot to foot with excited energy.

There was a loud rustling, and the group turned to see G'Aam and Wuyan unrolling a giant scroll outside the pavilion. It was so large that every single one of them could stand on it with their arms stretched wide and still not reach the closest Silhouette.

Neoi Syu continued as if she wasn't aware of the rippling concentration of the group. "Unfortunately, Cyo

B'Ahon can often outlive the written instructions they've shared, especially if not protected from the seasons." On cue, thunder rolled in the distance. The tutor smiled as large droplets began to drum against the scroll. She pointed at the yellow lantern above them.

"There is a famous poem written on this. It honors and names every single child from the gold province who has ever passed their Silhouette year." She smiled as a few Silhouettes nodded excitedly, mouthing the words under their breath. "This lantern is a replica, of course. I update the one in G'Ilding once a year. I'll give you all a moment to take in their names."

Jack nudged Zhi Ging, his eyes comically wide.

"She really is going to have us match handwriting for our challenge," he whispered dramatically.

Zhi Ging snorted, shaking her head as Neoi Syu reached into her sleeve and placed a slim hourglass on the table.

"My challenge is simple. You have thirty minutes to transcribe this lantern's poem onto the scroll out there." She paused, waiting for the latest rumble of thunder to end as rain danced across the pavilion roof. "Your calligraphy must still be legible by the time this sand runs out."

Zhi Ging glanced out, frowning at the downpour. Parts of the scroll had already begun to sag, puddles of rainwater gathering in pockets. Neoi Syu turned, stretching a hand toward the silk fan. The bright scent of lemons burst through the air as she snapped it shut, revealing a hidden cabinet filled with brushes, inkstones, inksticks, and water droppers. "You can use anything from the pavilion to re-create the poem. Ready?"

The tutor clicked her fingers and a small flame erupted between them. Zhi Ging did a double take before spotting the fragments of flint. Neoi Syu held the fire against the tassels at the bottom of the giant lantern, the flames eagerly licking up to its paper body. She stepped out of the pavilion, only calling back as she vanished between lemon trees: "Your time starts now."

There was a second's pause, then the Silhouettes rushed to the cabinet. Kaolin knocked Zhi Ging's hands out of the way as he reached for a small brush. Cing Yau barreled into his back, sending a bundle of inksticks clattering across the floor, where they were immediately snatched up by other Silhouettes.

"What did you do that for!" Kaolin yelled as Cing Yau grabbed the last inkstick on the shelf and sprinted for the challenge scroll. Zhi Ging pushed her way through the scramble. She claimed a slim brush before frantically searching the fast-emptying cabinet for more inksticks.

"You can use some of mine!" Jack cried, waving a broken half stick of solid ink.

The Silhouettes raced out, peering back at the burning saffron lantern as they attempted to re-create the poem. The rain drummed across their backs, stealing away the brushstrokes of wet ink almost as soon as they touched the scroll's surface. There was a muffled cry, and Zhi

Ging turned to see Kaolin staring in horror at a sodden hole in the middle of his writing paper.

She nudged Jack and Hiulam. "Neoi Syu said we could use anything in the pavilion, right? Let's use the fan as an umbrella."

"Yes!" Hiulam yelped, her short hair now plastered to her face. They hurried back into the pavilion and unhooked it, wincing at how much of the paper lantern poem had already been consumed by flames. Once back outside they shook it open, and nearby Silhouettes clambered to squeeze under its wide protection, desperate to give their calligraphy a better chance. However, the silk fabric soon began to darken, and a thick citrus scent filled the air.

"It's no good," Jack cried as the storm thundered above them, water pouring down the sides of the fan.

"We have to keep it dry!" Zhi Ging sprinted into the pavilion, tugging one of the smaller lanterns loose. She crouched low as she ducked back under the fan, tilting the flame toward the damp patches of silk.

"I think it's working," Hiulam said, pointing at the rich yellow spreading back across the fan's surface.

"Give me that," Iridill barked, jostling over to tug the lantern toward the water threatening to drip on her section of scroll.

The lantern slipped out of Zhi Ging's hand, and she fumbled for it, knowing if it landed on the paper, no matter how sodden, they could lose the entire scroll. Iridill's hand shot out, small droplets of sallow wax splattering her wrist as she caught it. She winced and tried to brush them away, but the wax had already solidified in the cold air, leaving three raised crescents beneath her thumb.

"Nice going, you nearly made us all fail," Iridill snapped, her narrowed eyes flashing blue and green.

"You're the one who snatched it!"

"Wait, what's that?" Jack asked, pointing back up to the fan. There, slowly shimmering into sight, was a single sentence, the characters identical to the ones that had flowed across Neoi Syu's robes. It glimmered down at them in warm brown strokes.

Calligraphy is collaborative. To pass, write the poem together: one character per Silhouette.

The air beneath the fan erupted into chaos as the Silhouettes looked down in horror, scouring the scroll between their feet for enough space to restart the poem. Dark ink-stained puddles had already spread to the edges of the paper, leaving a single clean strip in the center.

There was only one chance to get it right.

"I'm a big fan of secret messages," Zhi Ging gasped, repeating the message that had twirled across Neoi Syu's robes. She shook her head in disbelief. *It had been a challenge clue!*

Jack turned back to the pavilion and grimaced. The yellow lantern was mostly ash now; only the upper third remained.

"How are we meant to do that?" Hiulam shouted. "Even with the fan, none of us have managed to get the ink to stay."

"I'm not failing because the rest of you ruined this scroll!" Iridill screamed, a furious nasal edge to her whining. She flung the small lantern back toward the pavilion in frustration. It hit a pillar, wax spilling out over the steps before its flame was snuffed out by a perfectly timed raindrop.

Zhi Ging stared up at the silk fan above them, her mind racing. *What am I not seeing?* She pressed her hands to her eyes and breathed in deeply, the scent of lemons sparking her lungs.

"I've got it!" Her eyes snapped open, and she pointed back at the dark brown message above them. "Forget the inksticks—let's write with what Neoi Syu used: lemon juice."

She spun her arms wide, pointing at the trees that surrounded the pavilion, each branch heavy with waxy yellow fruit. Several Silhouettes sprinted straight out, snatching at the lemons before racing back through the downpour to the relative safety of the fan.

"What now?" Hiulam asked, handing out lemons.

"We just need to dip our calligraphy brushes in and—"

"How are we meant to open them without a knife?" Iridill's drawl cut over her.

Zhi Ging hesitated, rolling the lemon Jack had just passed her between her hands. Under her rain-slicked fingers it was already difficult enough to just hold, getting the grip needed to tear it open would be impossible.

"We need to stomp them open," Kaolin cried, tossing his lemon onto the scroll. He raised his foot over it, and Zhi Ging's eyes widened, realizing what was about to happen.

"No!" she and Iridill screamed in unison, but it was too late. Kaolin's foot slammed down on the lemon, and it erupted, a cascade of juice streaming out.

Right over the last clean part of the scroll.

"What's wrong with you?" Iridill screeched. "I'm not going back to Fei Chui with my eyes still looking like this." She rubbed at her wrist, the skin around the wax now red and irritated. Suddenly, Iridill stopped, one finger directly above the largest wax droplet. Without a word she sprinted back into the shrine, emerging with a hand cupped over the top of her calligraphy brush. Iridill kicked the scroll aside, waterlogged paper tearing beneath her shoe, and swept an empty brush across the flat stones.

"I think the challenge has broken her," Hiulam whispered. "Should we get Wusi?"

Zhi Ging hesitated, then crouched down beside Iridill, eyes narrowed in concern. "What are you—"

"It's wax!" Iridill snapped, ignoring Zhi Ging's outstretched hand. She spun her brush between her fingers and tapped it on the ground. Rather than a dull thud, there was a faint plink. "The stone's cold so it's solidifying immediately. Which means the rain . . ."

"Can't wash it away," Zhi Ging realized in amazement.

"Exactly." Iridill's pale face twitched, and she looked down, red patches flushing her cheeks. "I'm not just here because of my father, you know," she whispered, refusing to meet Zhi Ging's eyes. "I might not be my brother Favrile, but I'm more than my father thinks."

Zhi Ging felt her stomach clench as she crouched next to her, the vicious comments Iridill's father had hurled at his only daughter during the mirror maze flashing across her mind.

She nodded slowly. "Even if your father cheated to get you in, you're the reason you're still here."

Iridill sniffed, then leaped up, her face carefully blank as if she hadn't heard Zhi Ging's comment. "Everyone, line up!" she barked, her usual scowl sliding back into place. "There wasn't much sand left in the hourglass when I went to get that wax. You need to write your characters for the poem now!"

"No wonder there weren't enough inksticks," Hiulam said as she hurried into the pavilion after Zhi Ging. "Neoi Syu never wanted us to use them!"

The Silhouettes raced back in, dipping their brushes against lantern candles, careful not to touch the flames as they swirled the molten wax. Soon the grove was filled with the sound of brushes industriously sweeping wax over stones. The only other sound was that of gold province Silhouettes chanting the poem out loud, repeating the verses for the others.

Zhi Ging didn't even notice the rain had stopped until she heard Neoi Syu's shoes clicking back across the courtyard. The tutor's eyes flicked to the destroyed ink-stained scroll, a faint frown etched across her face. She stepped forward and there was a sharp crack.

Iridill's wax character had splintered beneath her heel.

Neoi Syu bent down and snapped it free from the stone. She held it up, examining the brushwork with a lantern. Without saying anything, she lowered the character to the flame. Warm light shone through it, the clear wax shimmering like glass as she observed the silently watching Silhouettes.

She bent the glowing wax between her hands, twisting it into a new word. The tutor winked at the group, then flung the wax high, its new edges catching the sunlight now streaming between clouds. Its shadow stretched over them, a single word outlined across their faces.

CONGRATULATIONS!

CHAPTER 26

"All right, Silhouettes, time for your Chau."

The group followed Neoi Syu to an unassuming restaurant. A faded banner hung above it, each of the characters now so sun-stained it was impossible to read.

As soon as the doors opened, Zhi Ging was greeted with the most delicious combination of smells. The tiny restaurant had one large circular table that filled the entire room. A wizened waiter nodded at the group, placing down a final porcelain bowl with an efficient click. His arms were covered with patches of white, and for a split second Zhi Ging wondered if he'd achieved the chroma-shifting Mynah was still working on. However, when he stepped forward she realized they were overlapping streaks of dried dough. The patches crackled as he gestured at the stools tucked beneath the table, hidden under its wide spinning surface.

"Take a seat," he said. "The others are already here."

As Zhi Ging's eyes adjusted to the gloom, she spotted familiar figures seated at the back of the tiny room.

Mynah waved brightly at them, her cheeks flashing gold, as Pinderent smiled up at them.

Zhi Ging beamed, her attempt to race to them slowed by the need to squeeze past Oimaa and Hoi Dak, who were hurrying toward their own friends. "What are you two doing here?"

"Well," Mynah began, her eyes sparkling as she glanced back to Neoi Syu, who was now deep in conversation with the waiter, "as I argued last night, I *technically* also passed this challenge, just months before all of you. So if I have to repeat lessons, they might as well let me repeat Chaus. Neoi Syu appreciates a good debate; she'll agree once you can make your words work for you. And now that she's agreed, all the other Cyo B'Ahon will too," she added triumphantly.

"How about you?" Zhi Ging asked, glancing over at Pinderent. She couldn't quite imagine him arguing his way into a Chau.

He flushed, nodding at Mynah as Hiulam and Jack joined them. "Mynah did it."

"Well, I didn't talk to Neoi Syu alone. I brought Bucbou with me as backup. There's not much she and I agree on—"

"The only agreement being your dragon boat tryout was the worst Team Bolei's ever had," Pinderent interrupted, his eyes gleaming.

Mynah gasped theatrically. "Well, excuse me for attempting something new."

He snorted. "Holding your paddle upside down definitely isn't something anyone's tried before, or since."

Mynah swatted him away good-naturedly. "Anyway. I explained that Oimaa, Hoi Dak, and I were all going to the Chau, and it wouldn't be fair for Pinderent to be left behind. Not when he'd been working so hard to find a way to improve the dragon boats. Despite our little hiccup at the waterfall, Bucbou agreed and told Neoi Syu as much. Well, I say that. She just frowned and barked, 'Pinderent too.'"

"Wait," Zhi Ging said, waving her hands in mock confusion. "So does Neoi Syu appreciate clever arguments *or* the world's shortest sentences?"

Mynah's cheeks shone bright yellow as the others burst out laughing.

"Ah, whatever. Grab the seats we've saved before someone else swipes them."

The other Silhouettes had begun to shuffle around, holding their breath as they squeezed past where the table almost touched the wall. Neoi Syu, G'Aam, and Wuyan were forced to ageshift down to fit in the narrow space. Zhi Ging sat with her back to the kitchen door, the scents wafting through it making her stomach rumble. Jack pulled out a stool beside her while Hiulam squeezed in on his other side.

Zhi Ging reached forward and lifted her plate, noticing

a curious splatter of cobalt blue along its porcelain base. She jerked her hand back as the ink wiggled beneath her fingers, scooting away to the far side of the porcelain.

"Ah-ah." The waiter reappeared beside Neoi Syu, tutting. "Please don't touch the plates before the meal has been served."

Iridill smirked at Zhi Ging from the far side of the table, flicking her long hair over her shoulder. It had frizzed slightly from the rain but was still annoyingly glossy. All traces of their reluctant truce outside had clearly been washed away.

"Ready?" The waiter leaned forward once Neoi Syu nodded, his hand gripping the edge of the glass turntable. With a strength that surprised everyone, he spun the glass until the plates became a whirring blur of white and blue. The spinning seemed to gather speed as he vanished back into the kitchen before materializing with two trays balanced on each arm and a fifth expertly stacked above his head.

Zhi Ging and the others ducked as bowls and plates were thrown overhead, each landing on the turntable and adding to the swirling colors. The porcelain seemed to dance before them, the percussion rattle of dishes reminding Zhi Ging of the music that had swelled over Pingon's parade. Eventually the glass turntable slowed to a halt and her eyes widened in surprise. The plate directly in front of her now had her name inscribed across its surface in elegant blue strokes.

"The spinning, while fun, also gives the plates the chance to pick who they want to pair with for the meal," the waiter explained before turning to Zhi Ging. "You can pick up your plate now, miss. I recommend filling it with as much as you can."

"Ooh, look, there's choi yuen ngo hor," Jack said excitedly. "It's the one thing the homei spoons never get quite right." He leaned forward, placing a generous helping of the glossy beef noodles onto Zhi Ging's plate before adding a portion to his own. "The rice noodles never taste as good without the heat of a properly hot wok."

Neoi Syu watched on happily as the Silhouettes spun the glass turntable back and forth, filling their plates with garlic king prawns, tea-smoked chicken, and pan-fried pork chops. Golden pieces of mantou were used to mop up rich curry sauce, while others dipped the steamed-then-fried buns into saucers of condensed milk.

Zhi Ging eventually leaned back, her stomach comfortably full. "Good thing Wusi needed Malo in the sick bay again. I think he'd have kept eating until he fell asleep," she sighed, stifling a yawn.

"Oh, I've almost done that," Jack said, using his own wide yawn as a chance to take one final bite of noodles.

Neoi Syu chuckled from the other side of the table, and Zhi Ging realized for the first time that none of the Cyo B'Ahon had been given a plate. Instead, their new tutor was simply sipping from a small teacup. "Weren't you hungry?" she asked in confusion.

"Ah no, the banquet isn't your Chau; those are." Neoi Syu leaned forward and waved a clean pair of chopsticks at Zhi Ging's newly empty plate. The Cyo B'Ahon stood up, tapping a finger against her porcelain teacup for silence. The clear chime cut through all the conversations, and the Silhouettes turned to face her, Kaolin still mid-slurp through an extra-large helping of soup noodles.

"I hope you've enjoyed your meal, and now it's time to enjoy your Chau."

There were confused looks between the Silhouettes, and a muffled hurried gulp from Kaolin.

"While Ling B'Aan"—Neoi Syu nodded to the waiter—"is an excellent cook, it's his pottery skills that are the real marvel."

It's not flour; it's clay! Zhi Ging realized as he bashfully waved away the compliment with a white-streaked hand.

Neoi Syu pointed down at the empty dishes in front of them. "These are fate plates. Ling B'Aan's creations allow you to glimpse the future, a brief vision of a moment that awaits you. While there's no telling whether what you see will take place ten minutes or ten decades from now, I hope you'll agree this is a particularly unique way to end a meal."

There were squeals of excitement as the Silhouettes lifted the plates up, their inky names now smeared across the porcelain and transforming into illustrations in front of their eyes.

Pinderent winced, flipping his plate upside down and

266

shutting his eyes. "No way. I don't want to see myself back home. Nothing ever happens in Geng Zun."

Jack frowned as he tried to decipher the blue ink image now tracing across his plate. "Is that meant to be me?" He pointed a chopstick at a blurred figure floating high above a crowd. "Oh, maybe I'm going to learn how to fly! Won't even need the lantern to take me to the next challenge." He laughed, tapping at the plate to try to get his miniature figure to move. Although the crowd beneath him swayed, his illustration stayed statue-still.

"Maybe you decide to become an acrobat, like the ones at the last Chau?" Zhi Ging suggested.

"Ha, don't say that to Reishi!" He lowered his voice so only Zhi Ging could hear. "He'll be seriously unimpressed if I leave Hok Woh again."

Zhi Ging lifted her plate, turning it between her hands. Beneath a faint layer of sauce, the blue ink had begun to move, twisting into a thin ribbon. It stretched out across the length of the plate, a dragon's face appearing at its front. Its claws flickered in and out of view, as if the ink hadn't made up its mind.

"I knew it!"

Zhi Ging's head jerked up as Hiulam screamed from the other side of Jack. She was waving her plate triumphantly, leaning forward to show them.

"Look! It's our dragon boat, but it's at the *top* of the waterfall!" She tapped the cheering figures as she passed the plate to Pinderent. "Ugh, I can't see how we climb it, but at least now we know we make it." The girl's smile vanished as she frowned at Zhi Ging's plate. "Whoa, what's happening in yours?"

Zhi Ging looked back down. The ribbon was split in two now; one half was still a dragon, while the other had formed into a vicious snaking cord. They watched as the cord chased after the dragon, its movements twitching as if controlled from afar. It latched onto the dragon and coiled around its body, causing the creature to break apart, blue fragments falling to the bottom of the plate.

"Stop it!" Zhi Ging cried as the dragon roared in silent pain. The cord ignored her, twisting the dragon's body into knots, looping tighter and tighter until they resembled a single Pan Chang Knot. The knot pulled, and the two halves erupted, mercury ink seeping across the plate. Zhi Ging began to wheeze, suddenly feeling like there was an invisible claw squeezing her entire body. The plate juddered, but her fingers were frozen in place and she couldn't let it go. The ink surged up to form a split face: one half that of Niotiya, the other Ami. The former Dohrnii snarled at her, and cracks appeared across the porcelain surface, gray steam erupting from its fissures.

Ling B'Aan leaped up, his mouth open in horror. Neoi Syu raced over, ageshifting down but struggling to get past the other Silhouettes. G'Aam leaped onto the table, empty dishes scattering around him; he snatched the plate from Zhi Ging and hurled it against the wall, where it finally shattered. A white Pan Chang, outlined in mercury, slid from the plate's surface and slithered across the restaurant floor. Wuyan stamped down on it, and a harsh leaden light erupted under his foot, blinding the entire room. When the light faded, the Pan Chang had vanished, leaving a dark scorch mark burned into the restaurant floor.

Zhi Ging collapsed to her knees, pulling her arms tight around herself. There was no sign of the gold lines, but in the final seconds before G'Aam had pulled the plate from her hands, it had felt like the split-faced woman had been trying to tug them loose.

Neoi Syu crouched down beside her and gestured quietly for Ling B'Aan to bring some tea while G'Aam and Wuyan shepherded the other wide-eyed Silhouettes out of the room.

Zhi Ging stared at the scorch mark until her eyes began to water. Her heart pounded in her ears, blurring the tutor's words. Why had Ami's face appeared? Had the fate plate been warning her that Niotiya and Ami worked together? But she had already figured that out. What had it been trying to tell her? She reached a shaking hand out toward the shards of porcelain. A fragment of blue was all that was left of the two half faces, a narrowed eye glaring up at her from the floor. Zhi Ging shuddered as she flipped it over, its jagged edges biting her fingers. It made no sense; fate plates were meant to show the future, not remind her of old nightmares.

Ami was safely trapped in her past.

Wasn't she?

CHAPTER 27

The next morning, the Silhouettes filed into a hazy greenhouse. Large incense coils swung from branches above them, delicate ribbons of blue smoke drifting up to the glass ceiling before cascading back over the group. Zhi Ging kept her eyes trained on the incense, determined to ignore the concerned looks the others were still shooting her a full day after Neoi Syu had cleared up the destroyed fate plate. If she squinted hard enough, the curling incense almost looked like miniature sleeping dragons.

"Ignore them," Mynah whispered, stepping forward to block Zhi Ging from the worst of the stares. "Pinderent's already doing enough worrying for the entire group; we don't need you thinking about the vision too."

"It's not like I wanted to see Ami and Niotiya on my fate plate," Zhi Ging muttered while Malo huffed from her hood, flapping his wings to shoo the others' curious glances away.

"Are we sure this isn't the Flora tutor's classroom?" Hiulam whispered, ducking under a low-hanging branch. Pine trees soared high above them, while the incense decorating every branch filled the greenhouse with the heady scent of jasmine and sandalwood. Zhi Ging peered closer at the trees behind Hiulam, confused by what looked like dozens of black shells sprouting along its trunk.

"Weird-looking leaves," Jack muttered as he leaned forward.

"Are they collecting something?" she asked, pointing to the liquid glinting at the center of one of the shells.

Just then Neoi Syu stepped out in front of the Silhouettes, carrying a small woven basket filled with the craggy black petals.

"They're clamshells," the tutor clarified, plucking one from a nearby tree. "This is the first step needed to create the ink used for calligraphy."

"It's pine sap," Mynah explained as Neoi Syu poured the liquid into a miniature vase tucked between the tree's roots. "She'll show us how to turn it into inksticks in our last week."

The tutor gestured for the Silhouettes to follow her, leading them toward the desks in the center of the greenhouse. Rather than a blackboard, the rows of desks faced six large fans, each the color of a different province. Above them, freshly pressed inksticks hung from pine branches, the drying black tokens clicking gently while pale smoke shimmered between them. Several Cyo

B'Ahon specializing in Calligraphy were balanced on ladders, taking notes as they checked the quality of the latest batch. They waved down at the Silhouettes before returning to their task.

Neoi Syu handed her basket to a nearby Cyo B'Ahon, then plucked an inkstick down.

"When I first arrived in Hok Woh, the fourth province wasn't known as the gold province; it was still the ink province. Back then a gram of ink cost more than a gram of gold, but I've helped generations of non–Cyo B'Ahon refine ink until it was easier to create." She tapped the inkstick against her palm. "I like to keep emergency stores here. All it'd take is one prolonged drought, and the supply would become rare again. I'm very happy to be the reason the gold province never returns to its original name."

Zhi Ging stared up at the hypnotic movement of the black inksticks dancing above them like a starling murmuration. It had never crossed her mind that provinces could change. What would the glass province be without dragons? Villagers were afraid of them, but the Glassmiths wouldn't be able to create anything without them. If they vanished, would it simply become the jade province?

"Calligraphy is often seen as an art form and nothing more," Neoi Syu said. "Being able to communicate through writing is a silent but eternal echo. I'll teach you how to share messages with anyone you want and, more important, how to share messages with *only* those you want. We're going to begin this week by exploring the methods of communication unique to each province. You'll quickly see there can always be new ways to connect. My skill is one of the most collaborative. Take Tai." She gestured to one of the Cyo B'Ahon quietly inspecting clamshells. They paused, nodding at the Silhouettes before turning back to the shell in their hand. "Tai is working with Tutor Wun on a form of sky messaging where, on their signal, winds can be released to shape clouds into sentences that can be read by those below. These will be crucial as warnings ahead of natural disasters."

She began pacing in front of the desks, gesticulating enthusiastically. "For something more secretive, there are many discreet forms of calligraphy. Farmers living beneath the glass province's cloud sea have spent generations sharing messages written on individual grains of rice. While I, shortly after my graduation, created a form of writing that can only be read by women, a hidden language to help those in areas that continue to mistakenly underestimate half their population."

There was faint giggling among the girls as the lilac thread along Neoi Syu's robe twisted loose to write *Shh, don't tell the others.* The tutor winked at them, then ran her hands across the fans decorating the wall behind her. "Today we'll start with the porcelain and paper provinces. These are provinces that have thrived with calligraphy."

Neoi Syu snapped the blue fan shut. The glass behind it had been hollowed out, a tall thin vase balanced at its center. The porcelain was completely blank, with nothing decorating its bone-white surface.

"Who can tell me what this is?" she asked.

The class looked around, waiting for one of the porcelain province Silhouettes to answer.

Eventually, Cing Yau raised a hesitant hand. "It's a gangsan vase. Everyone in my aunt's town uses them."

"Would you like to read what I've written inside it?" the tutor asked, lifting the vase out from its hiding place.

Cing Yau blanched. "Oh no, I couldn't. That wouldn't be right," she squeaked, leaning as far back as possible while Silhouettes from the other five provinces looked between them in utter confusion.

"Those words only have as much power as I give them," Neoi Syu said with a small shrug before turning to the rest of the class. She lifted the vase high, balancing it casually in her left palm.

"For those from the northern half of the porcelain province, gangsan vases are a common sight. In fact you'll see several in every home you visit. When people from this part of the province turn eighteen, they create their own vase. From that moment on, they fill it with slips of paper, each one scrawled with a secret insecurity or regret." She began spinning her vase between her hands. "The hope is that once you've written it out, you no longer carry that worry with you. Instead the porcelain will hold it for you, protecting you from those thoughts." She nodded at another of the porcelain province Silhouettes. "Would you like to explain what happens later?"

He cleared his throat, his eyes never leaving the vase. "After you die, your family reads through the slips and burns every single insecurity. We did this for my grandfather right before I arrived in Hok Woh . . . ," he added in a small whisper before trailing off.

The Silhouette beside him gave him a quick one-armed hug before taking over. "Then, uh, they collect all the paper ash and mix it with water to make ink. This is used by the family to write out all the best things about the person who passed. They write everything they loved about them on the gangsan vase until all the ink is used up."

Zhi Ging could see several of the porcelain province Silhouettes blink back tears; even Cing Yau's eyes had gone slightly red. She felt a sudden pang of sympathy. She'd never considered that others in Hok Woh might have already lost someone. Aapau was now halfway through her Final Year, but at least she was still here, traveling around Wengyuen in the roaming pagoda.

Neoi Syu lifted the gangsan vase back up, high enough for the final row of desks to see it clearly. Zhi Ging could feel the porcelain province Silhouettes tense.

"Once all the love and unspoken praise has been written out across the vase's surface, many families then smash the vase. Either dropping it off a cliff or traveling to the porcelain moat that surrounds Pingon, the province capital."

"Why would you destroy it after all that?" Zhi Ging blushed as she realized she'd blurted the thought out loud.

"The hope is," Neoi Syu explained softly, "the loved one will finally be free. They'll see themselves just as their family did, with none of their private insecurities. The power of others' words can change who you become." The tutor placed the vase carefully back in its wall space, and Malo's head popped out of Zhi Ging's hood as the Cyo B'Ahon moved toward the paper province fan. He chirped in excitement, pointing to the illustration of the Omophilli pagoda at its center. Neoi Syu snapped the fan back, and Zhi Ging had to lift herself up from her desk to see what was concealed behind it.

Rather than an ornate paper cutting or even a scroll, there at the bottom of the hollow was a folded wad of paper.

"Now, who wants to explain to the rest of the class what this is? How about you?" She nodded at one of the youngest paper province Silhouettes.

"It's a letter-locked message," the boy murmured, his ears burning red as the rest of the class turned to face him.

"Exactly." Neoi Syu gestured for him to fetch the paper and pass it around for the others to examine. "Let's see if anyone can read its note."

Zhi Ging noticed with interest that the other paper

province Silhouettes barely glanced at it before passing the message on. Iridill snatched the paper from Kaolin and tried to unfold it, attempting to prize it open with a nearby clamshell.

"Never going to work," Mynah whispered in a sing-song voice, clearly knowing what their tutor was about to say. Her cheeks flashed pale yellow as Iridill finally gave up and tossed the paper to their group. Jack caught it first and after a few unsuccessful moments handed the paper over to Zhi Ging.

She held her breath as it dropped into her hands. The last time she'd touched something from the paper province, her mother's face had flashed across it. However, unlike the sodden paper dragon head, this felt like it had been carved from jade. No matter how hard she tugged, the folds refused to loosen. After a few more tries she passed it to Hiulam, feeling surprisingly disappointed. Eventually the letter-locked message made its way back to the first Silhouette.

Neoi Syu tapped it with a closed fan, counting out the folds along its side. "Most paper can only be folded seven times. However, generations ago someone in the paper province developed a technique to fold parchment eight times. Many believe it happened when spirits were still friendly with humans, before they ever needed to be summoned." She shrugged, unaware of the knot that had suddenly tightened in Zhi Ging's stomach. "Exactly how to create this eighth fold was kept a highly guarded secret from the other provinces and was only ever carried out by senior Matchmakers. That meant, until I worked it out for myself, the Guild could—and would—charge ridiculous sums to letter-lock a message." A look of disapproval flashed across Neoi Syu's usually warm expression. The lilac embroidery on her robes flickered to life, a furious tight scrawl muttering about the Matchmakers' greed.

"Since the eighth fold shouldn't be possible, it causes a temporary ripple in reality," the Calligraphy tutor continued. "If you look along the edge, you'll see that it's been carefully stitched together. Thanks to the eighth fold, these stitches are one thousand times stronger than steel. Even with a blade you wouldn't be able to open a letter-locked message if you weren't its intended recipient."

"How do you open it if you are?" Zhi Ging asked.

"Like this." Neoi Syu replaced her fan and took the message from the Silhouette's unresisting hand. The second her fingers closed around it, the paper began to rattle. A thin black thread unwound across its folds, racing backward along the seams. She pocketed it and carefully unfolded the parchment, snatching an identical black string from its center.

"What was that?" Iridill demanded.

"Any of the paper province students want to explain?" Neoi Syu smiled encouragingly at the class.

"Once you've folded it," a girl beside Jack began hesitantly, "you seal it by stitching a strand of the recipient's hair through the eight folds. Most people also add one of

278

their hairs to the middle of the letter so the other person can write back straightaway."

"Ew," Iridill scoffed in a stage whisper.

"Miss Seoipin, just because it's not something you're used to doesn't make it gross. I encourage you to experiment with things that are new to you."

Mynah snorted and pointed at the tutor's sleeves. For a split second, the embroidered lilac pine trees had unfolded into a sharp message. *Might I suggest manners, for a start?*

Neoi Syu folded the paper back up. "As you'll learn, all forms of communication have their limits. Letter-locked messages can only be passed between people who know in advance they need to communicate. I doubt many of you have a collection of your friends' hairs in your room."

"Nope, my friend just keeps a totally normal secret stash of clay voice boxes in her room," Zhi Ging muttered under her breath, while Mynah's cheeks flashed teal in her attempt not to laugh.

"They are also an impossibility for those born without hair or who have become bald," Neoi Syu continued, gesturing for the Silhouettes to take notes.

Zhi Ging's eyes flicked to Iridill. The girl was scowling now, her hands twisting through her long hair. Although others might mistake it for her usual bored glare, Zhi Ging could read her pinched features perfectly. Favrile, Iridill's brother, had lost his hair after being struck by dragon lightning. Did Iridill still speak to him? It had been years since he'd left Fei Chui.

Since he was forced *out,* a quiet part of her mind corrected. Iridill's father had wanted nothing to do with his only son once it became clear his hair would never grow back. Without hair that glowed near dragons, he could never become the next Lead Glassmith. Iridill's shoulders stiffened, as if she could feel Zhi Ging's gaze.

She took in Zhi Ging's loose braid, sneering at the haphazard plait. *No one would write to you anyway,* she mouthed, her left eye flickering green.

Zhi Ging gritted her teeth and forced herself to turn back to their tutor, her nails digging furious crescent moons into her palms. Every single time Zhi Ging came close to feeling bad for Iridill, the girl managed to remind her that *she* was the main reason Zhi Ging had hated her time in Fei Chui.

"After lunch, we'll work on potential methods to improve letter-locked messages," Neoi Syu continued. "However, before that, let's come back to the gangsan vase." She picked up the porcelain once more, raising it up in one palm. The other Cyo B'Ahon in the greenhouse stopped what they were doing, turning to watch the class in anticipation.

"Why wait until a loved one has passed on? We should share our message with them now. Also, why carry worries and fears for your entire life? I'm immortal—imagine if I held on to everything. The vase would crack and break with the number of slips I'd try to squeeze into it. Which is why—"

She turned away from the Silhouettes and hurled the vase at the thick glass wall, where it shattered.

Cing Yau squeaked, her eyes wide as slips of paper appeared among the shards of white porcelain.

"I break mine annually. There's no need to hold on. Words have power, and sometimes the most powerful thing to do is release and forget them." Neoi Syu smiled at the stunned class, then glanced at their empty scrolls.

"I hope your homework scrolls look considerably better when you submit them tomorrow." She snapped shut a smaller fan in the center of the wall and began marching between desks, placing a single incense stick on top of each Silhouette's scroll.

Zhi Ging raised hers to her nose, but there was no scent.

"The Cyo B'Ahon who choose to specialize with me are all working on new forms of communication," Neoi Syu said as she reached Hiulam. "Of course, we use our jellyfish in Hok Woh, but what about when we want to share messages that can only be read once? Comments we don't want passed through hundreds of jellyfish and in turn their Cyo B'Ahon? These incense sticks were the result of a centuries-long collaboration with the Flora tutor." She strode back to the front of the class. "After much trial and error, we discovered that messages could be preserved if written on strips of agarwood left to dry under a full moon. This bark is then crushed and the powder used to create incense sticks. Although"—for a second her expression perfectly mirrored Reishi's right before he made a particularly terrible pun—"I hope the contents of your first homework stick don't *incense* you."

Mynah snorted, but the others looked up at Neoi Syu in confused silence.

"Oh, right. I've not shown you how they work yet." The tutor sighed, holding a spare stick against a lantern flame. Once it began to glow, she blew out the tip of the incense, and silky blue smoke streamed out, curling into their homework instructions for the night.

"No need to write this down," the Cyo B'Ahon said as several Silhouettes scrambled to copy out the swirling instructions. "The incense sticks will repeat the instructions." She pointed at the slowly fading smoke message above them. "This is how we used to communicate in the original Hok Woh, before we had jellyfish. Originally the messages only appeared if the flame was blown out by a Cyo B'Ahon's silk fan. If it was blown out any other way, it would just burn like normal incense. They became a way for Scouts to leave messages behind for the next Cyo B'Ahon to visit the area. For you, though, these incense sticks will share your homework instructions no matter how you blow them out. Meaning there's no excuse to show up empty-handed tomorrow."

CHAPTER 28

A few mornings later, the dining hall was filled with excited chatter as Zhi Ging walked in for breakfast. She searched the packed circular tables for her friends while overlapping snippets of conversation bounced across the walls.

Mynah waved. "Over here!"

"What's going on?" Zhi Ging asked as she squeezed in between Jack and Pinderent. Malo leaped on the table beside her, immediately snuffling the closest breakfast bowl.

"It's Iridill!" Hiulam said, sliding across a bamboo steamer filled with cha siu bao. Zhi Ging frowned and bit into one of the fluffy pork buns. *I bet it's not to do with her being the paint thief.* The dough became claggy on her tongue and she struggled to swallow it, a heavy layer of resentment filling her mouth. Why was Reishi still protecting Iridill's secret? He had refused to answer any questions about when or how Iridill would be punished, despite Zhi Ging asking at multiple air rail sessions.

"Her eyes. They're back to normal," Pinderent explained. "Wusi spotted they hadn't flickered at all during the last two Cure Clubs, so she asked her to stay overnight for a check. Mynah and I heard them talking this morning and—"

The doors flung open to reveal a smirking Iridill. She batted her eyelashes, showing off her deep brown eyes as every other Silhouette went silent, swiveling in their seats to stare at her in awe.

"There she is, the curse breaker!" came Kaolin's booming voice.

"I knew it'd be you. I always said you'd be first," Cing Yau fawned. She looped her arm through Iridill's, beaming to be seen beside her.

"She's not first," Hiulam muttered, stabbing a chopstick into a siu mai. "She's just the first from our group of Silhouettes." She rolled her eyes as several others hurried past their table, eager to congratulate Iridill. She shoved the yellow dumpling into her mouth, her left eye flashing between blue and green as she chewed furiously. "Has everyone else forgotten that most of the older Silhouettes have had brown eyes again for ages? Some have already been sent home because they're cured. And anyway, it's Wusi and D'Amask who broke the curse. All she did was drink the same tea as the rest of us."

"What was that?" Iridill snapped, turning to glare at their table. Silhouettes parted like a shoal of anxious fish as she strode toward them, Cing Yau and Kaolin flanking her.

"She's clearly jealous," Cing Yau hissed from behind her right shoulder.

"Obviously." Iridill rolled her eyes before reaching down to snatch up an unused homei spoon. "You can't even get through a cup of elixir without crying," she sneered, tapping the spoon against Hiulam's forehead. "Guess you'll be stuck with creepy colorful eyes forever."

"So what if she is!" Mynah leaped up, her arm and cheek patches flaring as she slammed her hands down on the table. Malo ruffled his feathers beside her, his rainbow-hued wings raised protectively in front of Hiulam.

Iridill ignored them, turning to Pinderent. "I can see why *you* don't want the elixir to work. Once your eyes switch back, you're out. You won't remember any of us, but trust me, we won't either. You're the least memorable person in all of Hok Woh."

"At least he's actually won a dragon boat race!" Zhi Ging snapped, her heart tightening as she glanced back to Pinderent. When was the last time *his* eyes flickered? They hadn't all breakfast.

"Who cares?" Kaolin muttered as Iridill rounded on Jack.

"And you, I don't even know why you bother with the elixir. I bet you weren't ever even possessed; you were just born looking like that." Iridill wrinkled her nose in disgust.

"At least you won't need to see any of them at Cure Club anymore," Cing Yau crowed, her eyes glittering maliciously.

"What do you mean?" Iridill snapped, turning to her with such intensity that the other girl took a step back.

Cing Yau's mouth opened and shut noiselessly, staring at her in confusion.

"You're cured," Mynah barked, the patches along her folded arms a stormy gray. "You don't need to come to Cure Club anymore."

"You'll get the whole dorm to yourself," Cing Yau added, a desperate smile stretching tight across her face. "I'm so jealous. I'd give anything not to be squashed into the sick bay dorm, listening to Hiulam struggling with her elixir. Instead, you get to spend the entire evening doing whatever you want."

"Alone?" Iridill asked, a strange note in her voice as she twisted her arm out from Cing Yau's grip.

Kaolin nodded. "Yeah, you're so lucky! I bet no one else fully recovers for weeks too; it'll be like you're the only Silhouette in all Hok Woh."

Zhi Ging scowled up at him, the last of her cha siu bao now flattened under her fingers. Her and Jack's detention with Neoi Syu in the lantern archive was actually ending that week, not that Kaolin considered her a real Silhouette with her golden Pan Chang.

"Congratulations, you deserve it," Mynah muttered, a flash of coral bursting across her cheeks.

The homei spoon clattered to the table, and without a word Iridill spun around, the color draining from her face as she stormed out of the dining hall.

"WHAT DO YOU THINK THAT WAS ALL ABOUT?" ZHI Ging asked as she handed Jack the final handwriting sample. Malo was waddling between the trees, a miniature scroll tucked in his beak.

He shrugged, staring listlessly up at the lanterns above them. Zhi Ging took a step closer, watching how his eyes flicked rapidly between blue and green. He was the only Silhouette who hadn't spent all day guessing why Iridill hadn't come to class. Surely it would have been the perfect moment to show off her newly recovered eyes. Instead, Mynah had been asked to stay back after class, and by dinner Zhi Ging was already hearing ridiculous rumors that Mynah had said something far worse than congratulations that morning.

"Hey, are you all right?" she asked, nudging Jack's arm.

He sighed, unable to look at her. "I just—well, what if Iridill's right?"

"What?" She blinked hard, scarcely able to believe she'd just heard "Iridill" and "right" in the same sentence.

Jack began to twist a scroll, the dark ink flashing up at them as he curled it tight between his hands. "I know we started thinking I only Reverted because Ami possessed me, but what if that's not true after all? What if I've really always had eyes like this?" He hit the scroll against a low-lying lantern, the soft thwack muffled by the surrounding paper. "It's so annoying not remembering anything.

I thought coming back would help, but there's been nothing!"

"We could ask Reishi? I bet he—"

"No, I don't want him to know." He took a deep breath and turned back to Zhi Ging, his eyes now a constant shimmering teal. "Don't tell the others, but if it turns out I really have always looked like this, I'm going to leave. I only ever agreed to take Silhouette entrance exams to save up enough money to get a tent at the floating market . . ."

"So you could visit that silk province village." Zhi Ging finished his sentence for him. Snatches of Jack's apology as they left her Perception challenge months earlier flashed through her mind. "They're the only others who definitely have eyes like yours."

"Exactly. Maybe if I can talk to someone there, I can find out whether I really was possessed, or maybe"—he took a deep breath, finally turning to face Zhi Ging— "maybe someone there will know where I can find my family."

"Do you know how to get there?"

"No," Jack admitted, scratching the back of his neck.

They were silent for a while, staring at the hundreds of lanterns swaying from the silk province tree. Had any of those Silhouettes come from the village he was looking for?

Zhi Ging suddenly clapped her hands together, causing Malo to chirp in surprise, before turning to Jack with a large smile. "I know who we can ask."

"No, I really don't want any Cyo B'Ahon to know about this."

"They won't! Well, not a current one, at least." She spun on her heels, hurrying for the door.

"What are you talking about?" he called after her, gathering the lanterns and scrolls they'd matched over detention.

Zhi Ging paused with a hand on the door and turned to beam at him. "All we need to do is break into the Dohrnii's office. *Your* old office. I bet we'll find something there."

ZHI GING AND JACK STOOD IN FRONT OF THE frosted glass door, their hearts thudding as they waited for a lone jellyfish to float past. Once it was gone, she tried to slide the door open, but it wouldn't budge. Zhi Ging traced her fingers along its surface, searching for the frame edge, but it blended seamlessly with the walls surrounding it.

"One of the Cyo B'Ahon must have done something to seal it," she muttered in annoyance.

Malo chirped from her hood and raised one wing, flames sparking across his feathers.

"We're going for a stealth break-in, remember?" She shook her head with a smile, her hand passing harmlessly through the flame to lower his wing back down. "Turning the door into a glass puddle might not be the best way to do that."

Jack crouched down, a curious expression flickering

across his face as he peered at a circular indent in the center of the door.

"Let me try something." He placed his hand against the mark, and the glass gleamed, faint clicks echoing down the empty hallway as the door unlocked.

"Glass never forgets," Zhi Ging breathed, remembering Aapau's old adage. "It remembers when you were still Dohrnii."

The door slid back, and they stepped inside. The office was ice-cold, thin light shining through the walls to reveal a moment frozen in time. Ami's final cup of tea as Dohrnii still sat undrunk above a half-opened drawer. Zhi Ging shuddered as the Cyo B'Ahon's face flashed across her mind, smirking as she fell backward into the underwater waterfall.

"Let's try to find some of your old scrolls, then get back to the dorm. I . . ." Zhi Ging stopped.

There, behind the desk, was an opaque tank. It began to rattle, something solid thumping against the dark glass.

Marzi.

Zhi Ging had forgotten all about Ami's old jellyfish. She snatched a scrap of parchment from the table and scrawled a frantic note to Jack.

DON'T LET HIM HEAR US!

They began to search in silence, the constant angry thuds sending shivers down Zhi Ging's spine.

Suddenly there was a sharp clang behind her. Jack had climbed a reading ladder to reach some of the higher scrolls, but it had unhooked from the shelf. It now tilted backward, leaving him dangling above the tank by just one hand. Zhi Ging ran forward, but the final rung snapped just before she could reach him.

"No!" Her left hand shot out instinctively, and air rails blazed to life, solid gold beams filling the room.

Jack landed hard against one and quickly climbed down, staring in awe at the gold frame surrounding him. "How did you do that?"

"I'm not sure. Reishi and I never got anywhere close to this . . ." Zhi Ging trailed off as Malo flew to one of the higher air rails, hopping between beams in delight. She followed underneath him, her now-gold-lined arms outstretched in case he slipped.

Crack.

Her heart dropped as an air rail shot through the opaque tank, shattering the glass. Water spilled out, pooling across the floor and seeping into her shoes. Zhi Ging dropped her hands, and the gold beams vanished.

"No, no, no." She raced forward but it was too late; the tank was empty, with no sign at all of the captured jellyfish.

Marzi had escaped.

CHAPTER 29

Sintou glowered at the two Silhouettes in front of her. Seven other Cyo B'Ahon were gathered around her, Reishi and Yingzi among the inner circle. Malo poked his beak out of Zhi Ging's hood before quickly burrowing back in, squirming as all eight immortals turned to stare at him. The white flame behind Sintou's office walls now hovered directly above them, a blinding spotlight on Zhi Ging and Jack. Zhi Ging shuffled uncomfortably, trying to scrunch her hands into her sleeves to hide the gold lines that still covered her palms.

"Did you believe I had sealed Ami's office for no reason?" The Head of the Cyo B'Ahon's voice was terse as she examined a shard from Marzi's former tank.

"I just wanted to—" Jack began.

"It was my idea." Zhi Ging stepped forward. "I thought that maybe we could help Jack remember his time as Dohrnii."

"No memories are retained after a Cyo B'Ahon chooses

292

to Revert. It's an irreversible removal. You were warned multiple times before you made that decision, Jack. I appreciate that you don't remember now, but your recklessness—both when you chose to leave your position as Dohrnii and tonight—has put all of Hok Woh at risk."

"But what if he didn't really make that choice!" Zhi Ging blurted out, her cheeks burning as the Cyo B'Ahon turned the full force of their gazes on her. "Think about it: you were also going to Revert," she plowed on, speaking directly to Sintou's shoes. "But that wasn't really your idea, was it? It was Ami convincing you it was your choice. Well, what if she practiced with Jack first? It'd make sense to get rid of the current Dohrnii if she wanted his job."

The room was silent. After a few seconds Zhi Ging risked looking up. Sintou had shut her eyes, her face deep in concentration.

Jack opened his mouth and the Cyo B'Ahon held a gnarled finger up, commanding silence. Above them, the flame flowed back down the walls, removing its harsh spotlight on Zhi Ging and Jack.

"Gertie and I already took that into consideration when I allowed Jack to return as a Silhouette. However, Ami was not involved in tonight's incident." Sintou opened her eyes, deep creases running down either side of her mouth as she frowned at Jack. "Regardless of the intentions, you both deliberately chose to break into the Dohrnii's office."

The door behind Zhi Ging slid open, and Ai'Deng

Bou hurried in, stepping past the Silhouettes to bow in front of Sintou.

"Well?" the Head of the Cyo B'Ahon asked, her expression tense.

"Still no sign of Marzi. I've put the other jellyfish on high alert, but there's been no sighting of him anywhere," he admitted.

"Let us know the second he's found. Until then, G'Aam and Wuyan will continue standing guard in front of both dorm doors, in case Ami's jellyfish plans to attack either group of Silhouettes," Reishi added from beside Sintou.

Jack's face crumbled. "I'm so sorry," he croaked. "We really didn't mean to do any of this."

"Actions, not apologies, are what's needed right now, Jack," Yingzi scoffed, fingers drumming her metallic crane's leg.

"Now now," Reishi sighed. "We could have listened to Ai'Deng Bou's original advice, moving Marzi to a more secure room months ago."

"No other Silhouette has ever formerly been Dohrnii, though," Yingzi snapped back. "No one else could have unlocked the door's seal."

Sintou slammed her hand onto the checkers table, causing Zhi Ging and Jack to jump, while several Cyo B'Ahon ageshifted down in shock. "Enough! I don't want to hear it."

In the strained silence, everyone heard the faint clink of metal hitting glass as three gray tokens slipped from the hexagonal table, rolling forward until they hit Zhi Ging's shoe. She crouched down to pick them up, her gaze sliding past Sintou's outstretched hand. Five of the checkerboard's six points were now covered in piles of gray tokens. Only Omophilli's pagoda remained visible on the sixth point, the mother-of-pearl glinting.

"What are these?" Zhi Ging murmured, placing the tokens in the center of the board.

"That's not necessary for you to know," Yingzi began, before quickly shutting her mouth as Sintou raised an eyebrow in warning.

The Head of the Cyo B'Ahon gestured for Jack to join Zhi Ging by the board.

"I want you both to understand just how much damage you've caused by releasing Marzi." Sintou considered both of them in turn, the air becoming so thick with blame that Zhi Ging found it difficult to breathe.

"Each of these," Sintou said, sweeping a hand over the piles of metal tokens, "tracks reports of recent spirit attacks across five of the six provinces. Attacks that took place after Ami fell into the underwater waterfall."

"But that doesn't make sense; she was the Fui Gwai. Why are the attacks still happening?" Zhi Ging asked, looking around the Cyo B'Ahon in confusion.

"It's not the Fui Gwai," Yingzi muttered, glaring so hard at the tokens that Zhi Ging was surprised they didn't burst into flames. "It's a new eight-legged sand spirit. One the Folklore tutor has never encountered."

"The key difference between previous spirit attacks and these new ones," Reishi added, "is they're now exclusively targeting Silhouette-age children. Not a single adult has vanished since Ami's disappearance."

Sintou continued, "Only we Cyo B'Ahon know what really happened to her. No one else in Wengyuen will have heard about the underwater waterfall. If the Matchmakers really were working for—or with—Ami, they may be enjoying their new unrestricted freedom." She gestured to the tokens. "The rate of spirit attacks on children spiked the week she vanished."

"But what do the Matchmakers want children for?" Zhi Ging asked quietly, the metal tracks stretching into darkness flashing across her mind. *Dippy and I never found out what was at the end of that tunnel . . .*

"That's what we're still trying to work out," Sintou admitted with a sigh. "We're also yet to solve how the Matchmakers have gotten sand spirits to obey them."

"You said five of the six provinces," Zhi Ging said slowly, her eyes drawing back to the empty Omophilli pagoda. "Why aren't they attacking the paper province?"

"Are the Matchmakers avoiding children from their own province?" Jack wondered out loud.

"Either that or they're simply more familiar with their home province. They know which children can be taken without notice or creating a fuss," Reishi murmured.

"Each of these"—Sintou lifted a token from the porcelain province pile—"represents ten missing children." As she twisted the gray token in the light, names appeared scratched across its surface.

"Whatever Ami and the Matchmakers had plotted, it's definitely ramping up," Yingzi continued. "We now need to hope Ami was too paranoid to share the final stages of the plan with them in advance."

"A while ago, at dragon boat training, one of the captains mentioned fighting the sand spirits. Would that . . . ?" Zhi Ging trailed off as Sintou began to shake her head.

"I've already explained it to him multiple times. Although we can ageshift, we mustn't forget we're still just human. No matter how many centuries a Cyo B'Ahon spent preparing, there'd be no guarantee they could take on a spirit and win. Even if every Cyo B'Ahon in Hok Woh was involved, there's still an infinitely larger number of sand spirits across Wengyuen's deserts. Our best way to stop the sand spirits is to stop the Matchmakers."

G'AAM NODDED AS ZHI GING AND JACK APproached the dorm. He slid the door open, his eyes scanning the dark corridor behind them for any sign of Marzi. Zhi Ging stifled a yawn as they slipped past him. The discussion between Sintou and the others was still raging, and it was only after Malo had started snoring in her hood that Reishi had suggested the two Silhouettes head to bed.

"Night," Jack murmured, swinging his arm in an exhausted wave before dragging his feet to his room.

The dorm was almost completely dark now; even the Silhouettes who loved midnight snacks were fast asleep. The only room still lit up was Iridill's; a bright glow beamed down from the upper floor.

Zhi Ging shook her head, feeling bad for the Silhouettes on either side of her. *That light's much worse than someone snoring.*

Just before she turned for her door, Zhi Ging spotted someone creep out of Iridill's room. As the figure closed the screen door behind them, their arm lit up in a warm glow of light. Zhi Ging gasped, unable to believe what she was seeing. The person's arm was covered in colorful patches of yellow and blue. *Mynah?*

Confusion swelled inside Zhi Ging, stinging bubbles of hurt knocking the air from her lungs. She raced to the wooden ladder, her eyes never leaving her friend as she pulled herself up the rungs two at a time. Mynah had never sneaked out to visit her after moving to the sick bay dorm. Why was she secretly hanging out with Iridill?

Zhi Ging landed with a thud on the upper platform, not caring if she woke anyone up. Mynah's eyes widened as she spotted her, and every single one of her patches went pebble gray.

"What's going on?" Zhi Ging demanded, betrayal slicing down her back like shards of burning ice. "Since when are you two friends?"

Mynah winced, the glow from Iridill's room highlighting Zhi Ging's hurt scowl.

"We're not!" she hissed back, her eyes darting to the screen doors around them. "It's complicated. I'm not meant to say . . ." She broke off, pointing toward Zhi Ging's room.

The two Silhouettes climbed down the ladder in silence, Mynah leading the way past the low-burning fire.

"So when did this start?" Zhi Ging muttered, slumping on her bed while Mynah quietly slid the screen door shut behind them. "Let me guess: It's something *else* I missed at Cure Club?"

"No! I know we were possessed, but that doesn't mean I suddenly think she's nice; no curse is strong enough for that. It's just"—Mynah sighed, tracing a hand along her arm patches as she sank into a crouched squat on the floor—"I'm the only Silhouette who gets what she's going through."

"What do you mean?"

"Reishi and Sycee brought Iridill up to the sick bay a few weeks ago. After you and Pinderent caught her as the paint thief. They had a long, whispered conversation with Wusi, then came to fetch me. I'd already been trying to listen from the dorm door, so my fake yawn probably wasn't too convincing." She shrugged, her cheek patches flashing lime green. Mynah turned to Zhi Ging then, the corners of her mouth drooping down. "Do you remember when we first met? You asked about my patches and I explained I had vitiligo. Well, I don't mind them now, but honestly"—she sighed again, tugging at the edge of her

299

sleeve—"the first few times I spotted the patches in my reflection it felt weird. Like it wasn't really me. Does that make sense?"

"'Course," Zhi Ging said softly, unfolding her arms and wrapping one around her friend. She had felt just as strange the first time the gold lines had swirled across her fingers, but at least those had faded away.

"Well, that's how Iridill felt."

"What do you mean?"

"Her eyes," Mynah explained, pushing up from the floor. Her reflection rippled in the frosted glass wall as she began to pace. "Her eyes only turned blue and green because of Ami's possession. At least my vitiligo was never caused by someone else."

"But you all got blue and green eyes," Zhi Ging grumbled. "It's not like everyone in Hok Woh was staring at her or the other Silhouettes gave her a horrible nickname." The sting of years of being called NoGlow and teased for not having hair that lit up near dragons washed over her. *Maybe it's about time Iridill learned how that feels.*

"That's the thing," Mynah explained. "No one had to. Every single thing someone could have whispered behind Iridill's back, she was already saying to herself."

"I don't see why that . . . Anyway, it doesn't matter. Her eyes are back to normal now."

"I'm not explaining this well. Where have we not scrubbed . . . ?" Mynah added under her breath, before grabbing Zhi Ging's arm and pulling her out of the dorm.

They came to a stop a few minutes later in front of one of the last remaining stripes of bright yellow paint, its surface glowing against the mirrorlike glass.

"What do you see?" Mynah asked, turning Zhi Ging to face the blank wall behind them.

"Um, a jellyfish?" she guessed, nodding at the single passing jellyfish, who waved politely back at them.

"What else?" Mynah pushed, her eyes almost comically wide as she tapped pointedly at the glass.

Zhi Ging frowned, watching her eyebrows furrow together in front of her. "Oh!" she yelped. "My reflection!"

"Exactly. Now imagine something about you had changed, and you hated your reflection each time you walked to and from class." Mynah slowly spun Zhi Ging back to the yellow line. "Can you see why she did this now? It had nothing to do with trying to get you kicked out of Hok Woh."

Zhi Ging peered at the line hovering just above her forehead and shook her head. "Not really," she admitted, watching Mynah's eyebrows shoot up in confusion.

The other girl frowned at their rippling reflections, then crouched down so they were the same height.

"Oh, Iridill and I are taller than you. Shut your eyes and stand on your toes . . . Now open them again!"

Zhi Ging obediently followed her friend's strange instructions, then gasped as she opened her eyes. Of course.

"I can't see my eyes anymore," she whispered, reaching out to tap the yellow line. No wonder Reishi had understood once he ageshifted to Iridill's height. The lines painted across Hok Woh hadn't been random after all. Instead, each one had been carefully painted at Iridill's exact eye level. Meaning she never had to see her own reflection. Never had to be reminded of Ami's possession.

Zhi Ging thought back and the pattern behind the painted lines became suddenly, blindingly clear. Over the past months, there had been flurries of new lines every few weeks. She hadn't really paid them much attention, beyond using them to avoid Cure Club chat. If she had, she might have noticed that they appeared after every challenge, when the Silhouettes were assigned a new tutor. Each time Iridill had to walk down different corridors to a new classroom.

Zhi Ging got back off her toes. Her reflection in the glass looked different now; the scowl was gone.

"I'm not saying what she did was right," Mynah continued, "and Sycee made that pretty clear when she spent an hour screaming at Iridill in the sick bay, but I can understand why she did it. It's not easy to suddenly find your own face uncomfortable."

"I'm sorry if you ever felt like that, Mynah," Zhi Ging murmured.

Her friend shrugged. "I can't imagine being without my patches now; they're part of me. That's why Reishi changed my detention from scrubbing paint with Pinderent and Hiulam to spending an hour every night talking to Iridill, trying to explain that her eyes didn't change who she was." Mynah sighed, shaking her head as she led them back to the dorm. "I assumed my detention would finish today once her eyes went back to normal, but apparently not."

"Is that why you had to stay back after class?"

"Yeah. For some reason Iridill seemed to forget that the whole point of Cure Club was to lift the last of the possession. Apparently"—Mynah lowered her voice as they stepped past G'Aam back into the dorm—"when she stormed off this morning she ran straight up to the sick bay and started screaming at D'Amask for not warning her what would happen once she drank her final batch of elixir."

"Of course she did." Zhi Ging rolled her eyes as she followed Mynah back up the ladder.

"Wusi managed to calm her down eventually, and that's when it all came out." Mynah paused as she reached the first platform, pulling Zhi Ging up behind her. "Iridill didn't want to leave Cure Club. Not because she was going to miss everyone, but because she's scared to be by herself. When Ami turned us into thralls, most of us were still together in the banquet hall, but Iridill was alone. She was on her way back from the bathroom when she was attacked."

Zhi Ging glanced at the glowing room beside them. "I didn't know that."

"Neither did I. She never shared it with anyone during Cure Club. Wuiyam's now offered to help remove the fear from her memories, but it'll take time. Until then, she'll have to rely on this."

Mynah quietly slid Iridill's bedroom door open, and Zhi Ging's jaw dropped. Every single surface, from the floor to ceiling, had been coated in a thick layer of glowing yellow paint. Iridill was curled up in the center of her bed, her knitted yellow scarf clutched tight between her sleeping hands like a safety blanket.

"I helped her finish painting it this evening," Mynah explained, holding up paint-spattered palms. "It's the only way she agreed to be alone." She closed the door gently, then turned back to Zhi Ging, her expression serious. "You can't tell any of the others about this. Wusi swore me to secrecy."

"Of course. I don't want Sycee coming after you too, but"—Zhi Ging hesitated—"why were you still here when I got back? Surely it didn't take that long to paint?"

Mynah bit her lip, her cheek patches fading to stormy blue before continuing. "Iridill didn't talk to me for the entire two hours we were painting, but just before I was going to leave she told me something. I got the feeling she hasn't even admitted it to Wusi or Wuiyam yet . . ."

"What? What did she say?"

Mynah paused, then puffed out her cheeks.

"Her eyes going back to normal? It's not made her feel better. It's actually made things worse. At least before, when she accidentally caught her reflection, she sometimes wouldn't recognize it as herself, but now . . ."

Mynah's voice was barely loud enough to hear even when Zhi Ging leaned in. "It's made me scared of the elixir working. Iridill told me that now when she spots herself in the glass, it reminds her of being trapped on the other side, a frozen thrall caught inside the water-filled walls of the catacombs."

Zhi Ging winced and squeezed her friend's hand tight. "If that happens to you, I'll help paint every wall in this entire realm."

CHAPTER 30

The next night, after another unsuccessful detention matching Silhouette handwriting to lanterns,
Zhi Ging made her way to Reishi's lab for her now
joint air rail sessions with Pinderent. Although she could
make them appear for more than a minute at a time,
weight continued to be the main issue. The air rails refused to reappear as strongly as they had in Ami's office.

"Bucbou's sure they're the answer," Pinderent said as
he slid open the lab door. "Hiulam was bragging about
her waterfall fate plate, so now she wants Team Bolei out
first once training restarts at the end of this week." The
teak dragon boat had been propped against several tanks,
and Malo flew to the top before wriggling into a sitting
position. Zhi Ging chuckled as the little phoenix slid
down the length of its wooden frame, both wings flung
out joyously. Ever since Wuiyam's first class with the spiral staircase, Malo had become obsessed with seeing what
else he could use as a slide.

"Ah, there you are." Reishi waved before leaning back over his desk, moving small figures across a map of Wengyuen. "Please go ahead. I'll join you in a moment."

Zhi Ging glanced across at Pinderent, and he shrugged. They set to work, lowering the dragon boat to the floor, much to Malo's dismay, and began flicking through Pinderent's latest ideas.

"I like this one," Zhi Ging said, pointing at a detailed sketch of a giant silk lantern attached to the dragon boat. "Also, it means we don't have to rely on my air rails."

"But was it on Hiulam's fate plate?" Pinderent asked, peering closely at the illustration.

"I don't think so," Zhi Ging admitted, "but her plate only showed us on the other side of the waterfall. What if we released the ropes right before that?"

"I do think the answer's something to do with silk, but it's still not quite right." Pinderent sighed. "What did you think of the hydrophobic pebble idea?" he asked, handing Zhi Ging a rough sketch of metal paddles studded with the water-hating stones.

"Maybe, but I'd be worried the paddles would just shoot out of our hands," Zhi Ging said, scrunching her nose. It was hard enough keeping waves from snatching their paddles away. Would she really be able to hold on to one that was actively trying to avoid the water?

"Yeah, that needs a bit of work." Pinderent glanced across at Reishi, who still showed no sign of joining them. "I guess we can practice with the air rails again until he's ready?"

Zhi Ging shuffled to the center of the lab and shut her eyes, knees bent as she strained to keep the air rails solid beneath her fingers. In front of her, Pinderent and Malo attempted to maneuver the dragon boat onto the single golden beam without it snapping.

Whatever Reishi was working on, there were faint pops every so often as he ageshifted down, trying to solve the puzzle in front of him. Finally, after forty minutes, Zhi Ging and Pinderent gave up, red in the face from the effort of trying to hold on to the air rails and lifting the teak boat.

"Do you think he's forgotten we're here?" Pinderent whispered, nodding at the Cyo B'Ahon.

"I don't know how." Zhi Ging shook her head. "The tanks rattle each time the boat slams down off an air rail." The jellyfish in the tanks closest to them nodded vigorously, pointing tentacles at the numerous puddles now splattered across the lab floor.

"Maybe we try again tomor—" Pinderent began, the end of his sentence vanishing inside a yawn. "Sorry," he said. "I've been up since six this morning working on ideas. I really want to help solve the dragon boat problem before I'm . . ."

He trailed off, and Zhi Ging felt her heart tighten. Only getting to spend time with Pinderent at air rail sessions and dragon boat training wasn't enough.

Their conversation was interrupted by a loud sigh from Reishi. He stretched and rubbed his eyes before abandoning the map, placing it on Gahyau's bubble before gesturing for the jellyfish to return it to a bookshelf beside the two Silhouettes.

"What's that meant to be?" Zhi Ging asked in confusion, pointing at the map as Gahyau hovered next to her, searching for a space on the crammed shelves. "There definitely isn't a lake halfway up the jade mountain." Up close, the map wasn't a Wengyuen she recognized at all; each river and lake had been drawn in the wrong place. The waterfall that had filled Bucbou's every waking thought for months didn't even appear on it.

"This is a map of what's beneath Wengyuen's surface. It's every tunnel and cave across the six provinces." Reishi frowned, drumming his fingers along the tanks as he walked toward them. "At least, all the ones we're aware of."

He pointed at several new-looking lines on the map. "I've been updating this with the other Scouts ever since I recovered, trying to work out where the Matchmakers could have hidden the chi—" He stopped, suddenly aware of Pinderent staring at them.

"Let's finish for the night. Pinderent, you're happy to bring the dragon boat back to its usual stepping stone, yes? Thank you very much." The Cyo B'Ahon waited until a very flustered Pinderent vanished down the corridor, the boat's wooden tail thumping against glass, before turning back to Zhi Ging.

"Shouldn't we warn the province rulers? Let them know what's going on?" she asked.

"It's complicated. Quite a lot of them are considerably closer to the Matchmakers than they are to us. We only visit to host the Silhouette entrance exams, and some rulers get very offended when their children aren't selected." Reishi sighed and ageshifted back up to fifty. "We can't reveal anything too soon. Once the Matchmakers know we suspect them, we lose our advantage, small as that is. Right now it's difficult to know which rulers we can really trust. Any one of them could use the information to try to win favor at the next Matchmaker Ceremony."

He paused, his eyes suddenly narrowed in thought.

"Zhi Ging, you're eleven, right? This was your first Silhouette Scout exam?"

"Well, it was my first exam, but I'm twelve. You didn't come to Fei Chui the year before, remember?"

Reishi went pale and rushed to a basin on the other side of the bookshelf. Gahyau shot after him, landing in the water with a splash. He held out his tentacles as the Cyo B'Ahon scrawled an urgent note on a slip of rice paper. Before Zhi Ging had a chance to read it, ink rippled through the jellyfish's body, and he shot into the glass wall.

Malo chirped uneasily, snuffling Zhi Ging's leg. She lifted him up, watching Reishi with growing concern as the Cyo B'Ahon began to pace.

"What is it?" she asked, unsure if she wanted to know the answer.

Reishi glanced at her, opened his mouth, then shook

his head. "It's best if Sintou explains," he said, waving a hand at the lab door.

Zhi Ging turned to it, her heart pounding as the minutes counted down.

Eventually, the lab entrance flew open, the Head of the Cyo B'Ahon striding into the room. Every single jellyfish bowed as she walked past, the water in their tanks rippling to reflect her golden robes.

"I've not been summoned out of my private office by anyone in five decades, and now it happens twice in two months. What's going on, Reishi?" she demanded, her eyebrows raised.

"I know why they're searching for her," he said in a quiet voice.

"What?" Zhi Ging yelped, glancing between the two Cyo B'Ahon. Ice-cold recollection spilled down her spine. Reishi had kept something hidden all those weeks ago back in the sick bay, when Jack had asked what had been on the Matchmakers' scrolls.

Reishi finally stopped pacing and pulled something from a nearby bookshelf before handing it to Zhi Ging. "I'd been hoping we could protect you from this." She took the worn parchment and stared at it in confusion.

"I don't get it. This is just the arrest warrant the Lead Glassmith put out for me." For a split second, hope bubbled through Zhi Ging. Maybe there was nothing to worry about after all; maybe Reishi had forgotten she already knew about them.

"Take a seat, Zhi Ging." Sintou's strained voice shattered that hope.

"The Matchmakers were using these arrest warrants back in the cavern. Checking the faces of each child they'd kidnapped," Reishi said with a grimace.

"Why?" Zhi Ging's question came out as a faint croak.

"Your mother's paper-cutting power will nearly be spent now," Sintou explained, her mouth a thin, somber line. "Ever since Ling Geng, the first in your line to have spirit magic, the ability to cut reality from paper has never lasted more than thirty years. This year should have been the Matchmaker Ceremony, where you, Zhi Ging, took over from your mother, officially becoming the new paper cutter in the pagoda."

"But you're not there. Obviously." Reishi took over. "Meaning the Matchmakers now have no one to offer at this month's ceremony."

Sintou nodded. "Which explains why they're desperately searching for you."

"So they're not just looking for me because they think I stole the paper cuttings from Pingon?" Zhi Ging winced as another question seeped into her mind. "But why are they keeping the other children?" she added in a small voice. "They're not releasing them even after they're obviously not me."

Was this her fault? Were these kidnappings happening because of her?

"We've not worked that out yet," Reishi admitted,

tracing a finger across the maps' tunnels. "But I suspect it's nothing good."

"We Cyo B'Ahon used to rule over all of Wengyuen. After our influence faded following the attack on the original Hok Woh, the Matchmakers leaped into that role." Sintou glowered, deep lines burrowing across her cheeks. "Although some could argue they'd been enjoying power for centuries, subtly pitting the provinces against one another—despite our work to prevent conflict. It's in their Guild's interest for there not to be friendships or alliances between the six provinces."

"They only benefit when the provinces are fighting for the paper-cutting powers," Reishi agreed. "Not once has any ruler considered the fact that, rather than competing every twelve years for exclusive access, they could instead share the power. None of them will accept a smaller amount of cuttings, though." He frowned and crossed his arms, a dozen jellyfish mirroring his movement in the tanks behind him. "The Matchmakers have fueled this competitive mindset, and I doubt they'll simply let the power they've carefully built up over decades go without a fight. Something big is coming, and I suspect it'll be revealed at the Matchmaker Ceremony."

"What can we do in the meantime?" Zhi Ging asked, her heart racing.

Reishi glanced across at Sintou, who narrowed her eyes and nodded.

"I think, Zhi Ging, we need to have a serious discussion

about keeping you in Hok Woh until after that moment has passed. Sintou and I need to decide whether it's safe for you to take part in the next challenge."

WHEN ZHI GING CREPT BACK INTO THE DORMS, IT was silent apart from the faint crackle of the fireplace. Malo had refused to leave her side since Reishi and Sintou's revelation, and he now bounded headfirst into her room, wings spread protectively in case any Matchmakers were lurking inside.

"I think we should be safe in here." Zhi Ging turned her attention to Neoi Syu's latest homework incense stick. *Maybe it won't be too bad to miss the next challenge,* she tried to convince herself. She could spend the day with Pinderent, and Mynah would be thrilled to become a Cyo B'Ahon before her again. She lit the incense, yawning as blue smoke unfurled from its tip. Her instructions filled the air, sentences bumping gently against the walls.

Zhi Ging scrawled down the details, sighing as she realized Neoi Syu had listed several books to read. She'd have to go back to the library for most of them. Once the final sentence had drifted up from the incense stick, the characters began to diffuse, the blue smoke spreading like water.

Zhi Ging inhaled deeply, a calming scent of jasmine rising from the azure haze that now tinged the lower half of her room. She glanced down at Malo. The little phoenix had fallen asleep beneath her desk, his wings flailing as he fought sand spirits and Matchmakers in his dreams. Through the blue smoke, it almost seemed like he was swimming. Zhi Ging smiled, wondering if this was how he'd looked inside his egg, back when Reishi had first mistaken him for a jade stone rolling along the river toward Fei Chui.

Zhi Ging reached a hand through the haze to ruffle his feathers and froze, an idea swooping into her mind. Her breath caught in her throat and she leaped back, flinging her screen door open and racing toward the sick bay. She sprinted past a confused-looking Heisiu and shook Pinderent awake. Before the bleary-eyed Silhouette even had a chance to open his mouth, Zhi Ging grabbed his sleeve and pulled him out of his bed and back to Reishi's lab.

"I know how we can keep you in Hok Woh. Permanently!"

CHAPTER 31

"Quick, training starts any second now." Zhi Ging gestured frantically to Malo as the little phoenix hurried across the teak, a hammer clutched between his wings. Pinderent crouched on the platform, triple-checking silk knots while racing through the checklist under his breath.

They had spent the past three days and nights working on the boat while everyone else thought they were in the sick bay, contagious after catching something at air rail research. Only Mynah knew the truth, her cheek patches flashing golden as she heard their plan and cackled. The updated dragon boat now bobbed in the water beside them, a newly risen gibbous moon shivering against the waves.

"What have you done?!"

The two Silhouettes spun around to see Bucbou glaring at them, her eyes wild with fury. Gwong took one look at their captain's flaring nostrils and quickly stepped back. Crew members from the other five teams craned around Bucbou, several ageshifting down in shock when they spotted the strange new contraption tied to the platform. Zhi Ging and Pinderent flinched, trapped under the force of the Cyo B'Ahon's stare.

"Well? You have ten seconds before I send you on a one-way lap to shore and seal Hok Woh's entrance behind you."

Hiulam appeared beneath Bucbou's waving arms, her nose crinkling in bewilderment as she took in the transformed dragon boat. "I thought you were still too sick to come to class?" She peered at them in confusion. "I was going to visit you both after training. Jack's already on his way to the sick bay."

Zhi Ging felt a rush of guilt for lying to her friends, but she and Pinderent had needed all the time they could get. Even then, they hadn't done it alone. Before she could answer, Iridill elbowed Hiulam out of the way, scoffing loudly as she took in their additions to the boat.

"It looks more like a giant carp than a dragon now," she sneered, delighting in Pinderent's still-frozen expression. "Look at those red splotches," she added, raising her voice in exaggerated horror as she pointed to the thick patches of carved lacquer that now covered the boat's new roof. "They look like bloated fish scales."

Zhi Ging glanced back at their hard work and had to admit Iridill was right. The boat had been completely reconstructed; its glass dragon head was now hidden under a curved wooden dome. She and Pinderent had initially wanted to create an egg-like structure; there hadn't been enough crates in the equipment room, however, so the boat's dragon tail still stuck out beyond the edge of the dome, transforming its shape into that of a large oblong fish. It really did look like a carp.

"Where did you get that carved lacquer from?" Bucbou hissed, her voice a whisper wrapped in steel.

Team Tsadeu murmured behind her, their eyes flicking to the stepping stones.

"I promise most of the carved lacquer dragon head is still okay. We just used its horns . . . and a couple of its whiskers," Zhi Ging said, inching away from the furious Cyo B'Ahon.

"To keep the new half waterproof," Pinderent added in a dry croak. He pointed a shaking finger to the top of the wooden dome, which had significantly more patches of lacquer.

"Um, I would recommend you both explain yourself as quickly as possible," Yuttou murmured, pointing at the cracks that had started to appear across the whistle clutched in Bucbou's hand.

A cheerful humming rippled toward the group, and as one they turned to see Reishi emerging from the darkness, leaping between the stepping stones. A trail of miniature jellyfish led by Gahyau bounced in a line behind him, hammers and nails jangling merrily from the tops of their bubbles. He skidded to a stop when he spotted the crew members surrounding Zhi Ging and Pinderent, tools splashing into the water as jellyfish crashed into his back.

"Ah!" he squeaked, ageshifting down under the fierceness of Bucbou's glare. "I forgot you liked to show up to training early."

"I thought I told you never to touch a dragon boat again after I kicked you off the team," Bucbou roared, slicing her paddle through the air toward the transformed boat. "Two foolish Silhouettes I can *almost* understand, but why were you helping them?"

"We've solved the waterfall problem!" Zhi Ging cried.

Every single pair of eyes snapped to her in disbelief.

Hiulam was the only one to smile. "My fate plate, it's finally happening," she whispered, her eyes widening with excitement.

"How is this better than the original dragon boat?" B'ei Gun asked, waving his oar to the raised curve of the dome. "You've effectively ruined any and all aerodynamic structure it had."

"Yes, but you're not going to rely on air!" Reishi babbled, jumping from the last stepping stone to press down on the boat's new dome, causing it to seal shut against the original teak. "Once Zhi Ging and Pinderent showed me their sketch, I knew their idea could actually work!"

Bucbou narrowed her eyes, her gaze focusing on the

two Silhouettes. Zhi Ging swallowed, knowing the captain was remembering their last disastrous attempt with the silk dragon boat. There was a pause, and her knuckles loosened fractionally. "Go on."

"No team's been able to scale the waterfall by rowing up its surface; the force of the rapids is just too strong," Pinderent said, his hands shaking as he mimicked its steep vertical rise.

Several crew members winced, nodding as they remembered their plummets back into the dark ocean.

Zhi Ging took over. "But before I came to Hok Woh, Malo here was able to climb up a waterfall to find *me*." She lifted the little phoenix off the wooden dome. He ruffled his feathers, looking smug as he nodded at the confused Cyo B'Ahon.

"Well, of course, he can fly. Are you trying to tell us this dome is a giant wooden wing?" B'ei Gun asked, prodding its surface.

"No, he reached me when he was still an egg," Zhi Ging said slowly, frustrated at the interruption. "He was able to roll up a waterfall by sticking as close to the riverbed as possible." She paused, then turned to Pinderent, nudging her friend as he stepped forward.

"And that's how we'll beat the waterfall," he announced, his eyes gleaming. "Not by fighting the strongest waves at the top, but by battling the weakest ones at its base."

They held their breath, waiting for Bucbou's reaction.

Even the other teams turned to face her, silent until she shared her verdict. The seconds seemed to stretch, the only sound that of waves hitting the dragon boat's hull.

"Let's try it." Her voice was curt, but the moonlight caught a flicker of excitement flash across the captain's face.

Reishi whooped, ageshifting back up, while Zhi Ging and Pinderent shared a shaky smile.

"If this really works . . ." Pinderent broke off, the hope catching in his throat. The tips of his ears and nose were bright red, as if they'd just finished a punishing set of anti-current drills.

"It will," Zhi Ging whispered back as they unlatched the dome and held it open for the rest of Team Bolei.

Hiulam flashed them a look of amazement when she ducked under the dome to reach her regular seat. "I can't believe you're not both swimming to shore right now. Hey!" she exclaimed, running a hand along her paddle. "You polished these. I've never seen the wood shine like this."

"That's not all we've done," Zhi Ging whispered so only Hiulam could hear.

On the platform, Bucbou snatched at Reishi's robes before he could sidle back to the safety of the entrance stepping stone. "Not so fast," she barked. "You worked on this too, so you're sitting in on the test ride. If this doesn't work, I want all three of you within screaming distance."

Reishi winced, his eyes darting to the distant beach,

and Zhi Ging bit back a laugh, knowing exactly what he was thinking. Even the shore would be close enough to hear her shouting.

Bucbou gestured at the gap between her and Pinderent's seats, and Reishi ageshifted down, squeezing into the narrow space. Gahyau and the other jellyfish followed after him, perching along his shoulders and the top of his head.

"We won't need the dome until we're at the base of the waterfall," Pinderent called out as Gwong stretched up to pull the wooden structure over them.

They rowed out, B'ei Gun scowling after being ordered to prop the dome up with his oar. The other teams hurried to release their own boats from the hidden stepping stones, eager not to miss a second of the underwater attempt. There were distant cries as the dragon boats sprang free, but the words were drowned out by the sound of boats splashing down hard against the waves.

Zhi Ging felt her heart thumping as they reached Seoizyu. The enormous jellyfish waved, sending seawater cascading down before she performed a languid tumble, flipping to stretch her tentacles over the stacked bamboo towers.

In the sudden silence that filled their dragon boat, the only sound was the tumbling rapids of the newly created waterfall.

"Now what?" Hiulam asked, trying to look past Reishi. "How do we get to the base?"

"Um, so, like I said, we only took a small bit of the carved lacquer dragon head," Zhi Ging began, suddenly relieved she wasn't sitting beside Bucbou. "But we did take all of this." She reached under her seat to reveal the paper dragon head, its origami jaws folded into a conspiratorial smile.

Hiulam snorted and leaped up, sending their entire boat rocking as she tried to peer back at Team Syun Zi. However, without the usual light of the race-night jellyfish, the other boat was nothing more than a blurred shadow.

"Remember my first race, when the paper head almost dragged us under?" Zhi Ging explained quickly, watching two furious mauve patches appear on Bucbou's cheeks. "Well, this time we let it!"

"If we soak the paper dragon head, then attach it to the front of the boat, the extra weight will drag us down," Pinderent explained in a single rapid squeak, leaning as far away from Bucbou as he could.

She snapped her head to him, eyes narrowed. "And what do we do on the upper side of the waterfall?" the Cyo B'Ahon barked. "Are we expected to blindly navigate underwater for the rest of the mission?"

"No, once you've finished your climb and reach the upper river . . ." Reishi trailed off, glancing back at Zhi Ging.

She paused, then lifted a thin sliver of silk. It caught

against the moonlight, revealing a curling ribbon that coiled around the dragon boat's tail before vanishing into the water. B'ei Gun jerked away from the silk, glowering at it as if it'd personally offended him by not being visible earlier.

"Promise you won't get mad?" Zhi Ging asked, attempting to smile at Bucbou.

"No."

Malo ducked low in her hood, hiding from the Cyo B'Ahon's steely expression as Zhi Ging soldiered on.

"Well, we lined the bottom of the boat with hydrophobic pebbles. Hundreds of them."

"I see." Bucbou turned her glower to the jellyfish covering Reishi. "I suspect you had help carrying them from the shore." Gahyau had the decency to look sheepish, sinking to the bottom of his bubble while others twisted their tentacles together, pretending not to understand her accusation.

Reishi coughed politely, causing the bubbles around him to wobble. "It doesn't matter how the pebbles made it across the stepping stones. What matters is they're currently covered by folded layers of silk. Once you know you're on the upper side of the waterfall, Zhi Ging can untie the fabric and the pebbles will push away from the water, shooting your boat back to the surface."

"After that, we can also remove the waterproof dome and turn it back into a dragon boat," Zhi Ging added, hoping her exaggerated hand movements would bat away

any questions, but Bucbou was not one to be easily distracted.

"And where exactly did you get this silk?" she asked in
a tight whisper.

"I, uh, does it matter? I think—"

"Zhi Ging." The Cyo B'Ahon glowered at her.

"The new silk dragon head, but only a few strips from
its snout and mane, I promise," she added in a rushed
voice.

This time, both Hiulam and Yuttou leaned sideways
out of the boat, trying to spot Team Si Cau. Gwong bit
down a smile, shaking his head in disbelief as Bucbou
shut her eyes, drumming her fingers along her paddle.

Finally she exhaled sharply. "Let's test it."

Zhi Ging sighed with relief.

Reishi spun around, his features wobbling through the
layer of bubbles, and mouthed the word "now." She nodded and quickly slipped a crumpled scroll into the paper
dragon's mouth before Bucbou could see, then passed its
head to Gu Sao, the team's Drummer.

He took it reluctantly, then lowered the dragon head
into the water. The paper began to bloat, its thin sheets
absorbing the seawater. He slapped the mulchy creation
across the front of the glass dragon head, and Zhi Ging
immediately felt their boat dip forward. Reishi shooed the
jellyfish overboard, the faint splash of their bubbles bursting as they landed between waves sounding like rain. Pinderent peered intently at the water level as they began to

tip forward, and a few seconds later he signalled for B'ei Gun to lower the dome.

The wooden frame sealed around them with a solid clunk, leaving the team in pitch dark. Zhi Ging held out her left hand, waving invisible fingers inches from her face. The carved lacquer might have sealed the water out, but it also stopped any moonlight from filtering through. There was a faint rustle as Malo spread his wings, delicate flames appearing along the tip of each feather. In the light, Zhi Ging saw that both Gwong and Gu Sao had also been holding their hands close to their faces. They smiled sheepishly when they spotted each other.

"Are we meant to feel anything—" Hiulam began, then jerked forward into Yuttou as the boat tilted sharply, the plunge pool currents dragging it down toward the ocean floor.

"Use your paddles!" Zhi Ging cried, her voice muffled as she tried to lean away from Gwong's cloak "We want to hit the bottom of the waterfall as quickly as we can."

Bucbou's eyes suddenly widened, and she slammed a hand to where her paddle jutted between the original dragon boat and its new dome. "You've only sealed the frame with carved lacquer! Release the hydrophobic pebbles. Our paddles are blocking it right now, but the second we move them, seawater will flood the boat."

The other Cyo B'Ahon began to shout, and B'ei Gun ageshifted down in horror.

"It's okay!" Pinderent tried to yell over the chaos, but his voice was drowned out by Gu Sao's screams.

"Stop!" Zhi Ging roared as the boat thudded against the bottom of the plunge pool. Malo clapped his wings together, and the dragon boat flashed with warning light. "We already worked that out. Look." She pointed with one hand as she rowed her paddle back and forth. There was no sudden rush of water. Instead a thin ribbon of seawater seemed to flow directly around the paddle, as if examining it, before draining back out to the ocean.

Bucbou narrowed her gaze and bent low until she was eye to eye with her paddle. The wood gleamed in the light of Malo's feathers. "What type of polish is this?" the Cyo B'Ahon asked suspiciously.

"Um, we might have borrowed a little bit of the glass dragon head too," Zhi Ging admitted.

"What?!" Bucbou spun around, stretching past Reishi to run a protective hand over its head. The dragon's glass horns, mane, and whiskers were all still in place. The captain paused, then turned back with a wary expression.

"Just its fangs," Zhi Ging explained. "We only needed a couple to seal the paddles."

"The glass works the same way as the entrance stepping stone," Pinderent explained. "We made hollow tubes that the paddles fitted into. You can row like normal, and no water'll get in, it'll just flow into the hollow glass, then out again."

"Is there *any* dragon head I'm not going to have to replace?!" Bucbou shook her head, but there was a flicker of amusement in her eyes now.

"There's also a small amount of the gold dragon's whiskers missing," Zhi Ging confessed. "We needed something to weld the hydrophobic pebbles in place."

Malo glanced guiltily at his flaming wings, trying to casually tuck them behind his back.

"And there might be a few loose porcelain dragon's scales between the silk and the hydrophobic pebbles, just in case the fabric got waterlogged too quickly," Pinderent added, not meeting Bucbou's eye.

The captain snorted as their boat continued to be pulled forward by the current. "All six, perfect."

"We realized we needed all of them to make the climb work," Pinderent said.

Zhi Ging flashed him an appreciative smile. There had been no "we" about it; the final plan had been completely his. After she had woken him up with her idea to go *under* the waterfall, it had taken Pinderent another five hours and sixteen scratched-out scrolls to work out exactly *how* to build a dome that wouldn't flood. All she and Reishi had done after that was follow his instructions.

Suddenly, water began to drum hard against the teak. The boat jolted as if they were being attacked by howling dragons, watery talons clawing the wooden frame.

"This is it! The base of the waterfall." Bucbou's eyes

gleamed as she lifted the whistle to her mouth. "Time to see what this carp can do!"

Paddles rattled against bamboo as they hit the first stand at the base of the makeshift waterfall. Zhi Ging felt every bone in her body judder from the force of the rapids roaring down around them. The entire boat shuddered as they pushed upward, the water rushing into the hollow glass a foaming white chaos. Reishi was forced to hold on to the base of Bucbou's seat to stop himself sliding the length of the boat.

"Argh!" Hiulam shrieked, suddenly shaking a clear glass tube. "My paddle's gone! It caught between two pieces of bamboo and slid out."

Zhi Ging's stomach dropped and she saw the color drain from Pinderent's and Reishi's faces. *Why didn't any of us think about that? What else have we missed?*

"Listen up!" Bucbou shouted. "If your paddle hits resistance, let the rest of the team know. We'll need to row backward to release it." The Cyo B'Ahon's eyes flicked between the two halves of the boat, calculating their chances of reaching the top of the waterfall.

"Hiulam, the left side of the boat will be stronger now. Share Yuttou's paddle and make sure we balance the power of each row." Bucbou frowned, the light from Malo's feathers deepening the creases across her forehead. "The last thing we need is to get trapped spinning in circles under the waterfall."

Yuttou ageshifted down to make space for Hiulam and the two of them heaved hard against the single paddle. The team was silent as they battled up the waterfall, their arms straining against the currents as they hunched forward. Zhi Ging felt a flutter of relief each time their boat thumped between the stands, inching higher despite the waterfall's best attempts to force them back down. Soon there were only two stands left to climb.

Reishi suddenly sat bolt upright, wiping a hand across his cheek. "Did anyone else feel that?"

The others turned to him, expressions freezing when they spotted his face.

It was covered in droplets.

As one, Team Bolei looked up and saw the teak dome begin to crack. Malo flapped his wings in panic, beads of water sizzling on his wings.

Zhi Ging's heart dropped. *No, no, no!*

"Release the silk!" Bucbou roared, abandoning her paddle and lunging past Reishi toward Zhi Ging. She tugged hard on the fabric, every single crew member swiveling to watch it slip through a minuscule crack by the dragon tail. Once it slid through, B'ei Gun slammed a hand over the space, but water still spurted between his fingers.

"Any second now." Pinderent's face was pale, his eyes wide.

"Please tell me you three thought of a backup pla—"

The boat erupted out of the water, the dome snapping

loose as panels splintered and fell backward to the depths. The wooden carp transformed back into a dragon boat as it thumped down on top of the sixth bamboo stand.

There was a moment of stunned silence, then cheers erupted from the boats below.

They'd done it; they'd scaled the waterfall.

CHAPTER 32

Zhi Ging looked around at her team in a daze. Every single Cyo B'Ahon had ageshifted down once the hydrophobic pebbles kicked in. Even Bucbou looked no more than thirteen years old.

"It worked!" the captain roared, ageshifting back as she scooped up Malo and spun the little phoenix in the air, his still-flaming tail feathers leaving a trail of mist. She looked at her team, a genuine smile lighting up her face.

Zhi Ging stepped into the center of the boat, gesturing for Pinderent and Reishi to join her. *This is it. Time to keep my promise.*

"It's all thanks to Pinderent," she began. "He's the one who worked out how to build this boat. Reishi and I just spent the past few days collecting hydrophobic pebbles for him. Even if he can't become captain, he deserves to stay in Hok Woh. Without him, we'll never be able to re-create this dome for the other dragon boats. Especially since—" she took a deep breath and met Bucbou's eye— "I just realized I *accidentally* put his sketches into the paper dragon's jaws before we started. For safekeeping." Bucbou's mouth dropped open as Zhi Ging plowed on, Reishi struggling to keep a proud smile from his face. "I know Pinderent can't stay here as a Silhouette"—she gulped, feeling a fresh wave of guilt for being the reason he failed the Concealment challenge—"but what if he doesn't? Sintou said we'd help all failed Silhouettes find new apprenticeships. Well, what if Pinderent stays on to train as a dragon boat specialist? Even if some of the Cyo B'Ahon don't think he has the skills needed to become immortal, he has all the skills needed to improve our boats."

"And you've said it yourself loads of times: Team Bolei's never had a better Pacer!" Hiulam added, leaping up beside Zhi Ging. "No one cares more about dragon boat racing than him."

Pinderent flushed, smiling appreciatively at his friends while Bucbou raised a single eyebrow and considered him.

"Well, I definitely don't want Reishi back as the Pacer beside me," she muttered.

Zhi Ging held her breath, desperately hoping she'd done enough to keep Pinderent in Hok Woh.

"Sand spirit!" B'ei Gun suddenly cried, shattering the hope-filled moment as he jabbed a finger at the underwater waterfall. Its border had been surrounded by a shifting gray creature, eight limbs twisting out from its knotted, faceless body. A deep, steady hiss carried across the ocean as a solitary orb floated above it, as if guiding the spirit. *What is that?* Zhi Ging squinted, and her stomach dropped.

Marzi.

Ami's jellyfish sank beneath the surface of the underwater waterfall and the sand spirit moved forward, forming a twisting helix directly above where he vanished. The five other dragon boats raced toward it, Pacers' and Central Paddlers' arms blurred as they churned through the water. On the stepping stones, the Drummer from Team Si Cau herded Silhouettes back to the safety of Hok Woh. Zhi Ging leaned forward, and suddenly their boat thudded against bamboo. Seoizyu had pulled her tentacles loose from beneath them, leaving them stranded at the top of the now-dry tower. Within seconds, the giant jellyfish had caught up with the other dragon boats, protective walls of water swelling around the charging Cyo B'Ahon.

Bucbou roared and began to scale the stand.

"Don't!" Reishi shouted, catching her arm. "What are you going to do when you reach the bottom? You can't swim out there."

"Try me," Bucbou snapped, her eyes never leaving the tight spinning circle of sand spirit limbs.

Suddenly the underwater waterfall erupted upward, transforming into a geyser of dark roiling currents. Seoizyu wrapped her tentacles around the charging dragon boats as waves exploded out, threatening to capsize the Cyo B'Ahon. The sand spirit pressed tight against the geyser, gray limbs stretching wide across the water as it twisted into a new shape.

Zhi Ging's mouth dropped open as the geyser coiled into a bloated version of the Pan Chang Knot that Ami had snatched from her cloak months ago. Flames filled Malo's body, and the phoenix rose protectively above Team Bolei. The Pan Chang–shaped geyser pulsed, and the sand spirit peeled back to reveal a writhing white dragon. It snapped its jaws, swallowing two of the spirit's tentacles, then slammed its tail hard against the ocean surface, sending a tidal wave back to the bamboo tower.

Bucbou leaped up and pinned Zhi Ging and Hiulam against the bottom of the boat seconds before water roared over them. The entire tower creaked ominously, their boat tilting toward the steep drop before the bamboo righted itself.

"Pinderent!" Zhi Ging scrambled out from beneath Bucbou's grip. She blinked hard, salt water stinging her eyes, struggling to make out the faces in front of her. *Why can I only see two shapes? Did he fall overboard?* Zhi Ging clambered to the front of the boat, and the larger figure broke apart as her vision cleared: Pinderent sheltered between Reishi and Gwong.

"I'm okay," he croaked, a dazed look on his face.

In the distance, the dragon snapped at the boats still

circling beneath it on the ocean surface. Its head caught beneath moonlight as it snarled, exposing long fangs, and Zhi Ging felt her entire body go numb.

She recognized the dragon.

It had the exact same mercury eyes as the one that had attacked her on Fei Chui's jade mountain. Zhi Ging raised a shaking hand to her hair and felt with horror the sudden fizzing of glowing strands beneath her fingers. Her knees collapsed beneath her and she thumped down hard. *How is it here?*

Cyo B'Ahon from Team Chi Hei and Team Tsadeu were forced to abandon their boats, diving into the water as the dragon clamped teak frames between its claws. It curled its talons, and the two boats splintered, wooden fragments crashing between the other boats as they raced to lift crew members out of the water. The dragon leaned forward, whiskers coiling around the yelling Cyo B'Ahon, then jerked back, its head snapping to the stacked bamboo tower.

It reared up, its long body rising impossibly high, blocking out the moon and plunging Zhi Ging and the rest of Team Bolei into darkness. The dragon turned to face them, its jaws wide as lightning began to crackle in the back of its throat. Zhi Ging froze, her entire body suddenly back on Fei Chui's glass terraces. There was a loud whistling, and one of Seoizyu's tentacles shot past the dragon, pushing Team Bolei's boat off the tower and out of the lightning's path. Zhi Ging screamed, her hand snatching Hiulam's seconds before they plummeted backward into the water.

"Silhouettes to me!" Bucbou spluttered, her face the first to burst through the waves. She grabbed Pinderent by the back of his hood before racing one-armed to Zhi Ging and Hiulam. The dragon snapped in frustration as more of Seoizyu's tentacles began to lash around it, attempting to drag it back to the underwater waterfall. It clawed against the jellyfish, reducing her to a shower of seawater, then shot toward the porcelain province shore, what was left of the sand spirit clutched in its claws. It was only then that Zhi Ging spotted a figure crouched between the dragon's horns, steering the creature while a gray jellyfish floated beside her. Every boat went silent as the same realization crashed over the Cyo B'Ahon, even more suffocating than the tidal wave.

Ami had escaped the underwater waterfall.

CHAPTER 33

"Silence!" Sintou called, raising a hand covered in deep purple burns.

The shouting Cyo B'Ahon immediately went still.

"I want one voice and one voice only. Bucbou?"

"We thought the Fui Gwai—Ami," the captain corrected herself furiously, "only had the power to turn humans into thralls, but she seems to have control over a dragon too. We have to stop her immediately; no one is safe until we do. How are ordinary shoresiders meant to fend off a dragon attack?"

"But was it a real dragon? It looked like a Pan Chang first," Sycee interrupted, her robes still dripping with seawater.

"Definitely real," Zhi Ging muttered, her hair no longer glowing.

"We need to warn the province rulers, at the very least," the captain of Team Tsadeu added. "Reassign all Scouts and give them a protective role in their original home province." He waved a hand at the map of Wengyuen pinned to Sintou's hexagonal table, water droplets leaping from his sleeve and staining the pale parchment. "I've been saying this for weeks. More and more children have been going missing thanks to the sand spirits; what happens now that Ami's back?"

"How did she make a deal with the sand spirit from inside the underwater waterfall, anyway?" Team Si Cau's captain demanded. She paced up and down Sintou's office, her race cloak dragging across the floor as she ageshifted down in concentration. "What if she can turn that dragon into anything she wants?"

The group spun around as the doors flung open, a twelve-year-old Reishi ageshifting back up as he approached them.

Sintou nodded then turned to the captains. "Reishi and I need to speak with Miss Yeung, alone. Pou Pou will contact your jellyfish once we're done."

Bucbou and Sycee began to protest, but Sintou curled her hand tight, and the white flame trapped beneath the glass roared up, temporarily blinding everyone in the room. "You can present your strategies then. Right now you're dismissed."

Zhi Ging sneaked a glance at Reishi as he stepped aside for the captains. His face was drawn and pale. In fact, he looked even worse than he had when recovering in the sick bay.

"I think this is my fault." Zhi Ging's voice came out in a dull thud once the room had emptied.

"Marzi escaping?" Reishi raised an eyebrow in confusion. "Well, yes, but we've had Ai'Deng Bou's jellyfish searching for him all week. You couldn't have predicted, or stopped, Ami's reappearance tonight."

"No, not that." Zhi Ging twisted the golden Pan Chang Knot pinned to her cloak, worrying it between her fingers. It had been bothering her ever since the underwater waterfall had first erupted, twisting into an all-too-familiar white Pan Chang.

"What is it?" Sintou asked, turning to her.

"Reishi and I spent months trying to find the air rails. But until recently I couldn't really feel them. I thought maybe being underwater made them harder to sense, or there were more back in Fei Chui." She shook her head, remembering the number of times she'd tumbled past jellyfish tanks and onto cushions in their search. "But what if I actually couldn't find them again because of my Pan Chang?" She twisted her new knot between her fingers. "I never got a regular red one."

"You got one Ami made especially for you." Reishi's eyes widened, the realization causing him to ageshift down further to ten. "What if she put some sort of curse over it? Not a possession but . . . some form of spirit magic suppressor." He waved his hands, oversized robes flapping as he fought to find the right words.

"It would explain why you struggled to find additional air rails after arriving in Hok Woh," Sintou said slowly, her eyes narrowing in agreement.

"I bet that's why they only flashed up for a second during my Fauna challenge. Ami's Pan Chang was muffling my ability to feel them, blocking my powers. But what if that wasn't all it was doing?" Zhi Ging's eyebrows scrunched up as she tried to untangle the thought out loud. "What if it worked more like a net, stopping the magic from escaping but also keeping hold of it?" She glanced between the two Cyo B'Ahon. Reishi's face flickered as if attempting not to ageshift again. "What if it didn't push the magic back into me? What if the white Pan Chang was also stealing it?"

"If you were releasing a little bit of spirit magic each time we tried to find an air rail . . ." Reishi trailed off, horror slicing through his words.

Zhi Ging shut her eyes. Ami's gloating face as she vanished beneath the churning rapids filled her mind. It finally made sense. "We had research sessions every evening until my detention. I gave Ami a way to escape the underwater waterfall!"

Sintou sank into her seat, a deep frown etched across her features. "That would mean Ami benefitted each time your gold lines emerged."

"But she also told me to avoid them," Zhi Ging said in confusion, a headache biting into her temples. "She once

341

asked me not to do anything that would make them appear."

Reishi gestured for her to take the seat across from Sintou. "Maybe Ami thought the Pan Chang simply suppressed your power, only realizing its real potential later. She must have started to wonder when you were still able to make the air rails appear, even if only for a second." He shook his head. "No wonder she was willing to take the gamble with the underwater waterfall."

Sintou gave a furious snort. "I should have sealed the underwater waterfall, not her office." The Head of the Cyo B'Ahon drummed her fingers against the map, then carefully rolled it up, revealing a crumpled letter beneath the scroll. "This arrived for you earlier today. Neoi Syu returned it to me when you didn't attend class. Again." She held it out to Zhi Ging, her mouth drawn into a tight thin line.

Zhi Ging's breath caught in her throat as she opened the letter, recognizing the soft sweeping characters. It was from Aapau.

Zhi Ging,

I'm so glad you're safe in Hok Woh, although that means that ban daan of a Lead Glassmith has been keeping my letters for months! I've half a mind to send this roaming pagoda back up the jade mountain and crash through his precious glass terraces until he posts them—although Sintou tells me you've already done some damage there!

This arrived today in the beak of a white starling. My eyesight must be fading faster than I realized in my Final Year; it almost looks like it's made of paper. The little bird won't leave me alone as I write this, so I'll send a longer letter soon. Hope this reaches you in time.

Love,

Aapau

Zhi Ging flipped the scroll over but there was nothing attached.

"What was Aapau talking about? What did the bird send?" she asked.

Despite everything, she felt a small flicker of excitement. She could talk to Aapau again! That horrible morning when her guardian had been sent away in Fei Chui's roaming pagoda didn't have to be their final moment anymore.

Sintou pulled a small object from her pocket. Unlike Aapau's letter, this was a squat slip of paper made up of tight folds. "Do you know what this is?"

"It's a letter-locked message," Zhi Ging whispered, recognizing the strange eighth fold.

The Head of the Cyo B'Ahon nodded and placed it in her palm. The paper immediately began to wiggle, unfurling like a lotus bud to reveal the protected message, while a thin black strand unwound along its sealed edges.

Zhi Ging held it up, realizing with a jolt that the message was written in the same dark-purple ink that had told her to use the weather wax in her Concealment challenge. This time, however, the handwriting was rushed, smeared as if a sleeve had brushed across it before the ink dried.

Zhi Ging, do not let the Guild find you.

Spirit magic flows through you, stronger than it has in any generation.

The strength of that power is my fault. I will never forgive myself for trusting her and cursing you.

You are my daughter, but you were brought to life, not born.

If your spirit magic is taken, you'll fragment.

You began as a paper cutting.

CHAPTER 34

The two Cyo B'Ahon stared placidly at her, unaware of how Zhi Ging's life had just shattered.

"Well, what did the message say?" Reishi asked. His expression morphed to concern when he saw her hands begin to shake. He continued speaking, but Zhi Ging couldn't hear a word; each ragged breath of air calcifying in her lungs threatened to crush her.

She blinked hard at the letter, then without warning barreled out of Sintou's office. Her legs picked up speed as she stumbled blindly through Hok Woh, barely noticing the Silhouettes and Cyo B'Ahon she bundled past in the twisting corridors. Her body led her back to the lantern archive and she burst in, throat burning as she struggled to catch her breath.

In the silence, the paper lanterns of hundreds of Silhouettes swayed in the branches. Zhi Ging marched to the closest tree and slammed the letter hard against its trunk, several lanterns thudding down around her. She shut her eyes, pressing her forehead into her knees as she sank down, arms clutched tight around herself to protect against the shuddering breaths that rattled down her spine. Time seemed to congeal and stretch as her mother's revelation tore through her.

I'm a paper cutting.

I'm not real.

Zhi Ging groaned and buried her head deeper while tree roots dug into her back.

What if I stay right here? As long as I don't move it doesn't have to be true. I can still be normal. It only has to exist here and in Sintou's office; the rest of Hok Woh is safe. It won't be true until I leave this room.

Eventually, Zhi Ging's breathing settled, although her heart continued to thump out of time. The door slid open as her feet began to prickle with pins and needles, and Jack and Malo stepped inside, relief on both their faces.

"There you are," Jack said softly, sinking down beside her. "Reishi's been looking for you everywhere. What happened?"

Malo patted Zhi Ging's shoes as she looked up. Her voice withered, the words crumbling to ash in her throat as she took in Jack's concerned expression. *Once I tell him, it'll be true everywhere.*

She silently handed him the creased letter, her gaze slipping to a fallen paper lantern caught between tree roots. *Is spirit magic the only difference between me and that lantern?*

"Whoa." Jack's voice was small as he finished the letter. "Are you okay?" he asked tentatively. He hesitated for a moment, then leaned over, pulling her into a tight hug.

She watched their reflections in a daze, wondering why she didn't feel angrier. Jack had also learned who he really was a few months ago, but that had helped him rediscover somewhere he belonged. Everything was more complicated for her. What if this was the only room in Hok Woh where she actually belonged? Sitting in the dark with the rest of the Silhouette paper. A strange laugh burbled up her throat. *I'm more related to these lanterns than to anyone in Wengyuen. They could be my paper cousins.*

"I need to talk to her." Zhi Ging blinked hard, the sound of her voice surprising them both. Each word had been calm and sure, nothing like the hundreds of questions currently screaming through her mind.

"Who? Sintou?"

"No, my mother. I think she tried to reach me months ago, back before we even found the other Silhouettes." Zhi Ging shook her head. So much had happened since she had spotted that paper starling on the clifftop. Would they have learned about the Matchmakers and sand spirits sooner if it hadn't vanished during Dippy's cloud ceremony?

Jack was silent for a moment, then he pulled a small piece of sesame brittle from his pocket. He snapped it in half and offered a piece to Zhi Ging. "What about the

Matchmakers' Guild?" he asked softly, his eyes darting back to the letter. "What if they find us first?"

Zhi Ging winced and clenched her eyes shut, desperately searching through the thoughts and fears ricocheting through her. A wisp of an idea curled past and she tugged at it, pulling it closer. "Maybe," she began hesitantly, only opening her eyes once the idea began to take shape, "being with my mother in Omophilli's pagoda is actually the safest place for me. It's the only part of Wengyuen the Matchmakers won't be looking." She blinked, Jack's last question finally filtering through. "Wait, what do you mean find *us*?"

Jack bit into his half of the brittle, the caramelized sugar snapping loudly as a smile spread across his face. "You didn't think I'd let you go by yourself." He leaped up, his eyes dancing between green and blue as he held out his hand. "And you're right, Ami'll also think the Cyo B'Ahon won't let you out of their sight now. It's not like her escape was subtle. She'll be convinced you're stuck in Hok Woh, which means the Matchmakers will too."

Zhi Ging grabbed his hand, and Malo bounced into her hood as she stood up.

She took a deep breath, matching his smile. "Sintou was already thinking about keeping me in Hok Woh for the next challenge. Which means we should go now, before you officially find me."

Jack grinned. "Luckily I know where they hide the

lanterns for the Silhouette challenges. We could borrow one and be back this time tomorrow. We might not make it back in time for dinner"—he laughed as he was interrupted by Malo's shocked chirp—"but I think it'll be worth it!"

THE SUN HAD STARTED TO RISE BY THE TIME THEY spotted Omophilli on the horizon. Dark clouds curved around the city, their shadows rippling over nearby fields. Jack steered the lantern while Zhi Ging clutched their shared hoop and tried to hold in a yawn. Neither of them had wanted to risk sleeping while they soared high above the trees.

"Wait, are those clouds carrying something?" she murmured, rubbing her eyes before peering at a strange dense shape to their right.

Jack drew in a sharp breath, squinting at the twisting gray. "It's not a cloud. It's a sand spirit."

Seven of the spirit's eight limbs were coiled around its knotted body, a sleeping child trapped in each tentacle. As the spirit flew against the wind to the capital, thousands of gray grains trickled over the children's faces, streaming over their cheeks like a never-ending army of ants. Its eighth empty limb lashed from side to side as if scouring the paper province for one final catch. The spirit curled away from a rising sunbeam, and one of the children's faces tilted upside down, causing his eyes to open.

Zhi Ging yelped and Jack tugged hard against the rope, jerking them to a stop.

The child had the gray eyes of a thrall.

Zhi Ging slapped a hand across her mouth, but it was too late; she had caught the spirit's attention. It froze, then slowly turned to them, rising so they could see the pointed cluster of knots at the center of its faceless body.

Its eighth limb stretched forward, the shapeless gray sand mutating into a gnarled claw. Jack urged the lantern higher as it shot toward them, and the spirit's talons closed just beneath his feet. The spirit's hissing grew louder as its empty claw curled back toward its tangled core, the sand shuddering as it transformed into thick pincers. Malo chirped frantically, his left wing caught in Zhi Ging's hood as Jack tried to push the lantern out of reach. The spirit's new pincers shot forward, snapping through the air, and closed around Zhi Ging's cloak. She screamed as it pulled her backward, causing her to dangle upside down from the hoop.

"No!" Jack kicked out as two more spirit limbs surged forward, thrall children still clamped in its tentacles. His foot hit the pincer trying to take Zhi Ging, but the sand simply surged around him, re-forming over his shoe and slithering past to clasp her wrist.

Zhi Ging shrieked as gold lines erupted along her arms, brighter than she had ever seen. The rest of the spirit's tentacles lurched forward greedily as bright iridescent color began to spread across the pincer.

"It's stealing my power!" she screamed, frantically

trying to shake herself free. Malo finally broke loose from her hood, flames roaring across his wings to engulf his body. He screeched and dived down, snapping at the spirit limb. The pincer disintegrated, and the rest of the spirit toppled backward, reeling through the air. Malo beat his wings at the recoiling spirit, the strength of his flames sending molten glass crackling over its core. The glass surged across the faceless spirit's matted, knotted body, and it erupted, shards glittering down around Zhi Ging. The spirit's remaining limbs twisted free, contorting like panicked snakes as they raced away from Maloto Omophilli, the children still clutched tight.

"Are you all right?" Jack asked, his face pale as he struggled to pull Zhi Ging back up into the hoop.

"I—" Zhi Ging stopped, interrupted by a sharp hollow tapping. They turned slowly and saw the eighth limb, frozen in place beneath a thick layer of solidifying glass. The last remnants of the sand spirit rattled furiously against its new cage, a swarm of angry gray mites searching for a way out.

"Don't touch it," Jack warned, and Zhi Ging flinched, gold lines glinting on her outstretched arm. "If we break the glass, that limb is going to come straight for you. Hang on, I have an idea." Jack leaned forward and pulled a small paint pot from his pocket. The mites followed his finger beneath the glass, vibrating angrily against the surface. After a few moments, Jack leaned back and examined his handiwork.

He flashed her a quick smile, his eyes flickering between green and blue. "Might as well warn the next person." He adjusted his grip on the lantern.

"Let's keep going; we want to be through the Omophilli gates before too much of the city wakes up." Jack's eyes lit up as he spotted a familiar collection of fluttering twilight silks just outside the city walls. "And I think I know who can help us get in."

CHAPTER 35

"What are you two doing here?" Gertie beamed as Zhi Ging and Jack barreled into her tent. "Has Reishi finally accepted that no Chau could beat the floating market?" Her smile dropped when she took in their disheveled appearances. The old woman's wrinkles deepened and multiplied, a worried frown spilling across her face. "What happened?" she asked, her eyes narrowing as she spotted the torn fabric along the bottom of Zhi Ging's cloak.

"Sand spirit," Zhi Ging wheezed, still struggling to catch her breath. "Thralls . . . taking them . . . into Omophilli."

"Malo turned one of its tentacles to glass," Jack added, tossing the crumpled remains of their travel lantern into the corner. "It's frozen by the edge of Songsyu Forest." His frown was almost as furrowed as Gertie's. "Ami's back. A sand spirit released her from the underwater waterfall last night."

In the sudden silence the only sound was the faint rustle of paper as a line of order ants set about trying to patch up the damaged lantern.

"Not a Chau, then." Gertie's eyes flicked between them. "In that case, I definitely need an answer to my first question. What *are* you two doing here? There's no way Sintou allowed you out once Ami escaped."

Jack glanced at Zhi Ging, unsure if she wanted to tell Gertie about the letter. "We need to get into Omophilli without anyone realizing who Zhi Ging is."

"Why?" Gertie folded her arms and raised a single eyebrow. Zhi Ging could suddenly imagine what the old woman must look like when someone asked for an unreasonable discount. Or any discount.

Malo nudged the back of her ear, encouraging Zhi Ging to tell the truth.

"I need to talk to my mother." Zhi Ging pulled the crumpled message from her pocket and handed it to Gertie. The woman's eyes raced back and forth along the lines before gently folding the scroll and handing it back to her without a word.

"Didn't you see the last line?" Zhi Ging asked cautiously.

Gertie paused for a second, then smiled, shrugging. "So what? I began as a baby. Do I still look or act like one? Neither of us is what we started out as."

Malo chirped, his feathers ruffling with warm color.

Gertie nodded at him. "And he's not a jade stone any-more either."

"I guess." Zhi Ging felt her shoulders loosen slightly. She hadn't realized how tensed they'd been since she left Sintou's office. "But what if I use up all my powers?"

"What if you never do? You don't hear people shore-side worrying about when they'll use up all their dawns. Well, not many, at least. In the meantime, we can pretend you're my great-aunt." Gertie turned around, rummag-ing in the jumbled piles that towered around them. She handed a heavy jar of Crease Cream to Zhi Ging. "Oh, heavier than that, dear," she added as Zhi Ging tentatively smeared a small amount across her nose. "Otherwise you'll only hit twenty."

The old woman gave Malo an appraising look, chuck-ling as the little phoenix's beak dropped open in surprise at Zhi Ging's transformation. "Would you like some too?" she asked, holding a large dollop on her finger.

The little phoenix hmphed and jumped out of reach.

Five minutes later an unrecognizable Zhi Ging stood beside Jack.

Gertie pressed a slim wooden cane into her newly gnarled hands.

"Will I really need this?" Zhi Ging asked, bending her knees experimentally. They didn't feel stiff or creaky at all.

"The cane's for your protection," Gertie explained,

revealing a jade stamp sealed into its wooden base. A carving of a green bee glinted up at them, and in the tent's warm flickering lantern light it seemed to wink at Zhi Ging. "Stamp someone with this, and my bees will come to defend you against them."

"Where are they, anyway?" Zhi Ging asked, suddenly noticing the absence of Gertie's crown of weather-wax bees.

"Dippy will be giving them their breakfast right now." The old woman's features softened, a proud smile lighting up her eyes. "That boy's a marvel with them. I'm half tempted to enter them as a double act in tonight's closing ceremony. It's a chance for all six provinces to show off their most impressive performers," she added, spotting Zhi Ging's blank look.

"Yeah, and which province will you pretend to be from this time?" Jack turned to face Zhi Ging, snorting. "Gertie claims to be so old she doesn't even remember which province she's originally from."

"Cheeky! For all we know, you could be even older than me!" Gertie winked at Zhi Ging. "I was born before Wengyuen named its current six provinces, so I belong to whichever one suits my mood." She began walking back to the tent entrance. "Come on, let's find Dippy."

They wove between silk tents until they reached the edge of the floating market. There, dotted along the road to Omophilli, were hundreds of little emerald squares in a perfect straight line. Dippy sat cross-legged beside them, his back to the group as he ran his hands over the squares.

"What are those?" Zhi Ging asked.

Dippy jumped, the sound of her voice breaking his concentration. He looked confused until Gertie waved the jar of Crease Cream and mouthed, *Zhi Ging*. His face broke into a beaming smile and he scrambled to his feet, purple freckles swirling across his forehead.

"Zhi Ging! How've you been? Come have a look, this is so much better than cloud carrying." He flung an arm back toward the road. She crouched down beside him, laughing in delight when she realized what the emerald squares were. Every single one of them was a miniature weather-wax blanket covering a sleeping bee. A few snored gently, snuffling beneath their blankets, while the one closest to Zhi Ging waved a sleepy foreleg in greeting.

"We use my bees for most of Wengyuen's bigger festivals and ceremonies. Their stingers can help pin visitors' shadows in place, stretching out after them while they roam around, rather than being stuck in a line," Gertie explained, pointing at the soft black ribbons fluttering out beneath each blanket. "It means travelers from other provinces don't have to line up overnight before the city gates open, and it also saves us from traipsing up and down carrying trays filled with goods from our stalls." She nodded at a nearby tent that swayed with the sound of overlapping snores. "Vrile managed to rent out every single one of his hammocks last night. Everyone's here for the Matchmaker Ceremony, to see which province gets the next twelve years of paper-cutting powers."

Zhi Ging and Jack exchanged a look. *It won't be any province if we can help it.*

A couple of bees wriggled beneath their blankets, dawn light glinting against the squares of weather wax.

"They only need these overnight; the sun keeps them warm enough during the day," Dippy explained, crouching down to help the bees roll up their blankets before nodding toward the snoring tent. "Once the visitors reclaim their spots in line, Gertie's bees can unpin their shadows."

He carefully tipped the miniature blankets into an empty jar strapped across his back. Zhi Ging realized that, rather than clouds, every single jar was now filled with items for the bees. Dippy caught her eye and smiled, clinking as he pointed at a glass jar that had been converted into a large terrarium bursting with purple flowers. "Just in case they ever get hungry. I worked out last month that bergamot is their favorite."

"Didn't I tell you he was great?" Gertie said, waves of pride beaming off her. "I suppose we have you to thank for ruining his cloud ceremony." She winked at Malo, who had the decency to ruffle his feathers in embarrassment.

Zhi Ging winced as purple freckles drifted across Dippy's nose while he laughed. "Have you not found a way to remove those yet?" she asked, watching the dots swirl behind his left ear.

"No way! I'm not giving these up. Watch this." Dippy shook his left hand, and the freckles rattled down, bouncing along his arm to gather across his palm like a rich violet cloud.

"Name an animal," he said enthusiastically, holding his palm out between Zhi Ging and Jack.

"Uh, dragon?" Zhi Ging suggested, wondering what was going on.

"Easy." Dippy closed his palm, squeezing his fingers tight before rolling his wrist back and forth. He hummed to himself while he did it, Gertie's bees buzzing in harmony around them. A few seconds later, he opened his palm and the freckles had re-formed to create a shifting purple constellation, a dragon made from dots drifting along his palm.

"No way!" Jack breathed as he leaned forward to tap the miniature dragon.

"That's not even the most impressive bit," Gertie added, nodding above their heads. Zhi Ging looked up, and her mouth dropped open. Above them, the weatherwax bees were mimicking the freckles perfectly, hundreds of shimmering green bodies floating together to create a life-sized dragon.

"That's not all they can do either!" Dippy babbled excitedly as the purple dragon curled along his arm. "The freckles work like a compass too, always pointing southwest. Watch." He flicked his wrist and the dragon tumbled back into a series of purple dots, flowing toward the center of his palm. Zhi Ging leaned forward to watch, the tip of her braid brushing Dippy's hand. The freckles fluttered forward, dancing and spinning directly beneath her hair.

"Huh, that's weird. They don't normally do that." He shook his wrist again, but the freckles refused to budge, swirling as close to Zhi Ging as they could. "Guys, southwest is the other way," he whispered, trying to shoo the freckles to the other side of his palm.

"Maybe they were always pointing to a person," Gertie murmured, looking at Zhi Ging curiously. "Hok Woh *is* hidden beneath the waves of the southwest."

Worry flickered across Dippy's face, and Zhi Ging gently closed his palm around the freckles, the purple dots spilling over his fingers to be as near her as possible.

"Don't worry," she whispered. "I wouldn't take them even if I knew how. They're yours." She smiled at him sheepishly. "Hopefully they make up for you never knowing your cloud shape."

"What are you talking about? Dippy got his shape," Gertie called over her shoulder, bending to examine the repaired lantern that order ants had brought out for her approval.

"Really?" Zhi Ging beamed with relief. "How? Were the bees able to collect the scraps of your original swaddling cloud?"

"They didn't have to." Gertie shook her head proudly, tucking the lantern under her arm before coming to stand beside Dippy. "He created his own cloud shape. Unlike the rest of Wun-Wun, relying on twigs and smoke to decide their future, Dippy decided for himself." She placed a hand on his shoulder, smiling down at the boy. "When he chose to use the last of his cloud to help others, it revealed exactly who he's destined to be. That escape slide for the Silhouettes was Dippy's cloud shape. He's not going to be a cloud carrier or a cloud stitcher; he's going to be a guardian. Helping others across Wengyuen. And it's going to be my absolute honor watching him grow into that role."

Dippy flushed at the warmth of Gertie's praise.

"Guess I don't need to feel bad for going back to Hok Woh, then." Jack laughed, his eyes flashing green and blue as he nudged Dippy in congratulations.

"Don't worry, you're missed too. I'll even offer you the same discount I give Reishi when you visit as a full Cyo B'Ahon in the future. You'll be the second-ever person to get that."

"Wow, the zero-point-one-percent discount? What an honor." Jack snorted as Gertie ruffled his hair.

The old woman turned back to Dippy then, her eyes darting between the snoring tent and the Omophilli entrance ahead. "Dippy, stay here to collect the shadow line money. I need to take these two through the gates before the first tour."

"See you in a bit." Zhi Ging waved at him as they hurried past, Malo twisting in her hood to say goodbye to every single one of the still-dozing weather-wax bees.

"Why are ordinary people lining up for the Match-maker Ceremony?" she asked, struggling to keep pace with Gertie. "Won't the Matchmakers just choose which-ever province ruler offers the most, or does everyone get a chance to try to win them over?"

"Ha! Those *gu hon* Matchmakers only care about hoarding wealth," Gertie scoffed, "which is why every-thing they sell is soulless and flat. They'd never willingly part with anything that's actually valuable."

"Except they outsell the floating market every year," Jack noted with a grin, clearly recognizing the start of a well-worn rant.

"They steal my ideas and ruin them!" Gertie huffed. She patted her white hair, and the bees swarmed, nestling into her familiar emerald crown. "Anyway, they only out-sell us because provinces think it'll help buy them favor if they spend more money than they have on Matchmaker products. That unoriginal Guild saw I had bees, so they *had* to use butterflies." She shook her head in frustration, her hair vibrating as several bees shook their forelegs in mirrored annoyance. "They've been fooling villagers out of hard-earned money for decades, convincing them those butterflies can predict when you'll find your soulmate. It's utter nonsense, of course; everyone knows butterflies can only predict weather changes and boat races."

"Don't people eventually realize the predictions aren't real?" Zhi Ging asked.

"The only thing that Guild has more of than money is

excuses! If anyone dares to complain that their butterfly didn't lead them to a soulmate, the Matchmakers will turn around and say, *'Oh that means you made a mistake; you must have turned down the wrong street or eaten at the wrong restaurant. It's your fault you missed them; nothing to do with us. However, since you're here, would you like to buy another one and try again? Prices have gone up since your last visit, but finding your soulmate is priceless!'"*

Gertie was marching furiously now, Zhi Ging and Jack forced to jog to keep up with her while she continued to rant.

"The reason the floating market *floats* is because anyone who wants to have a permanent shop in Wengyuen must pay a monthly fee to their Guild. Not that any of that is ever shared back with struggling stores." Gertie's scowl deepened, her crown of weather-wax bees now so agitated that strands of hair were lifting up around her. "Let's get you into Omophilli, Zhi Ging. And if we can annoy the Matchmakers while solving where the sand spirits have hidden the thralls, even better."

"Gertie once admitted her parents originally sent her to train as a Matchmaker," Jack whispered to Zhi Ging. "She ran away every month until they finally released her. She was lucky too; they don't let junior Matchmakers leave anymore."

"Do they have their own version of Reverting?"

"I don't think so." He winced. "From what Gertie says, the Guild has too many secrets to trust anyone ever leaving. If they did offer a memory elixir, I have a feeling it'd be about as safe as the one Ami used."

Zhi Ging shivered and glanced back at the stretch of grass where Ami had held their Perception challenge. The area was completely covered by tents now, with no hint whatsoever of the mirror maze.

The main entrance to Omophilli was a thick wall that curved into an arch, its ceiling covered in a dramatic painting of six dragons locked in battle as they fought to reach a paper-white pearl. Each dragon had been painted a different province color, and Zhi Ging's eyes caught the paper province's purple dragon, its tail coiled protectively around the pearl.

"Shouldn't there be guards here?" she asked, dragging her eyes away from the vicious battle. A solitary man nodded at them from a blanket spread out at the far end of the entrance, chalk-filled porcelain bowls dotted across its surface. He eyed Malo with mild curiosity as the little phoenix sniffed the bowls, searching for secret sunflower seeds.

"There's no need. The outer mile of Omophilli is built like a maze. It's all the protection the city needs," Gertie explained, politely shaking her head as the man raised a bowl to them. "The guided tours won't begin for another two hours, so it should be nice and empty for us now."

"It doesn't look like a maze . . . ," Zhi Ging began, looking at the tightly packed storefronts and restaurants around them. Brightly decorated signs hung over every window and door, the wooden boards proudly proclaiming they had the best food in the entire city.

"Look at that noodle shop, then count to ten." Gertie led them down a narrow path that twisted sharply away from the entrance. Before Zhi Ging had even hit seven, they had passed two identical shops.

"Thanks to the Matchmakers, the paper province now has the least creativity in all Wengyuen. They had a chance to create a dream city, something even the greatest Cyo B'Ahon minds couldn't design, but instead the Matchmakers sold the paper cutting advantage to others. Why let their own province benefit when there's money to be made?"

Zhi Ging grimaced as they passed the fifth bakery with identical yellow signs advertising fresh egg tarts. The repeating pattern of shops was feeling less and less entertaining as Gertie led them through winding alleys.

"What are those?" Zhi Ging pointed at a series of colorful chalk markings on the wall beside Jack. Once she stopped, Zhi Ging realized most of the buildings around them had been marked, overlapping layers of chalk stretching along walls just above her eye level.

"The guided tours through Omophilli's outer mile are expensive, and they usually double the price during the Matchmaker Ceremony," Jack explained.

"Those who won't or can't pay try using chalk to find their own way through the maze." Gertie nodded at more chalk markings covering the lower half of the ninth green-doored mahjong store they'd passed. "In theory, you can add unique chalk symbols to work out whether you've already passed a certain loop of shops. The problem is . . ." She reached around the corner and pulled a small boy out by the back of his shirt. His ears burned red and he dropped a small sliver of chalk from between his fingers. "Some of the more *ambitious* local children have realized they can make money as emergency guides if they smudge or redraw travelers' symbols." She let go and the boy snatched up his chalk, flashing Malo a quick smile before disappearing down another alley lined with four identical dumpling shops. "When that happens, the poor traveler usually ends up spending more than if they'd just paid for the official tour." Gertie chuckled, shaking her head.

"How do you know your way through, then?" Zhi Ging asked.

"Oh, I joined a guided tour decades ago."

"And you just . . . remember?" she asked, trying not to sound skeptical.

"*I* don't." The old woman smirked, patting her hair. Between her fingers, emerald bees buzzed industriously, whispering directions in her ear. "Omophilli's outer maze might be difficult for us, but it's nothing compared to a beehive."

CHAPTER 36

The group emerged from the outer maze and squeezed into the crowded streets of central Omophilli. Here the buildings finally became distinct; the unique storefronts were jarring after they'd only seen the same ten shops on a loop.

Trees sprouted in the middle of paths, transforming already narrow alleys into single-file twisting walkways.

"Each of these trees is older than the buildings around it. That's the one thing previous generations of paper province rulers got right," Gertie said, placing a palm on the nearest trunk. "They respected where their trade power came from. They didn't rip out trees just for the sake of a straight path." The old woman glowered back over her shoulder at the outer mile. "That maze marks the exact point the Matchmakers became the unofficial rulers of Omophilli."

Above them, strings of purple paper cuttings streamed

along every branch, paper creatures floating out to the rooftops on either side of the alley. Zhi Ging peered up at the strands of fluttering starlings, wondering if her mother had created them.

"Those won't be official paper cuttings; your mother's are always white," Gertie murmured, reading Zhi Ging's questioning expression. "The Matchmakers made it illegal for anyone in the capital to use white scrolls for cuttings. They have to use dye-stained scrolls, which coincidentally"—her face twisted into a scowl—"only the Matchmakers have a permit to sell." She shook her head in disgust before expertly squeezing between a gap in the crowd that even Malo would struggle to fit through.

Zhi Ging and Jack hurried after her, their attempts to keep up slowed by a bakery line that snaked around two corners, the smell of pandan chiffon making Zhi Ging's stomach grumble. Instinctively she placed a hand into her hood. The last thing they needed was for Malo to chase after another bun.

"Where are we going?" she whispered as Gertie darted through another razor-thin gap in the throng. Zhi Ging slowed her steps to a labored hobble when nearby faces stared at her in surprise, her cane clutched uselessly under one arm. She scolded herself, embarrassed to have already forgotten she currently looked older than Gertie thanks to the Crease Cream.

"Zhi Ging, you and I are going to pretend to be Jack's elderly grandmothers. If any of the Matchmakers ask, we're eager to find his future soulmate. Hopefully in the bustle of the Guild Hall none of them will notice when we leave without buying one of their ridiculous butterflies."

THE GUILD HALL SPRAWLED ACROSS THE CENTRAL square of Omophilli's trade district, a hulking wooden structure that was more extension than original building. The sight of it made Zhi Ging shiver. Despite its multiple red pillars, the final structure resembled a spider, its bridging corridors rising up like tightly arched legs, ready to pounce.

The post pipe curled to the back of the building, a steady stream of letters and parcels flowing inside. For Zhi Ging, the glass seemed to hum ominously as mailbags swept through it, the pipe hinting at a larger web concealed behind the arachnid architecture. Omophilli's pagoda whirred behind the Guild Hall, its pointed top barely visible behind the hall's gilded roof.

"That's why nothing flies over Omophilli, not even clouds," Jack murmured, nodding above the twisting pagoda. The air above it shimmered, noticeably darker than the clear sky, as if dawn hadn't reached it. "The Omophilli half of Ling Geng's original paper-cutting pagoda has been spinning ever since the other half was taken by the Lead Glassmith. Most people think it's still trying to find its missing half. This pagoda used to be the highest point on the Omophilli skyline, but its constant spinning means it's sinking farther into the ground each year."

"Is the Guild Hall connected to it?" Zhi Ging stood on her toes, trying to see more of the whirring tower.

"Officially, no—there's a large courtyard that separates them," Gertie whispered. "But there're rumors of a secret tunnel that only the Matchmakers have access to."

Their conversation stopped as they joined those waiting to enter the Guild Hall. Matchmakers marched up and down, occasionally snatching bags for inspection.

"Stay hidden, Malo; we can't let them see you." Zhi Ging felt the little phoenix nod in her hood, his beak tugging the fabric into a cocoon.

The line crackled with strained, tense silence, and it was thirty minutes before they finally reached the front. They stepped toward a bored-looking Matchmaker who slouched in a booth beside the entrance, a long scroll spilling down across the cubicle floor.

"Province," she drawled, without even looking up.

Zhi Ging and Jack exchanged a panicked look.

"Porcelain province!" Gertie exclaimed, a new and rather unconvincing twang to her words.

"Occupation?"

"Eh, beekeepers." One of the weather-wax bees peeked out from beneath a strand of her hair and gave Zhi Ging a little wave before Gertie patted him back into place.

"From the *porcelain* province?" The Matchmaker finally looked up, raising a thin eyebrow in disbelief. She opened her mouth to ask another question, but then her eyes flicked to the horde of people still waiting to be let

370

in, and her curiosity was smothered by the sheer length of the line.

"Line four," she barked, pointing to a blue line that veered sharply down a corridor to the right of the entrance.

Zhi Ging hurried after Jack and Gertie, trying to remember to hobble as they joined the back of the porcelain province line. She anxiously patted at her face, wondering how long she had until the Crease Cream wore off. Steam filled the wide corridor as junior Matchmakers trundled between the province lines with metal trolleys piled high with steamed buns. Her stomach tightened as one was offered to a long-haired boy in the silk province line beside them. *What if they're filled with spirit sand?*

The line shuffled along the corridor, eventually reaching the main Guild Hall. Zhi Ging staggered to a stop, almost dropping her cane. The entire space was built like a giant butterfly house. The air around them rippled with a constant shimmer as multicolored wings fluttered between the six lines. Jack's eyes widened in amazement as a kaleidoscope of butterflies with carved lacquer wings swooped past.

Beside him, Gertie brushed away silk-winged butterflies that fluttered around her hair, their antennas twitching in confusion at the sight of her emerald bees. "Don't touch their wings," she muttered as other visitors turned to wave at a group of porcelain-winged butterflies. "They were designed to be extremely fragile, and if you accidentally damage one, the Matchmakers will charge you more than a year's salary to replace it."

Zhi Ging watched as the butterflies floated up to the ceiling, their delicate porcelain clinking with each wing-beat.

A colossal chandelier swayed gently above the center of the hall. Long blue candles covered its surface, the glass ornaments and sculptures that decorated each arm cloaked under thick layers of cerulean wax.

"That chandelier's been burning with exclusively blue candles for the past twelve years, to represent the agreement between the Matchmakers and the porcelain province," Gertie explained. "Tonight, though, all provinces will have a chance to make a new bid."

Zhi Gig frowned, unable to take her gaze off the swaying chandelier. There was something disconcerting about the shapes created by the dripping wax. The way the butterflies crawled over the chandelier, their wings flashing in the light, made it almost look alive.

"There she is. Eyes down, Zhi Ging," Gertie hissed.

Zhi Ging glanced over Gertie's shoulder and felt her stomach tighten. There, leaning over a balcony at the back of the Guild Hall, was Niotiya. The Matchmaker's cold, shark-like stare ran along the lines, evaluating each person who stepped into the hall. Her eight mercury rings glinted as she snapped instructions at other Matchmakers and pointed at unlucky visitors, who were quickly whisked away. Zhi Ging shivered, ducking her head low, despite the Crease Cream. *What if she recognizes me?*

She took a deep, shuddering breath, risking one final glance at Niotiya. The sight of the woman's kingfisher-feather headdress and red robes settled like stones in the pit of her stomach, fear mixing with vindication. Zhi Ging tightened her grip around the cane, twisting it in her wrinkle-covered hands. Now that she could see the Matchmaker's outfit up close, she was certain it had been Niotiya lurking behind the spirit attacks at both Pingon and the waterfall.

"Remember the plan," Jack murmured beside her. "Once we're given an appointment number, we'll be sent to wait." He nodded at a sprawling crowd directly beneath Niotiya's balcony. "It's the only spot where she won't be able to see us. We can split up then and try to find a way into the rest of the building."

The group continued to shuffle forward until they were at the front of their line.

"My name is Dourie; what match may I make for you today?" a Matchmaker droned, her flat smile disappearing as she took in their scuffed clothes. Her lips pursed and she curled a hand around the coin box on her table, pulling it pointedly out of reach. Dourie rolled her eyes at a passing Matchmaker, the butterfly hairpins studded through her severe bun rattling as she shook her head.

"Our poor darling grandson!" Gertie launched into a

long wail, causing half the hall to turn and watch. Even a passing group of glass-winged butterflies paused, hovering in the air above them. "He herds bees all day but has no skill for herding hearts." Behind her, Jack went bright red, his shoulders shaking as he slammed a hand up to his mouth. Those lining up on either side of them murmured in sympathy while Zhi Ging bit down on a smile. Only she seemed to realize he had gone red not from crying but from trying not to laugh.

"We've traveled all the way from the gold—"

"Porcelain," Jack coughed.

"Ah yes, the porcelain province, to find his match. I do hope one of these beautiful and oh-*so*-original butterflies can help." Gertie paused as a carved lacquer butterfly landed on her nose. "Shame none of these delightful little creatures have green wings. Was that color too tricky for you?" For a split second, Gertie's white hair flared red as hundreds of hidden emerald weather-wax bees stuck their tongues out at nearby butterflies. The Matchmaker narrowed her eyes, and Zhi Ging nudged Gertie aside.

"Please excuse us, we're not used to talking to powerful folk such as yourself," she cried, matching Gertie's wailing voice as she bowed low.

A strange expression flashed across Dourie's face, and she peered at Jack with a new calculating gleam in her eyes.

"You don't say. Where exactly in the porcelain province did you say you were from?"

"Oh, it's just a tiny little village." Zhi Ging desperately tried and failed to remember where any of the porcelain province Silhouettes were from. "Most haven't ever heard of it."

"Fascinating." Dourie's thin smile coiled back across her face. She rang a small bell and a junior Matchmaker hurried forward, placing a steamed bun down in front of them. The woman held it out to Jack, its all-too-familiar red seal blazing up at them from the center of its soft white dome. Niotiya peered down from her balcony, watching him with a strange hunger twisting across her face.

"No thank you," Gertie snapped, pushing Jack behind her. "He's already had breakfast."

Dourie stood up, her robes hissing as they unfurled behind her. She leaned forward, stretching an arm past Gertie to hold the bun directly beneath Jack's nose. "I insist."

Zhi Ging looked around in panic; at least three other Matchmakers were watching now, their frowns deepening with each second that passed without Jack accepting the bun. How could he avoid eating it without revealing they knew the truth about the buns? Zhi Ging tightened her grip on the cane Gertie had given her. Would it be safe to use it in the Guild Hall?

She tried to catch Gertie's eye, but the old woman was staring up at the ceiling, her forehead creased in concentration. There was a sudden flash of emerald green followed by a heavy splat. Dourie looked down at her hand in confusion. A large globule of blue wax had fallen from the chandelier to land directly on the offered bun. Zhi Ging's eyes shot up and spotted one of Gertie's weather-wax bees peeking down at them, its forelegs covered in freshly melted wax.

"Oh dear," Gertie said quickly, snatching the spoiled bun and slipping it into her pocket. "Well, he can't eat that now. And you know what, I've just realized we've forgotten to bring our money, so there's no way for us to pay for an appointment. We'll come back later." She grabbed the back of Jack's collar, raising her free arm in a dramatic wave that hid the bee as it shot back into her hair.

Zhi Ging scurried after them, the cane shaking in her hand. She glanced back when they reached the corridor. Although the main hall continued to bustle with crowds, a ripple had spread across the room. Every single Matchmaker had stilled, peering after them with identical frowns etched across their perfect faces. High above them, Niotiya drummed her ring-lined fingers against the balcony rail, her narrowed unblinking eyes following them out of the hall.

CHAPTER 37

"Well, as stealth missions go, that probably wasn't one of my best." Gertie bustled them down an empty alleyway, checking over her shoulder for following Matchmakers. She stepped toward a narrow strip of wall between a closed noodle shop and a store that sold hand-carved mahjong sets, then vanished. The wall rippled as Gertie's face reappeared, a floating hand gesturing for Zhi Ging and Jack to follow her.

"Quickly now. Once Minfun's opens, people will be lining up for noodles all day."

Zhi Ging pressed a hand against the wall and laughed as thousands of miniature glass beads swallowed it whole. She pushed through the closely packed strings, and Jack appeared beside her seconds later.

"What are these for?" he asked, tapping the beads. From the other side of the curtain they could see the empty alley clearly, as if all that separated them was a single sheet of thin glass.

Gertie smiled, and the bees emerged from her hair, swirling up the narrow stairwell.

"The beads keep the butterflies out; their wings are too wide to slip through. We don't want any clinging to our cloaks and silently listening in." Her smile fell as she began to climb the narrow steps. "Far too many people across Wengyuen have happily accepted butterfly bouquets from the Matchmakers. They never stop to wonder why they've been given such a *valuable* gift." The woman shook her head in exasperation. "They may not have paid for the butterflies with gold, but they're paying with their secrets."

Malo chirped nervously from Zhi Ging's hood, burrowing into the fabric in search of stowaway butterflies.

They stepped into a sparse room, and Gertie marched toward a bare table, gesturing for Jack to hand her a wooden bowl. The old woman pulled the wax-stained bun from her pocket and ripped it in half. Gray spirit sand spilled out, and she slammed the bowl over it, both hands pressed down hard as the table began to rattle. Tendrils of gray sand tried to claw out from under the bowl, but Malo pecked at them, his wings smoldering in warning. Eventually the sand stilled.

"Why were they trying to get me to eat that?" Jack asked, his face pale.

"I don't know. But you weren't the only one in there offered one." Gertie's frown deepened when she looked across at Zhi Ging.

"What is it? Is there a butterfly on me?" She patted both cheeks, then groaned. The Crease Cream had worn off.

Gertie tutted to herself while she searched through empty cupboards. "You'll have to stay here until a new batch is ready, Zhi Ging. In the meantime, Jack and I will try to find those who did eat the buns." Gertie placed Malo on top of the wooden bowl, and seeing Zhi Ging's crestfallen expression she added, "Once the new Crease Cream's ready, you can join us. I promise."

ZHI GING PULLED THE BUBBLING MIXTURE ACROSS the table until moonlight streamed through the window and over its surface. She paused, glancing back at Gertie's scrawled instructions.

"*Step Fourteen: fold in the moonlight.* What does that even mean?" she muttered.

Malo tilted his head to the side and waved an imaginary ladle between his wings, wobbling enthusiastically from the top of the upturned bowl.

"If Bucbou saw that technique, she'd have you kicked off the team," Zhi Ging snorted before copying his movements. The moonlight stretched like honey, catching against the ladle before vanishing beneath the mixture's surface, its light now radiating from the center of the pot.

Malo kicked his feet smugly, banging the side of the bowl until the trapped gray sand rattled in protest.

Zhi Ging replaced the lid, then flopped down into the room's only armchair. "Now we just have to wait for it to cool down." She smiled encouragingly at Malo. "Maybe I can sneak out and get us some dinner first." The scent of Minfun's noodles had filled the small room all day, until Zhi Ging wasn't sure if it was her stomach rumbling or the mixture bubbling away. The little phoenix nodded in excitement.

Suddenly a dark shape scraped across the window, leaving streaks of rattling gray sand on the glass. Zhi Ging ducked, her heart hammering as its shadow passed over the room. It had to be a sand spirit.

Malo chirped in alarm as the wooden bowl beneath him began to rock, the sand from the bun desperately trying to catch its attention.

Zhi Ging only risked peering over the armchair once the shadow had passed and moonlight spilled back into the room. Her mouth dropped open in surprise as she watched it through the window. It was one of the tentacle-like limbs that had broken free earlier. There was no child in its grip now, though. Instead, heavy patches of sand fell in chunks as it lurched down the alley.

What happens when it runs out of sand? she wondered as the gray tendril lumbered on, its erratic movements causing it to hit a string of dragon paper cuttings, large clods breaking off as it fought to untangle itself.

It was difficult to feel scared of the sand spirit when it looked like this. There was a flicker of gold as the tendril slipped from an invisible air rail, landing with a thud on the worn pavement.

"Guess it's not just me who struggles with them." Zhi Ging stepped back and lifted the Crease Cream lid. Steam surged out, filling the room with the scent of steeped oolong tea and blooming freesias. She dipped a finger into the pot and traced a line across her hand.

It still wasn't ready.

Zhi Ging bit her lip. This could be their best chance of finding out what the spirits were up to. She hurried to the door. "Malo, let's go! I bet—"

She cut off, finally realizing why Gertie had placed Malo on top of the wooden bowl. It hadn't just been to stop the sand escaping, but to stop *them* from sneaking out. Even if she held the bowl down with something else, Malo had been snapping at escaping grains all day, forcing them back. He chirped sadly and Zhi Ging took a deep breath.

She'd have to follow the spirit alone.

ZHI GING CREPT ALONG THE DARK STREETS, GRATE-ful that most of Omophilli was busy enjoying feasts ahead of the midnight ceremony. She followed the spirit tendril, a steady stream of sand now spilling from it as it struggled to navigate the twisting alleys.

By the time they reached the trade district, the tendril was noticeably smaller, with several paper cuttings clinging to what remained of its body. It ignored the Guild Hall entrance, lurching instead toward the back of the building.

Zhi Ging held her breath as she hurried after it, careful to keep to the shadows in case someone chose that moment to look out.

She scurried around a corner just in time to see the tendril attempt to slither through a fake wall panel. A string of paper dragons caught against the wood, and the spirit pulled hard, trying to tear itself free. There was a subdued thud as the last of its sand finally ran out, cascading down around the panel.

Zhi Ging crouched, waiting for the tendril to re-form in miniature. Instead the only movement was the tangle of paper cuttings rustling in the draft coming from the secret entrance. She inched forward, careful not to touch the sand as she peered around the panel. Ice-cold air rattled along the length of a narrow tunnel, sending goose bumps along her arms.

There was only one way to find out what the spirit tendril had been so desperate to reach. Zhi Ging glanced around quickly, then crawled into the gloom.

The tunnel curved down, and soon a bitter cold seeped into her. In the faint half-light, her breath appeared in front of her, not as soft clouds but as solid spheres of white that crumbled into snow. Eventually she emerged through a trapdoor into a murky cellar. As her eyes adjusted, Zhi Ging realized the walls around her were spinning, a heavy constant burr as wood ground against soil. She took a step forward and jumped as she heard a hiss by her feet.

The sand spirit!

Her head jerked down and she saw the string of paper dragons coiled around her right ankle. They must have caught against her shoe when she'd started crawling. She kicked the string loose with a shaky laugh before stepping toward the wall. Zhi Ging held her palm inches from its rotating surface, the air beneath her fingers crackling with energy.

Gertie had been right: there was at least one tunnel connecting the Guild Hall to Omophilli's pagoda. She peered up at the ceiling and her heart began to race. *Is my mother somewhere upstairs?*

She looked around, searching for a door, and spotted a narrow glass box in the center of the cellar. Zhi Ging crept toward it, confused by the cold that seemed to seep across its surface. The top half of a large hourglass was suspended directly above it, heavy metal chains holding it in place while a thin clear funnel stretched down into the box. The hourglass was filled with slate-gray sand, and although its main funnel led into the box, more glass tubes spread out along the upper half of the cellar and curled away from the spinning walls.

Zhi Ging couldn't help flinching. With its bulbous gray body and tentacle-like funnels, the hourglass looked like a monstrous jellyfish. She turned back to the box. Beneath its smooth surface, the inside was covered in thousands of thin scratches and what looked like . . . handprints.

She raised her hand and held it above a mark. The palm print was the same size as hers. Although the box barely reached her waist, at some point there had been a child trapped inside. It was a cage.

Suddenly, Zhi Ging heard muffled voices drawing closer. She looked around in a panic, searching for somewhere, anywhere, to hide. She pushed away from the cage, but the second her fingers brushed against the surface it clamped her palm in place, stinging her skin. Zhi Ging bit down a yelp as she struggled to pull free. It wasn't made from glass at all; the cage was solid ice. The voices were growing louder now—she could almost make out their words. In seconds they would step into the cellar. Zhi Ging tugged with all her strength until her hand came loose from the cage's freezing grip, and she collapsed backward, breathing hard.

She rubbed at the ice burn on her palm as she scrambled to her feet, spinning in a frantic circle until she spotted a narrow ladder stretching up between the hourglass funnels. She raced up, quickly reaching the top of a wide bamboo canopy. The floor swayed beneath her as she began to crawl forward, the thick metal chains that held the hourglass in place clinking.

Zhi Ging forced herself to still before inching across the canopy, desperately searching for a way out.

Ahead of her a peculiar haze shimmered up from the center of the bamboo. Zhi Ging crawled toward it, blinking down into the soft glow. A circle had been carved into the wooden canopy, revealing the open top half of the hourglass. Just like the cage below, it was carved from ice, the air around it humming with a faint blue hue.

Zhi Ging frowned suspiciously at the iridescent grains that filled the hourglass. *It definitely looked gray from below.* She leaned forward, and a paw shot out from beneath its surface, clasping her left palm. Zhi Ging jerked back, her mouth open in a silent scream as the paw fragmented, colorful sand crumbling back into the open hourglass. Gold lines swirled between her fingers, and Zhi Ging turned to check her palm. Her breath caught in her throat as a single golden word glinted up in her own handwriting.

Help.

Zhi Ging's eyes darted between her hand and the now-still sand in confusion.

"I really wish I'd brought Malo," she murmured, curling her hand into a fist. Beneath the canopy, the cellar door flew open, and cold harsh light flickered up through the bamboo. Zhi Ging pressed her face between the cracks, her heart pounding as she watched two figures stride in. It was Niotiya and Dourie.

"It's getting weaker," Niotiya snarled, her blue headdress jangling angrily as she stormed in. "And it's already useless to us during the day. We should have captured a second spirit weeks ago. This one will barely make it through tonight's ceremony."

Dourie nodded dutifully, pulling her red robes tight as they stepped deeper into the freezing room.

"What is *this*?" Niotiya crouched low and plucked something up between two pinched fingers.

Fear turned to icy shards in Zhi Ging's stomach as the Matchmaker held up the string of dragon paper cuttings. *Why didn't I shove it in my pocket?!*

"Where has this come from? Dourie, check that all tunnels are sealed." Niotiya peered around the silent cellar as the other Matchmaker hurried to the spinning walls.

Zhi Ging pulled back sharply as Niotiya's attention turned to the canopy, her narrowed eyes darting between the hourglass funnels. There was a triumphant cry from Dourie followed by the sharp *screech* of a bolt being drawn across the trapdoor. Time seemed to slow as the two Matchmakers nodded at one another.

"Well," Niotiya called out, her voice echoing as she raised a lantern high, her features falling into deep shadows. "It appears we have a guest. You should know entry into the Omophilli pagoda is expressly forbidden."

Zhi Ging went pale as their footsteps stalked toward the ladder. She looked around frantically, but there was nothing else on the bamboo canopy, no place at all to hide. The platform shook as the two Matchmakers began to climb toward her, the light from their raised lanterns surging ahead of them.

Beside her the hourglass jolted, and the sand pulsed pure gold. The paw reappeared, urgently beckoning for Zhi Ging to hide beneath its surface.

Heart pounding, she glanced between the paw and the

advancing Matchmaker light; the tops of their lanterns were already visible. Zhi Ging took a deep breath and grabbed the outstretched paw.

Short talons gripped her wrist, and Zhi Ging was wrenched down, sand swallowing her whole.

CHAPTER 38

All sound above Zhi Ging became muffled. She held her breath, scared of filling her lungs with iridescent grains as the paw pulled her deeper into the hourglass.

"There's no one here." Niotiya's disembodied voice floated down through the sand, disappointment oozing from each word. "Are you *sure* that trapdoor wasn't latched?"

"I thought it wasn't." Dourie's voice wavered, suddenly unsure. "Although the paper cuttings might have blown in earlier, when it was that new junior Matchmaker's turn to sweep up. She never does a good job."

Dourie tutted, and Zhi Ging felt the canopy sway as the two women climbed back down. Only then did she turn to face what was on the other end of the paw.

A sand spirit.

Although it initially had no features, grains of sand began to swirl around, building a face until it resembled a stout lion cub. It was slightly shorter than Zhi Ging, and it stared at her down its broad snout, a curled mane emerging like a tight halo of sunbeams behind its pointed ears. The spirit floated in the center of the sand-filled hourglass, a stocky paw scratching at a thick white knot that vanished beneath its mane.

Zhi Ging winced as she recognized the rope's pattern. It was identical to the one Ami had used to escape the underwater waterfall. The spirit was trapped inside the tight loops of a large white Pan Chang. It pressed its flat nose against her palm, its thick curled eyebrows tickling her fingers.

"What are you doing in here?" Zhi Ging whispered. She ran her hand along the spirit's mane, tugging at the heavy rope that tethered it to the hourglass. The sand spirit wagged its short tail in excitement as she pulled, but then it yelped. Its body crumbled to gray sand as the white loop tightened punishingly, jerking out of Zhi Ging's grasp.

"Sorry!" she cried as the spirit shakily rebuilt its lion cub form, noticeably smaller than before. It lowered its head between its front paws, its mane now hanging limp.

"What can I do?" Zhi Ging asked, tucking her hands behind her back in case she accidentally hurt the spirit again. It looked up at her with large glittering eyes that made her feel like she was staring into the midnight sky. The spirit raised its short tail, unfurling it to hit the inner ice of the hourglass. It shivered, then began to draw, using its tail as a thick brush.

Gray sand formed the scene's background as the sand spirit appeared high above a desert, bounding between clouds while two larger spirits watched on.

Suddenly, Matchmakers teemed across the dunes, ripping sand from the desert surface and sealing it in carts carved from ice.

The sand spirit howled, paws scrambling, as it lost its grip. Its tail stretched down, the young spirit's powers tethered to the sand now stolen by the Matchmakers. The two larger spirits tried to pull it to safety, but the younger spirit crumbled, its sand cascading into a waiting cart.

Zhi Ging's heart clenched tight. Clearly the Matchmakers hadn't just been stealing human children. She blinked, then peered closer at the scene sketched in front of her. There, standing by the cart, was a woman dressed in white robes. *Is that Ami?*

"When did this happen?" Zhi Ging asked, pointing at the miniature figure. "How long have you been trapped here?"

Before the spirit could draw its reply, it was wrenched down. Its short paws scrabbled around the edge of the funnel, desperately trying to keep itself in the hourglass. Sand cascaded past Zhi Ging, dragging her down with it. She flung an arm out, biting down a scream as her already ice-burned palm hit the hourglass's frozen surface.

"Hold on!" Zhi Ging stretched her free arm to the sand spirit, but it was too late; the spirit was being pulled down through the ice funnel and into the hollow cage below. She twisted, sand pressing down around her as she pushed her face to the ice, trying to spot it below her.

The sand spirit now cowered in the far corner of the cage, trying to avoid the sneering Matchmakers. Niotiya clutched the other end of the white rope while Dourie pulled a pair of masks from her robe.

"Right, who's next?"

"We're down to the last child," Niotiya snapped. "Ami hasn't sent any in months. We never should have trusted a Cyo B'Ahon."

Zhi Ging cringed. If either of them looked up now, they would spot her immediately. She tried to inch back, but the weight of the collapsed sand pinned her in place.

Niotiya snapped her fingers at Dourie, and the other Matchmaker nodded, scurrying backward out of the cellar.

Zhi Ging held her breath, trying to twist to the door, when it flew back open. Dourie had reappeared, dragging a dazed-looking boy behind her.

Zhi Ging's eyes widened in horror. It was the long-haired boy who had accepted a bun in the line earlier.

Niotiya smirked, breathing in deeply as she ran both hands along the length of her ornate headdress. "Ginsau is packing as we speak, ready to flee the city." A cruel sneer spread over her face. "Some Head Matchmaker she turned out to be. This is what happens when you allow titles to be inherited; the original strength becomes diluted through years of comfort. Ginsau had to make a deal with

Ami over a decade ago just to keep her control as Head Matchmaker. Soon I won't even need her." She grasped the top of the cage, not flinching as her fingers closed around the slim carved bars of ice. Niotiya wrenched the top up, then snapped her fingers at Dourie, gesturing for her to lower the boy in.

"Ginsau might be willing to lose her power, but I'll create a new paper cutter. I'm going to be the first Head Matchmaker in centuries to deserve the title." Niotiya slammed the lid back down, the sound echoing across the cellar and rattling up the hourglass.

"But the last seventy spirit attempts haven't worked," Dourie began. "How do you know this one . . ."

Niotiya glared at her until the younger Matchmaker blanched, lowering her head in apology.

"No one thought trapping a sand spirit was possible before me. Not even spirits will harm me now, not while I hold one of their own." Her eyes hardened as she took in Dourie's downcast face. "Don't be so arrogant as to expect I've shared my full plan with *you*. Even if I don't create a paper cutter tonight, the other provinces will still pay."

Niotiya pulled on a mask, concealing her features behind a sheer gray veil, and Dourie followed suit. Their faces swallowed, they stepped to either side of the narrow cage. As one, Niotiya and Dourie began to pull the rope back and forth, dragging the sand spirit across the cage between them. The spirit howled, desperately trying to avoid the boy now curled in the center. Its claws scratched against the ice each time the rope swung it back through the cage.

"Enough!" Niotiya snapped after a few moments.

Dourie turned to her, wheezing.

Niotiya marched back to the door, and Zhi Ging felt a flash of relief. *Maybe they're giving up.*

Instead the Matchmaker reached into a narrow vase and pulled out a gleaming rod of ice carved to resemble a bamboo cane. The room was silent as she strode back, each footstep a deafening click as she closed in on the spirit. She glared down at the slate-gray lion cub, adjusting her grip on the cane. "You should have learned to stop misbehaving long ago."

Time seemed to slow as Niotiya brought the cane down, slamming it expertly through the narrow bars and onto the lion cub's paw. In the last second before it hit, the spirit looked directly up at Zhi Ging, its eyes wide and pleading. Then it erupted, sand exploding outward to consume the cellar.

CHAPTER 39

The sand settled, leaving everything covered in a thick layer of gray. Ash-like grains sloughed off the spinning walls to collect around the Matchmakers' feet. Zhi Ging tried to peer through the dense sand that now covered the hourglass, but the shapes beneath her were blurred. She tapped the inner ice, trying to knock a patch loose as two figures leaned over the cage. Zhi Ging held her breath as small fragments tumbled down, revealing the scene below.

The boy was now hunched between the Matchmakers, coughing frantically while Dourie kept hold of the white rope.

Niotiya flung a paper scroll and scissors into his lap. "Vase," she barked, snapping her fingers in front of the boy's face. "Cut out a vase."

"I—what?" He shivered, then sneezed; a cloud of fine sand billowed in front of his face, much to the Matchmaker's disgust.

Zhi Ging gasped as thin streaks of gray swirled across his cheeks while he rubbed his nose. The way they twisted was identical to her own gold lines.

"She said cut out a vase!" Dourie snatched the boy's hand and forcefully closed it around the scissors, dragging it across the scroll.

A clumsy outline of a vase appeared and Niotiya snatched it up, shaking the paper cutting loose. The two Matchmakers watched in grim silence as the roughly cut shape floated down to land between their feet.

"So be it," Niotiya hissed, crushing the ordinary cutting beneath her shoe. Her eyes narrowed and she turned to Dourie. "Take him away. He'll be like the others soon."

The other Matchmaker nodded and grasped the boy's arms. His movements were jerky now, his limbs unbending as she hurried him out of the cellar.

Niotiya waited until their footsteps had vanished, then adjusted her blue headdress, its border of carved lapis lazuli butterflies clinking beneath her fingers. "Wake up," she ordered, shaking the white rope.

Gray sand gathered between the Pan Chang loops, tumbling over itself until the spirit reappeared, its lion cub ears pressed flat in fear. It reared up to the hourglass, its paws trying to squeeze back up the funnel.

"Not yet." Niotiya held the rope tight and tore eight thick strands from the spirit's mane. She tied them together, twisting the strands into an ugly tight knot. Eight gray tufts swayed in the center of the tangle, and Niotiya ripped them free. She curled each one around an out-stretched finger, smiling to herself as they warped into mercury rings.

Zhi Ging watched in horror as Niotiya flung what remained of the knotted strands into the air. The tangle stretched as the Matchmaker curled her hands into fists and it transformed into a hulking eight-limbed creature, identical to the spirits that had attacked before. Zhi Ging grimaced, watching as all traces of the lion cub's gentle coiling mane vanished and it shifted into a monstrous faceless spirit. *No wonder that strand was desperate to get in. It was trying to get back to the lion cub—back to its real self.*

"Come with me," Niotiya ordered, all eight rings glistening as she spoke. "There's time for one more child before the ceremony."

Once Niotiya and the tangle of spirit strands had left, the lion cub soared back up to the hourglass.

Zhi Ging scrambled to make space for the spirit as it began licking the paw Niotiya had hit. She realized with horror that there were numerous patches of dark sand along all four of its paws.

"How many times have they hurt you?" she asked in shock, reaching out to stroke the spirit's mane. It spun around, its hackles raised as it snarled at her. The spirit roared, sending a thick plume of sand forward that wrapped around Zhi Ging and ejected her from the hourglass. She thumped down hard onto the bamboo canopy as the sand in the hourglass rippled and darkened to a deep pitch black. It was clear the spirit wanted to be left alone.

Zhi Ging hesitated, her hand hovering above the open hourglass. "I'm sorry." She leaned forward, cautiously patting the inky surface. A warning growl rose up through the sand, and the dark grains pulled tight, the top layer stiffening to become as solid as stone beneath her fingers. She pulled back, stuffing her hands into her pockets to show the spirit she understood. Something smooth rolled against her left thumb, and she fumbled for it, scrambling along the heavy cloak lining until her hand closed around the REMedy pearl. Zhi Ging beamed as she pulled it free, relieved she'd never used it.

"Here," she whispered, dropping it gently into the center of the dark hourglass. Small seams of iridescent sand rippled beneath it, lapping against the pearl curiously. "Wusi, one of my tutors, said these pearls can help people recover while they sleep. I don't know if it'll help regrow your mane, but hopefully you won't be as sore." She paused, scanning the hourglass's dark surface, but the spirit remained silent, the earlier iridescent lines fading back to black.

It was only as Zhi Ging began to climb down from the platform that she spotted a flicker of movement. A small paw rose tentatively out from the sand, curling around the REMedy pearl to pull it back beneath the surface. The hourglass lightened as the pearl vanished, returning to its former slate gray. In the faint blue light cast by the ice, the earlier gold lines glinted along her palm. They were fainter now, but she could still see *help* etched across it. Zhi Ging clenched her fist tightly around the word, making a silent promise.

She would find a way to free the spirit.

"ZHI GING! WHERE DID YOU GO?" GERTIE GRABBED her the second she stepped back through the bead curtain. "Jack's still out searching for you." The weather-wax bees buzzed frantically above her head. "Go, let him know she's safe," the old woman ordered the bees, holding the glass beads aside for them.

"I'm sorry. I thought I'd be back before you. But I've worked out what the Matchmakers are up to. Sort of. I—" Zhi Ging broke off as Gahyau came bounding down to her. He nuzzled his bubble against her cheek, his unique version of a hug. She laughed. "When did you get here?"

"About an hour ago," Reishi answered, appearing at the top of the stairs, waving a half-eaten skewer of siu mai. Malo wove between his feet, the little phoenix's eyes never once leaving the bright yellow dumplings. "Lucky for you, Gertie sent one of her bees to let me know you and Jack were here. Otherwise it would have been a furious Bucbou coming to fetch you right now."

Zhi Ging followed Reishi upstairs and took a seat at the table. Its surface was now covered with detailed maps of the Matchmakers' Guild Hall, notes scrawled in thick ink along the sides. Scattered between scrolls were plates stacked with scallion pancakes, rolls of cheung fun drizzled in peanut sauce, and soft-boiled tea eggs. Her stomach rumbled.

"Minfun always makes sure to bring some food up before he closes shop for the night." Gertie smiled, handing Zhi Ging a bowl of spicy dan dan noodles. "Now, what were you saying about the Matchmakers?"

The two adults were pale by the time Zhi Ging had finished telling them a shortened version of what she had seen. She deliberately left out following the first spirit strand but suspected Gertie was expertly filling in the gaps from the way the old woman was tearing a scallion pancake to shreds. Reishi drummed the side of the table, his hoeng pin tea untouched beside him.

"Did either Matchmaker say where they were taking that boy?" he asked, frowning at the map in front of him.

"Niotiya said something about adding him to the others." Zhi Ging's nose crinkled. "But that doesn't make any sense. Why would they keep the children even after the experiment failed?"

The table fell silent, trying to work out what the Matchmakers had planned.

"I think these kidnappings are because of me," Zhi Ging admitted quietly a few moments later.

Both adults turned to her in surprise.

"What makes you think that?" Gertie asked, her voice gentle.

"Niotiya's trying to create a new person with paper-cutting powers." Zhi Ging pushed the last cheung fun around her bowl, the thick white roll sliding from side to side. She'd been replaying the Matchmakers' conversation in her mind. "The Matchmaker Ceremony happens every twelve years, right? I'm meant to be the one the provinces bid on this year, but my mother helped me escape when I was still a baby. She won't have enough paper-cutting power left for the next twelve years, though." Zhi Ging took a deep breath and placed her chopsticks down. "I knew that, but I never thought about what would happen next. I guess I thought the Matchmakers would just stop the ceremony."

She stood up, her gold-lined arms catching the lantern light as she began to pace the room. "We thought the Matchmakers were just searching for me, trying to get me back in time for the ceremony. But there's a group of them trying to re-create the spirit curse." Zhi Ging shut her eyes as her jumbled thoughts finally came together. "They're trying to repeat the original conditions inside that cage: getting someone to swallow spirit sand, just like in Omophilli's origin story. But the spirit they've caught, I think it's too young." She winced, the lion cub's terrified expression flashing through her mind. "It's just scared; it wouldn't let me near it afterward."

"Wait, you came into direct contact with the spirit?" Reishi asked, ageshifting down in shock.

"It helped me hide from the Matchmakers." Zhi Ging

traced the word still shining up from her palm and held it out for Gertie and Reishi to see. "It doesn't want to be doing this. Not the kidnappings across Wengyuen or the experiments in the cellar." She turned to face them. "We have to help the sand spirit escape too, not just the other children."

Gertie frowned, scratching her chin, as Reishi said, "Absolutely not." He returned to his usual age as he shook his head. "Spirits are known to be vengeful, and they can't differentiate between human faces. It wouldn't be able to tell if you were a Matchmaker or an ordinary Omophillian. What if we set it loose, and it attacked someone?"

"But it recognized *me*. It knew I wasn't a Matchmaker," Zhi Ging argued. "And I saw it try to avoid the boy. I think it *can* tell the difference."

"We can try to help the spirit, but only after we've found the missing children," Reishi sighed, trying to soothe Zhi Ging's frustration. "I'll send a message to the Folklore tutor back in Hok Woh. He can get the spirit to safety, but it'll have to wait."

"How are we even meant to find the children?" Zhi Ging could hear the disappointment leaking into her voice, but she couldn't help it. Why couldn't they help the sand spirit first, since they knew where it was being kept?

Thanks to her mother, she had spirit magic in her. Would Reishi have left her to the Matchmakers if he thought she was more spirit than Silhouette?

Reishi pointed at the scrolls on the table. "Gertie and I suspect they're in the Omophilli pagoda itself. In the hours leading up to the Matchmaker Ceremony, all private buildings across the capital are meant to open to the public. All *except* the pagoda."

"Only Matchmakers are allowed in and out," Gertie added.

"What's our plan, then?" Zhi Ging asked. "Do we disguise ourselves as Matchmakers?"

"No." Gertie peered out of the window, her face illuminated by lantern light. Excited snatches of conversation filtered up from the streets below as people gathered ahead of the ceremony. "Now that we know there *is* a secret tunnel, I say we break in during the midnight announcement. There's less than an hour to go, and it'll be our best chance to search the pagoda without bumping into any Matchmakers. They'll all be at the main ceremony, enjoying being the center of attention."

The group leaped as the glass curtain downstairs shattered, the sound of smashing beads filling the air. The door burst open, and the bees swarmed in, vibrating loudly as they streamed around Gertie.

She turned to the others, appearing gaunt as every single line on her weathered face pulled tight, accentuating her horror.

"It's Jack—the Matchmakers have him."

CHAPTER 40

They sprinted into the alley, Malo soaring high above them. Zhi Ging raced ahead, ignoring Gertie's and Reishi's cries as she slipped between the crowds now filling Omophilli's streets.

If I'd just waited, Jack wouldn't have been taken.

Images of the caged boy flashed through her mind, his features flickering to become Jack's.

Loud music boomed along the streets, cymbals and drums fighting with firecrackers and fireworks to be heard. Zhi Ging tried to push past the crowd as it wound through the city, but the never-ending throng seemed determined to stop at every single snack and souvenir stand that lined the already narrow streets. She felt her panic rise when the press of celebrating travelers suddenly picked up speed and splintered between two alleys. Zhi Ging was swept toward the left path, and when she managed to turn around, there was no sign of either Gertie or Reishi. Malo dived back into her hood, and Zhi Ging heard the panicked cry of a father calling out his daughter's name. Her vision swam as claustrophobia set in, unsure if the girl had simply slipped free from his grip or was another last-minute victim like Jack.

Finally the teeming mass of people dispersed, their voices echoing and magnified across the trade district's central square. Zhi Ging stumbled, dazzled by the bright lanterns that studded every roof.

A cluster of Matchmakers stood on a makeshift stage in the middle of the square, their feet level with the crowd's faces. The Guild Hall chandelier floated between them; the entire structure was draped in swathes of silk, its newly polished surface ready to be revealed at the end of the ceremony. Above it a kaleidoscope of porcelain-winged butterflies kept the chandelier afloat, thousands of forelegs clasped around its chain.

"Move it!" a man behind Zhi Ging barked, pushing her roughly aside as a sedan barged past.

Malo chirped in anger from her hood, the tips of his wings starting to spark.

"Don't," Zhi Ging hissed, her eyes darting across to a pair of Matchmakers prowling through the crowd. "We can't do anything to catch their attention."

The little phoenix huffed, his eyes narrowed as he watched the man deliver the sedan to an ornate ceremony box on the far side of the stage.

Six decorated boxes had been arranged in a crescent around the Matchmakers' stage, their colorful lanterns illuminating the province delegates within. Zhi Ging crouched low as a woman leaned out of the glass province box, ordering a skewer of bing tong wu lou from a passing vendor. The hardened sugar syrup shone in the lantern light, making the skewer of strawberries gleam as if they were made of glass themselves. Zhi Ging ran an anxious hand through Malo's feathers. *How many people in that box have seen my arrest warrant? What if the Lead Glassmith is in there?*

The music came to a sudden stop, and Niotiya appeared on the stage, an ornate cloud collar glittering against her red robes. Its overlapping curved silk petals stretched out toward the Matchmaker's shoulders as if two large embroidered butterflies had landed on her.

Confused whispers rippled across the watching crowd.

"Only the paper cutter is meant to wear that," a nearby vendor hissed, his tongs hovering above a tray of fried dumplings. "Why has *she* got it on?"

Zhi Ging's stomach tightened. While everyone else was staring at Niotiya, eight Matchmakers had slithered up from beneath the stage, gray masks covering their faces. Their sleeves hung loose as they swayed from side to side, like snakes ready to strike. Above them on the stage, Niotiya clenched her hands into fists, eight identical gray rings glimmering on her fingers. Zhi Ging's eyes darted back down to where the eight Matchmakers' feet should be and instead spotted thin trails of sand twisting back beneath the stage. Panic crackled down her spine, and she began to push forward, desperate to unmask the spirit strands before they could attack.

"Welcome!" Niotiya said, her voice cutting through the murmurs filling the square. "Tonight's ceremony will be quite different from any you've ever attended." She smirked and brushed a hand over the cloud collar. The chandelier behind her chimed as the porcelain-winged butterflies raised it higher. "Ginsau is no longer Head Matchmaker. From this moment onward, that position is *mine.*"

Surprise rippled through the province boxes and several of the Matchmakers onstage glanced at each other in concern.

"What does that mean for our already submitted bids?"

Zhi Ging's head jerked up. She'd recognize that nasal voice anywhere. The Lead Glassmith was scowling out from the glass province box, the red flush across his nose a clear sign he'd begun celebrating an expected win hours earlier. He banged an empty glass against the box's wooden sill, clearly frustrated he'd spent the past week trying to impress the wrong Matchmaker.

Niotiya ignored him, a sneer curling across her lips as she turned to the other delegates. "Rather than a single province paying once every twelve years, from tonight onward you will *all* pay an annual Matchmaker fee, with a fine for whichever province contributes the least."

The six boxes erupted, two delegates from the gold

province roaring with laughter at the ridiculous suggestion while a carved lacquer delegate shook his head in obvious disgust.

"That wouldn't be fair at all," a silk province leader blustered, glowering at the blue stand beside him. "That would mean the porcelain province getting paper cuttings for twenty-four years."

"Absolutely not!" the Lead Glassmith agreed. "If everyone has access to the paper cuttings, they have no value. We refuse to pay. I officially withdraw our province bid."

"Quite right." A tall woman in the carved lacquer province box nodded. "You can't fine us all if we refuse this ridiculous new system."

Delegates from all six stands turned back to Niotiya, their eyes gleaming in collective triumph. She stared at them, twisting one of the silk petals on her cloud collar. In the sudden silence, every single person across the square heard the faint snap as she tugged it loose. The Matchmaker curled her fist around the petal, crushing it.

"You're not listening," Niotiya said crisply, her contemptuous tone piercing their confidence like a blade. "At no point did I say *any* of you would receive paper cuttings."

Confusion spread through the boxes, and Zhi Ging felt her stomach drop. They were too late; whatever the Matchmakers had planned, this was it.

Niotiya blew the crumpled petal to the delegates in a mocking kiss, and the chandelier's silk coverings fell away.

Panicked screams echoed across the square as people realized what they were looking at. Rather than ornate carved sculptures, the chandelier was now covered with hundreds of glass children. The crowd surged forward, frantic parents reaching up to their stolen sons and daughters. Zhi Ging felt her heart stop when she spotted Jack dangling from the closest chandelier arm, a thin ribbon looped around his frozen wrist the only thing stopping him from crashing down onto the stage.

"Release them!" Gertie was suddenly racing past Zhi Ging, rage radiating from her. The old woman tugged her hairpins loose, thrusting each one at a waiting weatherwax bee. They swarmed above her, pins pointed directly at Niotiya.

"I wouldn't do that if I were you." The Matchmaker smirked, snapping her fingers. "Hurt me or my butterflies, and I'll let the chandelier fall."

The chandelier clinked, the glass children swaying precariously as the butterflies raised the structure higher.

"Lord Rhus, have you spotted your daughter yet?" Niotiya said, pointing at a small glass girl, no more than five, hanging by a thin red ribbon. "Oh, Senator Cin, there's your nephew—the only male heir to your family's gold mines, I believe?"

"This must be some sort of trick," the woman in the

carved lacquer province stand cried, though her face was pale. "You commissioned the Glassmiths to create these; they're not real children."

"How dare you!" the Lead Glassmith roared, turning to her with a crimson face.

"Let's find out, shall we?" Niotiya said, her smile peeling back to reveal sharp teeth. She flicked her wrist, and the butterflies released the chain, sending the chandelier hurtling to the ground.

CHAPTER 41

"No!" Zhi Ging lurched forward but was knocked to the ground as a stampede of frantic limbs surged ahead, hands reaching desperately for the plummeting chandelier.

Gertie's weather-wax bees swerved down, forming a protective shield around her as Malo struggled to help her up.

Niotiya watched the swell of horrified faces racing forward with cold amusement. At the very last second, she snapped her fingers, and the butterflies caught the end of the chain, stopping the chandelier inches above the stage's wooden floor.

The crowd froze, scared to move.

"As I was saying . . ." The Matchmaker strode along the stage, smirking at the ashen-faced delegates. "There'll be an annual fine for the province that pays the least. I suspect you've worked out by now what that fine is. If not, I'm sure you'll quickly learn."

Zhi Ging saw the Lead Glassmith's eyes dart back to the chandelier, frantically counting the number of green ribbons.

"To keep it interesting," Niotiya continued, winking at the woman from the carved lacquer province, "no province will know what the others have paid. That will only be revealed at the new and improved annual ceremony."

There was a scream from the edge of the stage as a Matchmaker was pulled backward into the crowd, two furious pairs of hands grabbing the bottom of her cloak.

Niotiya tutted, frowning at the interruption. "You see, Dourie," she said, addressing the struggling Matchmaker directly, "that's why I never shared my entire plan. You always were a fool."

Niotiya turned back to face the square and stretched her fingers wide. The eight knotted spirit strands rose up, their decoy Matchmaker robes tearing to reveal twisting gray limbs that towered over the crowd.

"Zhi Ging, get *back*!" Reishi cried out over the crowd, his voice breaking.

She spun around, searching for the Cyo B'Ahon, but he must have ageshifted down.

The eight strands began to coil protectively around Niotiya, the stage rattling as spinning gray sand caught against the rough wood. One of the stage panels came loose, and Zhi Ging froze, feeling a blast of all-too-familiar chill rush out through it. She dived forward as Niotiya turned to face the delegates, narrowly avoiding one of the circling spirit strands. Beneath the stage, the air was bitterly cold.

Zhi Ging crawled forward, her hands and knees sinking into a thick layer of snow. "Hello?" she whispered into the gloom. "Are you in here?"

There was a faint whine, then the muffled sound of soft paws hitting ice. Zhi Ging hurried toward the sound until she found the spirit, its lion cub body now squeezed inside another ice cage. The knotted tangle of strands controlled by Niotiya hovered directly above the cub's cage, gray sand cascading down as its eight limbs whirred inches above Zhi Ging's head.

"Don't worry, we'll get you out."

She nodded at Malo, but the spirit cowered as the phoenix's wings blazed into flames.

"It's okay," Zhi Ging murmured, trying to reassure it. "He won't hurt you."

The spirit shook its head, its tightly curled mane uncoiling and recoiling in panic. Above them the strands began to shimmer; the heat from Malo's flames caused the sand to congeal, thick seams of glass trickling across their surface.

"You're made from heat-sensitive sand!" Zhi Ging gasped, realization dawning on her.

The Matchmakers must have captured the spirit from the desert where she'd had her Concealment challenge.

Malo chirped and snuffed out his flames, plunging them back into darkness.

Zhi Ging knelt beside the spirit and placed her left hand on its cage, ignoring the cold that bit into her fingers. No wonder Niotiya's experiments hadn't worked. All that heat-sensitive sand needed to transform to glass was a single sunbeam. Once the gray sand had been absorbed, anyone's body temperature would have been more than enough to turn the sand, and themselves, into glass.

Above them, the stage creaked as Niotiya's voice rose over the sound of the spinning strands. "And, for those of you who think your children are safe . . ." The Matchmaker paused and Zhi Ging felt the ground quake beneath her. Blinding light shone down through the trapdoor as she and the cage began to rise up to the stage.

Niotiya's smile dropped when she spotted Zhi Ging crouched beside the spirit. Her shock hardened into fierce recognition, and one hand clutched tight around her cloud collar. "You!" she hissed, lunging forward.

Zhi Ging scrambled backward, but her left hand was still frozen against the cage. She flung her other arm high, her mind filled with nothing but a desperate need to protect the spirit. Her trapped hand pulsed, and Zhi Ging felt the word "help" sear across the ice.

An earsplitting crack echoed across the square as a golden air rail pierced the cage, shattering the thick ice.

The sand spirit blinked, then cautiously lifted a paw to the knot around its neck. The white rope slithered to the floor, split in half by the air rail.

Niotiya froze, her horrified eyes staring unblinking at the destroyed knot.

The spirit reared up, its booming roar that of crashing sand dunes. It lost its lion cub form, transforming into a vengeful desert storm that erupted outward.

Thick walls of sand thundered past Zhi Ging, the worst of the churning storm parting around her. The swirling tempest knocked several Matchmakers from the stage, tearing through the panicked crowd before snatching the eight knotted strands in the air.

The spirit returned to its lion shape, its claws slicing through the crude tangle that tied the sand together. It growled in triumph as the strands flowed back into its mane, the buildings that surrounded the square trembling from the noise. It turned to Niotiya then, baring its teeth.

The woman scrambled backward, frantically trying to remove the gray rings from her fingers. She flung seven back at the spirit before leaping from the stage, elbowing her way through the terrified crowd with her right hand possessively clutching the final ring.

Zhi Ging snatched at the fallen rings before they could roll off the stage. The spirit thudded down, leaving sand-blasted pawprints across the wooden slats as it prowled toward her. She held the collected rings out, her hands shaking as it loomed over her.

"Zhi Ging, get away. It thinks you're a Matchmaker!" she heard Gertie cry as weather-wax bees tugged desperately at her sleeves.

The spirit sniffed at the abandoned rings, then growled as it stretched its jaws wide. A thick sandy tongue rolled out and lapped them up, the contact causing Zhi Ging's arms to fizz as gold lines erupted out past her wrists toward her elbows.

The spirit purred deeply as the stolen sand returned to its body. It looked up then, its eyes narrowed on the escaping Niotiya. Sand roiled across its body, and it transformed back into a swirling squall that shot forward, gray sand cascading over the screaming crowd.

Zhi Ging spun to watch it, but at the very last second it twisted away from the terrified Matchmaker and shot into the Guild Hall, the heavy front doors shattering like kindling.

A tight silence filled the square as everyone held their breath, unsure of what was about to happen. Zhi Ging stood on the stage, her legs trembling as the chandelier swayed high above her.

The post pipe at the back of the Guild began to rattle, and the spirit thundered through it. Its sandy body pressed tight against the glass, leaving jagged trails of gray until it had stretched the full length of the pipe, and its lion body vanished. The water in the post pipe began to hiss and boil, trapped steam causing the entire structure to rumble. The heavy brackets that held the post pipe in place buckled, a piercing screech echoing across the square as the glass rose.

The fleeing crowd ducked as serrated glass screws

began to rain down, each one as sharp as a lion's fang. Zhi Ging pulled Malo out of the way as several embedded themselves into the stage, vibrating where they landed.

Above them, the post pipe twisted in the air, thick glass writhing around itself. Zhi Ging screamed as it transformed into a glass dragon, gray sand pulsing between its scales like angry veins. This was what her fate plate had tried to show her! The dragon raised its head and boiling steam erupted from between its glass jaws. It tested out its new tail, wildly thrashing what had been the end of the post pipe. Tiles shattered beneath it, roofs crumbling as if they themselves had been made from sand.

Lanterns tumbled down, their candles catching the delicate paper to become plummeting fireballs. There was widespread panic in the square now; every way out was clogged with those trying to flee down the capital's narrow alleys. Abandoned food carts lay on their sides while delegates scrambled out of their boxes. The dragon swooped down into the crowd, pinning a junior Matchmaker between its talons. The girl screamed as its long glass whiskers raced across her hands.

It's searching for the final ring! Zhi Ging realized with a jolt.

"It's not her!" she screamed from the stage. "That's the wrong Matchmaker." The dragon flung the girl aside, its tail coiling in frustration as it turned to Zhi Ging. She gulped, tripping over what remained of its ice cage as she scrambled backward. Malo leaped in front of her, his wings crackling with heat.

"Get off the stage!"

Zhi Ging twisted her head and saw Reishi and Gertie pushing against the crowd, desperately trying to reach her. Before Zhi Ging could reply, the dragon's tail thumped down, breaking the makeshift platform in half. The force of the glass pulverized the wood to dust and Zhi Ging fell backward off the collapsing structure. Reishi and Gertie were suddenly cut off from her, their faces distorted on the other side of the glass tail. The dragon lowered its snarling face to her, the burning remains of lanterns caught between its horns.

"It's me," Zhi Ging squeaked, trying to hold out her gold-lined hand, but the *help* had vanished from her palm now.

The dragon's eyes narrowed, no sign of recognition flickering across its features.

Zhi Ging shuddered, her terrified face reflected in the dragon's pupilless glass orbs. *Does it even remember being a lion cub?*

The dragon reared up, boiling steam erupting between its fangs. Its snaking body was now completely clear, its glass scales clinking as it tensed for attack. It lunged at Zhi Ging, its jaws open wide, and she leaped out of the way as Malo flared up and unleashed the full force of his flames.

Through the blazing light she saw the dragon twist; its

mouth snatched at the chandelier chain instead, porcelain butterflies shattering between its teeth. Time seemed to slow as Zhi Ging watched the dragon swing the chandelier high. Children glinted above her, frozen faces illuminated by moonlight.

Their ribbons stretched tight as the entire structure spun three times, arcing through the air before beginning its plummet back toward the ground. The dragon roared and opened its jaws wide, swallowing the chandelier, and the children, whole.

CHAPTER 42

The dragon shot into the air, glass children tumbling down the length of its gleaming water-filled body. Reishi wrenched Zhi Ging out of the way seconds before its tail swept past and wooden splinters cascaded over them. Beside him, Gertie summoned her weather-wax bees, arms raised like a general as they swarmed past her. Malo swooped after the glass dragon, his beak snapping at its tail. Suddenly the phoenix chirped in surprise, tumbling backward before stretching a wing up toward the dragon.

Zhi Ging followed his gaze and gasped. "Wait, look!" She caught Gertie's arm, pointing to the dragon's stomach. As if caught in a mirage, the children were beginning to shimmer, shedding thin sheets of glass from their bodies like snakeskin. The shards shattered against the dragon's hollow body, transforming back into the spirit's original sand. Zhi Ging yelped as Jack blinked, color returning to his face. Around him others began to wake up too, their voices muffled by the thick glass. Her relief vanished as water rushed over them; the trapped air pocket that had protected them slid away as the dragon spun in the air.

"We've got to get them out before they drown!" Zhi Ging shouted as Jack was swept up by the current, his hands struggling to find a grip inside the dragon's smooth post pipe body.

"We'll have to distract the spirit first," Gertie instructed, her bees billowing behind her like a glittering cape. "We can't risk panicking it. If it thinks it's in danger, it'll turn more water to steam."

The dragon twisted above them, its slender whiskers coiling through the air as it searched for Niotiya and the final sand ring.

"That's not our only problem," Reishi muttered grimly, ageshifting down as he pointed at gray scales that had begun to appear along the dragon's glass body. "It's confused. The spirit is drawing power from the sand originally used to create the glass post pipe, but that sand mixing with its own will have shaken its grasp of reality." He released Gahyau from a silk pouch, frowning. "I doubt it now remembers if it's a sand spirit disguised as a dragon or a genuine lightning-breathing creature trapped within a glass shell. At any second it could shake that first reality loose, transforming the post pipe into a real dragon."

Zhi Ging and Gertie looked up in horror. Long stretches of the post pipe were already becoming opaque, heavy gray scales pressing through the outer glass as the dragon moved. They were forced to duck as it swooped low across the square, its talons inches from their faces. Jack and the others tumbled past, crashing through pockets of air as the water surged in sync with the dragon's twisting movements.

"It doesn't get to do this," Zhi Ging muttered, her hands curling into tight fists as she scrambled back up. The post pipe had already claimed too many lives back in Fei Chui, its narrow pipes responsible for countless drownings over the years. "You should've left me alone once I got to Hok Woh!" she shouted up at the thrashing post pipe. "Reishi didn't help me escape you, and my mother didn't hide me from Matchmakers, just for others to get hurt instead." She took a step forward, her voice now stronger than any air rail. "I'm done running away."

Malo landed on her shoulder, his eyes narrowed in silent understanding.

Before Reishi or Gertie could react, Zhi Ging nodded, and the phoenix spread his wings, lifting her up to the dragon.

She grabbed onto its tail and began to climb, her fingers scrabbling between slick glass scales and rough gray plates that scratched her palms like sandpaper. The dragon spun in the air, sending Jack and the other children racing past beneath her, splashing as they struggled to keep their heads above the roaring water.

Zhi Ging sped up, her eyes darting between the rapidly disappearing patches of glass, searching for one of the post pipe's mailing hatches.

There! Tucked behind the dragon's hind leg was a hatch, its smooth glass door rattling on its hinges. It was large enough to fit a waterproof mailbag, so the hatch would be more than wide enough for the others to escape. Zhi Ging scrambled for it, frantically knocking on the remaining stretches of glass, gesturing for the trapped children to swim after her. They followed her through the churning water, Jack's eyes flashing in understanding when he spotted the hatch. He raced forward, his feet frantically treading water as he raised both hands to the door.

"No!" Zhi Ging flung a desperate hand forward as gray scales rippled past her, bursting over the glass and sealing the hatch shut.

Jack hammered the inner glass, bubbles obscuring his face as another wave crashed over him.

Zhi Ging and Malo tugged frantically between new gray scales, trying to wrench the hatch open. Its handle came loose in her hand, and the dragon howled, finally spotting them. It jerked down, speeding toward the square as it tried to shake her free.

The water around Jack and the others began to bubble, heating up as the dragon writhed back and forth in confusion.

"Let go!" Zhi Ging screamed as Malo flapped his wings, trying to keep them in place. "If it attacks us, it'll hurt the others."

She released her grip around the dragon, spinning as she hurtled through the air. She landed hard against the abandoned glass province box, a cloud of dust billowing up around her.

Gertie and Reishi raced forward, but she held out a shaking hand, her eyes still fixed on the dragon as it thudded down in front of her, the five other boxes instantly crushed beneath its weight. It snarled at Zhi Ging, its antler-like horns darkening before her eyes. The dragon tensed as Gahyau darted past its snout, the weather-wax bees forming a solid glittering wall between it and Zhi Ging.

"Quickly now," Gertie hissed, the top of her face appearing at the side of the box. "Get down while it's distracted."

"But the others!" Zhi Ging flung an arm toward the dragon. "We can't leave without them."

"And we're not," Gertie urged. "Reishi spotted another hatch at the back of its mane. We just need to keep the dragon focused on the weather-wax bees while he helps Jack and the others out."

Zhi Ging hobbled to the edge of the box, then hesitated, her last words echoing in her mind.

"We can't leave without them," she repeated, her eyes wide as she turned back to the dragon, "and *it* can't leave without its sand."

"Zhi Ging, wait!" Gertie cried as she hurtled across the top of the box.

The dragon jerked back as Zhi Ging burst through the shimmering wall of bees, and out of the corner of her eye she spotted Reishi ageshift down in alarm, his yellow robes billowing around him as he froze halfway up the dragon's foreleg.

"You're searching for your final piece of stolen sand, right? Let me help." Zhi Ging looked up at the dragon, her heart racing. "I bet you can't leave Omophilli without it. *That's* why you keep flying above the square; you're still tethered to this city!"

The dragon snapped its jaws in frustration, then gave a single sharp begrudging nod.

"I'll help you find Niotiya." Zhi Ging took a step forward, both palms up. "But only if you promise to let the others go. I don't think you want to hurt them, not really. You weren't eating them, you were helping to hide them from the Matchmakers. Just like you did for me." She took a deep breath, trying to spot the scared lion cub underneath the dragon's hard features. "I think that's also why you turned so much of the post pipe's water to steam before you swallowed them; you knew they'd drown if there was no air at all."

A few of the dragon's gray scales crumbled back to glass as it considered her. An inner eyelid swept over its narrow eyes, and Zhi Ging's reflection was replaced with a shimmering echo of her face inside the hourglass. Behind the dragon's head, Reishi continued his careful climb while Jack swam through the now-still water, leading the others to the hatch hidden under its tangled mane.

"Deal?" Zhi Ging pressed, taking a tentative step to the dragon. It growled and bared its teeth, images of the Matchmakers flashing across its eyes. She shuffled back, her heart hammering, and both Reishi and Jack froze, their hands stretched toward the hatch. Zhi Ging bit her lip, cursing her confidence. Why would it trust her? The only humans it had met until now were Matchmakers.

Good thing you're not really human, then, isn't it? a small voice whispered in her mind.

Zhi Ging took a deep breath and looked back up at the dragon. "I'm not trying to trick you." She held out her left hand, gold lines glinting on her palm. "Until we get the last of your sand back, you can keep some of my spirit magic. Take it—we can share."

She gulped as the dragon bent its head to her, its snout snuffling her palm. It paused for a long moment, then raised a claw, holding it out toward Zhi Ging as the REMedy pearl appeared between its talons, rising up between glass scales.

"That's right," she squeaked with relief. "It's me."

The dragon wagged its long tail, and the glass hatch beneath its mane popped open. Reishi scrambled to pull the others out, Gahyau guiding the drenched children down to Gertie.

Zhi Ging held her breath, waiting until she saw Jack leap out of the hatch before turning her attention back to the dragon. Its glass whiskers traced gently along the swirling lines that covered her fingers, and the gold clung to them, rising up from Zhi Ging's skin like unspooling silk thread. She shivered, her vision blurring as the lines came loose.

For a split second, her hand seemed to flatten paper-thin as the dragon's whiskers wove the gold together, creating a perfect glowing orb. A strange wave of giggles bubbled through Zhi Ging as she watched her hand return to normal.

I just made a deal with a spirit. Turns out I've earned the Lead Glassmith's warrant after all.

"Stop!" Jack cried, racing under the dragon as its whiskers continued to tickle Zhi Ging's wrist. "You'll turn back to paper if it takes too much!"

"What?!" Reishi snapped as he raced toward the glass province box.

A thin gray streak slashed through the air, snatching the floating orb from between Zhi Ging and the dragon. It vanished into the shadows of a half-collapsed alley, where it illuminated Niotiya's face. The Matchmaker's robes were torn and covered with a thick layer of dust, the cloud collar hanging over one shoulder.

The dragon snarled, spotting its final missing strand:

the tendril tethered to the ring gleaming above the Matchmaker's knuckle.

"Well, look at that." Niotiya smirked, twisting the golden spirit magic as if examining a large gem. "There I was thinking I'd just be collecting province payments tonight. Looks like I also get paper-cutting powers for myself."

The spirit growled, its unblinking eyes trained on the woman's hand as the REMedy pearl vanished back within its claw.

"Oh, I've had quite enough out of you," she snapped, scowling as the dragon reared up. "In fact, I have all I need right here." She jabbed her finger at it, and the final tethered strand shot forward like a whip, piercing the dragon's glass body.

"No!" Zhi Ging screamed, but it was too late.

Cracks spilled across the length of the glass, and the dragon's anguished roar cut out as it shattered. What was left of the post pipe water flooded through the square, washing Jack, Reishi, and Gertie down another alley.

"You didn't have to do that!" Zhi Ging cried, cradling the broken glass dragon head.

Niotiya narrowed her gaze, her calculating eyes staring at the gold lines that still covered Zhi Ging's arms, their swirling pattern now magnified through the glass in her hands. Greed twitched in the Matchmaker's cheeks, and she pouted at the orb in her hand.

"A palm's worth of spirit magic really isn't much, is

it?" The tethered strand lashed out again, coiling tight around Zhi Ging and Malo. They were dragged forward off the box to float in front of Niotiya.

The Matchmaker leaned forward, her eyes fixed on the glittering gold lines. "I think I deserve a *lot* more."

CHAPTER 43

Zhi Ging struggled as the gray strand dragged them into Omophilli's spinning pagoda, the glass dragon head still in her arms. Its horns pressed uncomfortably against her stomach, while beside her Malo kicked furiously at the tendril swaddling them, its heavy sand snuffing out every flame before it could flicker to life. Zhi Ging strained her ears, trying to hear anyone who might be able to help, but the constant whir of spinning walls grew louder with each floor Niotiya climbed. Unlike the Fei Chui pagoda, with its split center decorated with vast panels of stained glass, the Omophilli half was covered in a thick paper screen that stretched the length of the tower, concealing them from the rest of the capital.

Malo nudged Zhi Ging with his beak as he finally wriggled a wing loose, his feathers blurring with heat.

"I wouldn't do that if I were you," Niotiya sneered, snuffing out the small flame between two fingers. "Do you really think we added *all* the glass children we had to that chandelier? There are dozens hidden across each floor of this pagoda. If you set things alight to escape, what happens to them? I doubt glass does very well after falling through several layers of burning wood."

The phoenix chirped, and the flames that had begun to spark on his wing vanished.

Zhi Ging twisted her head in confusion when they reached the top of the pagoda. There was nothing at the top of the staircase, just dozens of hanging silks listing the names of previous Head Matchmakers.

Niotiya tugged the oldest silk aside, revealing a heavy wooden door. She unlocked it, and the gray strand dragged Zhi Ging in behind her.

"Recognize your old room?" she asked, smirking as she lit a solitary lantern.

The gray strand wrenched Zhi Ging into a wooden chair, threading around her until she couldn't move. She ignored Niotiya, her eyes darting around the room as she frowned in confusion. *Where's the window?* There had definitely been a window in her memory that floated free in Hok Woh's catacombs. Her mother's paper-cutting dragon had flown her to safety through a window. Niotiya spotted her roaming gaze and tapped a section of wall beside her where the wood was slightly darker in color. "Do you really think we'd leave that after your escape?"

The Matchmaker placed the golden orb of spirit magic on top of a nearby cabinet. She smiled hungrily, then ripped her cloud collar off and rolled up her billowing

sleeves as she strode back across the room to crouch beside Zhi Ging.

Niotiya curled her ring finger, and the gray strand
stretched Zhi Ging's left arm out. The Matchmaker leaned
forward and tapped one of the lines twisting up from Zhi
Ging's wrist, her gray ring glimmering in the lantern light.

Malo snapped at the woman, struggling to break free
of the strand's grip.

"I'll have none of that." She tapped the ring and a miniature tendril unfurled from the strand, wrapping around
the phoenix's beak.

"Let him g—" Zhi Ging gave a sharp yelp as Niotiya
pinched her arm, trying to pluck the gold line loose. Her
skin burned beneath the woman's fingers, but the gold
stayed in place, refusing to lift up.

"I saw them come loose," the Matchmaker muttered,
giving Zhi Ging's arm another impatient tug. Zhi Ging
bit down, trying to ignore the pain as the woman's nails
nipped at her skin, pulling at the gold lines. Niotiya
scowled down at the glass dragon head still pinned between Zhi Ging's arms. "If that pathetic creature could
do it, so can I."

She snatched the glass from Zhi Ging and snapped off
its whiskers before hurling the rest at a far wall. A jagged
crack raced across its surface and the dragon head im-
ploded, large shards collapsing back to sand.

Zhi Ging froze, fighting to keep her expression calm,
as behind Niotiya the sand began to shimmer. The air

vibrated, the outline of a lion cub flickering across the rising gray sand before swirling under the cabinet.

It had survived!

Zhi Ging tried to spot the sand spirit between the shadows, but it was concealed within the dappled gloom. The only hint it was even there was a new faint hiss of tumbling sand, barely noticeable over the rotating walls. The thick paper screen spun past, and Zhi Ging frowned at it. Jack, Reishi, and Gertie would have no idea where they were, so it was up to her and Malo to help the spirit. She closed her hand around Malo's wing and gave the phoenix a small squeeze. Time to uphold her part of the deal. The spirit had released the others, so she had to help get its final bit of sand. But how would she get the ring from Niotiya while she was tied to a chair?

The Matchmaker dropped the glass whiskers onto a table, her knuckles whitening around the first one as she leaned back toward Zhi Ging. The woman clamped her hand over Zhi Ging's wrist and began dragging the glass along her arm. It scratched her skin, but once again the gold lines refused to budge.

Niotiya snarled, tossing the first whisker aside and snatching a new one. "Why isn't this working?!" she growled, prodding the next whisker along the edge of a gold line, trying to prize it loose. A purple vein in her forehead had now been joined by a second; two pulsing frown lines stretched tight toward her nose.

The solitary lantern dimmed as Niotiya made her way

through the pile of glass whiskers, her desperation growing with each failed attempt. Behind her the sound of
hissing sand grew louder.

Zhi Ging's arm became numb, barely registering the
glass as it prodded, jabbed, and poked her. Niotiya's tight
grip had left an imprint around her wrist, the Matchmaker's ring leaving a deep indent where it pressed into
her skin. Zhi Ging stared down at it, her breath catching
in her throat as the lantern's candle stub flared, releasing
one final burst of light before it extinguished. *That's it!*

The Matchmaker paused in the gloom, finally noticing the rising hiss. She frowned and began to turn to the
cabinet.

"Can't you see what's happening?" Zhi Ging laughed,
catching the woman's attention.

Niotiya glowered at her in suspicion, wrapping her
spare hand around the final glass whisker.

Zhi Ging wriggled, imperceptibly twisting her arm as
she nodded at the gray strand holding her in place. "Your
ring's been pressed against my arm every time you tried
to lift a gold line. A ring made of *spirit sand*. It's letting the
tethered strand absorb my power instead." She paused,
watching Niotiya's eyes widen in fury. "It's literally been
stealing it from right beneath your fingers," Zhi Ging finished with a wide grin.

There was a loud snap as the glass between the Matchmaker's hands broke.

"Haven't you noticed the strand's gotten larger since

you started?" Zhi Ging shrugged. The lie was a gamble, but it would be hard to tell in the current gloom.

Niotiya raced to the cabinet, the golden orb wobbling precariously as she wrenched a drawer open in search of a new candle. Behind her Zhi Ging pushed hard against the gray strand tying her to the chair, straining to twist her arm sideways. There were almost no gold lines left along the back of her arm; they'd long since vanished back beneath her skin.

"I can feel it taking more power!" Zhi Ging called out in exaggerated fear.

Niotiya snatched at a candle and screeched as she took in Zhi Ging's arm in the new light. There was only one line left.

Zhi Ging kept her face carefully blank, her heart racing as Niotiya howled and wrenched the ring off, hurling it past Malo's head. It bounced off the spinning wall and rolled across the floor, coming to a stop beside the cabinet.

In the sudden silence, a heavy gray paw stretched out, its claws curling around the ring.

Niotiya stared at it in disbelief, her mouth dropping open; the gray strand flew up, releasing Zhi Ging and Malo as the lion cub erupted out from the shadows. It snarled at the Matchmaker as the last stolen strand coiled back into its mane, its entire body gleaming as it was finally made whole.

The spirit roared in triumph and leaped at Niotiya. She screamed, flinging herself flat on the ground as the spirit hurtled past. Its outstretched paws tore through the paper screen, the lights from Omophilli flooding into the pagoda for the first time in centuries. The spirit soared out into the air, its tail knocking the cabinet as it leaped for freedom. Once out of the pagoda it erupted, transforming into a blazing iridescent comet that vanished out toward the horizon.

"You really should pick your allies better, Zhi Ging. Spirits are wild creatures, with no loyalty to anyone. It's abandoned you." Niotiya picked herself up and began to cackle wildly. "Ami will help me extract what's left of your power. I can use that palm's worth to contact her. She'll be here before sunrise. I—What are you looking at?"

The Matchmaker followed Zhi Ging's gaze, only to see the golden orb roll off the upturned cabinet and through the torn paper screen.

"No!" Niotiya lurched forward, her fingers outstretched, but the orb tumbled out of the room, unraveling as it fell.

The spinning walls jerked to a stop as gold threads spread out, revealing the missing other half of the pagoda. The Matchmaker leaned forward, clawing at the golden lines, but her fingers passed through them as if they were nothing more than glittering mist. She turned back to Zhi Ging then, her face a mask of undiluted fury.

"You think that's it? You think I'm just going to let that spirit go free? I'll rip up the entire desert if I have to."

Niotiya lunged toward her, and Zhi Ging leaped blindly out of reach.

Malo shrieked in horror as Zhi Ging's foot slipped and she stumbled backward out of the tower. Air whistled around her, then abruptly stopped, her body thudding into a net of shimmering gold. She scrambled to her feet, blinking hard as she looked around and then down.

Zhi Ging was standing in midair.

CHAPTER 44

Texture and detail rippled out along the gold threads as Fei Chui's roaming pagoda solidified beneath Zhi Ging's feet. Out of the corner of her eye, she spotted a glittering haze darting through Omophilli's streets, gathering speed as it raced toward them. A thunderous roar echoed up the pagoda stairs, and Niotiya spun around in bewilderment.

The door flung open to reveal the sand spirit, once again looking like a lion cub. The spirit growled at Niotiya, the sound disconcertingly deep for its small size. Its tail stretched long, curling past the Matchmaker to flick Zhi Ging's palm.

Her skin prickled, and she glanced down as the word "fire" rose up in golden lines. She frowned at it, trying to work out what the spirit wanted. Surely it knew they couldn't burn down the pagoda. She held her palm up to Malo, letting the phoenix read the word. He chirped uncertainly, equally confused.

Suddenly the lion cub lowered his head, his back arching and bending as he grew in size, his body stretching to fill the door. He looked up, a smile spreading beneath his broad snout, then released a giant fur ball made from sand straight toward the horrified Matchmaker.

Zhi Ging leaped back into the pagoda, understanding crackling through her.

"Malo, get it!" she shouted, pointing to the spinning ball.

The phoenix swooped forward, his flaming wings brushing the heat-sensitive ball of sand. It shimmered, sand bubbling as it tumbled through the air to seal the Matchmaker within a thick glass sphere. She howled, banging the glass as the spirit held a protective paw over its surface.

Behind the spirit, Zhi Ging heard footsteps pounding up the stairs, and Jack, Reishi, and Gertie bundled past the sphere toward her. The province delegates flooded into the room behind them, red-faced after storming up several flights of stairs.

"Are you all right?" Reishi asked urgently, his eyes widening at Zhi Ging's bruised arm, while Gertie pulled her into a tight hug.

"I've sent my bees to fetch Dippy. He'll bring ointments and bandages—What is *that*?!" she cried, finally spotting the glittering other half of the tower over Zhi Ging's shoulder

"I *think* it's a way into Fei Chui's roaming pagoda,"

Zhi Ging admitted, her dazed voice muffled against the old woman's shoulder.

Jack looked at her in relief, his eyes flashing back and forth until they were a near-constant teal. "I still don't really know what happened tonight, but I feel like I owe you a *lot* of mochi," he said.

"Uh, I think mochi, cheung fun, *and* my pick of homei spoons for the next month," she corrected with a shaky laugh, overwhelmed at having her friend back.

He ruffled Malo's feathers. "That's fair, although you're breaking the news to Mynah that she can't go first with the spoons."

Behind them Reishi turned to the Matchmaker still trapped in the glass, his voice now cold and sharp. "Niotiya, as Cyo B'Ahon and protector of the six provinces, I hereby place you under arrest."

"It doesn't matter. Ami will release me," the woman hissed, her wild features magnified within the sphere. "She protects those who are loyal to her."

"Ah, the way she protected the previous Head Matchmaker against your takeover?"

Niotiya went pale, her mouth opening and shutting as the realization sunk in. She had thought Ami's silence when she pushed Ginsau out had been a sign of the Cyo B'Ahon's support. What if it had actually been indifference? Or, worse yet, Ami was just like her. Abandoning and betraying allies once they were no longer needed.

Reishi turned back to the delegates, taking in their

furious expressions. "Given the hurt caused by the Matchmakers' Guild, I hereby dissolve all their existing rulings. Until they can prove their Guild is focused on beneficial matches rather than amassing private wealth, they will no longer have control over how businesses run in *any* of the six provinces."

Gertie beamed at this, clenching a fist in silent triumph.

"As for their current fortune," Reishi continued, "this will be shared among the families of every child who was taken." He paused as the delegates cheered, their eyes gleaming. Reishi held up a hand, the gold crane on his robes seeming to stare out at each and every one of them. "The fortune will be shared *equally,* with children of delegates receiving no more and no less than those of villagers from the farthest corner of every district." A few of the delegates deflated, but the majority nodded.

"There're more glass children in the pagoda!" Zhi Ging yelped, suddenly remembering Niotiya's earlier threat. "She said there're some hidden on every floor."

The delegates perked up, each hoping that meant more money for their own province.

"Wait." Zhi Ging turned to the caged Matchmaker. "Where's my mother?"

Niotiya's eyes narrowed in fury. "You tell me," she hissed, before flinching as the spirit smacked a paw against the sphere in warning. "She vanished three months ago— that's when Ginsau really began to panic."

"What?" Zhi Ging's eyes widened. Her mother must

be looking for her. Could she be on her way to Hok Woh right now? Would they have met if she'd just stayed in the lantern archive?

Zhi Ging looked at the lion cub, and her regret fizzled out. No, that would have meant the spirit staying trapped. And how many more children would the Matchmakers have continued to turn to glass? Zhi Ging glanced back at the gold-outlined pagoda behind them, a small hope bubbling inside her. *What if there's still a way . . . ?*

Jack followed her gaze, raising an eyebrow as his eyes flicked between the two halves of the tower.

"Given the heightened risk of escape," Reishi continued, "Niotiya will split her prison sentence across the six provinces. Starting with twelve months in one province before being moved to the next." He turned back to face the delegates, peering at them closely. "This will require you to work together, ensuring the Matchmaker's movements are kept secret. Once the final glass child has been found, we will organize which province will hold Niotiya first."

ZHI GING AND JACK HUNG BACK AS THE OTHERS filed down the stairs. The spirit rolled the sphere down the steps after Gertie; the cloud collar now shone brightly beneath its curled mane, the REMedy pearl pinned proudly to the center. A deep satisfied purr radiated off the spirit each time the thick glass bounced down another step, causing Niotiya to yelp and tumble inside.

441

When just the two of them were left in the room, Jack stepped toward the glittering outline of the Fei Chui pagoda. He tapped a shoe against one of the nearest threads, and his foot sank right through. He turned back to Zhi Ging, his eyes gleaming. "You can stand on these, right?" he asked in an excited whisper. "I thought I saw you when we were running to the pagoda."

"Yeah, they feel solid to me. I actually think it became *more* real when I was standing on it, if that makes any sense?"

"Well"—he raised an eyebrow and nodded at the golden door—"don't you want to see what's on the other side?"

Zhi Ging bit her lip, her eyes tracing the shape glinting in the night sky. "Yes," she admitted. "But what if it's just empty?"

"But what if your mother's on the other side? She had enough power left to escape, right? What if she's not in this half of the pagoda anymore because she stepped into the other half?"

Zhi Ging felt her heart lurch; the thought had been swirling in her mind, but she'd been too scared to consider it. The hope felt almost painful.

"Aren't you curious?" Jack asked.

Zhi Ging took a deep breath, joining him at the edge of the two pagodas. She stepped forward onto the gold, detail erupting beneath her shoes.

Jack yelped in excitement as Malo flew past to land on her shoulder.

She pressed her hand against the door, then turned back to Jack.

"Go," he said, waving away her concerns. "Like I said, I owe you. I'll share my homework scrolls with you once you get back to Hok Woh."

"Thanks, but I've already spent more time looking at other Silhouettes' handwriting than anyone ever should," Zhi Ging said with a snort.

Jack laughed. "All right, dramatic readings of my homework scrolls it is!"

She smiled at him, trying to memorize every detail of her friend's face, desperately wishing she could have a memochi of this moment.

Fei Chui's roaming pagoda could be anywhere in Wengyuen. *How long will it be before I get back to Hok Woh?*

Jack paused, as if reading her thoughts, and his eyes flicked to the gibbous moon hanging high above them.

"Hey, if you don't make it back before the next full moon, I'll come find you. I promise."

"I guess you do need at least one person in the audience for your dramatic readings. Say bye to Reishi and Gertie for me?" Zhi Ging asked. She gave a shaky smile as he nodded, the reality of what she was about to do suddenly hitting. "I'll see you soon," she whispered.

Jack waved, and she flashed him one final grateful smile.

The door slid open in front of her, and Zhi Ging stepped inside, vanishing as she passed through its shimmering frame.

AUTHOR'S NOTE

For anyone curious about Zhi Ging and Pinderent's solution to the dragon boat/waterfall problem, this was a nod to one of my favorite parts of Chinese mythology. Legend tells of a dragon gate at the top of a waterfall along the Yellow River. Brave carp attempt to swim upstream, and any that succeed in leaping through the dragon gate are transformed into dragons. This legend is also linked to the phrase "鯉躍龍門" (carp leaping over the dragon gate), which was used to describe someone passing the fiendishly difficult exams needed to become a government official (*almost* as tough as Zhi Ging's Silhouette challenges).

HOK WOH AND CYO B'AHON

D'Amask—Named after the damask rose. In the past, people would use rose water to help heal infected eyes. Some eye drops still include rose water today.

G'Aam [and] Wuyan—Cantonese: Guardian (監護人).
You need both those first two characters to create the word for "guardian," so of course I needed two actual characters to look after the Silhouettes!

[Tutor] Miraj—Distorted spelling: Mirage.

Neoi Syu—Cantonese: Women's Script (女書).
Okay, so I LOVE this so much. Neoi Syu writing was a secret coded script exclusively read by women. Some believe it was used for over three thousand years in the Hunan province, but it was only in the 1980s that people outside China first heard about it. (I personally only stumbled across it in 2023.) The characters look different from traditional or simplified Chinese characters, and the writing was passed down from mother to daughter, giving female friends a way to communicate more freely in a patriarchal society; messages that could only be read by other women were shared on fans, handkerchiefs, or headscarves. Look up *Nüshu* (Mandarin pronunciation) for more information.

Sycee—A currency used in imperial China that was made from silver (and occasionally gold) ingots that just so happened to be shaped like little boats.

Wuiyam—Cantonese: Echo (回音).
For anyone interested, I've based Wuiyam's outfits and makeup on traditional Cantonese opera. If you imagine Malo as a human, this is what you'd get!

CHALLENGES

Binlim [performance]—Cantonese: Face changing (變臉).
Stop reading this immediately and watch a video of a real
Binlim performance! The speed at which they can change
masks is nothing short of magic. Look up "bian lian"
(Mandarin pronunciation), and get ready to have your
mind blown.

MATCHMAKERS

Dourie—A distorted spelling combination: Dour/dowry.
Niotiya—Distorted spelling: Neottia.
Although orchids are typically beautiful, some versions
of this flower are actually parasitic! Neottia orchids don't
get energy through photosynthesis; instead they take their
energy from the tree roots they latch on to and give nothing
back.

OTHER WORDS

Ban Daan—Cantonese: Idiot/fool (笨蛋).
The literal translation is so much more fun, though,
because the two characters break down to mean "stupid
egg."
Bao Saan [festival]—Cantonese: Bun mountain (包山).
Some of you will be surprised to learn that this isn't
actually a festival I've dreamed up on an empty stomach.

Instead it's based on the VERY REAL, VERY COOL bun festival that takes place on Cheung Chau Island every year. People really do climb giant towers (over sixty feet tall) covered in fluffy steamed buns, aiming to fill their sacks with the most valuable buns from the top of the tower.

G'Ilding—The gold province capital is named after the art of gilding: covering a surface with gold leaf or gold paint.

Gangsan [vase]—Cantonese: Rebirth/resurrection/rejuvenated (更生).

Ling B'Aan—Cantonese: Head waiter (領班).

Minfun—Cantonese: Flour (麵粉).

Pingon—Cantonese: Peace/safe and sound (平安). The porcelain capital's name is a nod to the actual characters that are stamped on the buns during Cheung Chau's annual bun festival. The festival lasts four days, and ten thousand buns are sold each day!

Seoizyu—Cantonese: Droplet/dewdrop (水珠). Only Ai'Deng Bou could gaze up at the largest jellyfish anyone has ever seen and choose to give her that teeny-tiny name!

Wun-Wun—Cantonese: Transport cloud (運雲). There's actually a second meaning for the character 運: fate/fortune. So not only is Wun-Wun a practical village that lets others know its main trade is cloud carrying, the name also hints at the future-predicting cloud ceremony Dippy attempts at the start of the book.

ACKNOWLEDGMENTS

Authors are often warned about the "tricky second novel," and I have to admit, I was a little nervous opening up that very first blank page for *Rise of the Sand Spirits*. However, thanks to the incredible team around me, this second book turned out to be an absolute joy to write.

Thank you, first and foremost, to my editor, Nazima, who just completely and utterly gets my brain. I love our catch-ups and I'm eternally grateful for you listening to my rambling ideas and not panicking at all (at least not obviously) when I casually mentioned adding another fifty thousand words to my second draft. An ever bigger thank-you to you, Laura and Jennie for expertly steering that draft back down below a hundred thousand words without ever once making me feel like I was losing world detail or plot points. Thank you for all the late nights and weekends you've all dedicated to editing Zhi Ging's story—I see those timestamps! Thank you to both Nazima and Rachel for giving up your weekend last Chinese

New Year to help cheer on *Fight for the Hidden Realm* and for sitting with me while I de-frazzled over tea during a slightly mad (and self-inflicted) day of darting between North and Southeast London bookshops.

An unbelievably huge thank-you to all the booksellers across the country who went above and beyond with their window displays for *Fight for the Hidden Realm*. I loved chatting to all of you and discovering some wonderful Hong Kong connections, including a honeymoon at Waterstones Edinburgh and a son's visit ahead of his wedding at Waterstones Newcastle! Also, a huge shout-out to my two fellow die-hard Taylor Swift fans in Waterstones Manchester (The Trafford Centre), I hope your voices recovered slightly faster than mine did after going to the Eras tour. In London (and slightly further afield) thank you so much to Waterstones booksellers Ben, Cassia, Ellen, Emma, Ines, Isla, Maria, Rhiannon, Robin, Sean, Tara, and the entire teams at both Covent Garden and Welwyn Garden City for embracing *Paper Dragons* with such enthusiasm and making me feel so incredibly welcome—not to mention sharing your own book and bubble tea recommendations! A massive thank-you also to Urmi at Pickled Pepper Books, Brooke at House of Books & Friends, and The Little Ripon Bookshop for choosing *Fight for the Hidden Realm* for your monthly book clubs. I would also like to thank the bookseller *who shall remain nameless* who let me sneak out of their store with a gigantic A1 poster of *Paper Dragons* tucked under one arm and a Zhi Ging standee tucked under the other.

None of this bookseller support would have been possible without the constant behind-the-scenes hard work of Katherine and the rest of Hachette Children's powerhouse of a sales team! Thank you also to the incredible Marketing and PR team for everything you've done over the past two years: Beth, Dan, Jasmin (hope you're enjoying your travels), Katie (welcome to the team!), Lucy, and Nils. Your collective creativity honestly puts me to shame, and I can't wait to work with you on the next book in the series (by that I mean nodding in amazement and agreeing to each of your fantastic ideas). Thank you to Yuzhen Cai and Alison for constantly nailing it with the cover and chapter artwork—I'm so sorry I made you have to look up what a rat king was while explaining what the sand spirit should look like.

Thank you to Gemma, my dream agent/trusted sounding board/all-around-excellent human being. I'll never stop saying this, but *Paper Dragons* truly wouldn't exist without you. I've never met an agent who cares more about her authors, and now no event or interview look is ever complete without your fantastic jellyfish necklace!

Leaping across to Ireland, thank you, Siobhan T! You are one of the hardest-working people I've ever met, and I loved our day racing around Dublin bookshops. It always makes me laugh how you'll casually update me on some truly incredible coverage you've achieved as if it's no big deal. Having been on the other side, I know just how hard these are to get, so thank you! A huge thank-you to the entire team at Dubray Grafton St for putting together the best possible launch party for *Fight for the Hidden Realm*. It really meant a lot that you all gave up your evenings, and hopefully you all managed to grab a glass of wine for yourselves once the night was over. I can't mention my book launch without also shouting out my aunt, Ann, who almost single-handedly cleared out the bookshop's supply of copies! A massive thank-you to the incredibly friendly team at Children's Books Ireland— so glad I was able to meet you in person, Elaina and Jenny!

To my wonderful team at Delacorte Press, thank you for all your dedicated work on *Paper Dragons*. I know it can be trickier when an author isn't based locally, but you've knocked it out of the park, and it's brilliant to know each and every one of you is ever only an email away. Thank you, Ally, Colleen, Emma, Josh, Jennifer, Kelsey, Nichole, Michelle, Tamar, and Suzanne! Huge thank-you also to Vivenne for another stunning cover illustration; I'm in awe of how fast you work. To all my fellow London (and further afield) Bubblies in the Bubble Tea Network, I seriously couldn't imagine being an author without you guys. Thank you for always jumping in with answers for each and every one of my debut questions and for organizing consistently top-tier restaurant meetups. Thank you to both The Hong Kong International Literary Festival and International Literature Festival Dublin for taking a chance on a debut and inviting me out for events. Thank you to Avina in Hong Kong, who really *did* buy every single copy of *Paper Dragons* after my panel event at the HKLitfest—can't wait for you to finally teach me the rules of mahjong next time I'm back in Hong Kong! Finally, thank you to Finn for being one of my very first readers once proofs of *Paper Dragons: The Fight for the Hidden Realm* were out in the wild. Forever grateful for the nights you spent racing through the book after school and giving it such a glowing review! I hope you speed through this book just as quickly.

ABOUT THE AUTHOR

SIOBHAN McDERMOTT was born in Hong Kong and grew up on a steady stream of stories filled with Chinese legends and Irish folklore from her Chinese mom and Irish dad. She now lives in the UK and continues to order dim sum in Cantonese tinged with a distinctly Dublin lilt. *Paper Dragons: The Fight for the Hidden Realm* was her debut novel. The story was inspired by moments across her life: from childhood ferry trips between Lantau Island and Hong Kong, to traveling around Taiwan, Italy, and Spain.

siobhanmcdermott.com